THE BEAR HUNTER'S DAUGHTERS

Anneli Jordahl

Translated by Nichola Smalley

THE BEAR HUNTER'S DAUGHTERS

A TALE OF SEVEN SISTERS

HarperVia
An Imprint of HarperCollinsPublishers

Without limiting the exclusive rights of any author, contributor or the publisher of this publication, any unauthorized use of this publication to train generative artificial intelligence (AI) technologies is expressly prohibited. HarperCollins also exercise their rights under Article 4(3) of the Digital Single Market Directive 2019/790 and expressly reserve this publication from the text and data mining exception.

This is a work of fiction. Names, characters, places, and incidents are products of the author's imagination or are used fictitiously and are not to be construed as real. Any resemblance to actual events, locales, organizations, or persons, living or dead, is entirely coincidental.

THE BEAR HUNTER'S DAUGHTERS. Copyright © 2022 by Anneli Jordahl. English translation copyright © 2026 by Nichola Smalley. A Note from the Translator © 2026 by Nichola Smalley. All rights reserved. No part of this book may be used or reproduced in any manner whatsoever without written permission except in the case of brief quotations embodied in critical articles and reviews. For information, address HarperCollins Publishers, 195 Broadway, New York, NY 10007. In Europe, HarperCollins Publishers, Macken House, 39/40 Mayor Street Upper, Dublin 1, D01 C9W8, Ireland.

HarperCollins books may be purchased for educational, business, or sales promotional use. For information, please email the Special Markets Department at SPsales@harpercollins.com.

harpercollins.com

Originally published as *Björnjägarens döttrar* in Sweden in 2022 by Norstedts

FIRST HARPERVIA EDITION PUBLISHED IN 2026

Designed by Elina Cohen
Art © Olga Korneeva/Shutterstock

Library of Congress Cataloging-in-Publication Data has been applied for.

ISBN 978-0-06-333884-5

Printed in the United States of America

26 27 28 29 30 LBC 5 4 3 2 1

*if you have but
a forest
and
a stream
close by you,
you'll get yourself
food!*

    Sara Lidman, from *Kropp och skäl* (translated by Nichola Smalley)

In order to understand nature, we must allow nature to be born inwardly in its full sequence.

    Novalis, from *The Novices of Sais* (translated by Ralph Manheim)

Naked and steaming, they entered the house, bodies aglow like the sun-baked bark of a cherry birch.

    Aleksis Kivi, from *Seven Brothers* (translated by Dr. Richard Impola)

The Bear Hunter's Daughters

The Farm

Chapter One

You noticed them straightaway. From a distance they looked like anybody else selling wood, mushrooms, and dried hare meat at the market. Mostly, they would turn up in twos or threes, wearing flannel shirts and black leather jackets. It was the smell that accompanied them that stood out and made its presence known. A mix of resin, sweat, and unwashed genitals.

On the backs of their jackets was a drawing of a predator's eye, and above it, a gun. Under the eye was the number seven in roman numerals. Were they triplets? They looked the same: wide foreheads, unkempt, auburn hair that had never known a hairdresser's hand and probably hadn't seen shampoo in a long while. The only thing that differentiated these three was that one of them had a nose that looked deformed in left profile, probably a frostbite injury.

A cheerful murmur hung over the marketplace on the football pitch; a vegetable seller was trying to convince skeptical customers that mustard leaf really was the same thing as rocket. A young couple were mooching around, curious to know how the local bakery made the popular bark bread the older people turned their nose up at—they'd had enough during the war. I couldn't take my eyes off the sisters—I was drawn to them, circulating around their stall as discreetly as I was able. As they held out paper bags full of mushrooms, I noted rough, wound-gashed hands, long fingers, and dirt under nails. I wondered how many of the town's increasingly dedicated animal lovers they'd lost as customers by decorating their stall with the gleaming tails of beasts they'd recently shot. They flourished foxtails in the crowd's faces before demonstrating possible uses: slinging them around their hips and making obscene motions with their pudenda. Men who'd been persuaded by their wives to come along wore amused expressions that indicated the trip hadn't been a complete waste of time from their point of view.

The girls' signs were written in a spidery hand with poor spelling, as if they'd hired a seven-year-old for the task. *Bear meet. Sweet forrest raspberies.* I photographed them from a distance as they arranged bearskins, pointing my lens at the glow; their thin, hand-rolled cigarettes hopped about in the corners of their mouths. Sometimes they kept puffing on the stumps so long they could've burned their lips off. I stood by their stall, peering between two men who wanted the stallholders to confirm that the bear population had grown in the last few years. When I asked what they were charging for the wood and if they had a card reader I got a brusque reply about cash payments, without them ever taking their eyes off the men's hairy arms. The notes and coins from each sale were stuffed in a brown leather pouch they fastened with a cord. When everything was sold, they would each take out a hip flask from which they drank great gulps with a theatrical grimace. The onlookers laughed. It became a gimmick. Sometimes they offered the men at the front a drink.

The sisters' stall always had the most customers, the volume was always high: whistles and applause. At last, I stood alongside the broad-shouldered men and raised my camera to get the picture of the year, honing in on a scar that snaked from the corner of one of the girls' eyes to the corner of her mouth. In a flash the convivial mood switched to hostility. Their eyes moved from the men to my face: I remember the turning of heads as if in slow motion, how sparkle turned to deepest black, switched from coquetry to enmity. Six black holes turned on me. The one with the scar drew a finger across her throat. My legs trembled, my heart pounded, why hadn't I asked their permission? I usually do before taking pictures of people. I replaced the lens cap and hung the camera to one side. The girls went back to entertaining their audience, drained the last drops from their flasks, and without having asked I was unexpectedly offered a knockdown price for the last foxtail. A cloud of the stallholders' snarling energy engulfed me, invisible yet quite tangible, and to my astonishment my trembling hand held out a note.

I couldn't stop thinking about how they lived. They occupied my mind. What did they have for breakfast? What did they do if they got a toothache? I bought a notebook and wrote down my observations—when you write by hand the words are for real. I began to dig deeper, asking acquaintances and people around town. I bought another notebook, and mildly obsessed, I went further, inquiring with various members of staff at the local council. What did they know about the sisters? The answers were contradictory. Poor souls who couldn't function in society was the most common response. Christ, they've grown up without TV, computers, cell phones. For the last ten years no landline either. In all likelihood they could barely read, since they'd never gone to school. It was said that a teacher—who'd lost her job when someone found her threatening a pupil with a knife—had somehow been able to engage them, gaining the sisters' trust to the extent that the youngest at least accepted an ABC book. The girl was thirsty for knowledge and quick of mind, but after she'd learned to read, the teacher lost contact with her and was unable to reach her again.

Everyone agreed that things began to go really wrong after the girls dealt with their father's dismembered body when he was killed by a bear. That must have been an unholy sight. The animal lay mortally wounded, blood pouring from its mouth but still with a pulse, alongside the dead hunter. The father's mangled body and unrecognizable face bore witness to the battle that had taken place. The oldest daughter shot the bear, saving the animal from prolonged suffering.

The father had earned a reputation as a skilled bear hunter. People were perplexed by his endurance in making his long treks through the forest: he carried many extra pounds, growing larger and larger as the years passed. The few people who'd observed him in action described how the man's ungainly body moved like that of a sprightly orienteer over roots, logs, and stones. In the end, fame became a poison. Their father was accused of poaching, and the police were after him on several occasions, but he never showed up in court. The oldest girl had started attending school, something both her parents soon put a stop to. The whole family avoided contact with society, and their neighbor, the widow Niskanpää, whose farm lay six or seven miles from the girls', agreed to do their errands, buying necessary items, filling gas cans, and assisting with births. She'd been taught by her mother, who'd had a little healthcare training and later worked as a rural district Samaritan.

Periodically their father would hide in the forest from real or imagined pursuers. It's likely he came home at night and then set off deep into the woods again in the morning. After his death, his daughters found traces of him in tumbledown cabins and the spacious caves of the mountainous old-growth forest.

When death came, bringing with it great dismay, existence became unbearable for the single mother and the daughters still grieving their father; their loathing was mutual, aggression turned to violence. Not even Mrs. Niskanpää was admitted. A few forestry workers had seen the sisters roving about the forest, skinny and battered.

At the father's funeral, where the mother, Louhi, the girls' uncle Veikko Huovinen, and the neighbor Niskanpää, along with her son John, joined the seven daughters in saying their last goodbyes, Simone was the only one to fold her hands in prayer and sing along with the psalms, which she knew by heart. As each of them went up and laid a sprig of blue chicory on the coffin, not a single one cried, though it was impossible to mistake their deep sorrow. The oldest daughter, Johanna, stayed by the coffin longest, stroking the lid with her hand and making a guttural sound. When the ceremony was over, the pastor took Johanna and her sister Tanja to one side and said: *Think of your good fortune. You have a mother and a farm. Over the years I've heard of fatherless children living like scruffy rodents in the forest. You have a lot going for you.*

But little did those warning words help, the pastor told me as I sat before him with my notebook upon being invited to the rectory. After the father's death, he'd had some contact with the mother and one of the daughters, who wanted to keep their meeting secret from the rest of the family. During this time, trench warfare had broken out between the mother and her daughters. The pastor spoke of violence, and the otherwise tranquil man's lively body language showed that he was just as fascinated as me by the seven sisters. A mystery that could be illuminated from various angles. Just when we thought we'd pinpointed their pitiable social position, they dodged the pin and slipped through our fingers.

The mother loosened her grip on her offspring and lived at times with her brother, twenty miles from the farm. She was at home when she passed, leaving the girls to their fate in their father's poorly maintained, damp-ravaged farm with its damaged roof. It's hard to avoid un's and negations when describing the girls' lives. Many un-paid. Much un-repaired. The stove was full of debt-collection demands and threats of seizure from the bailiffs.

The pastor had knocked on the door and stoically tried to get them to pull themselves together and get on with their mother's funeral. When he set foot in the large farm kitchen, he was met by a sight that would pursue him through life. The dead woman lay on the kitchen bench. There were buckets set out to catch raindrops. Bowls of dried-up porridge and macaroni formed a mountain by the sink. Pizza boxes from floor to ceiling in one corner. Two hens pecked around on the rug of dog hair covering the wide planks of a wooden floor that had almost certainly been beautiful once.

The stench would have been even worse had not a pleasant fog of pipe tobacco and cigarette smoke hung over the kitchen. It put the pastor in mind of a pleasant puff he'd once savored before his breathing troubles started and his doctor told him how injurious to his health it would be to continue to draw down smoke into his afflicted lungs.

THROUGH THE FOG COULD BE SEEN SEVEN PALE FACES AND SEVEN tangled auburn manes that looked, from a distance, rather like a field of swaying bent grass. They sat around the kitchen table, in the center of which was a rifle.

Then suddenly, the pastor was in the kitchen.

"The fuck did you come from?" Tiina yelled.

Simone was considerably more polite.

"Good day, Father, please do come in and take a seat. Would you like a North State? They're the strong ones—we managed to get hold of the forbidden stuff."

She held out a green cigarette packet.

The pastor eyed it covetously, his arm twitched, but he resisted the temptation. He looked at the dead mother's body. Her face mild, mouth frozen in a vague smile. The few times he'd met her, her face had been heavy, her body weighed down. Now, for once, she seemed amused.

Gently, he lifted a cupped hand toward the sisters, saying, "You must have your mother casketed and laid in consecrated ground."

The sisters glared at each other. Took deep drags on their cigarettes. Aune took the floor.

"We'll carry her into the forest and lay her to rest by the swamp. Our mother's last wishes are the first thing we intend to fulfill."

"Then you must have her cremated," said the pastor.

Johanna exhaled smoke and looked at him with a wrinkled brow. "Cremated?"

"Burn the body and scatter the ashes. Anything else would be illegal."

"Do *you* burn it?" Tiina asked.

The pastor shook his head.

"That's done by the people at the crematorium."

Johanna grew blunt: "We burn things when we feel like it. In this house we take care of our own business."

"And that's going well, you think?"

Elga let out a peal of laughter and gave the pastor an appreciative look. Tiina glared at her, with not a clue why she was grinning. Johanna interrupted, "You can come for the body in the morning, so we have time to bid farewell."

"Ten o'clock. Thanks for the coffee," the pastor said from sheer force of habit, and fled that terrifying place fast and with a sharp longing for coffee.

After he'd related the conversation to me from memory, he looked very pleased with his acting ability and his detailed recall, and I resolved to record all my interviews from that point on. I wanted to have the words as authentic and vivid as possible, otherwise I would be forced to add color. There was one sister at least I hoped and believed I could persuade to cooperate and talk to me. She was astonishingly articulate, given she'd never been to school, but after our conversations it became clear to me that she hadn't conveyed anything specific that would bring my tale closer to the truth. You know, the kind of details that make a story come to life.

Inspired by the sisters, I've had a few porters as I sit here at my desk, delving into my imagination. Trying to formulate the heart of the tale in a captivating prologue. How can I put into words the physical violence, the sisters' coarseness, or for that matter, the beauty and capriciousness of nature? How will I handle the conflicting accounts? Many of the people I ask tell me a version of the story that is completely at odds with an "underprivileged children" narrative. In their accounts, the girls were unscrupulous characters embroiled in dubious dealings—so hardened they didn't hesitate to resort to brutal violence, even killing if they felt threatened. Everyone I ask warns me about them, telling me how handy they are with firearms. There are rumors, too, of two muscular dogs. Some report that the beasts were trained to attack—below the belt.

Why did the authorities give up? The answers I get are like legends. The rumors say that two social workers, who tried to contact the girls after their father the bear hunter's death, were locked in an outhouse that functioned as an abattoir. There they were chained up and ill-treated with medieval torture implements. It is said that the girls even barbecued a man's amputated member and ate it for dinner.

SO, THE AUTHORITIES HAVE ABANDONED THEIR EFFORTS TO TRY TO get them to engage with the local council. In doing so, they've accepted the loss of much-needed tax income to this depopulated, impoverished small town, where empty shops have lined the high street since the paper mill shut down.

So far, the girls haven't been arrested while laying out the treasures of the forest on their market stall. Why? Probably a mix of the authorities' fear, empathy, and the need we all have for titillation.

You'll never see anyone in this small town come to life as they do when speaking of the seven sisters and their ways. The interest is such that I'd be a fool not to fulfill my dream of becoming a writer by committing the details of their lives to the page.

TO GAIN A FUNDAMENTAL UNDERSTANDING OF A PERSON, IT'S CRUcial to get a sense of their upbringing. How can anyone think they possess knowledge of a human being with no notion of who their parents were, the family's living conditions, their position in society?

You can't get away from your childhood—all your life it nips at your heels with a wolf pup's sharp fangs. During certain phases of your life, you look back to find a glow lighting you up from within, in others, everything seems wrapped in a darkness deep as the abyss. You understand, I'm sure, that the sisters' childhood years were a difficult puzzle for me to piece together, since the family had lived in isolation, and the girls' beloved uncle, Veikko Huovinen, who, with the irony of fate, was the namesake of that famous author, died just after the only interview I managed to get with him. The sisters' uncle was widely spoken of as a talented storyteller. In his dotage he was invited to speak at the coffee mornings held in conjunction with the annual general meeting of the local history association.

What can I, an amateur ethnologist, say with any certainty about the childhood world of these seven girl children? Not a lot. Well, this perhaps: it was surrounded by forest. High pines and thick spruces. Slender birches with chalk-white trunks close to the farm. The deep forest was their main home, not their small rye field. They abhorred every moment of plowing, harrowing, sowing, and harvesting: drudgery they associated with their mother's heavy step, swollen calves, and bad-tempered demeanor.

Badgers went fearlessly about their business as the girls bathed in forest tarns, romped in remote bogs, and quenched their thirst in the clear water of streams. The wood pigeon and the squirrel, on the other hand—not to mention the otter and the pine marten—learned, in time, to keep their distance.

Now let me at last introduce the sisters to you. It's impossible to present them as types: Grumpy, Bashful, Happy. You see, all seven of them are sulky and unsociable. They're happiest when gleefully pouring moonshine and home brew down their throats. Which, if

I'm honest, is a frequent occurrence. *Brännvin, the only vino worth the name*, they chorus, as though it were their very own drinking song. Johanna crows loudest of all—her body tolerates the largest quantity of alcohol before she crashes headlong to the floor. The oldest of the siblings, she has just turned twenty. And though she can certainly handle her drink, she can best be described as lucid and with a somewhat caring nature. That's not to say the younger ones don't find her self-righteous, or even censorious. They are filled with loathing every time she shouts: *Now, girls, let's do this properly. Together we can sort it out.* They find it especially galling since Johanna is not a particularly quick thinker. The youngest, the sharp-witted Elga, once told her as much, in her pert, prepubescent cocksure manner. This started a feud, an ongoing tumult between the two of them. And even today, the firstborn and the last one out have still not partaken of a much-needed peace pipe.

Tanja and Aune are not as alike as single-egg twins tend to be. Tanja is confident in practical matters, while Aune's hands fumble at their work, because she lives in her head and tells stories in the tradition of Uncle Veikko: both stories of her own and famous folktales. The twins Tiina and Laura are also very different, though they both have a tendency to clumsiness. Of course, Tiina is strong as a boxer, her body full of fire but seemingly lacking in motor skills. She sprawls wherever she goes, while Laura wavers along nearsightedly on paths known only to her, with the look of a somnambulist. It was Laura who pushed hardest for them to leave the farm and move out into the wilderness after both parents departed this life. She relates to the spruces as though they were her real parents.

Wait a moment. I forgot about Simone. She's the only one who believes, in a literal sense, in the Bible and in God the Holy Father.

The only one who would turn, in secret, to their mother. It makes the other girls' skin crawl to hear Simone fling the Word of God around, claiming to have seen Jesus and even the devil himself in all his glory. When it comes to Biblical tales, however, they all pay keen attention, viewing them as stories full of violence and adventure—where women are treated particularly poorly.

There's little to be said about the parents' childhoods. Hunger and hard labor from the age of ten. How on earth Heikki and Louhi met and got the urge to rub their naked bodies against one another's is a mystery to most. That the whole shebang was apparently repeated at least five times remains an even greater enigma. Although, don't most romantic couplings have screeching question marks hanging over them? Heikki and Louhi shared a home, yes, but they did nothing side by side and in harmony. Their duties were strictly divided as they undertook small-scale agroforestry with grazing cattle and farmed the fertile valley with its rye fields. Had it not been for the daughters, life would have been lived in complete silence.

The girls' howls and raucous laughter could be heard over the tops of the pines, yes—the cries really did carry more than seven miles, all the way to the bus station in town. Agile as cats, they rolled in the grass, in wrestling matches so rough that tufts of red hair flew into the air as noses ran with blood. When the neighbor's boy John Niskanpää lived at home, he'd sneak over to the sisters' farm, hiding in a thicket and watching them with binoculars through the hedge. John's observations have been invaluable to my work.

The trick to getting the girls to stop their earsplitting cries was the same as with dogs: diversion. The father would go into the porch, get a rifle down from the wall, walk outside, and stand beside his daughters as they pounded each other, apart from the youngest, whose job it was to keep score and declare the winner. The father aimed for the treetops and nailed a squirrel in one, and the animal fell from branch to branch to the ground, in a kind of slow motion. Six sweat-steaming, muddy sisters got up, all blood-streaked arms and lumps on foreheads. They followed their father, jostling for space closest to the powerful man-body, arms around him in conspiratorial intimacy, leaning their heads against their father's round belly and broad chest as he gently pushed the muddy girl-bodies aside, bent down, and grabbed the dead creature by the tail to lift its still-warm animal-body up into the sunlight.

"If ever there's a war or famine, this is what you can eat. Not a lot of meat on it, but squirrel brain is fatty and delicious."

Forming a ring around him, the girls listened carefully, paying heed to every movement; they aped everything their father did, like seven fox cubs. No, six. Laura walked alongside, as usual, listening distractedly and gazing at the sky as though she'd spotted something interesting in the treetops, though in reality everything blurred together. Their father would whistle for her when it was lesson time, and with apathetic posture and blasé countenance, she would obey. *It's good to practice on squirrels, they're hardest. Squirrels are never still.*

Each of them got to hold the rifle and aim at the branch where the rodent had sat—even the youngest got to have a go, needing help to hold the heavy gun. *Aim a little lower*, said their father, in his calm, paternal voice, *or you'll overshoot. But not so low you pepper the body.*

The skin had to be intact, otherwise it wouldn't be salable. Elga fired off a shot. A magpie dropped out of the sky.

Occasionally their mother would appear, seething with suppressed rage, to commandeer her daughters for help with the milking. In vain. Their mother spoke in scattered sentences, odd words stuttering from her mouth, and was met with seven tones of sneering laughter and their father's *Dammit, bitch, I'm teaching the girls to survive!*

Over the years their mother resorted to ever-cruder and more violent tools to compel her children to take part in the farm's daily chores—at the very least, freeing the cows of their milk. One time, with their father gone off to the forest on a bear hunt, Laura had answered her mother's pleas with a snarled *Crone's work. I'm going to be an artist, not a dairy maid,* she bellowed, stamping her foot. Elga repeated what her sister had said about women's chores, and said she was going to be a professor. At that point the devil got the better of their mother and she grabbed hold of Elga, forced her down onto the floor, then got down on her knees and struck the girl's rump hard seven times with a piece of wood. The mother's cheeks were flushed and she was panting, apparently high on her own severity. Then she got up, and with a decidedly musical rhythm, beat the older children about the face with a wooden ladle: quick, hard blows until the handle broke and blood ran from Laura's ear. Johanna and Tiina remained stoic from sheer malice, and persisted in laughing in their mother's face, while Elga was not yet able to hold back her tears.

The day would come when they'd all possess the mental fortitude to push their consciousness beyond pain.

HE'S COMING, FATHER'S HOME! JOHANNA CALLED OUT FROM THE PORCH, called out across the miles, and six sisters came running with sparkling eyes. Their father gave off the exquisite scent of pine forest, sweat, and bear blood. He walked straight into the kitchen, sat down in the wobbly armchair by the fireplace, threw his jacket and sweater on a chair, and pulled off his boots, shaking out gravel, pine needles, and birch leaves onto the kitchen floor. The littlest, Elga, climbed up onto his lap and snuggled into the bloody trousers. She leaned her little head against the sweat-yellow string vest through which bristled coarse chest hair, and inhaled the soothing scent of sweat from his armpit mixed with the sharp leather smell of his boots. Her father filled a pipe and sucked on it merrily as he brought the match to the tobacco. He took hold of his little one and placed her on his right foot, lifting his leg to form a swing. Now, as she bounced up and down in the air, Elga could hardly feel the ache in her bottom caused by her mother's cruel blows.

Ride, ride, ride the wild horse, this wee rider's got no spurs yet of course.

And with that, the killjoy mother's tricks were forgotten for a while.

EVERY MORNING, AS SOON AS SHE WOKE, JOHANNA WENT OUT TO the terrace where her father sat, shrouded in pipe smoke, gaze fixed over the treetops out toward the blue-gray mountain. He would take the pipe from his mouth and sniff the air in different directions like a predator, then nod at Johanna. She knew he had an inner radar that could sense from miles away where the bear was. *Can I come with you? Can I come with you? Yes, of course you can.* On these occasions, when they each packed a hunting bag and Johanna waved goodbye to six jealous sisters, she felt a dizzy rush as her power over her siblings grew. As the oldest, Johanna saw herself as suited to the role of leader, of top dog, well placed to learn her father's hunting secrets and telepathic connection with the bears. Her father came home with a bear so often that the coarse, flavorsome meat built the girls' strong bodies, their arms powerful, shoulders broad. The only one the protein and beer didn't rub off on at all was Elga, who remained a skinny thing. Perhaps it would change in a year or two, but she seemed to be of a different ilk, if graced with the same hair color. Did she even have the same father?

THE FATHER'S HUNTING PROWESS MEANT HIS WHOLE WORLD REvolved around the hunt and its practical and mental preparations: strategies for outwitting a taunted beast. Would he come home at the weekend with yet another felled animal? Increasingly he forgot about his beloved girl children during the little time he spent at home on the farm. He neither saw nor heard them, even when they were sitting in a ring around him, watching as he cleaned his rifles, greased them with lynx fat, and gulped porter. The next day, he'd be gone.

At night the girls lay on their bearskins, longing, whinnying, and calling out for their father in their dreams. In these dreams he would come home riding a gigantic brown bear. Tanja and Aune lay close together, holding hands. When Johanna felt sleep evading her, she would lie in her father's bed and breathe in the scent from his pillow. Their parents had long since begun to sleep in separate rooms—their mother in her own nook up in the attic. No one wanted to go up there—the attic room smelled of her nauseating, sour body odor. Muffled sounds drifted down. Was she shouting in her sleep?

On Elga's twelfth birthday, her father was out hunting. He'd informed the girls he was about to take on the most enormous bear he'd ever set eyes on, under such dangerous circumstances he didn't want a companion, particularly given the way they instinctively imitated him. Back on the farm they slouched around. Each day their games became more brutal from the pain of anticipation. Elga found herself being tripped, shoved, gashed, and trapped in snares. When she opened the door to the cowshed, she got a bucket of water over her head. Soaked and freezing, she was humiliated by the sisters' laughter and Johanna's *You had it coming, you disgusting little bitch!*

After their father's death, the shrieks of delight fell silent: no wrestling matches, no cow bingo. The hunting rifle lay in the center of the table like a relic—the gun's central presence replaced the father's spirit in the room. No one wanted the bear meat from their father's final fight, as though to eat it would be to eat of his body; instead, it was sold at the market. They kept the bearskin impregnated with their father's blood. The great head with its bloodthirsty glare and sharp fangs and the long, curved claws of its paws embodied the greatest loss of their lives. The bear's enraged expression lent a new purpose to the tatters of the sisters' lives.

After this defeat, nothing bad could ever happen to them.

SORROW BURNED IN THEIR BREASTS FOR A COUPLE OF DARK YEARS. THEY moved like somnambulists around the farm, nothing left over for fun and games. The only time the girls paid attention, the only time they ever allowed the corners of their mouths to twitch, was when Uncle Veikko came to visit—he even made their mother soften. A short ceasefire would endure between mother and daughters.

Veikko was well over sixty, and almost blind. He walked with a limp, supporting himself with a heavy stick. He recognized his nieces' voices, the way they spoke over one another, mostly without listening. He greeted them all in turn, from oldest to youngest: Johanna, the twins Tanja and Aune, Simone, and then the twins Tiina and Laura, and young Elga. Their uncle's voice was clear as he sat at ease in his usual storytelling spot, the firewood chest draped in beaver skin.

Castor, he said, stroking the skin. Castor was the Latin name for beaver. Important to know.

The sisters put wood in the stove and Tanja got a quiet, spark-free fire going. The bearskins were laid out, and they sat in a semicircle around their uncle. Then he began, and it sounded like a song come from a young man's throat. The well-modulated baritone of his voice, the rhythm, the pleasure he found in words, and then there it was: the story. They were transported.

Aune radiated concentration; she always sat nearest, right opposite her uncle, to be sure of catching every word, every emphasis, and every tension-building pause for effect. She carefully watched the gestures made by his veiny hand with its black thumbnail and its stump of a middle finger. Johanna listened with her eyes closed. Was she asleep? Tiina sat cross-legged, cracking her finger joints, then she stretched out her legs before lying on her front. Elga looked at her, irritated. When Tiina started doing press-ups she got a dressing-down from Tanja.

From his coat pocket, the girls' uncle took a stick of birch as thick as his wrist, which he cut into as he talked. Bears and elk emerged from his hands' memory of scale and form as he spun a yarn the sisters had heard before. The myth of young Aino, who drowned herself so she wouldn't have to marry the bearded old bard Väinämöinen. The girls wanted to hear that one every time, just like children asking for the same story. Though this group of listeners were teenagers, aside from Elga who hadn't yet turned thirteen, and Johanna who was twenty. If Veikko started with a brand-new story, he would normally be asked to tell an old favorite before he left. The girls would put in requests. *We want to hear about when Hagar was forced to go out into the Sinai desert.* Their favorite was the tale of Lemminkäinen's mother who patches up her son's drowned body and brings it back to life. On the bank of the Tuonela River she sits with her healing mother's hands on his naked, lifeless body... Then their real mother came into the kitchen and broke the spell. *Louhi, won't you sit with us a while?* said the silken-voiced Veikko to his sister. She shook her head, the stern lines of her face softening when she looked at her brother. *The milk truck will be here soon*, she said abruptly.

After two days of their uncle's rhythmic voice in their ears—tales that lasted from morning till evening with breaks for grilled sausages and saunas—they accompanied him home via a shortcut through the forest. A hesitant, slow journey: you couldn't make an old man take bigger steps. Here and there, the paths were criss-crossed with roots to stumble over and slopes steep and slippery from the rain, and they took turns carrying him over the obstacles. Each time they sat down on stumps and tussocks in the swamp to let him rest, he'd pick up from where he'd left off. Tales about the holes in moss-topped boulders where people had once lived. Fugitives, tramps, and unmarried women lived in these caves with their illegitimate children. He himself had played with the son of the forest whore, and he had a keen memory of how they'd sat in the depths of the cave's cold, moist darkness and competed at telling the most terrifying ghost story. It was all about imagining the most horrifying details. The boy's mother wasn't called the forest whore because she entertained men for money, but because she'd got pregnant by the headmaster of the village school: she was lady's maid to his wife. After that she was thrown out and met with nothing but no, no, no when she tried to rent a place to live nearby. No one wanted to be neighbors with a woman like that, because the bastard might carry a contagion that would spread to other children. So she took up residence, like many unmarried mothers, with her son in a cave.

If you want to nourish your stories, you must gather in caves, Veikko said as he rode like a boy on Tiina's strong shoulders and continued, in a jumpy, breathless voice, the tale of the friendly spirits of the forest: sprites, elves, pixies. They're rare, but those who become close friends with the forest sometimes meet them. Yes, the forest can kill, if there's a fire or a storm, or a bear attacks, but one thing is for sure: it speaks ill of no one.

On the long way home from their uncle's Aune tried to mimic his storytelling and was shamed into silence. By the time they'd walked a few miles, the internal drum kits of seven uneasy stomachs were protesting. They'd had no sustenance since breakfast, which had consisted of a boiled egg and a piece of rock-hard bread. The thought of the long journey ahead was torturous. Was their mother trying to starve them? She'd become even touchier since she became a widow. When they got back, the animals were mooing anxiously and stamping around in their own dung; in the kitchen, unwashed dishes were piled haphazardly, and tall ferns were growing all over the farm. A long-unwatered, yellowing monstera on the windowsill clutched at the moist windowpane as though trying to press its way out through the glass, out to lap up rain and fresh air. Their father's home felt abandoned, strange, even threatening.

Laura, who rarely ventured an opinion, had a compelling suggestion, "The old hag's nagging is poisoning our bodies. Let's head for the forest."

"She's dragging us down into her depravity," Tanja said. "Let's stand together and resist. If we plan carefully, we can live . . ."

Tiina banged her fist on the table.

"Yeeaah, let's move!"

"What would Veikko have said?" Aune said cautiously.

"Maybe we'll f-find traces of the old man out there," said Johanna, who'd been suffering from a stammer since their father's passing. "He drew me a m-map where he m-marked our rest stops."

The stammer vexed her, undermined the authority of her leadership. She realized immediately that the collective respect of her tribe was threatened. Elga's damn sneer.

"He's there in the forest to protect us," Simone said eagerly. "I can feel he's left signs. He's gazing down on us. Father, send us divine power!"

As usual, Elga made sure to have the last word.

"I reckon it's up to us to win power."

CHAPTER TWO

You know nothing of Finland until you've wandered through the deep forests, where the trunks of beautifully aged gray pines are clustered high up with bracket fungus. So the sisters dreamed of seeing the lush forests of the north, where only those with an intimate knowledge of the forest or adventurers with no self-preservation instincts dared set foot. Personally, I'm too much at home in my urban comforts to aspire to the sisters' spartan, physically demanding lifestyle—especially that which lay ahead of them. In order to write about it, I read up on flora and fauna, and studied the life writing of older Sámi people particularly carefully; they knew everything about harnessing the treasures of the forest, knew everything about surviving snow and cold and, of course, about hunting animals for food *and* being friends with them.

Johanna had packed her rucksack with a water bottle and some rice pirogs; Tanja carried a thermos of coffee, a wooden guksi, and some crispbread. Tiina had a hip flask, matches, strips of birch bark, and some snares.

A few miles from home, they approached the Niskanpää family's henhouse, and Johanna ordered the youngest, Elga, to slip her lithe little body in among the cackling bundles of feathers and stifling stench of chicken shit to gather as many eggs as she could while the older girls kept watch. There were cartons in a shed that adjoined the henhouse.

In the thick spruce forest you could almost touch the late summer heat. The sisters were tormented by mosquitoes, even though they'd covered themselves in beck oil. They walked and walked, until Laura and Elga started whining, wanting to rest. Sweat was running down their foreheads and Elga moaned that her legs felt like two broom handles. At just that moment, a forest glade opened up, at its center a large, sunlit stone that seemed to call out to them: *Girls, let me be your hearth!* The heat of the stone was a saving grace, since a fire would betray them to anyone on their trail. Aune broke the eggs on one side of the stone, which had a depression with a smooth, flat surface. Surely they would be fairly filling if fried in gun grease? Johanna seemed to expect the others to clean part of the stone of gravel, prepare the eggs, and serve her, while she trimmed the branches from a spruce and arranged them to form an impressive bed. She seemed to be under the impression that she, as troop leader, was working double and therefore deserved extra rest. Reclining, she watched the clouds scudding over the spruce tops as she waited for her fried egg and crispbread.

When they'd gobbled it all up and Tiina had burped her loudest, they heard a distant barking and their names floated over the trees: their mother's piercing voice echoed over muted male voices. They sat bolt upright and listened. It sounded like a whole crowd of people were out looking for them, but it was hard to determine how close they were. Johanna hid the heap of branches beneath a thick spruce, cleared away all trace of their presence, and ordered the sisters to ready themselves for flight. Then they jogged, one after the other, straight into the cool, dark forest. They passed swamps and made a detour around a marsh just as a heron rose, gliding off, with its straight body, to a less threatening place.

Fourteen feeble legs, fourteen bare feet beyond all imaginable function. After four hours, Elga fell whimpering to her knees and Tiina collapsed on a bed of moss. Black woodpecker. Jay. Not a peep from anyone trailing. Had they heard wrong earlier? Surely seven pairs of young ears couldn't mistake an owl for their mother's booming voice.

Tanja and Johanna staggered around, trying to find a suitable place to rest, and realized they were a few hundred yards from a forest tarn. They made for the lake, threw down their packs, tore off their clothes, and jumped in. Seven fountains. Tiina freestyled her way over to Simone. The girls splashed around and let out loud sounds of contentment. Even Laura got caught up in the games.

Renewed, they built a shelter and shared out pirogs as dusk fell and nocturnal animals rustled in the bushes. The hip flask passed from mouth to mouth, the drink burned and warmed them, the half-moon shone and was reflected in the water's surface. White bodies floated once again in the coal-black water, all apart from Aune and Laura, who thought it a little too cold. Elga held her nose and jumped in, and Tiina pretended to save her life before taking a hard grip on her little sister's head and holding it for a long time under the surface. Coarse laughter over terrified coughing and gasping for breath.

Afterward they huddled together, shivering, before bedding down their exhausted bodies, tightly packed in the sphagnum:

head on stomach, head on shoulder, entwined like puppies seeking warmth from their littermates. The sisters fell into a kind of deep sleep they hadn't experienced since their father departed. Is there a sleep so deep it borders on death? Not all of them were slumbering. Laura had trimmed a spruce with her whittling knife and made a bed for herself at the foot of the dense-growing tree's thick, sheltering branches, which hung down over a bed of Taylor's flapwort. She listened to the comforting sounds of the night: the squeaking of bats and the rustling of what she assumed to be foxes and roe deer.

Johanna was awoken by the sound of someone knocking on the door. It was a lesser-spotted woodpecker hacking a large hole in a pine, with a smaller nursery hole below the adult nest. It seemed the older birds wanted to sleep in peace. Half-asleep, Johanna stretched, straightened her aching legs, and realized that she was in the forest, right next to a wheezing Tiina whose armpits stank to high heaven. Woody's tapping went on; aside from that, she could hear nothing but her siblings' slumber and Tiina's grunts—she sounded like an old man when she slept. Johanna searched her rucksack for the last two rice pirogs. She munched one and looked out over the lake, where the dragonflies played and the morning mist had yet to lift. She gazed hungrily at the other pirog as it lay there looking delicious, but checked herself, experiencing an unusual, rather pleasing sense of equanimity. The others could share the last one. Hunger was their only concern in this beautiful place. Johanna took the snares out of the rucksack. If they followed their father's method, and set the traps in the morning, they would, in the best of worlds, have food for the evening. Though then, of course, they'd be forced to light a fire, and that might give them away.

Johanna dived into the lake, her morning swim waking the

others. Tanja and Aune yawned loudly and gave Simone a shake. Elga, who loathed early mornings, slumbered on, while Tanja and Aune slid down into the water and swam over to Johanna. Simone sat outside the shelter and folded her hands in a mumbled prayer. Laura crept out of her own, neighboring shelter, looking out over the tarn and her splashing siblings. She pulled on her boots, lit a cigarette, and walked into the forest, where she mooched about by herself—occasionally bending down and feeling the moss. She found some dark clay, which she dug around in, taking off her T-shirt and packing it full, pressing out the water before carrying the bundle a short distance and sitting down on an obliging stone. With careful fingers, she kneaded the lump of clay into a girl with a fox's snout.

The late summer day's tasks of setting snares and preparing for the evening's fire carried on without concern. Johanna's optimistic early morning plan worked out well. Some pigeons had wandered into cleverly concealed snares and without a word, the girls thought gratefully of their father in his heaven. Johanna lay down on a bed of moss and gazed up at the treetops; she found a comfortable position and hummed a pop song. Tanja trilled along as they plucked the feathers from the dead birds. Simone was building a bivouac of thin spruce branches, and a few yards away a fire was burning. Aune and Simone cooked the birds on spits over the embers, they had soot on their cheeks and their clothes were in tatters. A little apart from her sisters, lost in her own world, sat Laura, modeling a donkey.

The mosquitoes attacked. The sisters slapped and swore. Simone set light to a conk from a birch bracket, which gave off smoke that dispersed the swarms somewhat. While they waited for the meat to cook through, Aune told the story of the girl Aino, who was forced to marry the old man Väinämöinen: the tragic tale Veikko always returned to. They lusted after new details. Aino was told that it would be an honor to marry such a widely renowned man, one equal to the gods, who furthermore had a spellbinding, darkly sonorous singing voice that drew hordes of listeners. But young Aino preferred to drown herself rather than let a wrinkly old man's member inside her. Väinämöinen mourned his wife-to-be with her long, shining hair. He rowed out onto the lake where the girl had taken her own life and was met by a strong beam of light on the surface of the water. He glimpsed the young Aino, who turned into a silvery, shining fish, right down in the deep. The boat was close to capsizing when . . .

"Did she exist in reality?" Tiina interrupted.

"Of course," Aune replied softly.

"But she didn't turn into a fish. . . . You can't believe that, surely," Elga said.

"There are too many tales of that kind for me *not* to believe in them," Simone said. "Take the one about . . ."

It was clear fall was on its way. Dusk fell early, and the forest tarn was wreathed in swirls of mist. The sisters stared into the white air. Would they be given a sign? Was Aino down there, in the black water? Every damselfly that made patterns on the clear surface was a greeting from her. A dull whine could be heard as dusk brought down more thick swarms of mosquitoes over the sisters.

"D-d-don't scratch . . . blood . . . they'll all come," Johanna commanded.

"You might as well tell us to stop smoking," Tiina said.

The sisters scratched their bites, and their mouths watered as the game sizzled on the fire. Simone shared out the pieces of meat, which they grasped at hungrily with their fingers, burning their tongues and thumbs. When they'd devoured the pigeons they thought they'd never again be able to eat a bird's meat, never again be hungry. Johanna sent round the flask of brännvin. Tiina burped and farted a melody, challenging the others to guess the tune, while Elga wore a teenage expression conveying boundless incomprehension. She was keen to distance herself from the group.

"Right, I'm going to freshen my mouth up."

Elga tore off her clothes, jumped in the water, and blew great glittering bubbles, the tarn's very own jacuzzi.

Tiina followed her.

"I'm going to cool my ass down."

She vanished, swimming underwater so long that Johanna was worried she'd got caught in the water-lily stalks. Laura hopped up onto a stone and sat, dipping her feet in the cool water. When the others had finished bathing, she lowered herself in and swam slowly over to the opposite shore. The exciting thing about drifting across a forest tarn is that you never know what's beneath you as you go. A few Stone Age craniums, the odd human skeleton from a suicide, you can be sure of that. Bear skulls. A horse that went through the ice one winter when Veikko was young. Now the water was cleaning the girls' filthy clothes, which they hung up around the fire afterward to dry.

After bathing, they all stood naked in a ring around the flames, warming themselves. The older girls noticed that Elga's pubic hair had grown bushy over the summer and that Tanja's breasts had swelled. Johanna sent the flask wandering. When it was empty they fell silent and Johanna sighed. They all knew what that meant. They'd been waiting for the signal, and they sat down around the fire. Johanna climbed up onto a rocky mound and stood above the others. Laura angled herself away with her legs outside the ring.

"Wouldn't it be nice to be free of that c-crazy old bag back home?" Johanna said, entreating her band of sisters with her eyes.

"Thinking of killing her?" Elga asked with a lopsided grin.

"Nah, running away for good," Johanna replied.

The sisters in chorus: "Yeeeeaaaaah!"

Johanna hushed their cries and turned serious.

"Question is, will we survive the nomad's life in the long term?"

"Homeless people sleep under the open sky," Aune said gently. "Their skin is toughened by fall's storms and winter's brutality. We'll adapt to the conditions. We're no church mice. Our noble parents made sure of that. Veikko has taught us what he knows."

"The frosty nights are almost here," Tanja said. "The fall rains. We have to agree on a solution."

"The spruces are our shields. Imagine getting to live here with wolves and bears as neighbors," said Aune.

Johanna sat on her haunches and grew pensive.

"I b-believe . . . our dear father . . . up there on the mountaintops, smoking his pipe, has angels around him. You know what he s-said to me when we were out hunting and we slept in the hunter's lodge?"

"Noo-oo."

"I'll live forever. I'm with you always. Our empire is eternal."

"But can he protect us in a snowstorm?" Elga interjected, breaking the spell.

"The Holy Spirit protects us always," Simone said. "I at least know that, but our dear mother is surely scared to death right now."

"That old bag wants nothing more than to break all the bones in our bodies." Tanja spat.

"The stones in the forest are more tender than our bitch of a mother has ever been," Tiina said.

"A g-goddamn wh-whipping is what awaits us if we head back home," Johanna said. "She'll beat us to beef hash if she gets her claws into us."

Even gentle Aune grew coarse: "That hag is the very opposite of Lemminkäinen's sweet mother."

"Though of course, that mother had a son, not seven d-daughters," said Johanna.

The seven-headed troop fell silent and drifted into melancholy, letting the sounds of the night take over. The cold got to them, they shivered, and their lips turned blue, though of course that couldn't be seen in the dark.

Simone picked nervously at her toenails, doubt in her voice. "Time is running out. The nights are already frosty. We won't get hardened to the cold before fall. I can feel it in my bones: the devil will come for us if we stay out here. We'd do just as well to head home and get it over with, take our punishment. We'll head off at dawn tomorrow after sleep and a morning dip."

"We live p-pretty well at home with the river and the streams in the valley," Johanna said. "We have all the paraphernalia there for b-beer and brännvin. Good p-people, we'll plan to move next spring."

"Cellar-cold porter," Tiina added. "That's home for me."

"We can ask Veikko to live with us, then even Mother will soften up," Aune said. "Let these days in the forest's embrace be something to remember and to speak of when we grow old."

Simone looked up to the sky and clasped her hands piously. She said, "What does our poor mother intend to do? Has she gone back home and assembled a search party?"

"We won't get away with this," said Aune.

"We're robust. Together we're resilient," said Johanna.

"We'll make our way home at a leisurely pace, take the blows with dignity," said Simone.

"And we won't have to lie here like a bunch of sheep," said Tiina.

"But the sheep never goes vooo . . . luntarily to the slaughter," Johanna pointed out.

"We weren't exactly born with fur coats on our backs," said Aune.

"Let's clench our teeth and head back steadfastly. Every one of our arguments leads to that decision," said Simone.

Elga cleared her throat.

"My suggestion is that we mull it over for another day or so with our as-yet-unwhipped backs. What do you think, Laura, over there in the puddle with your mud bears?"

"I'm staying. I can work well here. You guys go home."

"You planning to eat mud?" Elga asked.

"Yeah."

"And what will you eat when the frosts come," Elga went on.

"Snow and old man's beard."

"Okay. One more day," Johanna said. "What have you squished together now then?"

Laura looked up at Johanna.

"Girl with bear."

IN THE MIDDLE OF THE NIGHT, JOHANNA WOKE UP WITH AUNE'S DIRTY foot against her mouth. Her shin was itching where the mosquitoes had sucked her blood. She heard rustling. Far off or close? Bears? Wolverines? Maybe wolves, scenting blood. Their old man had warned them about sleeping out with blood in their trousers. Tanja and Aune always bled at the same time. Their legs had been running with it while they were eating the barbecued meat. She sat up and listened tensely, but it was only Laura, coming out to pee. She was tricksy, Laura, but not the worst. In the nightmare Johanna had just woken from in a panic, all her siblings were like Elga: intractably pert. Was this how it was going to be? An unrelenting blood sport? Her nose was ice cold and she laid a hand on her rumbling stomach. It would be hard to wake up without bread and coffee, hard to get all the way home on an empty stomach. Here and there were sparse bilberry bushes with a few berries. The lingonberries weren't yet ripe. Uncle Veikko often told of Marjatta, who ate an over-fermented lingonberry, got pregnant, and gave birth to her son Suomi. Having children is not something for us, Johanna had long ago concluded. All that blood. Giving birth was not something she was planning on; Mom had done that for her in abundance. There was no way she was taking care of any more screaming brats.

How could God, if he indeed existed, punish a mother with seven daughters? What had Louhi done to deserve that?

Full of self-pity, Johanna talked silently to herself about her siblings' sense of entitlement—they did as they pleased and ridiculed her for what little order she tried to keep. *Someone has to take the role of leader, otherwise the group will break up and it'll be our downfall. People have treated us very badly, saying we live wrongly, but we're hungry for battle.*

There are weak spots, she conceded. One crack in the wall was Laura, who didn't really want to be part of the flock. *I'll keep an ever-watchful eye on her*, she thought, *even though I think she's harmless. She wanders around, closed to the world, with her stupid figurines. Stares bug-eyed when you talk to her, endures a telling-off in silence. The other crack is Elga. Any betrayal of the group should cost her more than a knife wound. The problem is that every punishment makes her more defiant.*

When had Johanna ever got to be rude and immature? It gnawed at her. Self-pitying, loud-voiced monologues flamed inside her: never getting to be the one who takes liberties. The weighty burden of the village elder as custodian: the price of being their father's chosen one. Each morning that she woke in her father's bed, the sheet and pillowcases of which still smelled of his shaving soap, she wanted to get up and sneak away from her duties. Disappear. Travel to Ireland. She'd always dreamed of it—the steep, moss-topped cliffs and the wild sea. People drank black beer and whiskey and they were sound, not too grand. But English? Can someone who can't read travel? Her short time in school had shown how she was made. She could never get a book to open itself to her. The same was true of their father, though he wouldn't admit it.

He'd managed to become famous anyway, and she, the oldest daughter, had tried to use everything he'd taught her in bringing up her sisters, but they just fooled around. There was an ounce of sense in Tanja, no jeering came from her direction. Nor any hard blows— side by side she and Tanja were she-wolves with steely claws.

Before Johanna drifted off to sleep again, a crystal-clear thought passed through her. This is how it is: In the beginning, the punisher is as fearful as the victim, unless, that is, the blows are fueled by long-suppressed rage. Then, it flows like a tango.

AS THEY APPROACHED THE RUNAWAYS' CAMP, WHERE CLOTHES LAY discarded here and there, Louhi ordered Killo and Kiiski to heel, to stop them rushing over toward the voices and the smell of smoke. Later, the girls would be astonished by the fact their mother had arrived with a man in tow. She'd knocked on the huntmaster's door and asked for help. He'd stepped up immediately—the search for the bear hunter's daughters would lend a thrill to his work. In the midst of all her anger, Mother Louhi felt a certain enchantment at walking through the forest with a well-built man who carried a rifle over his shoulder. He whispered that they should approach the girls' refuge with caution; they crouched silently some fifty yards from the camp. Waited attentively for the dawn that would light their way. When their mother heard Tiina's characteristic snores and grunts—and yes, she could match each sleeping sound to the right daughter—she nodded at the huntmaster. He gave a signal in return and they crept toward the girls' camp. The mother took a deep breath and unleashed in their direction a resolute, guttural sound that must have been audible twenty miles away.

Out you come, girls, game's up!

Seven bodies sat up and stared at each other. The dogs rushed over and greeted each of them, sniffing around the campfire and licking up scraps from the meal. Elga was quick to figure things out; she swiped away the branches and tried to run. In vain, because barring the way was a large man who seemed to have arms of steel. He caught hold of her naked body, gripping it tightly in his gloved hands, pressing it against him. The girls' mother rushed up alongside him, all rage and clenched fists.

And then there were seven shivering, naked girls in front of their mother and the huntmaster, who was a stranger to them. Their mother held out an arm, finger pointed.

Line up! Youngest first.

She held a guksi aloft and waved Elga forward. Her daughter shut her eyes tight and received two blows, one to each cheek. She shrieked, collapsed into a squat, held her face, and whimpered. The huntmaster shone the kind of oversize flashlight they'd otherwise only seen used by the police. Its floodlight beam was blinding. The sisters blinked in the sharp light.

Here with you, Tanja and Aune! Heel!

Killo and Kiiski barked at each blow. They ran around, confused and confounded at the pain being inflicted on their mistresses. The girls' mother got into the swing of things, and the strokes grew harder with each cheek. Simone, who looked at her mother with puppy-dog eyes, endured somewhat lighter blows. Harder again for Laura, who looked down at the ground.

When Johanna stepped up silently to be dealt her share of the violence, she looked her mother straight in the eye. A never-ending five-second reckoning of strength in which neither looked away. Johanna was the first to open her mouth.

"Where is he-ee . . . our be-beloved father?"

Her mother let out a peal of raw laughter, took another step closer, breathed into Johanna's face, stared right into her pupils. Into the dark blackness of her eyes.

"Don't you get it . . . ? He's dead. He chose the bear . . . and you can't bring yourself to accept it."

Her mother took a step backward. Gathered her strength. One blow. Two blows. They resounded on Johanna's cheekbones.

Johanna tensed every muscle in her body, cheeks flushed with rage, stoically suppressing any hint of a moan.

Her mother lowered her arm, stuffing the guksi in her rucksack. She looked at the huntmaster, giving him, with a nod, the signal to talk.

"Girls. Time for you to stop your dirty tricks. If you don't pull yourselves together, your mother—with my help—will see to it that you end up in a reformatory."

THE SKY BRIGHTENED, AND THEY MADE THEIR WAY SILENTLY HOME with heavy steps and hiccupping sobs from Elga. Their stomachs rumbled loudly. The sisters avoided their mother's gaze. Johanna tried to master her mounting rage. Tiina had caught an enervating cough; she kept spitting and clearing her throat. During the journey, their mother called them swine, scum, viper bait. She screamed at them to keep up, muttered and hissed that she cursed fate for not once permitting her to bear a child with a cock. God's sevenfold punishment, she said, looking in both anguish and accusation up at the sky. Though she'd claimed not to be a believer. Perhaps that was just while their father was alive, to avoid getting a fist in the stomach for speaking God's name.

They walked the whole day without a break—no, once they fell to their knees and quenched their thirst in a cold spring. They stepped into the spring, cooled the swellings and bleeding sores on their poor feet, soothed the spruce-twig scratches on their cheeks and brows. Laura let her guard down and whinnied, dragging her feet, delaying the party as she bent over the lingonberry bushes. Her mother gave her such a hard slap on the back that she fell headlong into the bushes and hit her chin on a stone.

The troop stopped again, swaying on the spot from exhaustion, and the girls' mother grasped Laura by the scruff of her neck and pulled her up.

"Almost home now," said the huntmaster, who was longing to get home to his dinner. "Hurry up, girls!"

They trudged on another mile or so. Then Louhi called out.

"Stop! Look! An anthill. Go over and spit, everyone. A really big wad, spit on the mound again. Good. Now rub your hands on the ants."

"Ouch, fucking hell," Tiina said.

"Stings like the devil," Johanna said.

"It's meant to sting. Ant piss heals most wounds," their mother said, rubbing Laura's chin.

Laura cried out in pain.

At dusk they arrived back at the farm. From the farmyard they hobbled up the stairs, wrenched open the front door, and headed straight for the kitchen with saliva running from the corners of their mouths. Their mother looked on as together they scoffed down three whole loaves of rye bread, fourteen raw eggs, and one smoked bear tongue apiece.

The force of their hunger made the girls eat so fast they kept choking and coughing. They didn't chew the elk-brown rye bread properly and it got stuck in their throats. They washed it down with so much porter they got hiccups. Elga held her stomach as her guts rebelled.

Their mother turned away with wet eyes, so as not to give away the unexpected twinge of gratitude she felt to have the wastrels back home again.

Thus ended the sisters' first escape attempt. A seed of freedom had been sown.

Chapter Three

Mothers and daughters. I need only write the words, and I, and surely many of you, read acrimony. Daughters can live their whole lives in antipathy toward their mothers and think that real life and big ideas are the stuff of boys, men, and fathers. In the clarity of life's final phase, many realize their self-deception.

These seven sisters, Louhi's daughters, would later come to see their mother with clear eyes, but we have a way to go until then.

After the escape, Louhi would disappear for days at a time, presumably to see Veikko, before turning up again, unspeaking, refusing to respond to questions. Silence as punishment is more dreadful than violence. After being kept awake all night by frightening sounds from the attic, Johanna realized that if their mother didn't regain her powers and begin to conduct her duties again, she, as the oldest daughter, would have to take parental responsibility. She decided to pull herself together.

Their mother had seen her work on the farm as her bitter fate in life. After her spouse's passing, she had no reason to slave away. But what should she do instead? Louhi's life had run through her fingers, and she could do nothing but sit with sagging shoulders, staring into the void—on the veranda, on a log in the forest, or in her favorite spot by the swamp.

WITH A HEAVY MORNING HEART, JOHANNA BURIED HER NOSE IN THE bearskin soaked in her father's blood. The warmth and the scent were calming. She dragged herself out of bed and stood on the veranda, peering into the mist that hung heavy over the rye field. She made her way down the steps and stumbled on the handle of a scythe cast aside by Tiina the Untidy. If she'd been unlucky, she would have been lying there, legs splayed, her ankles cut clean through. She had to be careful where she stepped so as not to trip over other discarded tools. The dogs followed her, right at her heels.

In the cowshed she noticed that the cows had grown so skinny their ribs were showing. They huddled close to one another with their bony bodies, making vague, nervous noises. Johanna gave them fresh water, and as she fed them potato skins and grass, she made up her mind. From now on, she'd keep an eye on her mother, following her discreetly to see what she was leaving undone.

She jumped at the sound of an engine from down on the road. Who could that be? She opened the leaking door to the cowshed, the hinge squealed. Out in the farmyard was the pockmarked guy who drove the milk truck. His cap was on backward with the peak over his neck.

"Where's the milk?" he asked, annoyed. He sensed he'd driven up to the farm in vain.

"Mother's ill," Johanna said, noting with surprise that she wasn't stammering.

"Hey, you could've rung!" he said crossly, turning on his heel and stalking back to the lorry, which could barely be seen through the mist.

Johanna heard the door slam. The man wound down the window and shouted, "Fucking riffraff!"

Tanja was tasked with doing the milking and getting the cows in some kind of order; better order, at least, than the kitchen. Together, Tanja and Johanna carried out the tasks their mother—to their dismay—no longer performed. Was their mother's neglect the result of forgetfulness brought on by sorrow, or sheer bloody-mindedness aimed at driving them all into a black hole? Johanna couldn't figure it out. She knew it wasn't an option to question her mother's behavior to her face. She had a habit of interpreting everything as a direct threat, an unalloyed criticism of her. Instead of explaining herself, she'd begin to reel off all the injustices, all the wrongs her daughters had perpetrated against her. She was right about some of it, but otherwise it was exaggeration on a grand scale. Johanna was keen to avoid arguments, but still wanted to be able to look at her mother with challenge in her eyes.

She stood in the middle of the farmyard and looked out across the fields. The rye was beginning to sag its shoulders; no harvest had been planned. The huntmaster had been right in his hard-voiced comments as he'd clutched the rifle in his powerful fists, dark hair on his knuckles. Their days of mischief were over. Otherwise, they'd be put away.

The sisters had to get it into their heads: an institution would be the end, Johanna thought as she woke them. She laid on a real spread, putting out coffee and rye bread buns with honey. She grabbed her father's rifle, held it fondly, closed her eyes, and felt an impulse to remove it from the table, but she let it go, leaving the gun in place. She whistled. Her sisters waddled sleepily in, one by one, Laura last of all with drooping eyelids and a bullish expression. The success of her summons gave Johanna a moment of satisfaction.

The sisters sat around the table, chewing, slurping, burping. Tiina rounded it all off with a fart. Johanna exhorted them: "Now, girls, it's time to do this properly. Unless we're *actively choosing* to run the farm into ruin and let the cows perish from neglect."

"Let's divide up the tasks," Tanja said. "However dull they are, they need doing."

Elga's face was suddenly shrouded in deep shadow; she looked like the world was ending. Laura crumpled into a self-protective hibernation.

Tiina held a clenched fist up toward the ceiling, "I'll drive the plow. Dibs!"

Johanna delegated the very dullest tasks. From now on it would be Elga and Laura who, with jerky, angry movements, carried out the jobs in the barn. They couldn't get away from it, they were counting down the years until this soul-crushing work would end. Tanja took on the kitchen and found unexpected pleasure in routine—the more monotonous, the better. She baked coal-black rye bread, while Johanna took the shotgun, to shoot for supper any game that happened to pass in front of the muzzle.

Tanja had made their evening porridge and managed to get it nice and smooth. Simone piously set out a sticky bottle of Polish fruit wine she'd found right at the back of the root cellar. The sickly sweet wine was passed round, and they drank in silence. Now and then came a gurgling sound from the attic. They stiffened, attentive. Instinctively, Johanna wanted to go up and check on their mother, in case she was ill, but she stopped herself. The tribe would see her as a weakling.

As they ate their dinner, they heard their mother whimpering in her bed. They looked at each other anxiously.

There wasn't a wild animal in the forest whose cry scared them like this did.

※

Six walking wounded with utterly done-in, aching bodies trudged into the kitchen. The sweat stench was unbearable. Scent is the underdog of the human senses, tolerant of the most challenging squalor. How else would sewage workers in major cities survive each working day? In the kitchen, the scent of bread fought for space with the stench of sweat. In a panic, Tanja searched through the pantry and kitchen for edible matter, finding nothing but salt gherkins, mustard, and brown onions. She put the jar of gherkins on the table and struggled not to think about how good it would be to have a little sour cream to balance the saltiness; that was a luxury they'd have to save for when the cows were back in top form. The sisters took their seats, each gnawing on a pickle while they waited for Johanna. They hoped she would soon appear in the doorway with a freshly slaughtered animal in her hand or over her shoulder. Or at least a pigeon they could take it in turns to pluck feathers from.

Tiina slapped her thighs when Johanna came home empty-handed with eyes lowered and tongue sharp. Like her father, she struggled with defeat. *Where's the old woman?* asked Tiina. Johanna looked at her siblings and pointed up at the ceiling. In the cellar, Tanja stated grimly, there was not a single potato, not even one tainted by mold. Johanna opened her eyes wide, placing the rifle, with exaggerated drama, in the center of the table. It was clear to her siblings that she was experiencing an inner avalanche. Johanna took a deep breath, then another, and then suddenly gripped the gun again, loaded it, aimed it at the door, and strode out. *Lord Jesus Christ*, said Simone, tiptoeing after her.

Tanja, Elga, Aune, and Tiina sat silently in the kitchen, ears pricked. They jumped when they heard a shot. The sound came from further away on the farm, not from the attic, as they'd first feared. Johanna could be coldhearted but she was no mother-killer. Tiina suppressed a vexatious sob and when the door opened, they sat still as sculptures. Johanna and Simone stood once again in the kitchen, Johanna with a dead squirrel in her hand. She thumped the corpse down on the table.

"The old man has spoken."

Tanja got up like some obedient wife from the farming communities of yore.

"I'll take care of it."

Simone was relieved Johanna hadn't committed an act of violence against their mother. Leaving everyone else to try to cook the small pieces of meat, Simone crept hesitantly up to the attic, a little afraid of what she might find as she rounded the curve in the steps. A foul, sour smell assailed her. The door was open and she peered in. Soiled sheets lay coiled around a pale-yellow mattress in one corner. Where could her mother be? Not in the attic, Simone concluded, inspecting every nook. Mouse shit, heaps of dead wasps and flies.

Simone made her way back down the creaking stairs to the kitchen.

"Is she sick?" Johanna asked.

"She's not there. But I know some secret places," Simone said.

The others looked at each other. Had that dried-up old bitch had secret places?

"She'll have to eat at some point," Elga said.

Simone went on searching. She called out over the farmyard. Called out in the barn. The poor cows with their swollen udders. Elga, what a fucking cheat! Had Mother gone into town to buy food and forgotten to let them know? The quad bike was still there, and all the rusty bicycles. Maybe their neighbor Niskanpää had taken her to the shop. If their mother had escaped to the forest, they'd be forced to search for her. Simone fell to her knees in the damp moss and held her stomach; she'd need food if she was to go on with her hunt. The squirrel must surely be cooked by now. Did squirrel taste like chicken legs? Simone swallowed the saliva that was welling up in her cheeks. On her way back she thought of Jesus walking on the water and pushed aside all thoughts of grilled sausage.

The sisters ate the meat slowly, tentatively. Squirrel, their very first time. They weren't exactly sick to their stomachs, but they were still prepared for a vomit-inducing aftertaste. They pictured the shiny, ruddy tail. Pictured the animal, brimming with life as it leaped from branch to branch as though there were lianas in the Finnish forests. The sisters chewed and chewed and admitted that their father had once again been right. There was nothing seriously wrong with the meat. Shame there was no way to make the tail edible. Shame the animal only had *one* brain. It really was fatty and delicious, just like their father had said.

"Tomorrow we must go in and do some shopping. How we're going to pay for it, I don't know," said Johanna.

These days she talked abruptly and carelessly when under

pressure, rather than stammering—that seemed to have disappeared since she took command of the family. Tiina walked up to her and started shadowboxing.

"Let's go down to the river and wrestle in the mud. It's been raining all night. Could be the last time in this life we get to have a little fun."

Five sisters rushed down to the river, which looked more than anything like a rivulet of dark brown water. Elga followed them with a cap on her head—her umpire's cap, she called it. Laura was carrying a bucket she intended to fill with pliable, rain-softened black clay before finding a place in the forest to work it. Soon the roars rose over the treetops, the dogs barked happily and rolled in the mud. Tiina backed into the forest and took a high, wildcat-like long jump. She landed on her behind, sliding several yards in the mud while her sisters hooted and cheered her on. Tiina stood up, reached up her hands, and roared at the sky, tore off the only rags she was still wearing, fell naked to her knees, and leaned back as she rubbed her crotch with brisk strokes, harder and harder, coming in fits, shrieking wildly as the secretions of her orgasm ran down her legs.

The sisters laughed, clapped their hands, and cheered her on. They didn't know the neighbor Niskanpää's son John was hiding in a bush with his binoculars a hundred yards away, thrusting, his member boring into the moss.

Five bodies were still tumbling around on the riverbank and the shadows grew long as the sun sank over the now-harvested rye field. The girls hadn't noticed that three hours had passed. Five bodies slick with river water, earth, and clay looked even more potent half-naked. Red-speckled breasts and thighs that hadn't noticed, in the heat of the moment, how the horseflies and mosquitoes had indulged themselves with fresh, fiery blood. Elga fetched cold porter and handed it out to the participants, who glugged it rabidly as she relayed the results. Tiina bounced around, howling, spinning a series of somersaults. Johanna glared, arms crossed, pigheaded as always at losing.

Laura snuck away from the shrieking, pulling the hood of her jacket over her head as she walked into the forest, and, dogs zigzagging ahead of her, reached the swamp. Darkness fell. She heard the comforting rustle of animals in trees and bushes, drew in the fresh air she was in greater need of than sausage sandwiches and beer. The dogs stopped and caught a scent; noses to the ground they followed a clear trail, fleet-footed, panting. Laura froze. The bear trail? She stopped and observed the dogs keenly. She'd survived meeting a bear alone without a weapon, but it was dangerous with the dogs; their tracking could frighten the bear into attacking. They made off across the swamp. Two harsh barks a few hundred yards ahead of her. Blurry pine tree. Indistinct meadow. She didn't want to think about the blurring, she needed to go to an optician. Food, cigarettes, and gas could be stolen, but not an eye test. As long as her vision didn't get worse—then she'd be lost. Her models required precision, and she had that up close. In the forest, everything bled together, like the yellowing, rattling aspen leaves in front of her.

The dogs must have scented a beaver or squirrel; she couldn't see anything that indicated there was something to bark about. She called them, but they whined and yapped far off by the swamp. Instinct told her to turn back as though her life depended on it and let the dogs run home on their own. She hoped they hadn't wandered into a bog and gotten stuck. Now they were barking even more urgently, howling loudly, clamoring. As she approached, she saw they were licking a tree stump. After a few more steps, she noticed some boots, her mother's worn-out boots with their uneven soles. Alongside was an overturned bucket of lingonberries. Laura trudged over to the lifeless body. Had she fallen asleep? Fainted? Her cheek was cold. When had she last stroked her mother's cheek? Had her mother permitted that when she was little? All she could remember was her sisters taking care of her as she toddled around the farm.

Her earliest memory, from the age of three, was of Tiina lifting her up into a rowan tree on their farmland, training her to sit and look out across their property. Tiina climbed up into the aspen beside her and shouted, *Wave!* Laura waved, wobbled, lost her balance, fell, winded herself, fainted—but she'd landed in a heap of leaves that saved her from serious injury.

To compensate for her poor sight, she had excellent hearing. She heard conversations from a long distance, heard her mother call to her father: *Laura gets lost in her own head. That's the injury from the fall.*

Laura sank down alongside the dead body with the dogs, who nudged and whined at this mistress of theirs, who'd been leaving their food bowls gaping empty of late. They shared the lingonberries, though the dogs preferred bilberries: for bilberries they would go diving into the bushes, but when they were really hungry, even lingonberries could be forced down. Darkness fell and memories whirled in her head. She saw a young Elga before her. She used to keep an eye on little Elga because her mother had rejected her—Laura had seen it, convinced it was the baby of the family their mother was most indifferent to. She was a mother who kept her distance, as though her offspring, despite their strength, were possessed of a weakness she was incapable of dealing with.

Laura's bottom was soaking wet. She made a final attempt, slapping her mother's cheeks and pushing down on her chest. No question that life had left her. She was dead as a doornail. The dogs buzzed around nervously, whining. *Killo and Kiiski, run home and fetch my sisters! Fetch Johanna, Tanja, Aune, Simone, Tiina, and Elga.*

She couldn't lie here all night, she'd get eaten. The dogs ran off and did their best messengering.

SEVEN SISTERS SPENT THE WHOLE NIGHT AROUND THE KITCHEN BENCH where they'd laid their mother's body; they wanted nothing to do with the attic room and its mouse-eaten bed. With folded hands, Simone mumbled a prayer. She went out into the farmyard and without asking the others, took the quad bike and drove to the parish village, where she hammered on the pastor's door. *That was damn unnecessary*, Tiina hissed in Simone's ear as the pastor walked in a few hours later and read the last rites over their mother. The dogs barked annoyingly in the porch and wagged their tails so hard that Laura took them out and shut them in the shed. She gave them each a squirrel bone to keep them quiet during the hour of parting. She had no desire to return to the pastor's God-talk. She felt an extreme craving for coffee and realized they didn't have so much as a piece of crispbread to offer. Salt gherkins probably weren't what a pastor wants after completing his deathbed duties.

In vain, the pastor tried to bring the dead woman's hands together in prayer. They fell back into their natural position at her sides. Then the pastor was left standing there, staring at the piles of washing-up by the sink and on the table. The slop bucket in the middle of the floor, covered with earth, pine needles, and grit. In one corner lay a large, chewed-up, old dog bone. In another, a forest of vodka bottles and gallon cans bearing a hand-drawn skull. The pastor tried not to breathe, the smell was appalling. He opened his mouth as little as possible when he said:

"I brought along a bag of raspberry caves. Do you have any coffee?"

"No . . . but we do have Polish fruit liqueur," said Johanna.

The girls stared at the bag of cookies, drool running from their mouths.

"Yes, please, that sounds like a good pairing," the pastor said.

He sat down, sharing out a cookie each and watching, with sorrow in his heart, how the girls tucked in. The pastor had never seen anyone eat as quickly as these red-haired orphan girls with their dirty, scratched faces. One of them licked the table free of crumbs like a greedy dog. Seven hand-rolled cigarettes lent a pleasant smell that was welcomed by the pastor's afflicted nostrils. He swallowed. That looked awfully good. But then he grew sad. Some kind of abuse had taken place here, he thought. The girls sitting before him with bruises on their arms and stained rags for clothes needed saving. The silence was broken by the one with the biggest biceps.

"You like our place?" asked Tiina. "We were thinking of doing up Mother's old attic room."

"I see," the pastor replied.

"But maybe we shouldn't have such lofty ambitions."

Tiina added a guffaw and looked with disappointment at the others, who weren't laughing along with her.

He looked at them, his expression open, not knowing what to say. He wanted to ask about the bruises and the hunger, but didn't want to embarrass them. Instead, a formal, default question passed his lips.

"Which schools do you go to—the younger ones among you?"

He'd learned, over the years, to always ask open questions, even if he knew the answers.

Seven pairs of eyes met his. Seven closed mouths. He stood up and thanked them. Johanna followed him and he suggested a meeting at the rectory. If he didn't make this happen, Mother Louhi would never be casketed. The girls had nothing to put toward the funeral or the wake afterward. Johanna nodded and agreed that she would come the following Monday. The pastor thanked the girls and as soon as they heard his car start, Johanna got out a bottle of brännvin. The last one.

"We need to calm our nerves. That Polish shit isn't good enough for connoisseurs. Savor every drop. Soon we'll have nothing to wet our whistles."

Simone suggested a psalm and was booed off. Instead, Aune started telling the tale of Lemminkäinen's mother. No one thought that story particularly fitting, and they were sick of hearing about the self-sacrificing mother and her stuck-up son. Simone's eyes were shifty. She looked at Johanna with concern.

"Did you really say the last booze? You'll need to buy yeast and potatoes tomorrow."

"We'll have to search every nook and cranny for things to sell," said Tanja.

"We need gas and coffee," said Tiina.

"The only thing of any value is the old man's rifle," Aune said.

Johanna snarled.

"Not a chance. It gives us food."

Aune wouldn't budge, went on in spite of Johanna's hard look.

"We can auction it. The bear hunting legend's very own champion shotgun. People will buy anything from celebs. I reckon we could flog his underwear too."

"I've taken it," Johanna said, hurt. "Keeps you warm overnight in the huntsman's cabin."

"Well, you others will have to come up with a better suggestion," Aune said guardedly, wishing at that moment that her band of siblings was restricted to her, Laura, and Elga.

They sat in silence. They could hear the hens cackling out in the farmyard. Tanja drummed her fingers on the table. Simone closed her eyes. Then Tiina leaped up and roared. Thumped a fist on the table so hard blood sprang from her knuckles.

"ARE YOU INVITING ANYONE ELSE TO THE FUNERAL?"

The pastor looked with amusement at Johanna, who'd wolfed down the sausage sandwiches and the checkerboard, the last of the seven cookies. She suppressed an impulse to lick the table clean of crumbs. She had some manners after all. The rectory's housemaid refilled first the pastor's cup, then Johanna's, with coffee. Johanna topped hers up right to the brim with cream. Held it as carefully as she could, but still managed to spill some on her shirt.

The pastor discreetly handed her another napkin.

"Uncle's dying, so I guess it'll be just the neighbor at the funeral, even though she's angry with us."

"Why is she angry?"

"We've stolen a few necessities. Eggs and so on."

"Could you apologize?"

Johanna sat in silence, making a sort of gurgling noise as she thought.

"The small chapel next to the church would provide a suitable farewell for your mother," the pastor said. "The church would feel too empty."

"There's a problem," Johanna said.

The pastor looked her in the eye, nodded, and waited for her to continue.

"She wants to be laid to rest . . . in the forest by the swamp. She had a tree there that gave her comfort."

"We must get your mother into consecrated ground. That's all there is to it. If that doesn't happen, neither the dead nor the bereaved will be able to find peace."

He looked at Johanna and waited in vain for a reaction.

"The small chapel, next Sunday at eleven. There will be seven of you, maybe eight. That's more mourners than . . . imagine how empty it is when a poor, childless widow farmer is buried. Then there'll be me and the cantor. Children are abundance; you are abundance."

Johanna nodded skeptically, looking out through the large, pristine window, saw the rosebushes in the garden and the prematurely yellowing leaves on the birch trees. She dipped her hand into the crystal water glass to rub away the coffee stain on the white shirt that had been her mother's.

The pastor tried to sound gentle and fatherly as he said, "You're of working age, but your youngest siblings must go to school. It's the law, you know that."

Johanna looked up and held the pastor's gaze. She was irritated by the pastor's soft voice.

"My father had bigger plans for us."

The challenge in her eyes made the pastor look down at the tablecloth. He cleared his throat.

"You don't want to be thought of as forest bandits, do you?"

Johanna looked at the pastor's coarse, bushy beard, in which were caught a few cookie crumbs.

Her large mouth broadened into a smile.

The stain on her shirt was gone.

THEY'D GATHERED IN THE KITCHEN, NONE OF THEM HAD THOUGHT TO invite their neighbor. More to the point, they couldn't bear the thought of the cleaning that would make that possible. They were all smoking anxiously. Elga coughed in the clouds of smoke and her sisters, who thought she should sort it out, glared at her. The gravity of the hour was upon them. It was clear to them all how much their mother had done while they were mucking around, breaking their arms, diving into the river, and driving souped-up motors. Now their survival was dependent on them alone. They were all crying out for help, but inwardly.

Their father's words echoed in Johanna's head: *Never trust the two "p"s: the pastor and the police.* She heard him booming at his daughters as he sat on a tree trunk. *All those people who follow their advice and believe they're wishing them well are crazy. There's no well-wishing, only ulterior motives. Remember that, my little fox cubs.* Johanna never forgot her father's rule. She refused the pastor's alms from the congregation's poor box. She expanded the rule to include an "s" and a "t": social services and the tax man. But their father had never let on about the seriousness of the "b": the bailiff.

Johanna saw the future before her in sharp focus. Very sharp focus. She saw pitfalls but also possible ways forward. She outlined them for her sisters.

"We have two chances of surviving as fatherless and motherfree. Keep living here and fix up the farm, running it so we can make some money from it. Or pack ourselves off to the forest. We can live on the croft in the wilderness."

Now that Johanna had made it clear that they were at a fork in the road, the mood in the room became electric, the cigarette smoke thick. Tiina tried to collect drops from empty bottles and gallon cans. They spoke excitedly.

"Let us gather our wits. We've got a roof over our heads here, and some insulation and fireplaces to help us survive the winters," Aune said.

"We've not let in the chimney sweep these last few years and we've been forbidden from lighting fires. If anyone so much as touches the kitchen stovepipe, the whole kitchen will be filled with soot. We've living inside a whacking great fire risk," said Tanja.

"Pah, there are seven of us. That's like two fire engines with their men springing into action," Tiina said.

"Without equipment. Were you planning to piss on the flames?" Elga said.

Johanna slammed her fist on the table and the chatter stopped.

"Speaking of wit, I hereby appoint myself foreman of this project. I'm your leader, chairperson, and chief. I'm also responsible for important things like weapons, ammunition, traps, and knives."

"The rain's coming into the attic," said Tanja, who'd taken the role of leader's right hand. "Who can fix the roof, get new roof tiles, and roofing felt? Elga, you're handy, and you, Laura, are good with a knife."

"I'll save my energy for other things," Elga said, her facial expression insufferable.

Johanna looked at her youngest sister with hate in her eyes.

"Watch it, rat. I'm saving my energy too—for the cane."

"I'm master of spirits. I'll keep tabs on the sugar, yeast, and hops. The whole distillery," said Tiina.

Johanna snubbed her. "We really need someone better suited."

"The fuuuuuck?"

"Someone who won't down it all."

"Name a single one of us who won't."

"I have a suggestion—" said Tanja, before being interrupted.

"We'll have a competition. The person who can neck the most beer can be brewery foreman," said Elga, suddenly constructive.

"Good idea," Johanna said. "But in that case, we've got to sell up first and get a food fund together. Our assets are the cows and the dogs. They're no good for hunting these days."

"Who the fuck's going to buy those bony goats you call cows?" Elga said.

Laura protested.

"I look after them. They're old. We won't get much."

"Okay," Johanna said. "The cows are yours. You take care of the poor starving creatures."

"Can we afford enough feed to bulk them up a bit?" Aune asked. "The wretched things are wasting away."

There was a silence around the table at the words wasting away. Tiina got up and traipsed around the kitchen. Tanja, who'd been building up to it for a while now finally got the words out.

"There's Mrs. Niskanpää, who we want nothing to do with, but in a real crisis she could be of use. Should we ask her for advice?"

Simone folded her hands and closed her eyes.

"Lord, tell us what is to be done."

"Hey, you can be the housewife. You get help from your God," said Aune.

Simone looked up, her brow furrowed. "Housewife?!"

"Cook, then. Someone has to get food and cook it."

Elga grimaced. "In that case, I'd rather not eat food made by us. Anyone know a tasty girl?"

"Let's think it over," Johanna said. She raised a finger in the air: an idea. "I know what we can sell: Mother's wedding ring."

"The old man got it out of a chewing-gum dispenser," Tanja said.

Tiina, done with her wandering, sat down so abruptly on a chair that one of the spindles on the back flew across the room. She raked her hands through her long, tangled hair. It was obvious she was thinking hard. Then she drummed on the edge of the table and said, "We'll start by heading into town and buying some frozen pizza with the last of our cash. If we get some food inside us, we'll have the energy to work."

"If we put our backs into it, we might be able to charm a cook into moving in here," Johanna added.

Elga looked at Johanna and said something uncustomarily affirmative, "You're the oldest, didn't you go to school for a term or something before everything came crashing down? Was there anyone you took a liking to? Is it possible there's a good woman in that shit heap of a town?"

Johanna pondered for a moment, then smiled bashfully.

"Yeah . . . I know one—Lygia."

"When did you last see her?" Elga asked.

Johanna pondered again while lighting yet another cigarette.

"One evening, maybe three years ago, late in August. The sunlight was soft, the shadows long and low, the forest smelled of cinnamon and nutmeg. The old man and I were out tracking a bear by the lake, and we heard the sound of splashing sounds. We thought it must be an elk bathing, but it was Lygia—I recognized her dark hair. She was swimming naked."

"And how did you know that?" Elga countered.

"She came up onto the beach to dry herself. The evening light was suddenly sharp and I . . . saw how she was made. You should have seen the soot-black bush between her legs. A real enchanted forest."

"I saw her once, though she was wearing a swimsuit. At the triathlon," Aune added.

Johanna stayed in the memory, her cheeks flushing.

"I saw her several times by the lake. She always swam naked. Always at the same time in the evening."

"So have—" Tanja ventured, but Elga was ahead of her.

"Do you know where she lives?"

"I asked the pastor. Not married yet. Lives by the square in town, works at the nursery school."

Elga shrugged. "So she has a job?"

Johanna didn't want to give up the spark of hope.

"Unless she thinks it would be nicer to live with us on a farm with rowan trees, a slope covered in blooming chicory, and a field of swaying rye. You never know with people. Especially not people in town."

"People in town have no sense of smell," Aune said.

"Boys who grow up in town have damaged scrotums with dead sperm," said Tiina.

"No one has seven children in town," Elga said.

"In town babies die in the womb," said Tiina.

Johanna stood up, clapped her hands, and demanded attention:

"Let's go in and do our shopping, and we'll look for Lygia when she leaves work."

Tanja was the second to stand up:

"Do we have any soap? Clothes that aren't filthy? Let's go down to the stream and wash."

Five sisters played clumsily on the way to the stream. Roaring, shoving, tripping. Tanja walked, deep in thought, after the loudmouths, and Laura sauntered after her, bringing up the rear. Tanja was breathing heavily, full of rage toward her sisters. *Self-satisfied*, she was muttering to herself, *but they don't even know it. Incompetent and conceited. Running their mouths.* How would it have been if she, Tanja, were the same, were as puffed-up? Her head was spinning: *I've got the patience of a saint, it's my best sport.*

She could see herself wandering around the farm old and heavy-bellied, like their father, *the beloved*. She remembered sitting with Aune, one of them on each of his soft knees. *He caressed me in a special way. He saw me: Tanja, his magical little girl. Did Aune sense it?*

Tanja looked intently at Aune's sinewy back as she strode toward the stream. Saw her as a girl: feeble and older than her years, while she, Tanja, her twin, grew ever stronger and more insolent. It was as though she'd been allotted double servings of egg and bear meat during their childhood. Tanja started to be drawn to her older sister, Johanna, they were more equal. Under her protection, Tanja grew in strength, while Aune was as much of a pushover as ever.

Just imagine a brisk walk to the stream encapsulating both a whole childhood and the infractions of the present. She tried not to think about the ways Johanna had disappointed her.

She thinks she's leading us; in reality, it's me. And Tiina has this idea she's a genius with motors, but I'm the only one who can see when the quad bike's tires need pumping up, when the chain of the saw is screaming for oil, or when it's so worn it needs replacing. If I hadn't been part of this tribe of misfits, all the machines and kitchen utensils would have broken. Even so, everything is collapsing around our ears.

The anxiety was gnawing at her. What would they do about Simone, who claimed to hear voices when there was not a sound to be heard? How could she have shared a womb with Aune, who sat around telling stories and let the others handle almost all the practical stuff? Tanja was irritated. Ordering Aune to fix the roof tiles would be like planning sororicide. She'd noticed that her twin sister had begun to tell stories almost as well as old Veikko, emphasizing the words like he did.

She'd probably have to hunger her whole life long for a nugget of gratitude. No one had said thanks when she'd unblocked the pipe in the toilet and stopped it overflowing. Man's work. But the worst of it: *I do the women's work too.*

Now Johanna was calling her from the stream.

"Tanja! Come on. Wash my back!"

AFTER THEY'D MOVED THEIR MOTHER'S BODY TO THE ROOT CELLAR, hunger struck. Over the course of the day, they'd collected up empty cans and found so many they'd have enough deposit money for pizza and beer. It was clear to them that people had fat wallets. They couldn't even be bothered to return their empties. They hadn't caught a glimpse of Lygia outside the nursery school. Maybe she was sick, or off work. That evening, seven somber sisters chewed cold Vesuvius and drank porter.

Together, they belched, smoked, and fumed. Elga said she wanted to be inducted into the art of reading, so that she could undertake to teach the others. Johanna was raging mad, calling Elga insubordinate, as per usual. She started going on again about what their father had impressed upon them, that people study in order to make other people their slaves.

"Don't you get it? We need to stay away from teachers, police, those old bitches up at social services, and ideally pastors too. They want to drive a wedge between us. The cantor as well. You and he are terribly alike, Elga. Why do you think that might be?"

Elga flew at Johanna and bit her arm, furious. Johanna boxed her youngest sister in the stomach, sending her flying backward. Elga got up again and lashed out furiously at the boxer. In the end, the other five sisters were forced to pull Johanna and Elga apart as they wrestled on the ground, tufts of red hair flying. Johanna stopped whirling her fists and calmed down, standing up straight and putting on a stern face.

Later that evening, Johanna laid the bullwhip demonstratively on the table alongside their father's shotgun. Aune managed to spit out the words everyone had been waiting for.

"We'll end up in the clink if we don't go to school. Meditate on that, forest lovers."

EARLY THE NEXT MORNING, ELGA SNUCK OUT OF BED AND GOT dressed, tiptoed out of the house, breathed in the fresh, damp farmyard air, jumped up onto the quad bike, and drove into town.

It was a long time since she'd sat at the controls, felt the cool air fresh on her face, noticed how her nostrils widened with the scent of pine needles. Out on her own at last. She took uneven, narrow paths where the dust whirled and the gravel bounced off her calves—she wanted to ensure no early-bird police officer would pull her over. None of the sisters had a driving license. *What would we want them for?* the old man had said. *Having a training course for driving is ludicrous; the authorities just want to make money from ordinary folk.*

The school was like a redbrick castle, just outside the center of town. Elga turned into the car park and parked the quad bike alongside a row of brand-new cars. She thought they looked like they were made of plastic. Why were all the cars in town white? She looked at her filthy sneakers, worn-out and covered in patches.

The screaming school kids in the playground sounded worse than the sisters when they had wrestling matches. She stopped on the steps, turning to look out across the playground, where the puffer jackets shone red, blue, and white. Noted the cozy lace-up boots with their tough soles, and the solid high-top sneakers. She turned back and walked into the building and was hit by a wave of stuffy air—plasticky linoleum floors and paper were unfamiliar smells. But then her nostrils flared: just inside the doors stood two older women with plastic cups in their hands. The smell of coffee made Elga's mouth water. She walked over to the women:

"Hi. I'm looking for the teacher."

The women—one a teacher, the other an assistant—looked at Elga and tried not to flinch. It was a long time since they'd seen a girl in such worn-out clothes. With such tangled hair. The bruises on her forehead.

"Who are you looking for?" the assistant asked.

Elga looked at the woman's hair. It was pale pink. She swallowed and steeled herself.

"I want to start school."

"Follow me," Pink Hair said, walking up some stairs. A long corridor, many doors with name plates. A bunch of keys jangled in the assistant's jacket pocket. Elga tried to read the names on the doors, but didn't have time to sound them out.

"Come in," said Pink Hair. "My name is Inkeri."

"Elga."

"Lovely name. My daughter's called Elga too."

Inkeri held out her hand to indicate the chair in front of the desk. *Have a seat.* She sat at the computer and tapped on the keyboard. Elga looked at the rows of colorful folders on the bookcase. No books. Inkeri looked up.

"What's your surname?"

"Leskinen."

Inkeri didn't flinch, which was the most common reaction when the Leskinen family was mentioned. The tapping went on and on: *This is taking a little while*, she said from behind the screen.

It took half an hour to get to the bottom of Elga's situation in life, because the name didn't bring up any results. Instead, she wrote down Elga's own explanation of why she'd never gone to school—that her parents were of the opinion children didn't need to. Inkeri pondered this awhile and then stood up.

"I'll have to consult the Head. Are you happy to wait? Fancy a cup of coffee in the meantime?"

She walked briskly out of the room. Elga munched a piece of chocolate cake and drank coffee from a paper cup while inspecting the photos Inkeri had pinned to a board: vacation photos from a taverna by the sea. Three children in swimsuits eating a banana split. A pale blue sea with fishing boats in the background.

Inkeri rushed back in with a folder under her arm. She sat down and flicked through it and found the document that confirmed just what the Head had told her. The school had attempted to reach the parents at the farm multiple times. Management had written to the Leskinens ahead of each term without any response, and even made home visits. It was at this point that Inkeri recognized the dead bear hunter's name and put two and two together: the school's management team had given up in the face of the man's threats. Now the destructive pattern would be broken, and the youngest, a twelve-year-old girl, would finally get to start school. In the best-case scenario, they'd manage to tempt back into education the four older siblings who were still of compulsory school age.

"So, that's that. You'll get a summons letter," Inkeri said.

A warm feeling spread through her when she saw how the girl exhaled, an inner light shining from her face.

ELGA SLEPT RESTLESSLY ON HER BEARSKIN THAT NIGHT. SHE'D lied to her sisters that she'd taken the quad bike out to search for cans to return, but that the homeless people must have got there before her. There were so many of them now, hoping the contents of the rubbish bins would enable them to get through the day. She managed to steal a few tea bags from the assistant's room, and some tiny containers of milk, so she'd have something for the others to see her bring to the kitchen table. The tea tasted vile—nauseating vanilla. She knew she'd get a beating when Johanna found out she'd sought out the school of her own free will; she was prepared for all hell to break loose, but she didn't intend to budge an inch.

Elga passed the mailbox every day. It was always empty. A week passed and she was ready to give up. Then suddenly, there in the box was a white envelope. She stuck it in her pocket to make sure her sisters, Johanna and Tanja in particular, wouldn't discover it and tear the envelope to bits like their father always had. She opened the letter in the privy. What did it say? She didn't know a soul who could read, aside from the pastor, and there was no way she was going to the rectory. She went resolutely back to the school, up the stairs, along the corridor, and knocked on Inkeri's door.

It opened. Elga stared at the giant hoops in Inkeri's ears.

"Hello. I'm busy right now. Did you want something in particular?"

Elga strode brazenly into the room and put the letter on Inkeri's desk. She pointed at the letter.

"What does it say?"

Inkeri realized the gravity of the situation.

THEY WOULD ALL HAVE ONE WEEKEND OF READING LESSONS, AFTER which Elga would be enrolled as a student at the adult education center, though her lessons would take place in her teacher's home. For security reasons, neither the public school system nor the adult education center wanted to have the sisters as students, as it would cause anxiety among parents and fear among the student body. Feelings of insecurity restrict learning potential, that's what all the statistics unequivocally showed.

The first person Elga told was Aune, who felt a rush she was incapable of putting into words, it bubbled and rippled inside her. Perhaps she herself might read and write some fine May evening, as the nightingale trilled and the fox cubs frolicked. *The tales in my head keep me going. Something great might happen if I can get them down on paper*, she thought, as she sat there smoking on the big rock by the stream.

If Uncle Veikko hadn't existed, I'd have let myself get sucked down into a swamp and taken pleasure in breathing my last. For the time being I write in my head. In there I can read and write. When night's darkness comes over me and I hear the hungry growling of seven stomachs, I write, practicing pauses and stress. The things Veikko put stock in. I tell the dogs stories, they lie at my feet, close their eyes, and listen. Open one eye cautiously when things get violent. Perhaps one day I'll write an adventure story, but I won't say anything to Elga. She's the language whiz. The doubt holds its tongue when I drink porter. When I see the forest stars on the inside of my eyelids, yes, then I become Väinämöinen himself.

Aune was worried about Veikko, who was in intensive care. His heart was about to give up. Mrs. Niskanpää had sent a message via the garbage truck. They'd also found out that would be the last time their bins got emptied. The waste management company could no longer be handing out alms. Enough was enough.

Aune sank into daydreams, wishing in secret that she'd been the daughter of Veikko, instead of her brute of a father. *After he was killed, my heart was lighter. To think of the way my sisters showed off in front of that boor, even Laura.*

Chapter Four

Many a joke was made over coffee cups and wineglasses about the bear hunter's daughters and their lack of education. Having met one of the sisters in the hope of initiating a conversation, I can confirm the obvious: just because you haven't gone to school, it doesn't make you a simpleton.

What the sisters did have in common was a helplessness when it came to that essential part of a functioning life: routine.

On T-Day, the day they were expected at the teacher's house, they awoke to frost on the windows and an uncomfortable feeling they had somewhere to be. No bread. Coffee all gone. Tiina launched a kick at the fridge door. It would have to be a beer and a raw potato each—they had to get some nourishment inside them.

Seven sulky mouths round the kitchen table. Seventy nimble fingers rolling cigarettes. Seven soothing threads of smoke. Raindrops drumming a tranquil melody in the bucket in the middle of the floor.

Johanna bent over and groaned.

"My tummy's playing up. It can feel I'm headed for torture."

"It'll be good for you to give using your head a try," Elga said, winking at Johanna to show she was joking.

"Hohoho, you wouldn't have survived a day without me, but we could live three hundred years without you."

"We'll see."

Elga looked at Johanna with as friendly a look as she could manage. She hadn't gotten a beating when she'd told them about the school and the teacher who was going to take them all into her home. It just so happened that Johanna remembered that very teacher from her short time at school, a fun woman and a good sort—the only one who'd managed to get Johanna to relax at her school desk. She was sure she would have been able to read her father's hunting magazines if she'd stayed in school a few more semesters. Perhaps now she could hope to one day read them?

HOW MANY PEOPLE CAN YOU GET ON A QUAD BIKE? TIINA ON THE steering column. Two on the seat, one sitting behind them facing backward, three on the little trailer. Johanna put her foot down, changed gears hard and jerkily. Tanja, sitting alongside her, smoked into the wind, inhaling the smoke as if she needed it to reach her big toe, and grimacing in concern over all the strange noises coming from the engine and gears. Would they have to steal another gearbox? Not much gas left.

Johanna called to her flock:

"On a day like today we must make an effort to behave respectably."

Elga smiled inwardly in the fresh fall air, Tiina was all knees as she lorded it on the steering column, while Simone sat misty-eyed with her hands folded—she'd been forced to have her own little Holy Communion in the kitchen that morning. Laura hugged herself, shivering in a battered jean jacket, staring out across the fields, into forest glades lit with clear sunlight. For her, everything merged into a single wash of green with orange dots. Elga whistled as she held on to the unwieldy hiking backpack packed with a pad of paper and some freshly sharpened pencils she'd bought with the deposit money from the bottles she'd returned, a heap she'd found in the woodshed. Black and sweet the beer had to be, to satisfy their father. He always scratched away at the label with its drawing of a bear.

JOHANNA MADE A SHARP TURN AND PARKED OUTSIDE THE TOBACconist's, and Aune said crossly that they'd be late, at which point Johanna snapped that she didn't give a damn, because she needed more cigarettes, and Aune said, *We can't fucking well be late on the very first day*, while Tiina shouted, *Buy fourteen!* Johanna opened the tinkling door and rushed into the little shop with its narrow aisles; Elga looked at her watch twice a second. Shouts were heard from inside the shop, then Johanna dashed out, leaped up onto the seat, and turned the key in the ignition. Two chunky women ran out of the shop, and before Johanna could start the engine, they pulled her down onto the tarmac.

No fucking way are you gonna steal smokes and hot dogs from us, you goddamn filthy cunts!

Johanna was winded by kicks to her back, and Tiina jumped down from the quad bike right onto the back of one of the assailants, hanging on tight like a battle-hungry chimpanzee. She in turn took a karate chop to the back from one of the assailant's companions. Tanja joined in; now there were five of them fighting. Laura stared dumbly at the tumult, and Elga observed matter-of-factly that they hadn't even brought a stick to hit them with. All this stuff about school had distracted them and made them forget themselves.

Noses ran with blood and one assailant spat out a tooth.

Stop fighting!

A man of at least forty came running round from behind the shop brandishing an orange hosepipe. He turned on the spray, and three red-haired women and two brunettes stood up, filthy and soaked to the skin, hands over their faces. They looked at each other, foreheads shredded.

Elga jumped down from the quad bike and stood in front of the tobacconist's broad-shouldered daughter, who was grunting with snot running from her nose.

"How much do we owe?"

The woman looked at her with contempt and doubled the amount. The notes were bundled into her aching hand.

"We don't want any fuss over this," said Elga.

JOHANNA DROVE, WET THROUGH, WHIMPERING AND DRYING HERSELF simultaneously with the hairy dog blanket that was kept in a side pouch. Tiina tried to rise above the pain in her back, but the grimace on her mouth stuck.

"So, you have money!"

Elga didn't answer. She looked at her watch and said:

"We're going to be half an hour late."

"YOU REALLY COULD HAV—" THE TEACHER, STANDING IN THE DOORway, interrupted herself mid scold when she saw the badly knocked-about bunch: wet clothes, black eyes, thickets of hair, bleeding noses. The oldest stood on the top step in boots that were almost in a state of decomposition. One of them was wearing a torn T-shirt from which her breast was peeping out; the girl beside her had a bald patch at her temple.

The teacher looked them up and down: a few of the younger ones on the bottom step were barefoot; they appeared to have been hosed down, but not beaten. Two of them were more slender than the other, bigger girls. One was of a delicate build, with a backpack on her back and an alert gaze, and at her side was a girl with a slouching demeanor and tired, squinting eyes.

"We were attacked by ruffians," said the eldest.

The teacher looked at the mangled personage at the front with sympathy and resolve.

"You must go to the doctor."

"Relax, we'll handle it ourselves," Johanna said. "You got any booze here?"

The teacher nodded. Went into the kitchen and came back with cleaning alcohol, bandages, and compresses. She passed them some towels and safety pins, and said, "Please dry yourselves thoroughly before you come in."

The teacher showed them to the bathroom so they could look over their bleeding wounds and clean off the dirt. Elga and Laura were standing in front of the mirror in the hall, staring in astonishment at their reflections, when the door to one of the rooms opened and a guy with glasses and a neon yellow T-shirt appeared in the mirror and said, straightforwardly, "Hi there. Welcome." He held out his arm to show them into the living room.

"My son, Matti—my assistant," the teacher said. "My name is Leena, it's great to have you here."

They jostled for space in the hallway and entered one by one, with Elga in the lead for once. Tiina caught a sconce with her shoulder, knocking it to the ground. Leena picked up the light and saw that it was intact, even the light bulb, which had been protected by its guardian angel, the fabric shade.

"Please, take a seat."

They sat, legs spread so their knees knocked against each other's, forming a circle. Tiina and Johanna leaned back on their chairs. They noticed that all four walls of the room were lined floor to ceiling with books. The teacher realized Tiina hadn't understood why she'd been given a safety pin. One of her breasts was sticking out, completely visible, through her shirt. Leena handed her yet another safety pin, patting her own chest to show her what it was for. Tiina stared at the teacher's breasts and then down at her own naked tit and put the safety pin through her earlobe. Leena called out to her son and asked him to lend her a shirt. He brought her a white T-shirt, then Tiina pulled her own, torn garment over her head, wiping her forehead and throwing it on the floor. Two bare breasts captured everyone's attention as Tiina pulled on Matti's shirt.

"Thanks!"

"Well, now then, welcome! I thought we could work through lunch, seeing as you came late. Do you have any ABC books?"

THE TEACHER LEENA HANDED OUT BOOKS, AND NOTICED HOW ELGA quickly wrote her name, as did Aune. Tiina drew a lion and Laura took a pen and wrote an "L" and an "A" and then a full stop. Matti let out a little whistle and smiled scornfully—and got a stern look from his mother. Even at that point, those sisters who were strangers to the alphabet felt a contrariness that would only grow.

So many questions to answer.

"Can you write your mother's name?"

Silence. Sighs.

"We've got a dog called Kiiski," Tiina said. "The other one's called—"

"Can you tell me the first letter?"

"Nope."

Leena rounded her lips and said: "Kayyy."

Johanna got annoyed. "Come on, it starts with Kiii!"

"'K' for cave man!" Tiina ventured.

"Almost! Now, what does the first letter in the alphabet sound like? Anyone?"

"Aaaa," said Elga.

Everyone joined in. Aaaaaaa.

"Like when we gargle with brännvin in the morning," Tiina said.

She didn't say that to distinguish herself or seem uncouth. She was thinking of their father, who was convinced that toothpaste damaged the enamel. Toothbrushes and toothpaste only existed to make people gad about, spending their money on unnecessary things. Greenlanders have the best gnashers in the world, their father used to say. They eat fresh polar-bear meat and never brush their teeth.

"Next letter."

"Beee," said Elga.

"'B' for beeelieve," Simone said, before any of the others could say anything. That sound was hers.

Laura interrupted: "I need the can."

"'C' for can," said Elga.

Leena nodded, and Laura got up and hurried out into the hallway.

"I'm coming with you," said Tiina.

And so it went on. One after the other, they trailed off to the bathroom. Then they needed a cigarette break, pronto. Johanna was incapable of sitting still. It seemed to her as though the words, the sounds, bounced off her wide forehead and back out into the room. Her knuckles tensed and whitened. She disappeared into her thoughts, wandering through a forest tinged orange with the fall. There was a fresh scent of pine as the sun burst through after an intense downpour. She followed the old man along the forest paths . . . and then was back in the room again, her heart beating backward at the thought of learning to read. She saw that the pages of Tiina's book were covered in black sweat stains, and that Simone was nodding along to everything the teacher said, even though it was obvious she didn't understand a jot, and didn't believe she'd ever be able to read. The will was there—she wanted to read Holy Scripture. As they sounded "J," Johanna shot up out of her chair, startling the others with her sudden movement.

"Listen. Good people. I've got b-better things to do than p-play the idiot. I'm going shopping. I'll be b-back to get you when the time comes."

"I'll join you," Tiina said, her chair crashing to the ground.

"Me too," Tanja piped up.

Aune, Laura, Simone, and Elga stayed seated. There was a calm, a common focus. While Aune and Laura were still struggling to sound out the letters, Elga was already starting to write. She and Matti were on the same wavelength—he wasn't at all as stuck-up as he'd at first seemed. When he stood alongside her, she caught a faint whiff of sweat, and she grew weak of knee and wavery of pencil.

She spelled something wrong. Rubbed it out. Rubbed through the paper.

The afternoon flew by. They all jumped when Leena clapped her hands together.

"Girls! You've come a long way in a short time. Let's have another go tomorrow. What you need now is a snack."

The sisters were each given a little bag containing a croissant, raisins, and an apple. They bolted the lot in less than a minute, the cores of the apples going down with the rest.

Then they vanished.

Once the room was empty, Matti wiped the crumbs from the chairs and opened both windows as wide as he could—airing out the stench of sweat.

THE QUAD BIKE WAS PARKED IN FRONT OF LEENA'S HOUSE. JOHANNA was drumming on the steering wheel and blowing bubble-gum bubbles. They were on time! Tiina was holding a ring of sausage, and a bottle of mustard was sticking out of her jacket pocket. Tanja was sitting on the trailer, facing backward, holding a stack of frozen pizzas and a sack of potatoes. Johanna waved her arms madly as the four sisters took the steps in one leap.

"Up you get!"

Tiina whistled as the quad bike was pushed to its limits, careening round street corners. The driver of a dark green SUV leaned into their horn when the un-roadworthy vehicle drove right through a red. Pedal to the floor past the square, through the center of town to Lygia's day care center.

"All the kids are out," Tanja said.

"Let's wait till she finishes," said Tiina.

Johanna slowed down, almost running over a farm cat that shot from nowhere like a black and white arrow up onto the pavement. They parked the quad bike outside the entrance to the school and marched around the block with Johanna playing the role of the alpha male, driving forward the weakest link: Laura.

"Will she look like . . . she used to . . . in school?" Tanja asked.

"I'll recognize the girl, don't you worry," said Johanna.

She stood by the fence and looked out across the crowds of children building forts or digging in the sandpit. The others wandered around with their eyes on the ground, searching for cigarette butts and old wads of chewing gum—a bus stop was a particularly good spot. On a patch of grass by the gate to the day care center, they stood in a line and had a competition to see who could blow the biggest bubbles. The parents coming to collect their children glanced suspiciously in their direction and walked more quickly into the building. One man with his hair in a little bun and wearing a bougainvillea-patterned waist-length jacket was about to park his bike with its child seat outside the gate, but when he noticed the sisters, he opted, with jerky movements, to take the bike inside the schoolyard.

Tiina grimaced.

"Imagine if we'd had that twit for an old man."

"Poor kid," said Tanja.

Johanna whispered, "There she is. Quiet now. Focus."

A woman in a thin vest and white sneakers closed the gate and crossed the road with her hands in her jacket pockets and wearing a concerned expression. Then seven redheaded bundles of muscle formed a wall in front of her.

"Stop!"

Lygia took a few steps backward and looked at the dirty girls. Something about them made her hold out her wallet, her hands shaking.

"Here! Take it!" Lygia said with a trembling voice.

Johanna stepped closer to Lygia, and coolly yet determinedly pushed back the wallet. After that, she held out a pack of cigarettes. Lygia shook her head and looked scared stiff as she stared at the girls, who must surely be over six feet tall, though one was skinnier than the others and another was small and slender like her. Her knees wobbled as the wall of broad, hard-muscled bodies stepped even closer. A gray-haired lady passed with a spring in her step, bending over every few moments to pick up cigarette butts that she put in a bag attached to her hip rather than smoking them. Tiina flicked a butt after her and Tanja followed it with a roar of laughter.

"Hey Lygia! Been a while," Johanna said.

"Do I know you?" Lygia said tentatively.

"Yep, we were in the same class in school. Johanna."

"Scally-Jo?"

Johanna grinned.

"You lived in the forest?"

Johanna nodded.

"And you left."

"I was homeschooled, in the forest. These are my sisters."

"What do you want?"

"We live near the tarn," Tiina said with a grin.

Lygia furrowed her brow and looked at the sisters one by one. Gestured helplessly with her arms.

"Where you like to swim naked."

"Er, what are you talking about?"

Tiina put on an innocent face.

"I wasn't the one spying."

Johanna turned to Tiina and indicated, with a murderous stiletto gesture across her throat, that she should shut her mouth. She said, "We have a lovely . . ."

". . . job offer for you," Tanja went on.

". . . at our place," Simone concluded.

"Job offer?"

Tanja got excited and laid out the bait.

"On our farm in the forest. About seven miles north of town. We need your help keeping the house. Cooking food. Hot dogs and mash. Toad in the hole. No funny business."

Simone took a step toward Lygia and put her hand on her heart. "Our dear mother recently shuffled off this mortal coil."

"I'm a day care worker," Lygia said, squirming with discomfort and the remnants of fear.

"We know," Johanna said. "Come visit us and taste our famous porter. We'll tell you more about our offer."

"I can barely cook a hot dog," Lygia said.

"You'll learn," said Tanja.

Tiina felt she'd been holding her tongue long enough, and steeled herself with a smile, even though she'd promised herself she'd never smile and show the gaps where two of her teeth were missing.

"An offer you won't want to miss."

Lygia turned toward the schoolyard, where the kids were playing on swings and in a fort with a pirate flag fluttering from the roof.

"I like being with the kids. Ask someone else."

Tiina stood very close and flexed her biceps.

"Fancy an arm wrestle?"

Lygia's eyes were panicked. Her voice trembled and broke.

"I've got to go home. My dog's booked in a puppy training course that's about to start. Let me go, please!"

Tiina took hold of Lygia's waist and lifted her right up into the air. Lygia whirled her fists, terrified.

"Puppy training course. Did you say puppy training course? What?"

"Give over, Tiina! Put her down. Let her go," Tanja said gruffly.

And Lygia walked—no, she ran—over to the parking lot and drove off with screeching tires.

Johanna's cheeks flushed. Elga walked over to her and pretended to give her a kiss on the lips, then got a fist in the stomach that bent her double.

"Stop it now, for fuck's sake. We've had a shitty day," Tanja said.

Johanna shoved her hands into her trouser pockets and made for the quad bike.

"This world stinks of rotten rats."

JOHANNA WENT TO PUT AWAY THE SHOPPING IN THE CUPBOARD AND the root cellar. No, not the root cellar. It stank of their mother's dead body there. It was time. They couldn't wait any longer. Tired, very tired, she put the partially defrosted pizzas on the table with seven bottles of beer. They ate from the boxes, while a hard rain drove against the windows and the leaky roof.

Tanja emptied the water out of the buckets when it splashed over the edge.

"The farmhouse is crumbling," Johanna said with a deep sigh.

"And we haven't a penny to our names," Aune added to the lament Johanna had begun.

Tiina did her best to lighten the mood.

"My plan is to brew some beer and moonshine and sell it at the market. We have to remember, the townies want what we have."

"I'm going to keep going to school. Soon I'll be able to do the accounts. Anyone who wants teaching can get lessons from me," Elga said.

The very thought of lessons put Johanna in a bad mood.

"I've got by for over twenty years without all that Ayyy, Beee, Ceee."

"Depends how you define 'get by.' Here you are, superannuated illiterate, knocking about in a dilapidated rat's nest. You . . ."

Whack! Elga took a right cross and crumpled in a heap on the floor. Tiina lifted her lifeless body and slapped her pale cheeks.

With steel in her voice, Johanna said, "You're wasting your time with this shit. As soon as the rain stops, we're all going to go and bury Mother under the birch by the swamp."

Chapter Five

What are the right words to say when burying your mother? How can a band of sisters stand united when they are at odds as to what their mother meant to them? I myself have stood by my mother's coffin, finding that the pastor's words rang false, while my siblings cried.

Are you allowed to feel relief at the death of your mother? I'll say no more about myself now, but it's the nature of stories that the reader writes their own tale between the lines.

More than one of the bear hunter's daughters felt liberated when their mother gave up the ghost. That didn't stop them feeling abandoned, but each of them kept that to themselves. There was an emptiness. With what can you fill that inner void?

FEET LIKE TWO BLOCKS OF ICE—HAD SHE LET THEM GET TOO COLD by the marsh yesterday? Johanna awoke once more with the disagreeable feeling of having somewhere to be. This couldn't be allowed to continue. Her back was stiff, her arm muscles ached and stung from all the digging.

The work would have taken all night if the tribe's strongest members hadn't flexed their muscles. Tiina and Johanna had done most of it, with Tanja's help. The others had *waggled the spades about like townie bitches*. They found that out and no mistake. All they had to do was *attack the roots with all their might*. It was all about that fighting mentality, the weak-armed ones were told. It took several hours to dig a proper, deep hole. Shallow holes in the ground attract wild animals.

Midnight came and a docile full moon gave them light to work by as they all beat their spades on the ground to flatten the surface. Now she was in the ground at least, though not consecrated ground, and not in a coffin. *May the old woman lie still in her grave*, said Tiina, and got a punch in the side from Simone, who looked up at the moon and down at the grave, dropping to her knees to begin a short prayer:

"Our beloved mother, by the swamp you so—"

"Nooo," Elga interjected. "Say something we can all agree on."

Aune made an attempt:

"Our mother by her beloved swamp. May death grant peace to your soul."

Simone went on:

"Seven daughters remember you well."

"Well?" said Tiina with a grimace.

Aune said:

"Your daughters remember you."

Laura placed a hand-carved, black-and-white painted dairy cow onto the patch of earth; she'd worked hard on the udder and teats. *Now, from where Mother lies, she can see the cow's underside and feel at home*, said Tanja. Johanna couldn't even get a sound out.

When at last Johanna had stretched out her aching body in bed, she was much too tired to sleep—her sisters' words were buzzing around her brain. What would she herself have said about their mother? A chill ran down her spine. She heard her siblings grunting and snoring and felt a flash of rage that they could slumber untroubled while she lay awake. She shoved Elga, who whinnied crossly, and still asleep, kicked Aune lying next to her. Elga had to be at the teacher's house at ten o'clock, and Johanna had promised to drive her because she needed the quad bike for the harvest. The engine of the old man's tractor was as dead as their mother. Even though she'd never admit it to Elga and the others, she still hoped that those hunting magazines would one day get read.

Her stomach lurched with another kind of anxiety: how do you keep time when your family has never owned a clock? The wristwatch Elga had bought at the market worked sometimes, mostly when it thundered. Where time was concerned, they went by instinct.

Clocks and mirrors make people unhappy, Mamma always said. She thought of her as Mamma, but called her the Old Woman or Mother in front of others. Mammas say so many things. They often say things of consequence, but you don't realize until a long time afterward, when you're grown up and Mamma is dead and buried. Johanna pictured her reflection in the teacher's mirror. She recalled shuddering with horror when she saw her mother's broad forehead and strong jaw mirrored in her own. She, who'd imagined a handsome face with clean lines, the opposite of her mother's coarse cheeks and wrestler's brow. How else would her father have been able to look at her with all his love? She breathed in the little that remained of her father's body odor on the pillow. The only one who had enjoyed looking in the mirror at the teacher's place was Tiina. Plus, Laura, funnily enough. She must be fucking blind.

And now she had to drive Baby Bossy to school, waiting on her like a bloody maidservant. She felt a sense of irritation that grew more brutal the more she thought of the system. S-Y-S-T-E-M, as the old man always said. All the authorities her father would speak of as though they were man-eating monsters. The system strips us of our principles. He was right about that. He was right about every goddamn thing.

Perhaps the authorities would be bolder now the bear hunter—and his misanthropic wife—had passed away. Johanna and Tanja kept coming back to this new kind of niggling anxiety that squirmed in their stomachs, spitting poison. Now they'd be forced to predict danger and parry with countermoves. They absolutely must take their new life seriously—the orphan's perilous journey.

Johanna got out of bed, her body creaking, at least a hundred years old. She looked at the calluses on her hands, then out the window, which was covered in yellow pollen. Is the weather going to start taking the piss now, she said out loud with a snort, right at the beginning of winter? She often talked to herself loudly, narrated whatever she was doing. *I'm going to get up now. I'm putting on my trousers. I'm taking the rifle.*

If she was going to lay claim to father's nightshirt and bed—the royal bed itself—she should keep quiet about things taking the piss, Elga thought as she lay alongside the others on a bearskin spread right on the cold floor where the wood mice ran about at night. Of course, they all preferred this to the idea of sleeping in their mother's bed in the attic: they had no desire to be suffocated by her lingering, stale smells.

Instead, they used their mother's bed as a place to put all the things they had no other place for—like a rusty old skirt warmer, those metal lanterns old biddies used to take to church in wintertime, back in the olden days. They'd sit there, listening to the Word of God and toasting their cooches. Who knows what we can use it for, Tanja had thought, surveying her inheritance after their mother's death.

Dry crusts, salt gherkins, and cigarettes for breakfast. The devil's vanilla tea turned her stomach with its sweetness. Johanna opened the cookie tin, took the last rusk rattling about in the bottom. Elga ate as she was packing her backpack, then she combed her hair and put it up in a ponytail.

"Come on! Don't fuss now," Johanna snapped.

"I'm using every tool at my disposal to avoid looking like you," Elga said, with one of her friendlier minx faces.

"You'll be wearing a skirt soon. It'll be a relief to hand you over to that stuck-up teacher woman."

"It'll be a relief to get out of this convict camp."

"Ask the teacher if you can move in with her then. You seemed pretty hot for Nerdy Niklas."

"His name is Matti."

They spent the journey in silence, Johanna with her foot down and a cigarette in her mouth. The air was frigid, but the icy roads didn't seem to bother her. As she sat there behind Johanna, sensing her sister's hot temper radiating, Elga was forced to keep a humiliating grip around her sister's hard, muscular stomach.

Johanna turned her head and talked over her shoulder:

"You'll have to sell some pussy to buy gas . . . and you'll have to drive yourself if you carry on as a Goody Two-shoes schoolgirl."

"Make use of your own fucking pussy. I'll have a real job soon. Then I'll wave bye-bye for good."

"We'll toast that day with the finest whiskey."

For the time of day, there was an uncommon number of people about town. Office workers on their way to work, sleepy school children running to get to their first lessons on time. Parents with whining brats on their way to nursery.

"This is it! Stop."

Johanna slowed down and turned around.

"Jump!"

"Stop!"

Johanna shouted, her voice cold as ice, "Jump, scaredy-cat."

She made a U-turn at the crossing just past the teacher's house and drove slowly back toward it again. Flashes of scenes from her childhood and the sisters' games. Johanna towering over her. A giant with hands of steel. Shoving. Shoving.

"You bastard."

"Jump, you chickenshit."

Johanna peeled Elga's hands from around her stomach.

"Jump, you boffin bitch!"

Elga lifted one leg over, let go, and threw herself off. She crash-landed on the tarmac, sliced open one knee, and lay there whimpering. Got up slowly, sat watching the quad bike disappear: a red dot getting smaller and smaller. Limped toward the teacher's detached house, holding the handrail as she went up the steps. She hated feeling weak, hoped when she rang the doorbell that Matti wasn't at home.

Leena flung the door open.

"Only twenty minutes late this ti—You're bleeding! What happened?"

Her effort at reprimand had been derailed when she saw Elga's scratched face and scraped knee.

"My watch has stopped."

"Come in! The clock shop on the high street changes batteries while you wait."

Elga didn't answer. She'd never gone into any of the shops on the high street. She'd only been to the market and the workshops on the outskirts of town. The tobacconist and the pizzeria where all the customers were men in oil-stained overalls.

Leena didn't want to ask whether they'd had any help with day-to-day necessities since their parents' passing. She wanted her relationship with Elga to be pure, to be about passion and learning. She could leave the other stuff to social services, she thought.

"You have to develop a relationship to time," Leena said. At once decided and gentle. "I'll help you with the watch."

"We don't need time where we live."

Leena took her arm and sat her down on a stool in the hallway.

"You should learn that sometimes precision counts. Otherwise you won't last long in any job, or any course, for that matter. Take off these ragged trousers. We'll wash them here and you can borrow a pair of Matti's in the meantime."

Elga gritted her teeth as Leena cleaned her bleeding kneecap with antiseptic.

"Ouch!"

"Well. What happened?"

Leena cut off a large piece of bandage and stuck it over Elga's skinny, bony knee.

"Slipped on the ice."

Leena looked skeptical, but didn't question it. Instead, she went into her son's room, coming out again with a pair of jeans.

"He's growing like a beanpole. If these fit you, they're yours. We were planning to donate them to the church clothing bank anyway."

Elga went into the bathroom, felt the fabric, smelled it. Laundry liquid. She pulled on the jeans, which fit perfectly. Her reflection said: tight but not too tight. Ow! The wound on her knee was painful.

Just as the last time she was at Leena's, she stared incredulously at her face in the mirror, studying the mystery that was her reflection. Went closer, smiled a little, enjoying her own image. She'd had no idea she looked so good with her red hair and sharp nose. Sure, she'd been aware she had a canny look about her, but not that she had a dainty mouth and, strangest of all, almond-shaped eyes.

Leena called from the living room and Elga rushed out.

"Please, take a seat!"

In the middle of the room was a school desk, and on it was a pile of books.

"Do I get . . . my own desk?"

Elga ran her hand over the lid of the desk and picked up a book to flick through. She looked up at Leena, with sunlight in her face.

"Your very own," Leena said. "You can leave the books here, if you don't have any homework."

Elga lifted the lid of the desk and looked inside. There were pens, an eraser, and an exercise book.

"The desks were being thrown out when I was working at a school," Leena said. "It pained me, so I relocated a few to my basement. They're so beautiful! Look at the care that's gone into making this one."

Elga nodded and wrote her name on the front of the exercise book, while Leena got a few things off her chest.

"Everything's digital these days. People can hardly write, let alone read. They just press a screen and let it run their whole life."

Elga nodded in agreement but didn't ask what a digital screen was.

"So, we're in agreement. Thousands of years of knowledge is being lost. Soon, kids won't be able to write by hand or read any text of length."

"That . . . doesn't sound good," said Elga tentatively.

"You got to the middle of the book last time. Now start sounding out the words from page seventy."

First a low mumble. Then Elga buzzed like a bumblebee. She droned softly—one page, two. Sounding out the letters. The words and sentences floated together into an irritating, black-speckled pattern. She had a sinking feeling; maybe even she would never be able to read properly.

"Don't force it. Look at every letter, enjoy the shape—see how the letters work together to create words. You're almost there."

Elga clenched her fist, fingers crossed inside it. She felt dizzy. A grinding headache. When had she last eaten?

Leena could tell when a student had run out of steam.

"Would you like some coffee? I certainly need a cup." She went out into the kitchen and banged about. The kitchen cupboards opened and closed. She came out with a thermos and a plate bearing two rye-bread rolls with cheese. Poured coffee into two mugs.

"Do you want milk?"

"Milk?" Elga looked perplexed. She shook her head, took a sip of the coffee. Didn't dare ask for a sugar lump.

After their coffee break, the miracle happened. It was the closest thing to a religious experience a nonbeliever can have:

A throttle opened in her head

light streamed in

she read,

slowly, hesitantly

Leena praised her. "This is going well."

A rush through her body:

She could read!

An even more pleasurable rush than the one she got after her fifth porter.

"Good! Now you can teach your sisters!"

"Am I not allowed to come to school anymore?"

Elga looked nervously and urgently at her teacher.

"If you want to, we can continue with more difficult texts. You should master the art of writing too."

"And math?"

"If you want. Matti is in charge of math. But first I want you to be able to read fluently."

WHEN THE SCHOOL DAY WAS OVER AND SHE TROTTED, STILL LIMPing slightly, out the door, Johanna wasn't there. She sat on the curb and waited, thought about her tormentor of a sister, who was now punishing her younger sibling by not turning up. Her hatred for Johanna was muted for a while by the joy of reading that was bubbling in her chest. It would soon be dusk, and she realized there was nothing for it but to start the long walk home, perhaps hitchhiking along the way, though everyone would go crazy if she did that. She limped on, thinking of the homework book in her bag, and her new jeans. And that evening, the frustration didn't completely conquer her, because she was different now: literate and wearing cute jeans that were in one piece and fit snug across her ass. As if reborn. Books were hers now. She floated along the road, today she could walk any tightrope—although she should hurry, or there was no way she'd get home before dark.

She'd been trudging along for a fair while when she heard the sound of an engine and stuck out her thumb. A quad bike came along, with a trailer full of bellowing, hollering young people. For once, she was glad to see her shrill sisters. They blocked out the evening sky above the town. Tanja was driving, Johanna was sitting down on the trailer, swigging cut brandy from the bottle, and Tiina was singing loudly while the other three, even Laura, were standing up on the trailer, dancing.

Tanja slowed down and Simone, who seemed to be the tipsiest one, toppled over onto the trailer bed.

"We're off to the fall tango at the Rec," said Tanja. "Jump on!"

"I want to go home," Elga protested. Her knee was aching and she looked accusingly at Johanna.

"Then you can walk," Johanna said harshly.

"Oh, come on!" Aune called, unexpectedly cheerful.

"We need a party," Tiina said. "God, your jeans are nice! Who did you suck off? The math genius?"

Elga didn't answer. She thought about how she'd soon be free of Tiina's exhausting potty humor. Her knee hurt as she clambered up onto the trailer with the help of Tiina's strong arms. Simone sat in one corner, trying to focus. Johanna managed to spill brandy on Elga and dragged her into the dancing, with Aune and Laura shaking their behinds in time. Johanna leaped up when Aune burned a cigarette hole in their mother's good white blouse. After Johanna had worn it to visit the pastor, she'd hidden it in the chaos of the linen cupboard—where you could find anything but clean sheets.

Elga took a bottle from Aune and necked the beer. She screeched: "I can read!"

"Fuck, that's amazing!"

Aune slapped her little sister on the back, making her choke and gasp for breath.

"I'll teach you, Aune," Elga said, clinking her beer bottle against Aune's.

"Me too," Laura piped up.

"Anyone who likes," Elga screamed out across the neighborhood.

"Won't be many of you," said Johanna.

"I can read the old man's hunting magazines to you before you go to sleep."

"Shut your trap, piss-flaps. Tonight we're going to have some fun."

THE MEADOW NEXT TO THE RECREATION GROUND WAS FULL OF cars—rows of carefully parked vintage models made it seem like a car graveyard. Groups of people of different ages stood around the vehicles, laughing and drinking before weaving noisily toward the park. From the forest came the sound of electric guitar, accordion, and a powerful male voice singing about roses and unrequited love.

Tiina jumped nimbly down from the trailer as the quad bike was still moving, then the others crawled off, and Elga asked Aune for help—the wound on her knee was pulsating. They passed the hip flask around, while Johanna drove off to park in a clearing in the forest. The Rec lay before them, lit by the gentle glow of colored lights, and there was a snaking queue at the entrance. The shadows were long in the September evening; the moon was as near full as the punters' bottles were empty. The birch trees looked like they were preparing to turn red and drop their leaves.

Five sisters crept around the perimeter and climbed over the fence while Elga and Laura snuck under. Seven cigarettes were lit and moved as one glow toward the stage. Girls in short-sleeved polka-dot dresses with cinched waists shivered beside boyfriends dressed in bomber jackets and stuffing hot dogs into their faces. The sisters held their noses so they wouldn't be driven crazy by the wondrous scent of the sausages. The mosquitoes struck; the sisters struck back. As they approached the crowd around the stage, Johanna said that if it had been up to their mother and father, they wouldn't have been allowed to do this.

"The old man always said . . . the moment you walk through the front door, the bailiff will be the first person you meet."

"What would life be without a little danger?" said Aune.

"He said this too," said Johanna. "Now listen, Tiina!"

They think they're all-powerful. They think they can keep us down. They think wrong.

"Do you really think anyone here works for the taxman?" said Elga.

"Everybody likes to dance," said Tiina.

"Thought those folks preferred the Stadt Hotel?" said Elga.

Chalk-white birch trunks, golden leaves. The glow from seven filterless cigarettes. Seven tangled masses of auburn mane. Five strong, thickset bodies alongside two slighter ones. Aune at the front, in a jean jacket and her mother's high-collared lace blouse, Johanna stomping after her in the old man's plastic sandals. Elga, whose new jeans were made for hip-shaking, was thinking of Matti. Someone like him would never go to a hillbilly blowout like this. Laura was dragging her feet in clogs. They formed a chain through the crowd, pushing aside pleated skirts and floral puffed-sleeve blouses. Clip, clop, high-heeled hop.

"Do you see what I see?" Tanja asked, leaning over to Johanna.

"Lygia is dancing."

"Ask her for a dance," Tanja said encouragingly.

"Hand me that bottle."

They hung out by the railings, staring at the various dancing styles, and the singer's red leather jacket with tassels on the pockets. Johanna and Tanja clapped after every song and took gulps from the flask. Tiina whistled loudly. Laura, Elga, and Aune stood a little apart, looking pained, while Simone had already headed for the forest to violently chuck her guts up. Tiina spotted her and pointed.

"Look, Simone's kneeling to pray in the bushes."

Johanna ejected a disapproving sound.

"For fuck's sake . . . a girl's got to be able to hold a little at least."

"And we're just getting started," Tanja said.

When the singer was joined by an accordion-wielding woman in a red beret, Elga whispered in Laura's ear that she was going to go out and have a lie down on the trailer. Laura surprised Elga by saying she wanted to stay there.

Johanna readied herself, putting one foot in front of the other.

"Right, I'm going to dance."

"Me too," said Tiina, putting her hands on her sister's shoulders.

They chose a spot close to the dance floor, pointing out the corniest dance moves.

"Check out Lygia. And that sack of potatoes she's hanging off," said Tiina.

"Oh, this song! I'll ask her to dance."

And Johanna marched fearlessly toward Lygia and the guy she was dancing with. Her partner stayed with her when the song ended, his arm around her waist, obviously confident that he would be her partner for the next song, another one, the singer announced, about unrequited love. The pair were smiling at each other, out of breath, when Johanna stopped in front of them—uncomfortably close, they seemed to think. They sidestepped her.

"Hello again!"

Lygia jumped when she saw Johanna, and looked nervously at her partner, who gripped her waist a little tighter.

"Hello," she answered, reserved.

"I want to dance with you," Johanna said.

"I'm dancing with Buster."

Lygia looked at her partner, who responded by taking her hand and holding it tightly.

"Just one dance. Come on!" Johanna persisted.

"I'm dancing with Buster!" Lygia said self-consciously.

Triggered by this resistance, Johanna refused to give up.

"Could you be any more boring? Dancing with the same guy the whole time. Don't you want to have a little fun?!"

"Please go away," Lygia said.

"What the fuck! We're old school friends."

Now Lygia's partner stepped in front of her. Locked eyes with Johanna. A hard stare.

"Learn to respect when someone says no."

Johanna couldn't tolerate that tone. She stared back.

"Buster, eh? Cool name."

A spark lit in Lygia's boyfriend's eyes, and he snarled at Johanna, "Fuck off!"

"Not on your say-so."

"She said no. Accept it!" said Buster.

"She wants to dance . . . I can tell," Johanna teased.

Buster clenched his fists and grew threatening.

"Hey, there's a whole crowd of us here. We'll make mincemeat out of you and your skanky sisters in two minutes."

Then Johanna flexed her biceps.

"Hahaha. We'll turn you into little pools of gravy in a second."

Buster took an iron grip on Johanna's arm and tried to drag her away from his girlfriend, away from the dance floor, through the crowd and out toward the hot dog stand. But there it backfired. Johanna gathered all her strength into a hard kick backward. Buster lost his grip. Johanna turned and launched a foot into his groin; he fell, whimpering, in a heap. At that moment, three huge bundles of muscle stepped in, taking hold of Johanna, who kicked like crazy and swung her arms. The three men dragged her out through the entrance, out into the parking lot where they were intending to sock it to her: *Fucking whore* was all one of them managed to utter before he was attacked from behind. Tiina jumped up on his back and knocked him into the gravel, putting him into an armlock. She hissed in his ear:

"There are lots of us. And we kill."

Tanja punched one of the men in the stomach, and Laura pulled out her knife on Buster, who stood motionless, staring at the short, sharp blade. She walked up to him and carved a warning in the form of a number seven on his forehead. Blood welled up in the cut.

Aune and Elga were attempting to keep track of the tumult. *Laura*, they called: *Go girl!*

Five bouncers ran up and tore Tiina off her prey, as she sat with one knee against the floored man's bull neck.

People were screaming and raging with sudden, collective courage.

Fucking slags!

Wild wives of Satan! Rot in poverty on your farm.

No one wants to see your vile faces here at the Rec.

Elga broke down, body shaking, snot running from her nose. No more school for you, said a voice in her head. That wonderful time started and stopped on the same day. Now she'd end up in an institution for sure. She snuck away from the fight, out through the entrance, and made for the quad bike. Simone had vomited up all the poison and her eyes and mind were once again growing sharp. She approached the rabble from the side with a long, curved piece of pipe she'd found in the forest, and that she'd been planning to take home—perhaps it would come in handy. The pipe was so heavy she could hardly carry it. How the maneuver played out was hard to ascertain in the aftermath. Simone's innocent, gentle appearance meant that no one suspected her of being a vandal. She charged, pole aimed at the bouncers. They backed off and ran into the recreation ground to seek shelter. She managed to navigate the pole in among the group of people, so that Tiina and Johanna were behind it. Simone held it out in front of her, and with a strength that must have come from the Lord God himself, she steamed forth like a raging beast toward the mob, letting out a great roar. The attack made the crowd disperse, freeing Johanna and Tiina, and then Tanja, Aune, and Laura.

Then Simone led her tribe through the mob. She opened up a passable route for her sisters. Jesus walked on water, she stuttered. Jesus can walk on water. Once the enraged crowd had dispersed—most of them wanted to get back to dance to the band's hit song—the sisters lumbered over to the quad bike, where Elga had been lying on the trailer, spread-eagled in fear. Now she sat up, ready to start the engine. Once they were all on the trailer, they made off, while Laura threw stones at the guys running after the vehicle.

Johanna looked at Simone in a way she'd never done before:

"Holy fuck, you're a warrior . . . Damn it, blood's coming from somewhere. I've got a whole in the back of my head . . . is the fucker bleeding?"

"Pass the booze, I'll clean it," said Tanja.

"The booze is all gone. Do we even have anything clean to bathe it with?" said Aune.

Everyone hunted through their pockets. All they found was snuff and cigarette packets. The road was narrow, and the trailer jumped and swerved. They were thrown from side to side.

"Let's get in the sauna and bathe our wounds when we get home. I've got a crater in my mouth. Have I lost all my front teeth?" said Tiina, opening her mouth wide.

"One—no, two," Tanja surmised.

TANJA WAS ALMOST TEAR-GLAZED AT THE SIGHT OF HER SISTERS' bloody lips, bumps on foreheads, and cuts on breasts and arms. They talked over each other, edgy. The flesh wound on the back of Johanna's head probably needed stitches, but a trip to the hospital was unthinkable. They'd be arrested.

"Get a little brännvin . . . a towel . . . bathe it, Tanja," Johanna groaned, close to fainting from the pain.

She lay down on the sauna's upper bench.

Tanja rushed into the house and searched. She found a pair of scissors. Returned with her heart in her throat.

"The only towels in this house are filthy. You've gotta cut away some hair, trim around the wound."

"An ordinary family would have had bandages and compresses," sighed Elga.

Tanja bathed with spirits and sphagnum. Simone poured water on the stove. The steam rose.

"You'll have to use the birch whisk on my unsullied skin. You're all red-streaked already."

"I'll never lash you. There's no way I'd give you such pleasure," said Elga.

"You're looking pretty rotten, Aune."

Aune was moving her mouth about. It creaked.

"Can't close my jaw. Think it's dislocated."

"You were just standing around staring," said Tiina accusingly.

"We got pushed. I fell and someone ran straight into me," Aune explained.

She was overwhelmed with panic: her jaw, her storyteller's tool. Was it all over?

"Oh, I can fix that," said Tiina, taking a firm grip on Aune's face.

"Nooo! Oww! Stopppp."

Aune twisted, howling and groaning.

"We work hard for our daily bread and wanted a little fun for once. Why do people detest us? What have we done to them?"

"Someone like me isn't even allowed to ask someone to dance," said Johanna.

"You didn't actually ask," said Elga.

"What was the name of that clown she was dancing with?"

"Buster," grunted Johanna.

"How the fuck could you sleep with someone called Buster?!" Tiina said.

"I'm going to carve a Buster," said Laura.

"The devil in disguise," said Simone.

When Tanja had finished bathing Johanna's head, she took a gulp and offered the bottle to the others. They sat silent for a long time in the mounting heat. Simone beat herself with the whisk. Tiina went out to the privy.

Then she rushed in:

"Come on! The moon is full and bloody. Let's get up on the roof."

The others climbed after her, even Johanna with her head injury. They stood on the roof anywhere they managed to find spots where the tiles were intact. Toasted the moon.

"What a weird light over town," said Johanna.

"Dirty yellow," said Laura.

"Have you thought about this," said Tiina. "We're bigger than that shit heap. People are awful, not a soul wishes folk like us well."

"I've been thinking about how everything people shout at us begins with the letter 's,'" said Aune. "The oldies shout spoiled brats, stink-rats, slatterns, swine, Satan's brats, swamp muck, scrub-lubbers, spruce-huggers, stray cats. The real old folk yell sub-parish hussies. What do the young ones shout? Slags, sluts, swamp cunts, stoat fuckers."

"What about all the h-words," Elga chimed in. "Hos, harlots, hen-pecked idiots, hay-sacks."

"Trees are never nasty," said Laura. "Nor hens."

"The forest's not always kind, dammit," said Aune. "That much we know when there's a storm, but bad weather always passes."

"Suffering ennobles the character, don't forget that, girls," said Simone. "Don't be afraid . . . our suffering has plans for us."

"How weird your voice has gone," said Tiina. "Sounds like you're sucking cock."

The darkness hid the hurt in Simone's face.

"I saved you today. Feel free to show a little decency."

"Do you seriously think you're some kind of heroine, Simone?" Elga asked bluntly.

"You're always talking about *others* being evil. What about you lot?" said Simone accusingly.

Tanja thought:

"We fight when we have to. We never exactly honored our mother. Otherwise we're pretty decent, I guess."

"We're like panthers. Only attacking in self-defense," said Elga. "We should have hit back and put the old woman in her place."

"The old bitch's mouth was a gateway to the kingdom of the dead," said Tiina.

Simone protested, "I beg you . . . I feel so much guilt about our mother it stings. Here! In my heart. The seven of us could have helped her get a grip, but we punished Mother and fawned over Father."

"I agree with you, Simone," said Aune.

"Father had a mother's embrace. Mother was a tyrant," Elga summarized. "Many people have suffered on this earth without finding it necessary to abuse their children."

"She had no one on her side, apart from old, emaciated Flora who could no longer be milked," said Simone, voice quavering.

"Sourpusses. Isn't it time we had a little fun?" said Tiina, who'd tired of the gloom.

Elga kept on going.

"What Louhi wanted most was to hand me over to some robber in the forest."

"Now we're the robbers," Aune observed.

"If we're really all that worthless, maybe it's good we're on our own," said Elga. "No one would give us a job. But I'm going to go to school and be a genius. I'll invent something that will scare the shit out of all of them, and then you'll see them treating us with respect."

"You can live alone with your books here on the farm," said Tiina. "When the wagtail returns, we'll lock up for good and take our meager possessions deep into the forest. To hell with everyone else."

"In the forest we're free spirits," said Tanja. "Find food, eat it, sleep. Keep the cold at bay and warm ourselves with a drop of the good stuff. That's all."

The pelting rain beat down on them. They stretched back their heads and drank the fresh water, lifting their arms and accepting the pummeling shower. Tiina let the water wash over the sores from the fight. She took off her trousers and stood on her hands. As rapidly as the heavens had opened, off turned the tap. The rain stopped and was followed by a clap of thunder; the lightning flashes came in quick succession.

"The thunder heralds our day of judgment," Simone intoned. "The great change is coming. We have to take drastic action or we'll end up in hell."

"I'll say it again, just as the old man did," Johanna said. "We have to keep the flock together. Not get loved up and let in outsiders who'll break us up. We've got to keep all the money in the family. We wouldn't have survived this evening had we not been seven sisters, sisters who close ranks in the face of impending danger."

"You're drunk again," said Tiina. "Starting with the oldie talk like the old man . . . impending danger. Nope, now I'm going to fix a barbecue and we can grill some sausages."

They sat in a ring around the fire. Soon the sausages, barely grilled on the outside, were eaten; the long wait for properly cooked food was not for them.

The night after the fateful evening at the Rec, Johanna dreamed she was fleeing from soldiers, escaping a hail of bullets by diving into a spruce-thick forest. Sharp branches lacerated her as she pushed deeper in among the spruces, and she began flailing for her life in her sleep while Tanja tried to shake her awake. Her mouth dry as sawdust. Her head a hundred-pound sack of rye. The pillow stained brown with blood.

"The sauna! Come!" said Tanja.

"Take a sauna, now? It's morning, drat it."

Tanja would not be deterred.

"Come on, I tell you!"

Johanna sat up, shuffled out of bed, grabbed the base of her skull. Ouch! The others trailed after her, apart from Tiina, who was still sleeping.

Out on the veranda Johanna was met by an unpleasant sight. The sauna was nothing but soot and ash. She had to sit down.

"Did we forget to put out the fire?"

"Did lightning strike without us noticing?" Aune ventured.

"Shame neither Mother nor Father concerned themselves with insurance," said Tanja.

"They were thinking of all the thousands people pay throughout their lives without ever seeing a penny," Johanna said.

"Of course, now would have been a good time to call the insurance company," said Tanja.

"We haven't got a phone anyway," Johanna said, cradling the back of her head with a grimace.

Soon they were all standing, heads hanging, around the heap of ash.

"Shame we won't be able to take a sauna this winter," said Aune.

"We should be glad the fire didn't spread to the house," said Tanja.

Simone looked up at the sky and said, "Everything is ash. What did I say yesterday about Judgment Day? This is yet another sign. To the wild forest. A sacred hermit's life."

"We'll have to ride out our last winter in this dwelling. It's been decided," said Johanna.

"Every board in the house is sagging, it will collapse soon," said Aune.

"Right in front of our poor eyes. I pray for us. Don't abandon us," said Simone.

CHAPTER SIX

Well, you can probably sense the noose tightening, but the sisters haven't lost everything yet. They have one another, the hens, the dogs; the quietly explosive power of community. The energy that carries them through the winter, feeds them on a meager rye harvest, fish, and game shot close to home. Selling skins and meat at the Christmas market, and moonshine under the counter. Withstanding together the chill inside the house; as luck would have it, a mild winter.

But however strong they are, with fourteen legs and fourteen arms, they can't take everything when they move, for now their decampment is approaching.

Those of you accustomed to packing for journeys would perhaps not consider packing an art that needs mastering. But in order to wisely stow away the things needed, one must have experience of travel, an ability to imagine future needs dependent on weather, wind, work, and rest. Moreover, there must be a certain degree of order to one's thoughts, and of course, bags suitable for the kind of journey. If it were possible to lump the sisters together on one point, it would be this: an ineptitude, nay, a helplessness when faced with the need to order and systematize things. Adherence to rules is beyond their ken.

In this period of decampment and anxiety the sisters lay awake at night and listened to the owls mating and the Niskanpääs' felines' horny caterwauling. They liked the sounds. Late winter was here. The year's first wagtail bobbed its behind in the yard as Laura sat drinking coffee on the veranda. She followed the wagtail's sudden dash with her eyes. The time had come. How would they manage to take everything they needed?

A move lends sharper edges to the place one will soon abandon. Laura let out the dogs and thought about everything she stood to lose. She had no need to miss the sauna, all that remained was the stove and a black patch of earth scattered with charred boards. A forest glade and a tree of her own were things she'd be able to find in the new place too. Her tools were the main thing, they weren't so heavy.

She played with the dogs, who let out playful little barks. It took nothing to make them happy; she shared with the dogs a delight in finding a well-formed stick. Even though stick-throwing was her worst subject. Why were her arms, of all things, so weak? Tiina's upper arms are as strong as my thighs, she thought. She imagined how they'd shared the space in their mother's belly, and how her sister had gobbled up most of the placenta. She imagined with revulsion how they'd both been pushed out through their mother's pudenda. Tiina forced her way out first, weighing more than Laura even as a newborn.

The dogs came to lie around her legs and rested their heads on her feet. Thankfully, Killo and Kiiski would be coming with them. She scratched behind their ears, they growled softly with pleasure.

She'd probably spoken more to the hens and the dogs than her sisters, even more than she spoke to Tiina. The thought of Tiina always sent her tumbling into the thorny bush that was the injustices of her childhood and youth.

Laura didn't think ill of her twin sister. She didn't think anything.

Tiina was unafraid of bloodshed. The more she injured herself, the stronger her armor became. She wasn't afraid of her sensitive skin like Laura was, terrified of everything that bled, stung, and ached.

When I fell and hurt myself, I would cry for Mamma . . . who never came. I would cry louder, louder, until my voice was breaking. When I yelled out, she would come, fuming, to tell me off. Sitting there bawling over little cuts and bruises. Did she ever lift me onto her lap and tell me everything would be okay? Tell me a little pain's not so bad? That pain passes.

Tiina boored her way about, incapable of entering a room without tearing down anything in her way. A vase on a table lay in pieces. A shelf of plates was rammed into; soon everything lay in shards on the ground. Tiina's hard fists made Laura crawl into her own head. In there a game played out that only she could join in with. An only child amid six riotous sisters. In her head all was calm and still, luckily. A mindful slowness is needed in the search for the best clay. Tiina, on the other hand, has never made her way slowly through the forest, no, the ground vibrates when she comes steaming along, fledglings tumbling from their nests, pine cones raining down.

The dogs, on the other hand. My real parents, my true siblings. The cows used to trot over as soon as they spotted her; they knew they'd get a scratch behind the ears. Now they didn't have the strength to walk, their backs sagged. There was no hay in the feeder, and cows didn't like pizza. What would they do with the cows when they took off to the forest? There was only one thing for it, and she didn't want to think about that. Johanna could deal with it.

The worst thing about moving to the abandoned house was that she'd be completely at the mercy of the others. Here on the farm, she could occasionally cycle secretly into town, sell a few quarts of bilberries she'd steeped in water so they'd swell up into great big orbs, then buy glazes and other things she needed for her little figures. How long would the pens, the wood glue, and the paint last in the forest? Two wills were at war in her breast. Her longing for the ancient woodland and the fear of getting into an even tighter spot with her sisters. She felt like an old man of the forest. A man who'd never been close to a woman aside from those elves with long spindly legs he carved from birch wood. I'll make fourteen figures a day and in the end I'll have thousands. When I'm an ancient old woman of forty I'll open a museum.

The front door squeaked and the veranda creaked as Aune stepped out with the coffeepot in hand. She sat beside Laura, stretched out her legs and wiggled her feet, refilled Laura's mug. Scratched the dogs behind the ears.

"The wagtail's here," said Laura.

"Then it's time," said Aune. "In a week, say Johanna and Tanja."

"What are we going to pack everything in? Pizza boxes?" asked Laura.

"Sacks. Hunting bags. Mother's and Father's backpacks. We'll have to be inventive."

"Seven bearskins are quite enough weight for a hundred miles," Laura said despondently.

"Throughout time people have moved about with packs and they managed," said Aune.

"Not all of them . . ." said Laura, blackly.

"I'm going to tell you a story I made up by myself. Or at least, I think I did. There was once a man who had so much anxiety in his belly he wanted to scream out loud. But he couldn't do that, other people would think him crazy, and then he might get locked up. Screams have to be kept inside. The man always longed for the cranes to arrive in April. They screamed enough for him too and it relieved the pressure in his chest. One day when he was walking through the forest and it felt like he was going to go to pieces from all the terror, he found a little tarn. Black water, white water lilies. The forest around it was fairly sparse, and there were a number of cranes gathered. They hooted and blustered and didn't notice that the man had lain down in the moss and was watching them.

"When they screamed, he screamed. He opened his mouth and bawled out all that was causing him pain. His breath no longer came heavy. He felt light as a charioteer, emptied of evil vapors. He screamed again and then the unthinkable happened. The crane standing closest heard the scream of this outsider. It rushed at him with jerky, threatening strides. Before he could jump up and run away, the crane flew at him and attacked his forehead. It hurt like crazy. *Sorry*, he said. *Sorry*. He gathered all his strength and got up and ran away from there. The crane returned to its comrades—or maybe they were siblings."

Laura's face followed the story, joining in with grimaces—her eyes grew bigger and bigger, her eyebrows pinched together, her mouth moving from a vague smile to dismay, to muteness.

"Get Elga to write that down."

"I can't bear Elga's self-satisfied faultfinding, but I inhale everything she teaches."

"She'll get her revenge now. For everything we've done to her. Soon nobody's going to dare call her Wee Slag."

"Yeah, Johanna will. She's as savage as Mother these days. Kicking out wildly like a teenager. She'll never learn to read. Some door in her brain is closed. Even Tiina can do a bit of sounding out, her name at least."

"I do and I don't want to go to the abandoned house," Laura said pensively. "I just know my stomach calms when I'm deep in the forest."

"You and I wouldn't be able to manage the farm on our own," said Aune.

Laura curled up with her head on her knees. She really must figure out what she might need out there in the cabin.

"Let's ask Elga to write us some packing lists. Then we can read the words at the same time. I think when we have something to gain by reading the words, it will come more quickly."

Tiina strode out onto the veranda and heard Laura and Aune talking about words and writing. She yawned loudly above her sisters' heads, took the steps in one great leap, and landed steadily in the old man's rubber boots, spraying gritty mud over the sisters. She stomped off in the direction of the forest, stopped at the fence, pulled down her pants, bent her body backward, and took a piss. Then she vanished in among the spruce trees.

On the last night the sisters slept an anxious sleep. Laura had sobbed over the shots from the barn, and her body was jerking with sorrow.

Simone anguished over the dead batteries in Mother's transistor radio, she wanted to take it. Tiina had realized they wouldn't be able to take the quad bike—it was useless over marshy ground and in dense forest. Elga didn't sleep at all, worried about needing more pens and writing pads. She'd never really believed the sisters would make such a big decision and actually see it through. If she had, she would have found a way to fend it off, perhaps asking Teacher Leena if she knew of anywhere she could live. There was no question of staying at the farm on her own, the roof would soon collapse. Perhaps she would have been allowed to live in the playhouse at the Niskanpääs' and continue her schooling, read difficult books. Learn math—with Matti. She wanted to chain herself to something in the house, but what? A few days previously she'd had the most exciting day of her life, and tomorrow her darkest would come. She lay on one side, switched to the other, lay on her stomach, on her back. She heard Johanna sigh, whinny, and talk in her sleep: *Is it you? Father, are you here with me?*

In the dream, which was uncommonly rich in detail, Johanna felt warmth. Her father lay behind her back, his great soft belly against her body. His heavy arm held her, his hand on her breast, his breath on her neck.

He whispered in her ear:

I'm blowing a path for you, my first warrior. Your sisters' guardian. You will lead them to their new realm. You'll guide them on their way with a firm hand.

A very firm hand.

The Cabin in the Wilderness

CHAPTER SEVEN

And then they were off. A psychologist friend of mine often says that a loved one's death, a divorce, or a relocation—in that order—are the most stressful things a person can be subjected to. The sisters' heads were swirling with wildly differing thoughts. For some of them the trek was much longed for, it gave them a feeling of freedom and lust for life. Others saw it as an involuntary flight into the unknown; the death row prisoner's apathy as they are escorted to their cell.

The father made good on his promise to watch over his progeny so they would find their way to the cabin in the wilderness. He and Johanna had gone more than halfway once, on a hunt. The dogs knew exactly where to go, they'd been many times.

From a spruce tree bearded with lichens, a snowy owl looked on as a wandering host of humans traipsed through agricultural land to narrow forest tracks. The owl counted to seven. What the spying animal did not know was that they would be journeying for seven days. They passed abandoned houses and barns that had grown gray and dilapidated, past harrows overgrown with brushwood, sun-bleached rusty tractors. Root cellars with caved-in roofs. Ahead of them two strapping great dogs wove across the track, reading scents as they went. Three of the humans carried rifles over their shoulders, four pulled carts so overburdened and poorly packed that pans, spades, and packs of snus tumbled off at regular intervals. One of them toted a cage containing two anxious hens—poor birds of a feather—as well as an enormous sack on her back that had the bearer alternately gritting her teeth and stopping to pant for breath. The owl soon lost them from view.

Through the telescopic sights of a Siberian jay, they were seen to abandon the tracks for dense forest. Soon they reached the ancient woodland with its aged, bark-free pines and stately spruces. The wanderers trusted the dogs to lead them in the direction of the abandoned croft after all their journeys there with their owner. They helped each other lift the wagons over large tussocks, trunks, and stones. The tallest of them, who walked at the head of the group, held a stick with which she prodded the ground ahead so the convoy didn't get stuck in some marsh and drawn down into it.

The sun sank, moist darkness fell. A bat landed by a plunging forest tarn and hung comfortably in a birch tree. It heard a chattering it couldn't make out. What kind of animal was this that had stopped by the tarn's beachy shore? The bat wished he could see.

The seven bipeds set down all their baggage, sat on a bed of blue anemones, hunching together in a ring as protection from the cold and from danger. This time it was the thrush who regarded these humans as they placed little white sticks with one glowing end into their mouths. They shared out bread and hot dogs, then they lay down, braided together, beneath a spruce tree. They lay close together and snuffled up into each other's armpits or with their heads resting on each other's stomachs. One of them crept through the undergrowth to her own spruce. The squirrel at its top released its droppings into the bed at the bottom where the dogs lay generating heat behind the human back. Guttural sounds and heavy breathing were heard through the night, so loud the black-throated loon fell silent. The animals that slept in the vicinity of the humans hoped that they would soon be on their way so the forest might regain its stillness and its familiar animal sounds.

In the morning, the people ate bread and splashed around in the tarn like drunken otters. Then they set off. The birds pecked at breadcrumbs, then their song rose to a fortissimo.

AFTER THIRTY MILES THEY BEGAN TO REALIZE WHAT THEY'D LET themselves in for, after fifty, the youngest in the group were about to give up. Elga moaned and groaned. Laura collapsed from exhaustion. The last few days were a trial, with open, bloody flesh wounds under their feet and on their heels, backs aching, legs numb. On a steep slope leading up to thick coniferous forest, the moss lay dark green and lush. Large outcrops of rock with tempting cave openings. Laura dumped her pack on the ground and slumped.

"On your feet," ordered Johanna. "It's only the afternoon. I reckon it's still a few hours to the cave the old man told me about."

Tiina took some of Laura's load and they set off again. *These boots were made for walking*, she sang. She repeated the line, imitating drum sounds with her mouth. When the drumming stopped they heard the sound of running water. The dogs rushed first to the lively brook, lapping it up. The sisters dipped their feet in the ice-cold water. They'd packed all the scoops, guksis, and vessels at the bottom of one of the backpacks; they cupped their hands and drank until their thirst was quenched. Washed the sweat from their faces while the dogs picked up a scent and split off along a crevice, disappearing into the mountain where they'd found a cave. Short barks: *Come here now! It's here!*

Tiina, who had the most strength in her muscles, strode after the dogs and called out to the others, "Tonight we'll have a roof over our heads."

"We need to cover another ten miles. Otherwise we'll never get there," said Tanja.

"What difference does it make?" said Elga.

Johanna stopped short.

"For once I agree with Elga. We'll set up camp here, put out some traps, and three of us can do a recce with the rifles. There's going to be a meat-fest tonight!"

They parked the wagons and set down their baggage at the mouth of the cave. Tiina cut away some brushwood and found the remains of a campfire. When she crept inside the cave she saw discarded bones and animal hair that was both red and dark brown. Simone followed her with a bundle of leaves, sweeping out droppings, stones, and twigs, then covered the ground in skins. Ready to faint from tiredness and with throbbing calves, she looked forward to resting. Laura too laid out her sleeping roll in the cave with the others', placing the hens' cage alongside. But they couldn't rest yet. Johanna, Simone, and Tiina headed out with the rifles and traps while Aune, Simone, and Laura gathered birch bark, willow brush, and sticks for the night's fire.

Elga toddled off on her own, hoping to find some damp moss to soothe her sores. It would be a case of grinning and bearing the pain on tomorrow's stretch of the journey to the cabin. Of putting up with the disappointment of her life. As she used the last of the tampons she'd stolen from Teacher Leena's house, she caught sight of some black grouse droppings: the curved shape of the shit. A nausea that brought tears to her eyes.

She'd been eight years old, it was her birthday. For Mother and Father it had been a day like any other, they never celebrated, but Uncle Veikko remembered her with a card.

Happy birthday, Johanna had said, handing her a half-full bag of cheese curls. So insanely good. She'd grabbed a handful and stuffed her mouth full, gagged and spewed up black grouse droppings on the kitchen floor. Got a walloping from Mamma while the sisters laughed.

The memory made her legs buckle in the soft moss; she fell right into its moist scent, picked herself up gingerly, trudged onward with effort, and found some lovely sphagnum by a murmuring brook. She dipped her swollen, bloody feet, enjoyed the relief. She felt icky, stared straight at a Baltic pine, into the trunk's rugged exterior.

Another time when she was nine years old, her back pressed up against a pine tree, the rope cutting into her chest. She whimpered. Johanna's sweet breath, she held out a sack in front of Elga, something was moving inside. Johanna held the opening tight, opening it carefully before Elga's eyes. A head stuck out. Snake. It wasn't a grass snake, she could see that from its vertical pupils. Johanna held the snake, brought its head up to the captive's throat, brought the head to her mouth, to her eyes. The reptile's cold eyes. Johanna's empty gaze as the fangs sought out the carotid.

Elga fixed her gaze on the clear water of the brook, the smooth stones on its bed. Once again feeling heavy bodies, hard hands. How little she was, forever the smallest. Shrinking from the violence, shooting verbal arrows instead, learning how to shoot for the heart.

Should she have stayed on the farm? Called for help? Somewhere within her she knew it wasn't yet time to free herself. Her sisters were her tormentors and shields. Freedom would come, she knew that. But how? Now hard, physical work awaited, practical jobs at the cabin. All the things she loathed. How would she be able to keep up her reading? What lay beyond her notebook? Writing on stone tablets? Perhaps some fine day she would escape.

She tried to see her face in the brook, but the surface was too much in motion. She wanted once again to see that she was something other than what the sisters reflected back at her. Brisk and repellent, she had thought, but she actually wasn't ugly. Not beautiful either, whatever that was. The word beautiful made her think of lynx.

She cupped her hands and drank the delicious, ice-cold water, jumping when she heard Johanna's dog whistle, it unsettled her as usual. She quickly picked some sphagnum, filling the backpack. The sharp sting of her sores as she made her way to the cave.

LYING ON THE SKINS IN THE CAVE, THEY BELCHED WOOD PIGEON. Laura staggered out to pee and saw the stars dancing in the sky. The vodka, the bird meat, and the protection of the cave calmed and pacified them. The dogs, guarding the entrance, were attentive to every rustle.

Johanna, who was lying on the bearskin impregnated with their father's blood, the head of which they'd cut off ahead of their move, widened her nostrils and drew in the scent.

"Can you smell it?"

"What?" said Elga.

"The old man's scent. Breathe in deep. Can't you smell it?"

She inhaled deeply and uttered a groan of pleasure as her nose reacted with a powerful delight, her nostrils fluttering.

"His pipe tobacco?" Tanja ventured.

"His spirit is here. Fine and strong," said Johanna.

"You're starting to talk like me," said Simone.

"If our father spent the night in this cave, it's impossible that his scent could still be here," said Elga. "Even an idiot can see that."

"Stop yapping," Tiina said. "Go to sleep. I don't intend on carrying your bags if you drop."

"Can you spell brain-dead?" said Elga.

"How the hell do you have the energy?" said Tiina.

Laura crawled in to lie in her spot at the very back of the cave, as far from her sisters as possible. She rooted around and around like dogs do to find a comfortable position. A soft plastic pouch fell from a cleft in the rock. She switched on her flashlight.

"Incredible! Look, it's the old man's pipe. The lucky pipe he always had with him on hunts. And tobacco. Put your light on, Johanna!"

Six faces gawked in Laura's direction as she opened the packet and inhaled the sweet scent. The others reached out their hands like addicts waiting for their dose of heroin.

Laura studied the packet carefully.

"There's more here."

A letter written on lined paper in black, chunky graphite from his logger's pencil. Sprawling letters. Drawings by each paragraph.

"Could he write? Or . . . did he have someone with him who could?"

Laura handed the sheet of paper to the reader, who sat up sharply. Johanna and Laura shone their lights on the message. The words looked like strange insects to begin with; Elga felt terror rise from her stomach to her throat. How would she be able to make this out? Had she already forgotten how to do it? Was the reading muscle something you had to train every day?

"Can't you do it? Read!" said Johanna.

My dear daughters. I hope you are strong and able. I'll be leaving soon, standing face to face with the biggest whopper I've seen in all my hunting days. My body is heavy, my knees ache, my vision is failing. The forest is a blur. When my eyes give up, my life will be over. Perhaps it's my nearsightedness that makes me fearless in my encounters with these beasts. I go on impulse when I aim, no one knows that about me.

The bear I caught sight of today was born angry. He got away. If I beat this towering thing, all other bears are harmless. If it kills me, you must get the bastard. Avenge your great father. But I hope you'll never have to read this letter. I hope to return here to the cave with the bear's body. To sleep on the skin and gather my strength ahead of the long walk back to you. Of course then I'll have wolves to contend with.

If you're in a pinch, know that I am nearby. I'm at the top of the pine tree, I'm in the pine bracket. I'm the cuckoo who calls your way. I'm in the bat who watches over you while you sleep. My eye is everywhere you make your way.

My warriors. My magnificent daughters. I've gathered a few important things at the cabin. It will be a surprise. Be sure to grow potatoes and rye. Hops of course, but you'll need to build a greenhouse for that. You can grow more than people think in forest plots. Just let in some light. Become better than me at fishing. And for God's sake—

though I don't believe in him like your Mother, that crazy woman—stay together. Unity is survival.

I detest rules, you know that. But I must give you some.

Give men the finger. You'll catch diseases, get little beasties between your legs and ruined, aching hearts. Men are like dogs when they find a stick. Rush around all dizzy and playful for three minutes, then the minute they catch another scent, they drop the stick. If you get in with men, you'll soon be tugging teats all day long, your breasts hanging. You're bigger than that. Stay warriors and live a good life.

Remember this! Treated well, the forest is your best friend. Consult the spruce and the pine about what they want. You'll be forced to kill animals. What else will you eat? But don't let yourselves get eaten. Remember what I said about blood and wolves. Other animals kill to silence their hunger. Wolves will kill for fun, and to pass the time.

You should avoid people too. They only spread plagues and weaken you. Don't let any social services busybody or statistician get so much as a little finger in the door. People who claim to want to do good for underlings, as they see us—cherish a special suspicion for them. They want to sow discord, put you in foster homes where you'll be beaten and violated.

They think they're all-powerful.

They think they can keep us down.

They think wrong.

You should know that the cabin lies beyond borders. They won't find you there. You'll be protected. You're in the true wilderness, not the pretend-wild that's been tamed by human hand. The social services biddies who hunted us have no right to stick their noses in now. Nor the bailiffs. You're free. Free to create a kingdom where you rule.

Live! Live strong and secure in the knowledge that your father is with you until the very end.

CHAPTER EIGHT

What is a home? A place where you feel safe and at ease, a place you want to take care of. But what makes one person feel safe strikes terror into the heart of the next; a few years ago I heard about a woman who grew up in Las Vegas, her father owned a small casino. Slot machines gave her a homely feeling, especially the tinkling and rattling of one-armed bandits.

One thing is for sure, it takes a lot to make a snug home when you live close to nature, in a forest that spreads for a hundred miles in every direction. Who is suited to which tasks, and who decides? Who washes up, who skins the game?

Humanity can be divided into two categories: people who seek out physical challenges and are energized by the stiffness and strains that come after a marathon, and those whose bodies are cowardly and who try by all means to avoid the buildup of lactic acid. Ideally they undertake their tasks slowly from a comfortable chair, just like me as I write this book. You can guess which sisters fit into which category.

But finally, in the gentle dusk and its earthy freshness, they found themselves at the cabin in the wilderness. Now the raw toil began.

How do you get people to give their utmost? Sometimes it takes a real struggle and direct threats.

PACKS THUMPED ONTO THE GROUND. THE SISTERS THREW THEM-selves down, the dogs lay panting alongside. The finish line had been reached and Laura walked a little way into the bush and vomited from exhaustion. She remained there on her knees, drank water, unpacked the dog bowls and filled them; the dogs' whisking, thirsty tongues. Tanja was the first to enter the house's single room. Sound roof, solid build, fireplace. A bunk along the short side and a little coffee-stained table. Two windows speckled with mosquitoes. A little room, oh so tiny. For one person, two at the most. How would they fit? They weren't exactly used to making themselves small.

Tanja hung a flashlight from a hook on the ceiling and dug out a dustpan and brush. She was a little astonished at herself for having packed cleaning equipment, but she wanted it to be nice in her own home: she swept the stamped earth floor clean of mouse droppings and small, dead birds. Laid out the seven bearskins and then sat on the great flat stone, the step that led to the cabin, listening to the evening sounds of the forest. Eagerly, the song thrushes sang their randy spring song, now and then letting their pessimistic brother the blackbird speak up in his gentle way.

Johanna passed round a water bottle and a piece of bread, and some for the dogs too, before hauling in her pack and commandeering the bunk. Someone had left birch bark, willow brush, and winter-dry pine cones. Was it father? Where was his surprise?

They made a few rounds of the house to look over their new property. Stiff, tired legs aching from exhaustion. The conifers were enormous, the conks of bracket fungi high up in the pines.

The spruces put out pale green shoots that the sisters picked and chewed for dessert. They noted with relief that the bilberry bushes grew dense. They stood still and listened. Heard running water and made for the sound. Fell to their knees by the wide, deep, eddying brook. When Tiina stepped down into the clear water she saw fish. What kind of fish could it be? Laura ran her hand over the black mud, dug, and squeezed. She'd never clasped better working clay between her fingers.

The darkness brought the chill—one is never so cold as in the spring. The cabin was thoroughly cold and raw. Johanna got up a calm, steady fire in the hearth. She didn't like it, but every time she lit a fire, a clear image of her mother came to her.

They sat on the furs and Tiina shared out smoked sausage and pirogs. The dogs got theirs and begged for more. The hens, glad to be out of the cage, hopped about among the breadcrumbs. Fourteen human legs and fourteen arms interlocked. Hot red cheeks. Auburn tufts in a great bush of hair.

"We must raise a toast to our new home. Our first home of our own," said Tiina.

"A den with six square sisters," said Elga. "What a punishment. Yeah, we need a drink."

"Can't even manage a sip . . . to celebrate," said Johanna. Her tiredness reached all the way to her coccyx and she was barely capable of speech. "We'll have to do it . . . tomorrow. Find . . . Father's surprise."

"We need to find a hiding place for the booze, rifles, and ammo," said Tanja. "Find out whether there's a spring."

"Divining rod. I'll sort the fresh water," said Laura.

Surprised looks from her sisters.

"Who taught you that?" asked Tanja.

"The old man, actually. He said you had to be quiet and try to make contact with pixies to find water. We'll need a toolshed, too, with space to do woodwork."

"And dry meat," said Tanja. "We've got food enough to get by for a week or so . . . if we don't gobble it all up."

"We're pilgrims who've reached the promised land. May our souls find peace," said Simone.

"You can always make something out of a life catastrophe," muttered Elga.

Aune summarized the situation as was her want. "We've just walked over a hundred miles. We've been brave. Our most faithful companions—our legs and feet—are aching. Let us rest and come together to work when we're feeling refreshed."

"Stop chattering, you self-important fools," said Tiina. "Otherwise you'll be fixing up a root cellar."

"Of all the soulless things a person must do to survive, I really don't think building a root cellar is the worst," Aune said. "Digging sharpens your mental facilities."

Tanja was thinking, picturing all the heavy work that needed to be undertaken.

"Digging. Plowing. Harrowing. Sowing. Harvesting. We have to do it by hand and I'll have to figure out how. Tomorrow I'll check the quality of the land around the house."

"The clay by the brook is the best kind," said Laura.

"Well, you can eat clay then," Tiina pitched in.

Johanna, who surprisingly seemed the weariest of them, raised her voice.

"As the oldest and wisest I'm asking you to stop talking shop.

Our father always said that as long as you get your sleep you'll have the strength to pull up any mountain birch you choose. By the roots! Sleep!"

Johanna stretched out on the bunk and looked down at the floor where her sisters lay entangled with the dogs. The hen cage was on the little table.

"Is the door well shut?" Johanna mumbled. "We've got twenty-eight bloody flesh wounds in here. That kind of thing makes wolves . . ."

A snore mid-sentence. The others had already fallen asleep. Simone was belly-breathing, Tanja dry-coughing, and Tiina hadn't even managed to grab her crotch and release some tension before sleep descended. Dreams drifted into one another. Johanna saw her father bare-chested, riding toward her on a grizzly bear. He shot a wild boar and a lynx in passing as he blew his daughters a kiss. Johanna held on tight to the old man's pillow, the very first thing she'd packed.

The sisters slept so soundly they didn't notice the animals that crept around the house, a fox, two wolves. The dogs sat up, attentive, and parked themselves by the door. Growled quietly. Got growls in response.

Johanna awoke first, shivering. Tanja had stolen the covers and was enjoying the warmth. The little windows were overgrown, it was impossible to see out. But the glass was intact, the roof sound, and the door closed well. So they were protected to a certain degree. The dogs lay together by the doorframe and looked up. The sisters, who'd intertwined legs and arms to hold in the warmth, looked meek as they slept, even Elga looked peaceful. Tiina kicked her man-size feet and whimpered. Laura had swaddled herself in her bearskin and lay stretched out on the floor. Johanna took pipe and tobacco from her hunting bag, tiptoed out onto the step followed closely by the dogs, and was met with a surprise: a white landscape. It must have snowed five inches in the night. At the beginning of May! Why do those in northern countries always forget that it can snow right up to the end of June, and hail tennis balls any time after?

The dogs romped delightedly in the snow. Johanna fetched her jacket, stepped into her boots, and stood for a long time on the step, sucking on the pipe and trying to imagine what her father had done when he welcomed the morning here at the cabin. He would have smoked his pipe of course, and drunk coffee, but right now the coffeepot was packed and she wanted this quiet morning time to herself before the cackle-crones woke up and the volume rose to that of a traffic jam in a metropolis of millions.

Silent morning. Tranquility. Amid all the untouched whiteness she saw animal tracks, and the dogs were already in the depressions, sniffing. What Johanna wouldn't give for all the information they snapped up in one sniff. She sat on her haunches. Her father had taught her to recognize most tracks and droppings. Here was wood mouse, fox—and wolf.

On stinging, aching feet she stumbled around the house, inspecting every part of it. Everything looked solid, even on the outside. Had the old man taken care of it, or other hunters? How many hunters were there in an ancient forest? Will they come here and be angry to find their hunting cabin occupied? Their father had spoken of researchers who'd ventured into the ancient forests and then acted all high and mighty at the university. Unexpected visitors could come to the house. We need to be ready, she thought, looking up at the sky as though the old man might appear somewhere up there. She would certainly be able to get along with hunters and fishermen, but academics, who'd spent half their lives studying at university and then got stuck there. What do you say to people like that?

She planned to check the integrity of the chimney during the day. One could always heave Elga up like a little brush to get out the soot. Johanna laughed to herself. As soon as Wee Slag opened her mouth, sarcasm dripped from it. An inner nerve pulsed powerfully. An artery in her throat swelled. No one had any use for that feeble little rat. She didn't have the sense to have a care. *And I was the one who saw to it that she got to go to school. Huh? You'd think she'd show a little gratitude.* Johanna's cheeks burned with indignation. Their father had left school at thirteen, but he still managed to become famous, sure shot that he was. Could he write too? Peculiar. It's not like he would have let someone else write the letter they'd found in the cave. And who else would have read the hunting magazines?

Imagine nobody realizing that she was closest to Father and that her grief was the deepest. She tried to teach his words of wisdom to her sisters, but they just kept spouting nonsense. Not a single word seemed to go in. Tanja at least seemed to have an ounce of maturity, no provocations from her. She had an inner armor. Guess she'd had to develop that since she'd shared a belly with that chatterbox Aune. We need to be warlike, Johanna decided.

She walked behind the cabin and traipsed into a dense thicket of pines interspersed with occasional droopy-branched spruces. Moss peeped through in places where the snow hadn't succeeded in laying its white blanket. She sat on the trunk of a gray pine that had fallen to the ground, fixing her gaze on the tree's rough skeleton arms. Could they be something for Laura? The snow was melting, the sky went from gray to pale blue.

It was clear to her that she and Tanja would have to work together and share the command, the two of them united in severity. To begin with, the butcher is as scared as the animal, but it gets easier. The butcher befriends his knife, his tools, and it all becomes everyday. Then there's food on the table. He tells his children: The blood that stains my hands red will make your tummies full.

Should they reward those who behaved, who worked with sweat and fury? Liquor, medals? Betraying the group would have to cost them. What form would punishment take? Laura would have to put aside her silly figurines. They needed four totem poles. To the north, south, west, and east of the house. As frightening as she was able, with the skeletons of dead animals, wolf jaws, foxes' eyes, and bear claws. Scare away any visitors.

She heard sticks snapping in the forest, someone was walking toward her. A limping, weary Tanja.

"The timber for the sleeping cabin needs felling as soon as we can manage," she said. Tanja had followed Johanna's footprints and sat down on a stone beside her to massage her tired legs. Her behind got wet, but that made no difference to her. When would the ill effects of the walk pass?

"It won't be possible for all of us to sleep in the cabin," said Tanja.

"It was only possible last night because we were already unconscious," said Johanna. "We need to get building as soon as possible. The nights are going to be repulsive with all that snoring, sleep-talking, and sour farts, not to mention Tiina's fucking whinnying every morning."

"She claims she does it in her sleep, that she has no control over it," Tanja said in a conciliatory tone.

"We'll push her out from now on. She can jerk off outdoors," said Johanna.

"She's got that damned itch on the brain and it's not like she's ever satisfied with one roar," said Tanja.

Johanna nodded.

"She gets on it again. And again. Drives me crazy."

They sat awhile in silence. Tanja massaged her calves and said, "Hey, I've been thinking. How are we going to get everyone to really work? There are five of us can fell trees, even if Aune and Simone have got puny arms."

Johanna appreciated the constructive approach: "Laura and Elga can fiddle about with the toolshed, their little craft workshop. And cutting undergrowth, digging out roots, and sorting out a proper potato field will all fall to them. They'll also prepare the skins for sale at the market in June. We've got a month. We'll have to make a list in our heads, you and I. Though how we're going to keep track of the days now we haven't got any batteries for old Mother's radio I don't know."

"I can be in charge of counting the days," said Tanja. "One thing's for sure: we'll starve if we don't hunt every day."

Johanna put a hand on her rumbling belly.

"I'll need at least one meal a day if I'm going to have the strength to work. I suggest you and me have a meeting here without the others every morning."

"What shall we do with the troublemakers?" Tanja asked.

"I won't rule out corporal punishment."

Tanja's brow furrowed. She said, "Was old Mother right?"

Johanna looked her soberly in the eye.

"Now we're here I have to give her that. How else are you and I going to keep a handle on that rabble?"

THE RABBLE WERE UP WHEN THE TRIBE'S LEADERS RETURNED from their planning meeting. The sisters had dug out some breakfast and were breaking pieces off a rye cake; the hens were pecking off crumbs. Johanna and Tanja flopped down and helped themselves. When they'd drunk the coffee Johanna got a focused look in her eye, she climbed up onto an enormous rock in front of the house. The snow had melted, the birds were tweeting in the trees. The rock made Tiina realize they'd forgotten to bring a spit. On the other hand, not even she would have managed to carry a heavy spit this many miles. Johanna stood on the rock's uneven top. Whistled so that Laura and Elga, who were stumbling around somewhere by themselves, would hear and be brought into the fold. They appeared in a glade and shuffled in, Laura with a tired expression, Elga with her sourpuss and that pointy nose that Johanna was sure belonged to another hereditary line. Simone was on her knees in the glade, deep in morning prayer, and saw from a distance that Johanna was waving to say: We are meeting.

Tanja immediately stood to the right of nature's own soapbox. Simone at the speaker's feet, Tiina standing with a cigarette in the corner of her mouth. Her coil of smoke united with Aune's. Johanna raised her voice to include Elga and Laura, who both stepped forward slowly. Johanna cleared her throat. It was clear that she'd long been readying herself to communicate, in formal words, something important to the tribe.

"I know things you don't know. Yes, it's true, Elga. That's how it is."

Elga rolled her eyes, buttoned her lips. She was readying herself for flight. She'd wither in this forest glade, and if she fled across the border to Sweden she might be able to go to school there.

Johanna paused, cleared her throat again. The sun burst forth and shone an intense spotlight on the house, setting the six thickets of red hair ablaze. Laura put on the sunglasses she'd stolen from Teacher Leena's house, picked up a hen and put her on her lap to stroke. The dogs lay in the warmest patch of sun in front of the steps.

"I want to tell you a little about our beloved father," said Johanna in a clear, strong voice.

"Yeahhh," called Tiina and Tanja.

"He had serious talks with me when we were hunting. He knew our path would be difficult. A great man spoke to his oldest daughter, his first huntress."

Aune sat tense, listening with great focus. Laura squinted and listened half-heartedly to her sister, whose outline was blurred. Johanna swelled her chest, rearing up above them, and spoke in a strained, formal manner.

"Our father is with us. Do you feel that?"

"Yeahhh!"

"Do you feel the power from his mighty body and his warming spirit?"

"Yeahhh!"

Johanna raised her arm and pointed at the sky where the white, fluffy clouds were scudding past in a blue sky.

"Our father wants us to live the simple life well. We should rise above needs that intrude upon us."

Johanna said nothing for a while, stood up straighter. Searched for breath in the depths of her belly:

"Our dear father, most beloved up in heaven. We are your humble servants. You protect us. Dear father."

"Amen," said Simone.

She mumbled to herself: *Matthew five-seven.*

Elga snorted. Tiina, who'd been sitting on the ground, creak-cracked the joints in her fingers, her thigh muscles vibrating.

Johanna intoned, "We must stay together. Stay close. No letting in strangers who might drive us apart. Seven is stronger than six. Father spoke to me during long treks and nights spent in hollows in the rocks. He elevated me to the role of leader. We should beware of men, he told me, just like in his letter to us. You need to know that no romantic relationship with a man has ever favored a woman, he said. Enter into no marriage. Hold on to your own money, your own possessions. Never try to save a man who claims to be suffering. He will only use your bodies to relieve his tensions. He will make you hand over money, quad bikes, vodka bottles. He grabbed hold of my shoulders and looked me straight in the eye: 'Take me at my word, you know I'm a man. A man of renown, no less.'"

Tiina interrupted in a loud voice, "Seems unlikely we'll find a man out here unless a bear takes a liking to us."

Aune and Tanja hushed her, stern eyes on Tiina.

Johanna went on: "We've chosen to live in a spot that's as far from people as it's possible to get, but dangers can still arise. Adventurers, scientists, drifters. The persecution we've suffered as a result of our renowned father will strengthen and refine you. You must be especially wary of sheep who seek you out, speak tenderly, wishing to save you—they are wolves in disguise. Believe no one who claims they will be able to help. It will lead only to ruin. Together you will be one with the forest, we leave no traces but pine needles and mud."

Johanna saw that Tiina had lain down, while Laura and Elga were whispering together. Even Tanja wasn't paying attention, she closed her eyes and nodded off.

Johanna redoubled her efforts, her voice powerful.

"AS LEADER . . .

"I will teach you to become supreme hunters, no nimble beaver will escape us. We'll become skilled at fishing for pike, perch, and char. Do not be too lazy to take what the forest offers you in the way of wild mushrooms, bilberries, lingonberries, crowberries, and bearberries. Wild raspberries are candy.

"Father said: 'Do not mourn me. Channel that power into building a sauna. The sauna offers consolation. In times of conflict, go into the sauna. The heat will still overheated tempers.'

"Sisters! Soldiers! Look at your feet. Look at your hands. No one can take them from us. Worship the power in them. We must honor and uphold one another. Who else will? And we must work. As hard as we are able. From now on, we must plug away from morning till night. The cabin is good and sound, but small. We'll end up beating each other to death if we have to keep sleeping so close. We'll clear the brush on the plot, dig a potato field, fell trees, and start building today. Everything must be ready by first frost. It will be a tough but glorious summer. Are you ready?"

"Yeahhh!"

"Are you my strong sisters?"

Everyone apart from Laura and Elga shouted, "Yeahhh." Aune answered half-heartedly. She was thinking about Johanna's talk, the intensity in her voice. Perhaps she was as good as Veikko. Though she was unctuous, her father-worship was getting silly.

"We dragged the chainsaw, oil, and extra chains along with us," said Johanna. "Don't go too crazy with the saw, Tiina! You've broken a lot of chains."

"How are our booze and cigarette stocks looking? We need rewards," said Tiina.

"Hard to say, could last until market day. We'll have to keep the market in mind as we work. Sell all the things townies want from the forest. We need a storehouse too."

"It's time, girls. Time to show our strength," said Tanja and looked at her companion appreciatively. "We'll split into teams."

"Laura will be construction supervisor. Tiina's huntmaster," said Johanna.

Tiina put her hand up, making a victory sign. Laura looked confounded. She took off her sunglasses.

"Construction supervisor?"

Johanna explained: "They design and lay out the building others will build. Elga will be your assistant."

Elga looked up, her head heavy despite its delicate form. Shrugged lamely even though she thought the job was exciting. Laura was dizzied by the fancy title, would she be able to live up to this?

"Then let's get going, my friends," said Johanna. "We'll eat fried eggs at midday, then we'll have a barbecue and drink a toast."

Tiina took off with the chainsaw, appointing Aune her assistant. Johanna loaded the rifle, hoping for success on the hunt with Tanja and the dogs. Simone dug a little pit and built a fireplace, then slung a sack over her shoulder and headed off on a walkabout to gather birch bark, willow brush, and sticks for the fire. She decided to set off from the rear of the house and strike a straight course into the forest, then turn around and come back the same way. Since her eyes were constantly looking to the sky, to the clouds, she got lost easily.

The sun was warm, the sweat ran from her brow; she walked for hours, finding treasures she put in the sack. She found a fishing lake with such clear water no char would be able to hide, and beside it a gently murmuring forest meadow of high bluegrass. She climbed a small hilly ridge: toward the horizon, perhaps five miles away, she could see a high mountain with a snowcapped peak. One day she would climb that mountain, find her way to the top, and look out over the vast expanse. Closer to God. Feeling the breath of angels on her neck. Ask the higher powers for mercy on behalf of her godless sisters.

Laura, left at the abandoned cabin that was no longer abandoned, felt a thrill of energy inside her. She must now scale up her gaze from micro to macro, from stick to log. She asked Elga if she could borrow pens and sketch in her notepad. Her sister replied stubbornly that she needed the pad and pens for her own studies.

"What am I going to draw on then?" asked Laura, disappointed.

"Stone. It worked fine once upon a time," said Elga.

The corners of Laura's mouth turned down, she recognized herself in Elga's reluctance to comply. They were diametrically opposed to their sisters, it was really they who should be twins.

"We'll have to buy lots of notepads when the wares are taken to market," Laura said.

Elga sighed and fetched the pad and pen she'd hidden under

her bearskin. Laura studied closely how the cabin's logs had been arranged to form a stable structure. How many were needed? She drew the cross corners. She made a sketch of how the roof was constructed. How did you get the windows in? Were windows needed? Would they have to be transported all the way through the forest?

"The cabin's built without any nails at all," she said. "There will be a fair bit of math. You're good at that. We'll need to find peat and really good clay."

Elga nodded bullishly.

"Guess we'd better wait for Tiina's timber delivery," she said.

"You want to see my sleeping den?"

Laura crawled in under a spruce that had taken root close to a little rocky hillock. Elga crawled in after her. The stone made a protective wall. Long, sweeping branches hung down to the ground, the tree's floor-length gown. Inside, she'd laid out spruce branches, covered with a thick blanket of bracken stems on which the bearskin had been laid, with her backpack as a pillow. She'd lined up pine-cone figurines and little girls made of clay on a flat rock. She'd dubbed her new home Spruceside.

Elga sat on the bearskin and inhaled the tree's scents.

"I want to get away from the others too."

"There are plenty of other spruce dens," said Laura.

"And the wolves?"

"We can share the dogs," said Laura. "They keep watch and will give good warning."

A hard thud outside the entrance made them jump. Someone stamped on the ground. Their father's boots appeared.

"What the devil are you up to?! Damned bumrats playing forts while the rest of us are working our asses off. You know what father thought of layabouts!"

"We're drawing a house. We've got pen and paper in here, see for yourself."

"You'll sit out here so we can see you're working."

Laura and Elga crawled out of the spruce den. Johanna looked down on her little sisters who were no longer little, though their muscles were meager as old women's. She swung a teasing boot at Elga's behind.

"Show some balls now. Work!"

The jute sack Simone was carrying over her shoulder filled up with birch bark, willow brush, sallow, and spruce and pine kindling. Her feet were beginning to throb, afraid they would be forced to go on a hundred-mile trek before they'd had a proper chance to rest. She could smell swamp. She pictured Mother Louhi sitting by the cotton grass and followed the fresh scent until a great swamp opened up before her. She picked up a long, sturdy stick, prodding the ground to ensure it was dry. There was a risk otherwise that the marshy wetness would suck at the soles of her plimsolls, drawing her deep into the swamp's dark nether regions to meet Mother.

She leaned against a wind-ravaged birch, was close to her mother, recalling the mild odor of her body blending with this fresh swamp scent. Louhi always washed herself carefully on Sundays. They would sit just as Simone was sitting now, leaning against a short, thin little birch. The daily service on the radio. Soft choral voices. Resonant psalms. Scratchy sounds and static buzz. The heathens have come to disturb us, Mother would say in irritation, unpacking the flask of coffee from the birch-bark knapsack. They would both drink from the lid, in which four sugar cubes were melting. Days of cloudberry, the preserve soft in their mouths. *Glorious is the E-earth, glorious is God's he-eaven.*

Simone hummed a psalm as she scanned the ground. Here by this great swamp, however, the cloudberries were few, she saw only the occasional unripe red fruit.

Where did Mother go? Was she up there among the clouds in paradise? Had she and Father made up? Her heart ached. Her eyes stung. She alone grieved, she alone sought God. Alone among sinners.

The sun disappeared behind the clouds; how long would it take before this pain in her chest gave way? Maybe the pain would always be there. She would have to find ways to bear it. She'd come and sit here as often as she could. Her sack was nearly full; brimming with self-pity she thought of the long walk back to the cabin with this heavy burden on her back. She looked up at the sky: the clouds were in a rush, and she began her journey home. She stopped, turned. She had to find a landmark so she'd recognize the swamp. There. That enormous, charred pine. She walked over to the pine and scored an "S," then a cross beside it.

She must have taken a fork off the main track, because she caught a whiff of sludgy water, rotten vegetation. Through the thicket she caught sight of a tarn, here and there last year's water-lily leaves. On the opposite side, a beaver lodge that reminded her of the work that awaited her.

What do other young people do? Go on fairground rides, play games on those computer things like what Matti the math genius had, sit in cafes and talk. Go to school, of course. The sisters' fate was work. Hard physical work. She wasn't built for it, this sensitive body. She sank down onto a fallen pine branch, looked out across the coal-black water, felt dizzy and hungry; she hoped Johanna and Tanja would bring home food. Dear Lord help us. She looked up into the clouds, which parted at that very moment, and a strong, thin ray directed its light toward the tarn, striking the surface. The little forest lake shimmered, glimmered, dazzled. Little birds twittered in every tree and the toads joined in, their bass notes completed the choir. Simone hummed along, wishing she had a better singing voice. She wasn't capable of swooping between low notes and high.

The light was so intense it hurt her eyes. She bent forward and grazed her palm over the surface. Got a shock, her whole body shuddered. She perceived herself as one with the tarn, the trees, the light. Someone was there, wanting to show her she was absolutely not alone. What would she do in the face of her sisters' blindness to the one true Father?

"Help me Lord to make them honor you. The bear hunter Heikki Leskinen was a little ant among the rest of us ants. Our mother was closer to God."

Then she shouted, "Help me to not surrender to the tipple on St. John's Eve. That life-threatening drink soothes hunger, the strain of work, the sorrow over Mother. The drink offers a short moment of joy to a darkened temperament."

A wave ran across the tarn, the ripple set the beaver's lodge bobbing. Simone felt a beam pass through her body from her scalp to her big toes.

She said loudly, "You will never walk alone."

Thrown back into the reeds: her face to the sky, eyes closed in the beam of light.

With Aune's help, Tiina had felled and trimmed three pines. Johanna and Tanja hummed as they carried home a deer with the dogs jumping cockily at their heels. The animals sniffed the body excitedly. The flesh would be perfect for St. John's Eve. Simone's wood made a fine bonfire. Laura and Elga had puzzled out how Tiina's pine logs should be arranged so that the sleeping cabin would stand firm.

Satisfied with the day's work, they drank all the brännvin, ate the whole deer. The cuckoo called, but the sisters didn't hear. They roared, laughed, sang ditties.

"She sells seashells on the seashore," Aune ventured and was met with six theatrically bored expressions.

"She slurps shots and sings she's a whore—" Tiina tried to buoy them up.

She stopped in the middle of a sentence and collapsed with a snore. It set off a chain reaction. When darkness fell, the sisters were sleeping in a heap by the campfire, sated and drunk. All except Laura, who'd crawled off to her own nest.

The pygmy owl skirled portentously at the dawning of Midsummer's Day. They were all woken at once by the dogs' hunting bark. Johanna heaved herself up and Tanja swayed after her. They called the dogs, which came running, wide-jawed and full of muscular power. By the cabin, one hen lay dead and mutilated. The predator had probably carried off the other one. They searched for tracks but found none.

"We forgot to put them in the cage," said Johanna, clutching her forehead. Her headache was pulsating.

"How could we?" Tanja said, stamping her foot hard.

"Now we won't have any eggs," said Simone, wringing her hands. "What will become of us?"

"Stop feeling sorry for yourself," Johanna hissed.

"Feeling sorry for ourselves won't help," Tanja added.

Simone sobbed: "I can't help my feelings."

Johanna lost her patience: "Feelings! What the fuck use do we have for feelings?"

Laura lay in Spruceside with a drum solo playing in her head, fighting back the urge to vomit. She heard the raised voices and realized what had happened. She made a firm and sacred resolution to never again abandon herself to the brännvin. Never let alcohol take command, though she took pleasure in allowing booze to let her disappear, disappear, disappear.

With an aching heart, Laura dug a hole and buried the hen near Spruceside. Thank God the dogs were unharmed. They lay down on either side of Laura, who swallowed. She wanted to hold on to the venison she'd stuffed herself with. The cuckoo called. Another cuckoo returned its call, seeking contact.

CHAPTER NINE

Sometimes in life you make a decision you bitterly regret. The sisters now made such a decision: the stronger ones would stay behind to work on the construction project while the more delicate ones went to market. It was a catastrophic strategy. Elga and Simone may have set off with a taste for adventure and a fervent desire to sell sell sell, but there was an underlying problem.

For someone who's never had anything but small change, and who has no idea of the market value of goods, it can be hard to set a price. But the hardest thing of all is to manage your money when you happen to have a pouch full and you're surrounded by temptation.

If I were to try to draw out the essence of this chapter, it would be that money is the root of much evil in this world. Throw sex and a reckless attitude toward alcohol into the mix, and suddenly you're standing eye to eye with the devil himself.

Elga loaded the cart with foxtails and beaver and bearskins. Simone packed fried wood-pigeon meat as trail fodder. Johanna and Tanja had determined that they would be the two to trek into town and sell the skins, and with the money buy as much as they were able to transport and carry. Simone's innocent appearance and Elga's cunning, head for numbers, and ability to write were the decisive factors. Johanna and Tanja had reasoned that the coarse-set ones were needed for the house building, while the other incompetents could stay at home and gather pine cones.

Johanna had lent her boots to Simone. Elga, who had the smallest feet of the sisters, had to make do with her taped-up sneakers. The jeans she'd got from Matti were now barely holding together. They were ordered to bring home vodka in a plastic container with a skull and crossbones on it, drawn by Laura when she was in a playful mood, which happened a couple of times a year. It surprised Johanna and Tanja that she now and then contributed something with her silly drawings.

Johanna issued an exhortation: "The trek mustn't take more than three days. You'll need to stay one night when you get there and count on it taking longer to get home when you're tired and have just as much to carry. It'll probably be seven days."

"The noun week would have done just fine," said Elga.

"A wonderful week here at home for me. Free of you."

"The sleeping cabin will be done by the time you're back," said Tanja.

"Don't forget to buy glue. Otherwise the animals won't have any eyes," said Laura.

"Concentrate on building the house and the totem poles, I told you!" said Johanna. "Brandy. Batteries. Ammunition. Have you written lists, Elga?"

She pointed to her forehead.

"The list is in here."

"If you forget anything, remember it's three months until the next market," said Tanja.

"Hot dogs and crisps. Sneakers. If you can get hold of boots, buy them," said Tiina.

"The old man's boots are indestructible. Johanna has them. We'll need six more pairs for the winter," Aune said.

"At least buy a pair in my size—ten and a half—since I'm the one felling trees," said Tiina.

"Mountains of dried yeast. Flour. Sugar," said Tanja.

"Books if they sell secondhand ones. Make sure the print's not too small," said Aune.

Then they wobbled off with backpacks and carts, like two well-laden Ardennes horses.

IN A STREAMBED LAURA SIFTED BLACK CLAY THROUGH HER FINGERS. A black woodpecker pecked out a nest in the pine alongside. Sawdust whirled. The clay softened and molded under Laura's gentle pressure, her hands' searching movements opening up a moment of calm. Perhaps calm was overstating it, the absence of anxiety would be more accurate. Anxiety ruled. It was like Johanna, domineering and erratic. All it took was for her to hear shouting and arguing from over by the cabin, where Johanna, Tanja, and Tiina were sawing and hammering as they built the sleeping quarters, and her nerves would flare up again. Never seeing anyone but her sisters. She'd seen eyes and mouths in stones and tree trunks. Stroked the spruce when it looked sad.

Now Tiina's work had turned her nasty. She was screaming and throwing things, crashing and banging about. Laura covered her ears with muddy fingers and kneaded. She knew what they were swearing about over there: they were mocking their weak, puny sisters who had the nerve to ride on the heavy lifting the more powerful sisters had dealt with like three strongmen. *We never hear a word of thanks.* Yeah, that's what they say when they think no one's listening. It made no difference that Laura and Elga had promised to build a toolshed with space for carpentry and a sauna. The yelling stopped, Tiina hammered and the woodpecker in the dead tree answered the hammer blows. Perhaps the poor bird thought it was an invitation to fuck. Laura had no idea how the mating game played out in the woodpecker's world.

So many mosquitoes. Sucking up what little blood I have left, she thought, smacking her thigh hard. Such a relief that Johanna and Tanja had decided to let Elga trek to the market with Simone. Elga frightened her sometimes with her penetrating gaze. Alongside Aune she was the sister Laura looked up to, even though she was the youngest. She couldn't give a fig what the others might come out with, but she trembled whenever Elga surveyed her clay figures and ranked them. *This elk is so alive; this bear is lifeless. What's the idea with this girl on all fours with her ass in the air?* How should Laura know what the idea was? *Maybe it was a naked crawling race in the spring mud by the brook?* No, it just happened: I let my hands lead me.

The lump of clay frightened her at times—it seemed to doubt her ability to shape any one thing. Right now it was pliable. The lump wanted to be a beaver. But the paddle-shaped tail would be tricky. Every day she longed for glue. Three figures to go till one hundred. Then I'll celebrate, she decided, but not with booze, never again with booze. She'd celebrate in secret with Elga and Aune, maybe Simone. When she showed the others, Tiina would always sneer: *Show us your tits, clay girl! Fuck her in the ass!* while Tanja took it as an opportunity to sleep, snoring ever louder and dribbling on Johanna.

Alone, forever alone. A kitten trapped in a basement. But it didn't bother her. She could whisper confidences in the dogs' ears. They were attentive, keeping every secret.

She gathered up the projects she had underway and hid them in a cave she'd discovered close to her own hiding place. The warblers sang along her way, the wood pigeon puffed itself up. The bilberries were large and almost ripe. The mosquito bites itched like hell. Clammy and covered in mud she was itching all over. She remembered Simone mentioning a tarn with velvety water, just past a great swamp. The blessed tarn, she called it. What Laura wouldn't give for a quiet swim untroubled by six loudmouths.

"Hello, tantalizing tarn," she cried when she reached it. She tore off her clothes and pushed off from a rock, gliding out into the ice-cold water, her body strong and lean. The sunlight found its way in, dazzling. The soft, dark brown water caressed her belly, thighs, breasts. The pines and spruces obscured and observed.

In the center of the tarn she stopped, treading water and looking about her. How many species were keeping watch on her right now? Perhaps some crows, a magpie, a squirrel, a marten. And the dam over there: Mr. Beaver. She had a habit of wandering around lakes and waterways to find their lodges, beaver skin was what people paid most for right now. Imagine if she could catch the beaver and astonish her sisters. Her foot caught in a slimy plant, wouldn't slip free, she tugged and tugged. Dived and had to use both hands to free herself from the sticky stems. She coughed, got a throatful of cold water. She swam on, turning at the opposite shore before swimming back to her clothes on the beach. Something moved on a rocky hillock. An animal? Gray fur. Not a wolf, surely? The animal peered out, sitting still, observing her. A dog. She squinted, saw the animal's outline more clearly. *Canus lupus familiaris*, that's what the old man had said about this species. He'd learned the Latin name. She remembered one time as he slurred, after a dozen porters, that that was his family, that was us: *Canus lupus familiaris*. The dog gazed out, seeming not at all interested in jumping in and swimming out to her. It sat like a clay figure—a well-formed one, Elga would have said. A powerful beast, not some enslaved soul. Had this creature broken its chains, running out into the ancient woodland and becoming wild? Good job she hadn't brought the dogs with her, there would have been a fight.

The final stretch, soon ashore. Would the dog come running after her, wanting to say hello? She felt its gaze on her face, her body, tried to swim fast. Ah yes, now she'd reached the stones and could crawl out. Were the dog's eyes resting on her naked rear end and narrow back, her tangled red hair? Great gray horseflies sucked like vampires. Her body shivered, gooseflesh all over. Damn pants tangling into themselves. Sweater on. Moving fast, hoping the dog would still be there, statuesque. She turned quickly. It was, but alongside *Canus lupus familiaris* stood a man. She jumped. He watched her. Was he going to rush over and push her down in the moss, pull off her pants and . . . would he smell of sweat, leather, and gun oil? Would he stand and walk away, leaving her with a salt-milk rivulet running from her crotch? Tiina had spoken loud and long about what happened when guys wanted a piece of you. Sometimes she used to leave the farm at night. No one knew who she was meeting.

The man was still looking at her, he raised his hand in greeting.

Heart pounding, she walked away with determined steps, deciding not to tell the others about the dog and the man.

Tiina was taking a break and had poured herself like a puma over the high branch of a spruce. How had she got up there? Laura wondered as she spotted her twin sister's broad back up in the trees on her way toward Spruceside. She looked relaxed for a change, her legs completely still. But it was obvious: inside, things were happening.

Tiina was dreaming of taking to the road on the quad bike. When would she get to ride a massive chopper into the sunset? Or a drop-top sports car, on a hot summer's evening. If we'd had the money, I could have been a motocross star, she thought with a trace of bitterness. Elga always said, in her snobby way, that Tiina was the personification of a failed sporting career. *Yeah, she can talk the talk, that girl, but I liked that*, thought Tiina, chewing hectically on a lump of resin, looking out across the forest along the now well-trodden path toward town. She said out loud, to no one in particular:

"Are they coming?" Then: "When are they going to come back so we can brew beer and bake bread?" And: "When are they going to bring the gas so I can trim the logs?"

She felt the way she had as a kid, waiting for their father to get home from the forest with bear meat and tales of the hunt. She would get to stroke his wonderfully scratchy cheek, then.

"NINE DAYS," TIINA GRUNTED FURIOUSLY WHEN SHE'D GIVEN UP AND jumped down from the tree. She went to help Tanja, heaving up yet another log onto the house.

"Idiots," said Tanja. "They must have gotten lost."

Tiina whistled in the direction of town.

"If they don't come tomorrow, I'm going to run into the forest to look for them."

"I hope nothing's happened to them," Tanja said, anxious. She pictured them, dead and mutilated in the cave they'd slept in.

When Elga and Simone come back I can stick the elk heads onto the girls' bodies, thought Laura as she crept out of Spruceside and waddled down to the brook to get more clay.

"What on earth is she for?" said Johanna in irritation as she tore the feathers from a ptarmigan. "A Laura lopes louchely, looking for clay."

"You were meant to be looking for water," she bawled after Laura. "Where'd you hide your magic divining rod?"

Laura turned and held up her hands.

"Oh, I forgot."

"See something through, just once." Johanna bristled.

"Where did Aune go? She was meant to be helping me," said Tanja, just about keeping her balance on the construction site, trying to lay a provisional roof. They needed gas for the chain saw, and new handsaws. Tiina had gone at it so hard a saw blade had broken in two.

"Aune!" She cupped her hands and shouted but got no reply. As usual, Johanna was swearing over her sisters' princessy ways, as she put it. Of course she'd be expected to bring home more meat for that evening, and Tiina had good reason to rest. How many trees had she felled while Elga and Simone had been gone? Her arm muscles were bigger than ever.

AUNE HAD FOUND A FOREST PATH SHE'D NEVER PREVIOUSLY TAKEN. It led to a lake ringed with leafy mixed forest. She laid her sack full of nettles at the water's edge. Nutritious soup, the old man always said. She rolled up her trouser legs, walked out into the water, negotiating slippery stones, and played awhile with the tadpoles.

A mild rain was falling. Isn't that when the fish are biting? She hoped they'd come home soon so she could get paper, pens, and perhaps a book to practice reading. Elga had promised her a crash course. She went through her mental lists of stories and poems. Yep, they were steady as the ground rock. She would remember them as long as she lived, she knew that. When she'd forgotten everything else, the stories would remain.

The raindrops on the surface were clearly audible, that's how quiet it was in the forest. *It would soon be winter*, she thought with concern. Soon there would be a deep layer of snow, then everything would be even quieter.

If I sit calmly in absolute silence I can hear the foxes mating in their burrow. I can hear the beavers making babies.

Sitting calmly in peace and quiet I can see the lynx's summer coat change to winter-white. I can see when the bear is sated and tired, ready to sleep for months on end.

Now she saw it: over there amid the pines, a marten hunted a squirrel. The marten was a master at leaping and swinging about in trees. Swinging like Tiina.

The float bobbed. A heavy fish tugged. Oh yikes, what was she going to do now? She pulled the fish up toward the beach. The char flapped for dear life. She smacked it sharply on the head and ran a sturdy branch through its throat.

A bite for five, at least.

"THEY'RE COMING!"

Tiina climbed down from her lookout on the pine and yelled:

"They're coming! They're here!"

And then there they were, back at the cabin, their heads bowed. Hollow-eyed, slumped, and filthy. They looked wretched, though Elga was wearing a new top and new sweatpants she'd turned up at the bottoms. Her feet were bare and covered with scabs and open wounds. Simone's boots would have fallen apart had the laces not been bound around them.

Five bustling sisters encircling the home-comers. Astonished eyes on floppy backpacks and a single, empty cart. Tiina slapped the backpacks.

"The fuck you done with all the stuff?" said Tiina.

"Tell me you've hidden it!" said Tanja.

"Were you robbed?" asked Aune anxiously.

"Robbed of our senses," Simone replied, shame-faced.

"Cut the crap," said Tiina.

"Have you arranged a delivery by horse?" Tanja ventured hopefully.

"If only," said Elga.

Johanna strode round and round the traitors. Looked at them with contempt.

"Was the journey home all one big feast?"

"The journey home was all one big fast," said Simone.

"But you've got new pants and a new shirt, Elga," said Aune encouragingly.

"Got given them" came the brief reply.

Tiina shook Elga so hard she collapsed in a heap on the ground. Simone kneeled and begged for mercy. She sobbed:

"Elga ran into the schoolteacher's son, the math guy. She stayed with him and he gave her his sweatpants."

Johanna put the toe of her boot against Elga's face. Crawling on the ground Elga caught the scent of leather.

"So you been whoring, Elga. You forgot the pact, you little cat in heat."

"Broke the code of honor," Tanja snarled.

"Letting a cock come between us," Johanna said.

Simone crumpled on willow switch–flimsy legs and Aune tried to revive her.

"She kept fainting in the forest," said Elga. "I thought she was dead. Water!"

Aune fetched a scoop of water and Laura held out two boiled potatoes. Elga drank so quickly her stomach cramped, and bolted the potatoes. Simone came to and quenched her thirst.

"Bread," Elga whimpered.

"*You* were meant to be coming home with bread and yeast," said a confounded Tanja.

"Did you bring the glue?" Laura asked, though she knew the answer.

Aune sat on the stone threshold and summarized: "So this is how it is. You've walked a hundred miles to sell our goods. You sold everything, but you've brought back no money and no shopping."

Tiina's eyes clouded, her nostrils flared, she grunted her bloodlust.

"You could put it that way, yes," said Elga submissively.

Simone sat on a tree stump, looking up at her sisters stoically, meeting their furious, threatening eyes, their fists readying for revenge. Sobbing, she said, "We had a big bag of money. A person should never have that . . . dreadful things happen to you . . . when your purse is full."

Johanna kicked the stump.

"And now we've got no food until Michaelmas . . . you've shown what idiots you are behind your pathetic, pious phrases."

Tiina spat at Simone. "We've built the sleeping cabin. We've been hungering for pirogs and sausages. And you come back empty-handed and freshly fucked."

Tanja rummaged through their backpacks in a frenzy. She found an icon miniature in one and a book with large print in the other. A thick one. "Don Qui . . . Qui . . ."

"Ho-tee," Elga said helpfully. "Kee-ho-tee."

Simone pointed at the icon: "That was a bargain, it'll look great over the stove."

Laura was keen: "That claret color. Look at the gold! I need paint."

Johanna shoved Laura, sending her sprawling.

"Don't you realize what you've done?! You've swindled your own sisters, whored yourselves, and dragged your family through the muck. What have I told you about not associating with outsiders?"

"You forgot my glue!" said Laura, sounding like an unhappy child.

"Your figures have more soul without eyes," Elga replied.

"Did you say soul? Did you of all people say soul?" Laura said with a quavering voice.

Tiina stamped around angrily.

"Here we are with no rum or hot dogs. And we've been working our asses off. Fucking hell."

"Tell me you at least have tobacco?" Tanja asked.

Elga held out a crumpled little packet of butts.

That's when the first kick came. Elga clutched her back, groaned, fell headlong onto the ground.

Simone begged for mercy.

"Get down and crawl with the adders," Tiina snarled.

"We're . . . a-already a-a-adder fodder," coughed Simone.

Johanna dealt the second kick. A boot in the belly. One kick quickly becomes a volley. Humans are built for repetition. A kick in the backside, another to the head. Soon blood was running from mouths, a tooth tumbled out. Wailing. Wailing replaced by screaming. The dogs howled in panic, Elga cried and sobbed. Tiina walked into the cabin to fetch the piss-pot, holding it above them. *Please. Please. No!* She poured out a thin yellow stream, evenly distributed slops. Sharp stench of piss. Elga roared, Simone whined, all her strength turned inward.

That night. The pain that night.

ELGA WAS WOKEN BY HER WOUNDS, WHICH HAD KNITTED IN WITH THE bearskin, leaving her stuck tight. The thought of tearing herself loose was too much. She managed at least to turn her face toward Simone's bed. Empty. Had she left?

Her eyes almost swollen shut. No point trying to move her arms and legs, which were numb from the long, arduous trek. The aching and stinging grew worse with each passing hour. No treatment, aside from the piss. Simone and Elga had been put in the main cabin, which was now the sickroom. The others were sleeping in the new, birch-scented sleeping cabin, which had a provisional half-roof of thick branches. Laura slept out in her Spruceside with the dogs.

Now Johanna loomed in the doorway, like a rock-hard giant. Not a glimmer of concern for her bloodied sister lying in agony on the bearskin.

"Where's Simone?"

Elga shook her head—or rather, she tried, her face so swollen she was unable to open her mouth. Not a sound passed her misshapen lips.

"Tell me where she is or I'll kill you."

Elga moved her head with a grunt.

"We'll see to it that you never talk again."

The full moon shone in through the window, shone on her wounds. The stinging. The pain: a blade to the temple, her cheek abrasive with stiffened blood. Simone couldn't even grimace; it was like wearing a plaster mask. Luckily, she hadn't lain on her bloody effusions. Thin scabs had formed. My skin, she thought. My poor, sinful skin. What's that noise outside? Who's stalking round the house? Who's creeping, calling to me? A low, low call. Wolf? Fox? Had hairy feet scented their way to blood-spattered ground? A face at the window. A human face: wild hair, one eye swollen shut, one eye staring straight through her. A crooked finger with clawlike nails signed: *Come here, come out.* She thought she heard a whispering: *Come with me!* In spite of her pain, she slipped soundlessly from her bed, stepped into her flimsy boots, bit her lip, and swallowed the roar of pain, creeping out through the creaking door. The dogs roused in Spruceside and looked out, accustomed to them going out into the forest to do their business. Strangely, they didn't growl at the hairy one. Simone managed to grab a top, which she pulled over her head with a whimper before wriggling into a pair of trousers. The crooked finger gestured from within a thicket; she followed the dark figure clothed in floor-length gray cloth, limping slowly, slowly, silently, silently into the forest, heading straight for the moon. Simone stopped and gazed right into the eye of the moon, feeling the calm of its rays. Sudden, clear thoughts and a clear voice that segued into unctuous ranting:

You want me to come to you, I'll come. You are the sun in disguise and I wish to warm myself by you. You are a cold sun that shines even on those who have broken all of God's commandments. I will walk to you with this bloody body, toward the mountain, climbing it with weary legs and ragged feet. At the top I will be close to you. Save me from my sisters, they don't believe in the God in the moon. Impenitent wretches. Save me from myself! Deliver me unto the penance that is due.

Only she and her mother believed in the Bible's words; they inhaled them in secret, free for a while from the old man's curses. Was it when Mother disappeared that she fell into the abyss? Dancing an ardent fox's dance for the eyes of the men at the market. Enjoying those hot gazes. *Tell me why the furrier's member felt like God our holy Father moving inside my inner spaces. Tell me!*

Moist pine-needle scent. Rustling in the thickets. Lynx in the trees, the predators' mouths watering over the bloodied flesh. The tawny owl hooted a welcome, with the full moon in fine fettle alongside its timid subjects, the stars. The father's eye that will not be forgotten. *I'm sorry I broke the pact. Can there be mercy?*

The spruces spoke to her of faithlessness. The spruces checked up on her, ensured she was making for the mountain on a penitential pilgrimage: she was to reach the very top. Closer to God, a clearer eye on the world.

Her poor head was bursting. Dear Lord, help my legs carry me to the mountain before the bad weather sets in. As unsteady as old Veikko or a newborn calf. She prayed that God would show pity on her weak frame, she must rest. Her throat burning dry. She must quench her thirst in a brook, soothe her wounds and swellings. Sleep awhile and walk again replenished.

No use in looking back. No future. Only an eternal present. And six sisters who listened lustily to the lashes Johanna unleashed on her back. The spirits came to them, hovering. You could be a pastor, Simone, her mother said as they sat by the swamp, listening to the daily service on the transistor radio, a faithful servant ever since her youth. Simone combed her mother's long hair, slowly plaiting; a thick braid reached to the small of her back. *The training's long*, replied Simone, who couldn't even read the Bible. She'd practiced every time she and Elga took a break during their long trek to market. As the rain beat down, she and Elga sat in a cave, reading. Why did she tense up whenever she saw the written word, her jaw clenching? Elga held her in low esteem, her sluggishness made her sister impatient. She had to suck up the harsh comments. Awaiting redemption.

You can read when you're older, her mother had said. *There are adult education centers where . . . We'll see, Mother*, said Simone, and told her about the voices in her head that bade her do evil. When Elga was little, Simone used to carry her on her shoulders, and the baby would talk and talk before she even had language. The voice in her head had said, *Take her to the river, take her to the river where the current is strong*. As though she were the daughter of Old Nick and not God's child. Recurring nightmares of horses drowning in the fen and attracting starving predators who sank their teeth into the body before the great beast had even drawn its last breath.

Her mother said she dreamed her daughters would kill her. They worshiped their father like a god and that god detested his wife. *Their poor souls are hollow, Mother*, Simone said, unable to fathom how they had turned an overweight old duffer with a filthy beard into the almighty. A godhead who forbade them to move beyond his circle, to go to church even. Her mother looked out at the tall, thick grass mixed with reddish brown fescue. *My daughters' hair, daughters' scalps, red like their father.*

Between sleep and waking she downed moonshine. *I drink to silence the voices, the brännvin makes them hum sweetly.* Then she floated like an angel above the earth.

She was woken by the trickling of the brook. She'd pissed herself. She removed her underwear and threw them away. Her legs ached, the wounds had calmed a little. She looked around her for the gray-bearded apparition. Gone. No one to show her the way. She hobbled on toward the mountain, eternally stumbling over stones and fissures, was this a day hike? The heavens ever darker, the winds more urgently raw. The pain in her back from Johanna's kicks, the aching jaw from her punches. But all her teeth remained in place. Her mouth dry, as though she'd licked clean a rug embedded with dog hair.

She sat down to recover, her breath was wild, running riot within her breastbone. She heard a far-off roar, limped toward the sound, boggy ground, her legs sank deep, but over there, a few yards away, was a small waterfall that broke forth from the mountain. She pulled at one leg—it had gotten stuck and came free with a plop—her shoe gone, sunk in quick clay. Looking up at the sky: please, help me, help me this last stretch, she uttered a howl and a soft moan, felt herself grow lithe and light, and tottered up to the waterfall. She lay on her stomach, dipping her face in the glittering, crystalline water. Great gulps, her head rushing. Saw bearberry bushes. Ate so many her stomach cramped, fell asleep in the glowing red undergrowth. Dreamed she was swimming, long, powerful strokes, gliding off to Scotland, climbing up on a rocky shore to be met by the mild-eyed, cheering masses. *Long live the queen!*

She awoke at dusk, a cold yellow eye staring from within a willow thicket.

She spoke sternly to the gray beast:

"I can smell your cold, rotten breath. Don't you think I know you're at my side with your scabby tail and bushy eyebrows, your slack, stinking tongue hanging from your maw. An impoverished sinner, yes, that I am, but I'm not yours and never will be. You can follow someone else, you've misjudged the strength of my faith because I committed mortal sin with the furrier. I lay against his breast, the musk-scented sweat of his armpit, I felt his hands around my backside, his animal tongue licking upper and lower lips, there's no one can resist, then. Anyone who can step out of that steaming embrace is not human. It's how we're made."

Old Nick's eyes never flinched. She attempted to search within. Why had two perfectly lucid girls waded so determinedly into the jaws of sin? She found herself back at the bar:

Cocktails with little umbrellas call for more cocktails with umbrellas. San Francisco tasted like the sun itself, the coins slipped with a rhythmic clinking from the sisters' fists onto the bar. One more sip of sunlight and all the men in the bar were kind and lovely. They were two jester queens, entertaining their people, they longed to laugh. How they bellowed with laughter as they danced their foxdance, the men whistled and bought all the skins.

Of course someone who has trekked far, gone all in, and succeeded must be allowed to celebrate. They didn't want the thrill in their bodies to end.

Had she ever felt happier than when she crept, intoxicated, into the furrier's arms? She saw Elga's eyes sparkle as she sat on Matti the math genius's knee, even she could fuss about and talk girly.

They got up and walked, intertwined, into the forest behind the restaurant terrace, while the furrier took Simone under his arm, wandering home through the summer night. Bearskins everywhere, zebra skins on the wall, colored lights and taxidermy. The smell calmed her, reassured her. The furrier lit a fire and poured her a cold, black porter to wash down the cocktails' sweetness. *Nice to meet a woman who goes braless,* he said. *Women's breasts should be free.* And so they tumbled down among the furs.

And the yellow-glowing predator's eyes crept closer, the rotten breath making Simone nauseous. Once again she spoke aloud to the inquisitive gray coat.

"I'm not planning to ride on your back, you naughty furball. Best foot forward over beast foot forward. You're begging for company. Nobody wants someone who has to beg for company. I know you're thinking about that damn word afterward. If only humanity could have been free of this darned killjoy, afterward."

When she'd opened her eyes, head pounding, in the home of the fur dealer, she'd nearly jumped out of her skin: a rearing bear with its paws up ready to attack. *There, there,* soothed the furrier. Her body tender, soft, and ticklish. The furrier, whose name she'd never asked after, lay on his belly, snoring once more. A thought flashed through her mind: the money, where did all the money go? Where was Elga? How can we go back empty-handed? But she wasn't yet ready to confront the awful truth; she crept under the furs, where the furrier's supporting beam stood erect, even though he was sleeping. She mounted it. And afterward was banished for a few hours.

The gray coat bared sharp fangs. Now it was time to walk through the darkness beyond paradise. When they'd stilled their trembling bodies, she went to the bathroom and vomited, it tore at her insides as though she were bringing up the little umbrellas themselves. The furrier drove her to the marketplace, where Elsa was wandering around on grass that had already been cleared of debris. She looked wretched. White-pale with red-flushed cheeks and black under her eyes, mouth swollen, neck covered in hickeys. They said nothing, knowing what awaited them. Knowing that their moments of divine pleasure would cost them dearly. But wait. Let those wonders be allowed to take command of the feeling of chaos, they each granted the other a beatific smile, the last in a very long time. Onni the fur trader introduced himself, he said he'd known their father and expressed his condolences for the man's passing. He took them back to his house to get supplies for their journey, then drove them a good way, until the narrow forest tracks took over. *See you at the next market, girls,* he said when they jumped out. *Give me first dibs on your skins. I'll pay well.* As he revved off she patted her backpack. He'd sent them on their way with smoked meat, rice pirogs, and black currant cordial. When his van was out of sight, she longed for him so much her insides were screaming.

Now, her heart pounded at the memory of Johanna's rage. And it was completely understandable. But how would Johanna have acted? If you've never had money, those little round pieces of metal can easily burn your fingers; they don't want to stay still in the darkness of the coin pouch, they want to be pressed between fingers, to sun themselves on the wood of the bar. They compete with each other over how many hands have held them. Now her stomach was as empty as that leather pouch. The sisters would have to hunt alone from here on in; she was resolved to give herself up to the celestial flock. She was going to go higher, to wander the expanses, toward lightning flashes, toward thunder, over the lingonberry tussocks, the willow thickets and roots that tripped, the swarms of midges whining and nipping. She sensed the tree spirits' collective concern at the storm winds that threatened, though they were restrained as yet.

The birds closed their beaks against the hard winds, but she would thunder into the wind, and speak.

"I'm stamping on your foot, Mr. Mountain. Do you feel my naked foot? I will climb up onto your scalp; like a nimble little mountain goat I pay no heed to the fine gravel and the huge stones that are rolling down from your peak to warn me."

She'd reached the middle and was forced to slow down so she wouldn't slip or fall back. She hoped she'd reach her destination before the heavens opened. A little further, she gripped a sturdy root fiber, a lifeline up to the top. Made it. She looked out across the expanse, bewildered. Up here, another season was in full swing—a snowy landscape: winter, watery hollows with thick ice.

The gray coat stood at one end of the root fiber, a cloud of sharp scent. Old Nick opened his mouth, a voice from the abyss, making her veins freeze: "God is evil in disguise. One day you'll learn this lesson."

Simone had an answer to that: "You sound like my kid sister. Go bother her instead."

She stood on the mountain precipice, looked out over the forests, looked up at the sky. Spread her arms and greeted the world. The people of earth, arguing, gobbling, boozing, stuck on the Devil's roasting spit. They might buy a flashy, six-figure car and be buoyed for a while, with a renewed lust for life. Impoverished souls. Holes in their souls.

She shouted: "Look into your hearts. Look into the well of your souls, brimful with sewer water."

Shouting and shouting, the forest answering. The forest always answered.

The forest was the answer. In a weaker voice that dwindled to a whisper, she said: "You townspeople, showing off, aping America—my sister Tiina's idol. But the country is doomed. You've betrayed yourself. Slaving away under the sick city skies, buying gift-wrapped forest scents when you could be sleeping on a bed of rushes, bathing in a waterfall. Woe betide your stale tap water, it's barely fit to wash your behind."

SHE SANK DOWN, THOUGH IN HER MIND THE IMAGES WERE STILL sharp. She could see the hurrying steps of every person, hear terrified, hunted hearts pound to both the east and the west. Unhappy souls with lifeless, sorrowful eyes. *It's burning, burning.* Not with quiet, purifying fire, but with towering flames.

The fall from grace was close at hand, with hail the size of tennis balls. The tornado would cleanse them all. A beautiful bolt of lightning would form a cross over the heavens.

She stood on trembling legs, hurled a stone at the evil gray coat, feeling the end was near. She whispered out across the expanse: "Speak to me, God. I've sinned to my very bones. Grant me forgiveness. Give Zion's sisters a harvest of rye to live on, potato sprouts that thrive in the forest, and luck on the hunt. They ask for nothing but food enough and for the lightning to strike far from their simple cabin."

God heard her. Saw her. And listened. She felt a powerful warmth that brought an all-encompassing calm.

In a rush of joy she formulated her final words:

"My mother's wish is fulfilled. I stand here, your preacher daughter.

"Angels, angels, come to me. I will stand with thee every day until the end of time."

Laudate Dominum

Chapter Ten

What are the bear hunter's daughters to do? Of course it would never enter their heads to contact a huntmaster or even Missing People, for that matter. The sisters didn't even have a telephone. In their new home they couldn't knock on their neighbor Niskanpää's door and ask for help. It concerned them more than they could have foreseen.

The clan's warriors appointed themselves to the search party for the runaway, but how dedicated is a search when the missing person is a pain in the ass who'd already been written off by the sisters' callous leader? And how do you appeal to someone who's mentally ill? Or to use terms the sisters were more familiar with: someone who's lost their marbles and gone completely nuts.

They left behind the incapacitated Elga and the two klutzes, one of whom would prove to be less timid than the sisters thought when she met a camera-wielding beaver aficionado by the tarn.

JOHANNA WHISTLED. TANJA YODELED. TIINA JUST ROARED.

The echoes in the forest sent deer and hares fleeing; they ran every which way as though there was a forest fire.

"Toward the mountain or the lake? What you reckon, Tanja?" Johanna asked.

"The mountain. She's always been a climber," said Tanja.

"Let's head for the mountain and spread out with a few hundred yards between us," said Tiina. "Look for tracks. Cigarette butts and blood."

"What did old Mother do when she tracked us after we ran away?" Tanja pondered.

"Rage led her to us," Johanna said bitterly. "What she did . . . and that stuck-up forest ranger the old man always hated . . . makes me furious just to think of it. But I have to ask you: am I like her?"

"Regret weakens you," said Tanja. "We stood by you. Even Laura who didn't get her glue sticks."

"Here we are, no sausages, no brandy," Tiina said, as if to get the adrenaline going.

"What if she jumps?" said Johanna, surprised to find herself worried.

"From the top? Impaled on some rocky outcrop and . . ." said Tiina, as Tanja interrupted.

"Ah, she's chickenshit. A talker."

"Okay, warriors," said Johanna. "I'll go straight ahead. You come at the mountain from the sides. Signal if you see anything."

"Check out the sky," said Tanja.

A blazing flash in the graphite sky, shortly thereafter a clap that shook their innards. The trio crept into the gap between a rock and the crest it rested against. A zigzag across the sky, followed by a terrifying boom, a dry spruce in front of them went up in flames. Would Laura and Aune hear their whistles and cries?

Then everything fell silent. The primal soul of nature was perfectly still: pines, spruces, willow brush unmoving. Poised. Ready. The victim was preparing for the kick to the groin their tormentor was about to deliver. Then came the rain, hard as iron, and at that very moment the wind picked up and flung the water into the crevice. The whipping drops were replaced by hailstones that soon became rain again.

The sisters crawled around, worming their way to shelter, scuttling into a larger crevice, protecting their soaking wet bodies and dripping manes. Thankfully, the lashing rain abated, and a gentle summer drizzle took over. Johanna lay under a tall, dense spruce with long branches. In the needle-lined den there was a scent of fresh piss, whether human or animal was unclear. Tiina trudged on, cursing, thrashing her arms, waving. Fist brandished at the sky.

In the cabin, Elga lay, whimpering from the pain of open wounds and a throbbing head. She tried to move her feet, flex her toes. Nauseating taste of blood, big hole where her molar used to be. Her face must be dark blue and swollen to the point of unrecognizability after Johanna's kicks. What a relief there were no mirrors in the cabin. She closed her eyes and tried to recall the giddiness of Matti lying on top of her in the grass. She wanted to continue her life with him, keep him inside her. She wished he'd gotten caught there for good. She dreamed of a life where new words, sentences, ideas filled the void inside her head and a man's penis filled the other holes. That's the kind of life that would make a person feel whole. She didn't want any others in her space. She didn't recall which author Veikko was quoting when he said that every encounter with another human being is an act of aggression.

Ouch. Owowow. If she focused hard, she could float above the burning and stabbing pains that beset her, and she thought that there was one person, perhaps two, who she didn't revile as she drifted off to sleep. Dreamed . . . awoke to the thundering of rain, grimaced in pain. Tried to bring her thoughts back to down-to-earth things so as not to give in and howl in agony. Knitted socks. Field peas. Field vole.

Sock
Pea
Pod
Vole

༶

Aune at Elga's side. She lit the paraffin lamp that was gasping for breath—a sign she wanted refilling. The flame was giving over to a spasmodic squeaking sound. Elga opened one eye. The other was sealed shut, hopefully not forever. *I have to be able to read, I have to.* The panic ran away with her. Aune's face in the play of shadows resembled a painting of a red-haired woman that had hung in the home of Teacher Leena.

Aune got up and, with a furrowed brow, checked the wounds and swellings on Elga's face.

"Can you sit up to drink some water?"

Elga opened her mouth a fraction and grunted, she made an attempt to shake her head. The door flew open in the raging wind, and Aune battled with it as the rain beat its way in, wanting to intrude into the cabin, wanting to raise the water level, to drown them. In the end she managed to force the latch down. She brought a cup of water.

"We should keep some straws at home. And a nurse to clean up after that roughneck."

Elga's brain sent smile impulses to her mouth, but the signal did not reach its destination. Instead, there was a faint grumbling sound. Aune tried to feed her arm in around Elga's neck, but retracted it when her sister let out an imploded shriek. With a teaspoon she offered Elga water as the rain thundered against the roof and whipped the windowpanes clean.

"Are you hungry?" Aune asked.

Elga raised her hand no. Her hand! Her hands! They were whole and mobile at the ends of her disjointed, stiffened arms.

"Were you robbed?" Aune asked.

Elga was looking right at Aune, but the darkness hid her eyes. Her hands said no.

"What happened? All the things we were waiting for."

Aune couldn't think straight after all the terrible things that had happened. So she kept asking the mute to tell the story.

Elga's index finger pointed at the stool by the bed.

"I don't get it," said Aune with a shrug.

Elga wrote in the air. Pointed again.

"Aha," said Aune.

She reached over and took the notepad and pen, putting them into Elga's hands. Eagerly Elga took them and signaled to the sister nursing her to turn to a fresh page. Aune lit a candle and flicked through the pad, flicked through to a clean page. Her eye caught on sentences she could read. *I can read!* A little in any case. *I can read! "One day . . . I'm going to . . . kill Johanna . . . with Laura's knife."* She turned the page. Stopped short as light streamed into the cabin followed by a clap of thunder that made her tremble. And she usually welcomed lightning. She turned the page and tried not to let on that she was reading, sounding out silently to herself: *I . . . want to run away . . . with Matti.* She couldn't read what followed . . . *Run away to a place where we can fuck all day long.* Well, there was a word she could read. Her cheeks grew hot and she searched for an empty page, embarrassed, holding the pad out to the patient who wrote with great effort, unable to lift her head and follow her own letters. She knew Aune could read the odd word. Yes and no. Hate and love. Read and story. Maybe more.

In the notepad: *You can have a story. Don't spread it!*

"Okay. I promise," said Aune, while her body trembled with excitement. "What's it about?"

The wild thing.

"Did you both meet guys?"

Yeah.

"You sold the lot and celebrated with booze?"

San Francisco.

"So you got smashed and the money started flowing?"

Elga's hand signed a yes.

"And you started buying rounds?"

Brown liquor. Whiskey.

"You boozed it all away and found yourself fucking," said Aune. "Hope you had fun," she said peevishly.

Fun fuck.

Aune was irritated by Elga's thoughtlessness.

"Didn't you think to give a flying fuck about us sitting here longing for pirogs, yeast, salt, sugar, flour, gasoline, paraffin, glue, and . . ."

Cocktails with umbrellas.

"So you're blaming umbrellas?"

Simone was in a party mood. I got caught up.

"You didn't think about the fact we're going to be forced to eat field peas and bark bread until the fall market?"

Never drinking again.

Silence, aside from the rain clattering against the window. Would the roof blow off soon? Aune shivered, stood up, looked out. The spruces were bending in the wind. An ancient spruce fell with a crash. Thankfully not toward the house.

"Goddamn awful weather for a search party," Aune said anxiously. "Who was Simone fucking?"

Onni the furrier. Could be good for business.

"Where's she disappeared off to? Did she say anything on the way home?"

Crazy. Raving. God this, God that. Up on all the rocks. Talking to her people.

"Has she run off back to the fur dealer, you think?"

Brutally beaten? No.

"And you? Lost count completely and spread your legs for some math genius."

You ever been madly in love and wildly horny?

Aune looked over at the window. The rain had relented a little, more cautious tapping against the window. She thought, with an abyss inside, a precipice she had no wish to plunge down into, that she would never wind up in the moss with a man's body above her. Hot breath in her mouth and a hard bulge working away against her crotch. Very different from fiddling with a spiraea's fuzzy blossom bud.

"If the old man had known . . . how badly we've messed up."

Elga moaned as the pain took over from the mental acuity that had momentarily soothed her torment.

She wrote on the notepad.

Robbed. That's what I told Johanna. Not that we'd boozed up every last cent. Don't say anything!

"What do I get in return?" Aune said bullishly.

You can have the story when I've written it.

Her handwriting grew illegible. Her breath came labored and rattling.

"On one condition," said Aune.

With great effort Elga wrote the last words, before she fell, whimpering, into a deep sleep.

Tell me.

"Write me into it," Aune said decisively.

How?

"Demonic storyteller. Big-time bard."

GRAY SKY, STREAMING RAIN AS THEY CAME ACROSS THE UNDERWEAR AND boot, and spotted a track that formed a gully up to the top of the mountain. Tiina, at the front, slipped down several times and Tanja hissed, *Concentrate, take it easy, you can't run up. Not even you.* Soon they were astonished—assaulted, even—by a bitter winter's landscape. Harsh, raw winds bit their earlobes and the gusts encircled their throats.

"Simone!"

They yelled, yodeled, whistled. The echoes their only reply.

Johanna shivered hopelessly: "Are we going to search every glacier, every snowdrift? We'll freeze to death in these rags."

"Don't be such a namby-pamby," said Tiina. "Quick march to keep warm, a couple of miles I'm guessing."

"What if she's done for? You were too hard on her."

"Shut it, Tanja. Just shut it." Johanna looked at her henchwoman with disappointment.

Thin crusts of black ice broke as they steamed forth and they found themselves knee-deep in the coldest water they'd ever taken a dip in. Wet and shivering they clambered out.

"Could she have built a snow shelter?" Tanja ventured.

They found her half-conscious on a bed of willow: bare, angry-red feet sticking out from the thicket. Eagles and gyrfalcons hovered above the body, taking off when the search party fell to their knees around their sister. Her heart was pattering, she wasn't yet dead. Johanna slapped her on the cheeks, held her nose and blew in warm air. Pressed hard in the region of her heart. Pressed harder as Tanja massaged and blew on Simone's frozen feet. Then Simone opened her eyes, and the first thing her eyes alighted on was Johanna. She stared in dread at her sister, whimpering in mortal terror. She looked up at the sky. Raindrops on her face:

"The goddesses of revenge are come for me."

Tanja whispered in Simone's ear: "We'll carry you home. Into the warm."

And Tiina carried her befuddled sister on her back down the mountain. Dusk was falling as they reached the forest.

The tenderness of soaring pines.

Elga was stacking wood for the winter along the side of the house to dry and carrying birch twigs, brush, and pine cones into the cabin. Hot days could be followed by cold, damp nights. Elga's body was still mottled purple from Johanna's boots and fists, one eye still so swollen she couldn't see out of it. Aune was humming and carrying stones for the root cellar they were building, and Tiina was smoking ptarmigan over green willow. Tanja was clearing up where the deer had been slaughtered and she belched loudly as she always did after eating a lot of meat. The dogs were dozing in the sun after their feast of offal. They moved into the shade as the July heat intensified.

Johanna had gone off with the rifle and snares. Simone, who'd been in and out of consciousness for two days and nights, peeped out shyly. When she got up out of bed, she emerged like some translucent forest spirit out into the clear air, moving about slowly, staying close to the house. She supported herself with one hand against the timber of the house, keeping a constant distance from the sisters, who noted her timorous expression. The sisters snuck uneasy looks at her. She'd been alternating between delirium and lucidity. Would she recover or grow ever madder? They didn't know how to handle Simone, didn't want to infringe upon the distance she'd marked out.

Simone put her hands together and said a prayer over the potato plot, after which she swept a healing hand over the little patch of wilting rye. Would there ever be a harvest with no greenhouse? So foolish to expect anything to grow at such a northerly latitude. There'd be no potatoes for Michaelmas—they wouldn't have time to fill out before the frost arrived.

When they gathered that evening they were all in a stubborn mood, some days are so hopeless they make a person surly. The sisters wanted the evening to be done, to go to bed and sleep off their ennui and ill humor. They lit a huge fire, chewing on dry pieces of smoked rabbit they pretended were dill-flavored potato chips. The roasted meat soothed the hunger pangs, but they missed the booze. If only Elga and Simone hadn't fluffed everything up they'd have had bread to eat with their meat.

"Here we are, throats dry and disappointed," said Aune.

She couldn't be bothered to tell a story, and the others couldn't be bothered to listen; she was the first to go to bed. A pipe stuffed with angelica was passed between the others, who stayed up a while longer.

"Let's hope St. John's Eve is worth celebrating next year," said Tanja. "We'll have the potatoes going, our little forest farm, a full root cellar. Good hunting, fruitful market days."

Laura was forbidden from fiddling about with art, as Tiina put it. She was forced to be of use. Making fishing rods. Carving and smoothing seven pairs of wooden clogs. None of them had realized, when they set off for the cabin, how they would long for footwear. Why had they thrown out the old woman's walking boots and rain boots? As though they'd wanted to be rid of their mother's scent quicker than quick.

Johanna demanded that Laura get started on the totem pole. She declared it urgent.

"Strangers bring with them evil spirits, they must be driven off with evil spirits," she said. "We need anybody who approaches the cabin to come face-to-face with the pole and be scared out of their wits. I've seen footprints in the reeds by the tarn. From somebody wearing boots with a coarse-patterned sole. None of us has that. I also found dog shit in a weird shade of red. We must demarcate our boundaries."

"Wonder who that could be," Tanja said. "I doubt they'd be after us."

"Not yet," said Johanna.

She thought out loud: "We'll have the pole and a pile of warning stones we can throw if anyone approaches. We can't afford warning shots—our powder has to last until the fall market. Tanja, you and I will go into town next time, to see to it that everything gets done properly. The question is whether Tiina should come along, or whether she should stay behind to be the muscle for these wimps."

"Aune can get a thing or two done, it has to be said," Tanja said, careful that her twin sister should not be tarred with the same brush as the others. "And Tiina can carry at least a hundred pounds of raw materials."

"You're right, Tanja. You're a smart cookie," said Johanna, and Tanja lapped it up.

LAURA WAS SURPRISED TO FIND HERSELF GOING POTTY OVER THE pole—cheeks flushed with the joy of creation, pure and simple—she felt amazing. Bearskin head, billy goat horns, bat's ears, dried bear's eyes, a deer bone for a nose and bear claws for a mouth. The last nail of functional size went into that. Simone circled the pole, following the work in silence with a heavy heart.

"Can you eat wolf meat?" asked Laura.

"Man shalt not eat animals that hunt with their claws," said Simone.

She spoke! *Those who can't talk to others come to me*, Laura thought, with a sense that she possessed a special power others did not. She looked up at Simone.

"Did Father say that?"

Simone shook her head: "No, the Bible."

Laura was in an asking mood: "Why does no one wear elk skin?"

"Lean meat. Poor, lackluster fur," said Simone.

"Why can none of us sew?" Laura went on. "We could sell fox-fur caps and beaver-skin mittens."

Simone lit up and smiled almost imperceptibly.

"I have contacts in the industry."

Laura looked up at her sister: her watery, dark eyes, her pale, pale skin. Laura smiled an affirmation. She waved away horseflies and mosquitoes crazed by the sweat of her labors, and said: "Will you come with me to gather some birch bark? Grab a sack in case we find quick clay."

Slip-away Simone, as Johanna called her, had no choice but to acquiesce when asked to fill the sack for the night's fire. She'd been restored to the fold, but there was tension in the air. Laura stepped into the first pair of clogs she'd made, though it took a feat of imagination to view them as worthy of a foot. She kicked them off—just as well to go barefoot. Totems were more fun than clogs.

"You need special tools, a particular kind of file," she said.

She tore bark and conks from the trunks of elderly birches and cut branches from bushes. They sat on their rumps in a bilberry thicket, popping the still-sour berries into their mouths. There were masses here. They should have brought a bucket.

"Let's not tell the others," Simone chomped.

Laura smiled. She looked at her sister earnestly and said she too might have made a contact.

"It's in the works, you never know," she said secretively.

Simone looked up in surprise.

"I may be able to get a message to the furrier," Laura went on.

"What would I say to him?" Simone said, her cheeks hot.

"That you want to learn how to sew skins. But you need to flee the tribe in secret."

Simone jumped up, then inhaled sharply. "Oh, my hip. I think all that kicking smashed it. I wouldn't be able to walk that far."

Laura got up and walked slowly, continuing the thread she'd started on.

"The fur dealer could meet you halfway. Maybe with a horse. Hell, I don't know."

"Don't swear. Please, not you too."

"Figure something out. Save your skin," Laura said obstinately.

When they reached the brook, she undressed, rolling round in the cold clay. Simone followed her example.

"This is perfect," Laura said, ecstatic.

And they walked, mud-streaked, home to the cabin with a sack full of pliable quick clay. The scent of smoked meat met them. The dogs scampered about, barking a frisky welcome.

Laura's shirt stank of sweat as she stripped off on the bank of the tarn. The totem pole was finished and her body was sore from the exertion. She stood at the water's edge, dipped her shirt, and rubbed. It wasn't exactly going to get clean without laundry soap, but perhaps a little cleaner. She hung it on a bare spruce branch, pulled off her trousers and looked out over the morning mist. The rock where the dog had been sitting last time was hidden. She stretched and imagined an observer, eyes surveying her naked body. She looked in wonder at her arms, which had grown muscular with all the carrying, building, sawing, filing, whittling. She looked at white, freckled breasts. Scratched the lumps and ragged skin where horseflies and mosquitoes had feasted.

It was strangely quiet: no birds, no rustling of animals, the water's surface placid as a cow. She slipped in, floated still and soundless as a canoe in a jungle river. Long, full strokes without disturbing the surface. She came here alone almost every day now to avoid the great waves her sisters caused. When she wasn't constantly made to swallow their splashes as she swam, her thoughts seemed to radiate out as though released by the water. All the things she dared not think about in Johanna's presence—Johanna could see straight through Laura. She might not be able to read letters, but thoughts were no problem. With each stroke she thought about what lay before her. She didn't have a single plan for escaping her sibling prison. Any ideas about running away and starting a new life ended abruptly in impossibility. With no schooling, money, place to live, where would she go? Give herself up to social services? An even more inhuman imprisonment awaited there. She would feel like a lost, profoundly unhappy elk in a block of flats. The old man had been right when he said their salvation lay in keeping the tribe together. But it wasn't easy. Two babies who'd shared a womb could be like a fox and a rabbit.

The mist had lifted. The tranquil dog's rock was empty. The beaver's construction works by the side of the boulder were growing larger and larger. She turned round, swam back. Beavers could become angry if they suspected a threat to their timber. Once Kiiski had been attacked by a beaver who bit him so hard on his back the poor hound was almost lost.

She got out, pulling on her trousers and the wet shirt. She walked along the shoreline and crept up to the unknown dog's lookout, heard noises from inside the forest, branches snapping. Was it the dog signaling to her to climb up and follow the sound? Creeping slowly along a well-trodden track, she saw a strip of light a few yards ahead: an opening into a glade. She looked out and there in a meadow she saw a tent. Two tents. Three. From the branch of a tree hung high-tech jackets, blankets, and sleeping bags. No humans in sight, nor any dog. Would she dare to sneak up and steal the jackets and blankets? She waited at the forest's edge, watching in silence from behind a thick pine trunk. The campers must have gone fishing or whatever else it was they were here to do. She crept through the undergrowth, slithering forward to grab a jacket, then crawled back through the long grass. Once she regained the forest she ran toward the cabin without looking back. As she approached she realized she'd have to tell her sisters about the camp. She didn't want to. She had to know who these people were for her own sake. What were they doing there? When would they be returning to civilization? Perhaps they had food to offer, something delicious she hadn't eaten in a long time.

She tried the jacket on. It came down to her thighs, the sleeves covering her hands. Not a winter jacket, but probably windproof. She folded up the sleeves. In the pocket was half a pack of cigarettes, a lighter, a bunch of keys, and a little box of licorice chewing gum. She sat down, lit a cigarette—it went straight to her head, spreading a pleasant feeling of relaxation through her body—she closed her eyes and enjoyed the feeling of being freshly bathed and smoke-infused. Another cigarette. Then all the gum at once. The juice, that delicious licorice flavor that passed all too quickly. You've got to have a big wad of gum, or else what's the point? She stowed the jacket in a hollow pine, arranging stones around the base in a special pattern.

Yet another night of smoked meat. In her imagination Laura was drinking a large porter with her food. While the others chattered away as usual and Aune spun some tired yarn that bored everyone apart from the teller, Laura was away in her thoughts, still by the tarn and the three tents.

Dusk didn't fall until midnight, but it never really grew dark. When they were about to go to bed, Elga said: "Is someone here stashing cigs?"

"There's been a reek of cigarettes all night," Tiina said.

Laura bit her tongue, face innocent.

"Longing for something can evoke that thing so strongly it feels completely real," said Aune.

"I've got the taste of beer in my mouth," said Johanna.

"Capricciosa," said Tiina.

"Sourdough crackers with Emmental," said Tanja.

"Fish pirogs," said Aune.

"Hot dogs," said Laura.

"We need to work harder," said Johanna. "We haven't got much for the market yet."

"A month left," said Tanja.

"We need more hunters," Johanna said. "Traps, snares. Fishing. Cunning. Is any one of us cunning? Nobody, if your dopey faces are anything to go by. What's your contribution to the market?"

She fixed her gaze on Laura.

"You can sell my pine-cone figures."

"Who the fuck's going to pay for that tat?"

"You never know," said Laura.

"You're not coming to town with us, if that's what you're thinking. You'd sink the whole group."

"What can I do then?" Laura said, disappointed.

"Are you completely soft in the head?! More totem poles. Clogs. Shoes, whatever. You have skins. The forest is full of wood," said Tanja.

"All the glue's gone, and the nails. Clogs aren't my . . . I'm not a . . ." Laura attempted.

"Just do it! Try harder!" Johanna bawled.

"Otherwise we won't survive the winter, you must all realize that," said Tanja.

"Gravedigger talk," Tiina said. "We're seven stubborn bastards, why shouldn't we survive the winter? A little snow and cold won't kill people like us."

"We can start with two words. Warm clothing," said Elga.

"You've already sorted yours. Swapping your cunt for pants," Tiina said.

"Johanna screwed that up," said Elga.

"Boots, winter coats, sweaters. Look at these rags we're wearing," said Aune.

"There's normally a few stands selling old castoffs," Tanja said.

"They normally smell like shit," Tiina grimaced.

"Gosh, you've gotten fancy, all of a sudden," said Johanna.

"That vanilla-y old lady smell makes me back right up," said Tiina.

"So buy a man's coat then!" Tanja said.

"Dudes wear theirs out."

Laura was gliding again through the milk-white fog, tacking between the lily pads. She dipped her nose and blew bubbles underwater, then came the silence, the tension. The feeling of once more having eyes on her. The eyes of the pines and spruces. The eyes of owls. Of dogs. Of humans? Men watching? A rustle on the shoreline a way off, she didn't catch what caused the sound. She swam a few strokes in the direction of the western bank and noted how the beaver lodge had grown in height, the busy creature was snaking in and out around the bound-together sticks and twigs. Imagine if they could hire that guy to build their sauna. She quickly swam out again, a little anxious of disturbing the beaver.

A straight course through the mist to a clear vista—not a soul on the rock. Soon at the shore, but what's that there? She squinted, strained her eyes. A little scaffold, or . . . she needed glasses. Now she could see, if a little blurred, a film camera on a tall tripod. The camera's owner had pointed the lens right at the beaver lodge. How much had she been in the frame? It must belong to the campers. Filmmakers, scientists, or some wilderness preservation organization. Should she go to the tents and return the jacket? The keys at least—if they'd noticed her swimming they must suspect her.

Craving a cigarette she walked toward the ancient pine where she'd hidden the jacket, noting the arrangement of stones she'd laid as a marker. She sat against the trunk and scratched her mosquito bites against the bark. There were huge bracket fungi growing high up on the trunk. Not even Tiina would be able to climb up that high to harvest the treasures. She smoked fast and hot, felt a little nauseous; lit another, stubbed it out. She inhaled deeply, catching a whiff of human sweat. Apart from her sisters, she'd had no human contact since the beginning of May. She was like a starving wolf, lurking among the trees, ready to pounce on a dog, a child, or a steak. She squashed two mosquitoes; one was already swollen with blood when it settled. Human blood? Beaver blood? She thought of the old man, who went on all the time about how humans not only acted in bad faith but spread illnesses too: in the best case a cold, in the worst, death. Was the blood in this little biter fresh?

She peered straight into the forest, the trunks were blurrier than usual. *You can't see a bear five yards away*, Johanna had yelled when she'd tried teaching Laura to shoot. Could she help the fact she was nearsighted? She'd always known there was no point asking her parents to take her to the optician. *Costs as much as an old Ford*, Father would have said. She'd adapted to her vision, worked with objects that were close to her. She hoped they'd be leaving for the market soon, she needed a break from Johanna's cruelty. A break from tiptoeing around, being on her guard, a little fearful at all times. A break from getting up in the middle of the night to make progress with her figures. She'd promised herself there would be three thousand by the time she was done for. Those fucking clogs took the biscuit. Clogs for clods of earth. The totem poles, on the other hand. Taking on a seven-foot pole was a new challenge. There were to be three more, one for each point of the compass. The fear: what if in the end, she couldn't see her tools, couldn't see the blade? All that would be left was to roll around in the clay.

    She crept over to the glade and squinted at the tents. A fire, around which sat three men in red caps with large visors. Three sturdy pairs of boots. A dog who got up and sniffed the air, looked in her direction. One of the men laid a hand on the dog's back. *Down!* The men were talking, holding mugs, drinking coffee, smoking. Perhaps it was an illusion, but the scent seemed to reach all the way to where she was hiding: coffee. She didn't want to think about it. She crept back to the tarn, where she dressed and set off for the cabin. Stood still a moment. Changed her mind. Returned to the forest lake.

    The mist had dissipated, the sun's rays on the mirrorlike surface of the lake with water striders making patterns here and there. Dragonflies with pale pink wings. To see the metallic colors of the body, she must look the dragonfly in the eye. By the tallest rock she saw not the dog, but a man with a red cap—he was looking into the camera. She froze. Should she turn and run? Heart pounding, she walked closer. In order to see clearly, she was forced to get really quite close. A short bark, the warning kind. Then the dog was standing a few feet in front of her. It looked at her, barked another warning. She sat on her haunches, held out her palm, the dog sniffed, then she scratched the dog's chest, a whipping, rough tongue in her face. If there was one language she spoke, it was the language of dogs.

Red Cap called:

"Kalle, heel!"

The dog lumbered obediently back to the man. Laura stood still. Should she dash back home or stay and say something? The man pushed back his cap and walked toward her. She saw his facial features more clearly. He was older, maybe as old as thirty. Or maybe he was younger, but looked older with the beard. His jeans sat loose on slim hips. She stared at his stout boots that probably protected his feet completely from the wet and cold. Then she looked down at her own sneakers, where her big toe was poking out, its nail black: Elga had fumbled a thick pine branch and it had crashed down right on her toe. Tanja had heated a sewing needle and punctured the nail, and a little fountain of blood had spurted up from the hole.

Now Red Cap was standing in front of her, saying hello.

"Hello," she answered.

The hello was right inside her, squeaky. It embarrassed her. Was it the pastor or Mrs. Niskanpää she'd last spoken to? She wasn't exactly loquacious in her sisters' presence either. It seemed to her that you should keep your words within, otherwise you'd give yourself away.

He looked at her long, tangled hair, which hadn't been washed since May, and barely even then. Shampoo hadn't exactly been the first thing they'd spent money on after old Mother died. He noticed her ripped jeans that could use a belt. She'd always been rangy, but never as thin as now. His eyes on her dark-blue toenail.

"Ouch, I bet that hurt."

She nodded, trying to retract her big toe like a cat retracts its claws to show it's friendly.

He looked into her eyes, which were no longer squinting.

"Did you want a swim?"

She shook her head.

"We're nearly done here. Our actors have done a beautiful job," he said contentedly, pointing to the beaver lodge. "They're fascinating, aren't they?"

She nodded. If she'd been of a more communicative bent, she would have told him about the beaver attack on Kiiski.

"So what are you doing out here in the wilderness?" he asked.

What was she doing? Gathering clay and pine cones for her models. What should she say? The hardest questions: Who are you? What do you do? Well, what *do* you say? She needed a well-rehearsed ditty she could reel off.

The man took a step forward and held out his hand.

"I'm Philip."

She took the proffered paw tentatively.

"Laura."

"Are you a biologist?" It was clear from his tone that this was the last thing Philip believed, but he wanted to get her talking.

"I just live here," she said.

"Wow. How do you survive the winter?"

She shrugged.

"Moved here at the start of May."

"And how do you spend your days?"

"Totem poles."

Philip laughed. Looked at her with even greater interest, as though studying a rare kind of bird.

"And what do you do with them?"

"We erect them and then . . ." she said, regretting that she'd said "we."

"Who's 'we'?"

"My sisters and . . . and . . . I don't actually dance."

After she said that, she had a vision of the old man, heard his exhortations. Saw Johanna on the rock, preaching the seriousness of the situation. Now she had to watch her tongue.

"Where do you live?" Philip asked with interest.

"That way."

She pointed in the opposite direction from the cabin. Toward the mountains.

"Do you hunt? We've not met a single other person, but we've heard dogs and rifle shots."

"I don't," said Laura.

He looked at her a long while, his face friendly.

"You want to come for a coffee? We've got a little camp on the meadow. I've only got instant, but it's the expensive kind, it's surprisingly good. And outdoors, everything tastes great, doesn't it?"

Not everything. Not everything at all, she thought. Bloody meat they hadn't the patience to cook through. Moldy bread. But coffee. Yes, coffee. The coffee they'd brought to the cabin was gone in a matter of weeks.

She nodded.

"Yes, please. A little coffee."

She walked in silence and the dog rubbed up against her as Philip told her there were three of them working on the film about the beaver, something part-documentary, part-feature film. It was intended to be both a portrait of a fascinating animal, and an adventure in the wilderness. "We don't shun the pastoral," he said with a cheeky glint in his eye.

Laura looked up and thought about how she didn't like pastors. She looked at Philip's hairy arms. She hadn't thought thin men could have so much hair. The old man's back, with a new spare tire each year, was like a rug. She felt exhausted, when did she last eat? Goose two days ago. Small pieces of smoked meat. Unripe blackberries in a secret thicket on the way to the tarn. Bilberries. She wished she could be Tiina, blabbering on, or even Elga. Aune most of all, she spoke so well. Aune would suit Philip. Laura had never even been alone with a man.

When they reached the three little tents, Philip gave her a tour: "Jouni lives here, he's our electrician, crazy talented with lighting. Not that practical though. He thought it more important to bring along a bottle of single malt for each of us than proper boots for himself. This is where Olli lives, our biologist. He should stop smoking. But hey, we all have our vices. If we stopped having vices, we'd stop being human, right?"

She nodded and smiled vaguely.

"We've been friends since college. We love working together. This is our third film. God, how time flies."

She nodded, listened.

"Take a seat, I'll boil some water."

He arranged the wood, added some spruce twigs, and lit a long match. The flame went out. A new match: not a jot. Another.

"Dammit, I wish Olli was here. He's our pyro guy. You each take a role out here in the wilderness."

Laura took the matchbox from him, leaned forward, and with practiced hands got a lovely gentle fire going.

"You're a dab hand, I see," Philip said.

He gave her a mug and the tin of freeze-dried coffee. She put in four heaped spoonfuls.

"Watch out! I normally put in two, otherwise it's too bitter."

He filled her mug with water.

"Don't burn yourself!"

She did. Her tongue felt pimply and numb. She held the cup with both hands.

"You want some sausage? A little bread? We're heading home tomorrow anyway, and we'd like to have as little as possible to carry."

The moment she laid eyes on the sausage, saliva flooded her gullet. It felt like there was a fountain in there. He cut a huge piece and passed it over. She put in the whole piece, chewing like a wild animal. His eyebrows shot up.

"When did you last eat?"

Johanna had come back from the hunt surly and empty-handed. Chanterelles. Delicious but no hungry soul is going to get full on them. Blackberries. But they won't fill your belly. They'd gone to bed early two nights in a row, feeble, dizzy from hunger.

"You seen any bears?" Philip asked when he didn't get an answer to his last question.

"A while back," she said.

"We found tracks yesterday. Really huge ones. Like this."

He held out his hands to show the scale.

"Where was that?"

"I can show you later. Fancy another cup? We could borrow a little whiskey from Jouni."

A sudden sparkle in Laura's dull eyes. Though she'd promised herself she wouldn't drink strong liquor.

Johanna and Tiina grimaced, holding a large log between them. With a roar, they heaved up the timber for the sauna-in-progress. The saddle notch would work, that much they were sure of. Packing with moss and clay was something the wimps could be tasked with.

Johanna spotted Laura.

"Where the fuck you been?"

"All of us have been here slaving away," Tanja said, sourly.

"And you . . . you've been swimming . . . you heap of shit," said Tiina.

Aune looked her up and down.

"But . . . you look an absolute state . . . have you been fighting a bear?"

Laura fingered the scratches on her face and tugged at her ragged T-shirt.

"I frightened him."

Johanna was all ears: "Quick, Tanja. A bear!"

She strode to the cabin, grabbed the rifle.

"Which direction?"

Laura pointed: "Past the tarn, near the lakes. Clear tracks."

"Tiina, fetch the cart. If we get the beast, we'll drag him home," ordered Johanna.

"Let's cross our fingers for a real blow-out tonight," said Tanja.

"The tracks were completely fresh, the bear scent was still there," said Laura.

"Guess they must be fresh if you fought with the bear yourself," said Elga.

"I feel dizzy . . . have to go lie down," said Laura and staggered off to Spruceside.

Her legs were quivering, especially up by her groin. Fluid ran from her crotch. The dogs sniffed, but charged out when Johanna bawled at them to follow. Her breath caught. She wanted to cry, but couldn't. She wanted to tell all, but was afraid of Johanna's punishment. He wasn't repellent . . . no, not at all, really. But still . . . it happened so quickly.

He'd plied her with pieces of salami and they'd laughed, he'd topped up her whiskey and sat close, close, his lips against hers, she stopped chewing, swallowed, his thick tongue moved inside her mouth. *I'll show you*, he'd said, and she'd lain on the ground and caught the scent of nearby bear droppings. The whiskey on an empty stomach had gone straight to her head—she was seriously drunk. It's easy to get someone who's dizzy down on the ground. Not violent, no, not at all, but a resolute strength in the arms. He put her hands over her head and pressed them down into the moss, not brutal, no, not at all, but determined. Heavy body pressing down on hers. Worn jeans pushed down to her knees, now torn even more. She wanted to scream when he entered her, but nothing came out. He grabbed her hair and pulled it. No, not at all hard enough for it to hurt, but she felt it, she was caught. His breathing, faster and faster, the scent of dung, a few hard, quick stabs and he hollered, sudden. His hand limp in her hair, he lay there, writhing his floppy dick around in the shiny mess that smelled sharper even than the animal droppings.

Whispered in her ear:

"This is our true nature . . . do you feel it? Animals among animals. My seed runs out of you straight into the moss. That's how it should be. How lovely you are."

He brought one hand to his groin and put his already-hardening member back inside her. Now it stung horribly. The pain of real panic as he began to thrust his abdomen. The whiskey had completely evaporated.

"Wait," she said. "I'm lying on a sharp stick."

He took hold of her body and tried to lift it up a little. Then she grabbed on to the flick-knife in her back pocket, inched it open, and held the sharp blade to his eye.

"What are you doing? Put that away."

His voice was hard, metallic, but also a little afraid.

"I'm not a rapist."

He sat back, a hurt expression, a twitch of disappointment in the corner of his mouth. He knelt to wipe his genitals with a bracken leaf, Laura still holding the knife.

"Put that away, I'm not that guy. Shame you can't enjoy it. I pity you. Right, up you get!"

She pulled up her jeans, got up and ran, ran, ran. No looking back. Close to the cabin she stopped to piss. It stung angrily, she cleaned her crotch with damp moss. Rubbed and rubbed. Her stride grew wearier and she tripped on a root that lay like an elephant's trunk across the game trail, cutting her knee open. She stumbled home with her heart in her mouth.

Aune knelt down in front of Spruceside, peering in through the opening. Laura lay there, her eyes lifeless and her hands protective over her stomach. Aune passed her a washcloth.

"Here! It's completely clean. Dipped in rainwater."

Laura bathed her face, the wound on her knee, and lastly, her crotch. She changed into her hiking trousers. Her heart was still pounding. She tried to breath slowly, calmly, but it was impossible with the racket in her head. Her thoughts were careening around. He wasn't repellent, no, he wasn't: his fine-boned arms, the powerful veins in his underarms, his hands with their long fingers. But he'd pulled her to him before she was ready, pushed his tongue in before she'd understood what was going on. What should she call it? She heard the old man's word of warning, Johanna's harsh formulations, she would stone the traitor. She would stay silent about what had happened, keep the phial of poison inside.

How would she have the guts to go and swim again? Maybe she could go to the lake instead, snag a pike to bring home. A real whopper that would be enough for seven hungry wretches. Then she drifted into sleep. A great brown bear rearing up, its genitals swollen, a rutting bellow, the paws dashing her against the ground. Her belly growing, big enough to burst. She gives birth to a boy with claws and a furry head.

Johanna's whoops of joy awoke her; she crawled out and it was like she was still in the dream as she saw the bear's body.

"Just think, we got the bugger. Big as hell, but we got it."

Johanna was jumping up and down in front of the house. Tiina ricocheted beside her.

"And then I found this in the meadow. One word: Teerenpeli."

She held out three almost-full bottles of whiskey and the sisters' eyes gleamed. All of them, apart from Simone and Laura, wanted to stroke the bottles.

"Savu. The best kind. Smoky," said Elga.

"Now we're good for the market. We'll have the bearskin and dried bear meat to sell," said Tanja with satisfaction.

Johanna held out a little berry-picking bucket.

"Got some smokes too. Half a tub of butts . . . seems we've had folk on our very doorstep . . . we need to get the first totem up this instant."

Johanna looked up at the sky. She put her hands together and closed her eyes, murmured, "Old man, captain, give us strength."

Tiina and Tanja chorused, "Give us strength. Strength. Strength."

Aune, Laura, and Elga gathered stones and Simone started digging, against her will. It hurt inside that her sisters were so heathen, creating these false idols, but, afraid of a beating, she tramped the spade hard into the ground.

Elga instructed: "Dig just here. Then it won't fall on the house if there's a storm, and its leering face will be seen by anyone coming along the game trail."

"Wish we had two spades," said Aune.

"We'll buy one at the market," said Tanja.

"And a hoe, if we're to have a better potato plot," said Aune.

"Look at this beautiful earth," said Tanja.

"Great, let's make the most of it. We need to extend the rye plot too," Aune said.

"On forest ground?" Elga said skeptically.

"We have to try everything," Aune said. "You never know."

"You never know anything," Tanja said.

Simone whinnied and clutched her back and hip. Her face twisted in pain. Aune took the spade from her, digging rapidly, chaotically, until she was laid out on the ground. Then Tanja took over.

"Look. What a sky," said Laura.

"Rain on the way. Typical. Just when we're about to have a barbecue," said Tanja.

"We'll have to do a rain dance," said Tiina.

"A rain dance is a dance you do to *bring on* the rain," Elga informed her.

"A bit further to go, Laura!" said Tanja.

Laura wobbled: "I can't . . . I don't feel . . ."

"Dig around that stone and we'll lift it out," said Tiina.

"That's not a stone. It's metal," said Elga.

She jumped down and dug with her fingers, pulling out a rusty metal container that she laid alongside the hole. They stared at the tin, looked at each other. Might it contain an unwelcome surprise?

"Open it!" Tanja said.

Shells, batteries, rolling papers, tobacco, nylon line, fishhooks, and a bundle of bills.

Johanna examined the discoveries in the box.

"Father's treasure. He left this for us. Dear Father."

Elga counted quickly.

"A hundred euros."

"So we can buy all the necessities," Tanja said as raindrops turned into a downpour. The sky had turned a threatening shade of purple.

"Quickly now! Up!" said Tiina.

Gathering their strength, they hoisted the pole, but they could have done with more of Tiina's brute strength.

"Fetch the rope!" called Tiina. Laura stepped up and the thick rope was wrapped around the pole, then fourteen hands pulled and pulled. Tiina grunted, Johanna panted. And the pole stood erect. Rocks were tossed into the hole, building up. Elga stamped down stone after stone to form a rampart.

Johanna took a few steps back and admired the tribe's totem. Her hands were throbbing.

"A toast!"

A bottle was held aloft, Johanna gulped its contents down and passed it to Tanja. They grabbed the others, which went from hand to hand until they were empty.

The rain thundered against the ground, the buckets they'd put out filled rapidly, and in the firepit a little lake formed. It drummed, splashed, gurgled. Clothes were torn off and thrown into the cabin. They ran out naked and hopped, hooting, around the pole, drinking the rainwater, washing their foreheads, rivulets along their throats, bellies, genitals.

Simone, still fully clothed, stood to one side holding her head to protect it from the devil she knew would be tempted, especially by this naked dance in the rain. She didn't want to see this depravity, so she backed into the forest and lay down in a crevice in the rock. She put her hands over her ears and closed her eyes tight, thinking of how she was growing more devout each day. Thinking of herself as a monk called Symeon. She felt more and more like that monk.

The sisters linked hands and danced around the pole. The dogs ran around them, yelping playfully. Quicker, quicker, galloping gawkily. With a merry-go-round shriek they fell in a heap. At that moment the rain stopped and the evening sun showed its face.

Exhausted, they sat around the fire, mouths watering over the grilling meat. The scent! The foam rose in the corners of their mouths, the saliva ran. Nobody thought to eat carefully, no one considered their stomachs, unaccustomed to food. Nobody thought about how untrained lungs can't tolerate as much cigarette smoke. Nobody thought about how strong liquor, which they hadn't drunk for a long time, ate away at starving stomachs.

They choked on their bolted food.

"Don't forget to chew now, girls," said Tanja.

"Shut it, Mom," said Elga, in a mocking voice.

Then they went, one after another, into the forest to throw up.

Aune waved her arms about.

"Go further into the forest, Tiina. We won't want that stench when the sun comes up tomorrow."

"Shut it, Mom," said Tiina.

Simone crawled out of her safe space, climbed up a tall trunk that had been lopped off halfway up and split into a curved fork. From a distance the disfigured tree looked like the world's largest divining rod. Was it the work of lightning? Or had hunters cut it that way? To what end? She sat in the fork and looked down at her depraved sisters. *I'm never coming down again,* she thought. *Never. I'm Symeon, the tree's missing canopy.* She spread her toes and fingers. *I am the tree.*

Laura made her way out of Spruceside to pee. It stung where the stream of urine splashed against her crotch. She picked some soft, moist moss to soothe the pain, and to stuff into her ears to muffle the yelling; Tiina was bellowing loudest as usual. Had the men left behind more than just cigarette butts? She must find the courage to go back there, must pluck up the guts to swim in the tarn. To find the jacket she'd hidden in the tree. She hoped it wouldn't smell of him. Philip. She repeated the name to herself. The sound was needle-sharp.

IT TOOK TWENTY-FOUR HOURS FOR THE OTHERS IN THE RUSSET-topped tribe to sleep off their excesses. Gooey eyes. Sticky mouths. Throbbing brows. Muttering and swearing, they set to building again. The afternoon heat was intolerable.

"Last to the tarn gets it!" shrieked Tiina.

"You trot along. I'm going to take my time," said Elga.

"I'll be along in a minute to kick your asses," said Johanna.

Six sisters' greasy hair blended in with the tall russet-colored grasses in the meadow. Laura brought up the rear and searched the areas flattened by the tents. Something glinted over there, she dived down onto her knees. Bottle caps. They might come in useful someday. A bottle opener. Hmph, they'd brought ten of those along from the farm. The only thing they had too many of. What about this? A bag of rock-hard cinnamon buns. She put those in her pocket. A cigarette butt, though it was smoked down to the filter. Toss that. Her forehead was moist, the dirty sweat ran into her mouth. The mosquitoes attacked, she staggered toward the tarn. Her vulva was burning. Imagine if he was still there, imagine if he'd just moved his tent to another body of water. Her body was racked with hot shivers.

From the tarn, the yells and hoots lashed Laura's eardrums; their screeching made her quake as usual. She got in from the other side and swam quietly a distance from her sisters' splashing. She glided under the water's surface: that depth, black as coal. The beaver's lodge offered a winter hideout for a whole family. Perhaps Grandma and Grandpa Beaver too. She swam toward the beach, climbing out where the camera had once stood. Sat and watched the beaver. Her headache had dissipated, her body was cool. She tucked her legs beneath her and rested her head on her knees. It didn't matter how she sat, it still hurt. She looked between her legs: vivid red and swollen.

Chapter Eleven

And now the fall market awaited them, with the growers' freshly harvested greens and root vegetables taking center stage. The sisters had worked diligently and were well-stocked with meat and furs. This time they opted for a role reversal and let the Amazonians head off into town, while the skinny ones stayed home to build the root cellar. Would they finally get hold of the basics they needed and live in relative comfort?

ON THE MORNING OF DEPARTURE, THREE BULGING BACKPACKS were leaning against carts over which skins had been stretched and fastened with rope. Tanja went through the packs to ensure nothing had been forgotten, while Tiina stamped like a racehorse at the gate.

Aune and Elga were getting ready to finish the roof on the toolshed. Johanna came and stood before them, feet planted wide, hands on hips.

"When we get back, you're to have built the root cellar."

"In less than two weeks?" Elga said with raised eyebrows.

"Right. There'll be a fine for delays," said Johanna.

"We'll need baskets, big and small," said Elga. "Someone will have to weave them. Simone can use that as a rosary. Where is she?"

"Simone!"

"Haven't seen her for ages," said Aune.

Johanna sighed in annoyance. "Has she fucked off to the mountain again? Did you notice how she was acting all pious when we were living it up? Pursing her lips at the booze."

"Psycho bitch," Tiina snarled. "We can't waste time coddling her. We've got to go."

Tanja rushed around searching, while Tiina clicked her fingers. Then Tanja came back, her face stricken.

"She's sitting at the top of a broken pine. Chewing her knuckles and spitting out weird words. *Mea culpa*."

"What did you say it sounded like?" said Tiina.

"*Mea culpa*. Whatever that means. And she's screaming, *Begone Furies!*"

"She's got that on the brain," Johanna said, pulling on her backpack, making ready to pull the cart.

"We're off. So long, suckers. Laura and Elga can take care of the loony."

"Wait a minute," said Tanja, stomping over to Spruceside. She grabbed a couple of boxes and loaded them with clay girls and pinecone elk.

"You never know. Could get a little small change for these."

I've got a new car and it drives just like a dream, Tiina sang as Tanja blew on a grass reed and Johanna played air guitar. Three pairs of legs moved fleet and full of yearning along the game trail toward town. For the moment, the unwieldy rucksacks felt light on their backs. It would be tricky to restrain themselves from eating their wares: smoked bear meat, wild raspberries, blackberries. Johanna carried the rifle, ready to down a wood pigeon or two for dinner.

"We mustn't dirty the bearskins when we're sleeping in caves," Tanja said.

"You're planning to sleep?" Tiina said. "What? Now we're finally on the road?"

"Not even the old man could manage a hundred miles without sleep," Johanna said.

"Here's hoping we sell it all," said Tanja.

"I've been thinking about something," said Tiina eagerly.

"Watch out," said Johanna.

"Let's add a little extra."

"What like?" asked Tanja.

"A show that will bring in the punters," said Tiina.

"You want to show your titties?" said Tanja.

"Babe. We're going to show all the titties we've got," said Tiina, holding up her top.

Johanna sniggered. "And you think those snippy townies are going to buy expensive bearskins after that?"

"Get the old guys on our side, and we open the fat wallets. Old aunties might love buying stuff, but it's mostly cheap tat."

Johanna nodded.

"Let's test Laura's shit out. Women love all those cute little things."

"Every time I see her lining up those little models I have to pinch my arm hard to stop myself stomping all over them," said Tiina.

"Old Mother wasn't much of a one for cutesy stuff."

"But she wasn't exactly like any other old wo—"

Johanna stopped so suddenly Tanja thudded into her back. Squatting by the trail, Johanna examined some peculiar droppings.

"Someone's vomited up a whole whatsit," said Tiina.

"Has it been discarded by a hunt? Could the hunters be nearby?" said Tanja, casting a look around.

"Stomach, intestines, fur. Don't you see what's been here?" Johanna said.

"A bear?" Tanja ventured.

"No, no, a lynx has been partying here."

She prodded the mess with a stick. "Fresh."

"So, there's a lynx nearby," Tanja said, excited.

"They can go like the clappers . . . we can't know for sure. If she's resting after her meal, she'll be able to see us now."

Johanna loaded the rifle and hushed them.

"Imagine if we came thundering into town with a lynx skin. The money would rain down."

"Shut it, Tiina!"

Johanna took a deep breath. They stood still as statues. Breathing soundlessly, all three. Then Johanna cleared her throat and howled so loud the others jumped and covered their ears.

"And you're telling me to shut my mouth," Tiina said angrily.

"The lynx's mating call. The old man taught me," said Johanna.

They howled as they walked for five or six miles, like a curious kind of tribal song. One time a lynx had answered them, but so far off they never would have caught up with it.

Silence in the forest. A woodpecker pecked. A dove cooed.

"Isn't it the wrong time of year for mating?" said Tanja.

"You never know," Johanna said dismissively. "Did you know

lynx fat is the best thing for greasing a rifle, and good for your hands too, when you've been working in the forest."

Johanna looked at her calloused hands, patterned with scratches and little wounds. Tanja surveyed her coarse, dry fists.

"Work gloves," she said, adding them to her mental shopping list.

"Sometimes I get an urge to punch Laura. Simone too," Tiina said. "There we are, felling pine, spruce, and birch trees, and building houses log by log, snagging our nails, pulling muscles in our backs, and there's Laura, fiddling about with her stick figures."

"She has no muscles, poor thing," said Tanja. "She can't help that."

"Anyone can get muscles," Tiina said.

"She was born spindly as a spider," said Tanja.

Tiina was contrary.

"And the other two? What about them?!"

"Aune tries," the ever-diplomatic Tanja said of her twin. "There's nothing wrong with her."

"I fall asleep every time she starts spinning one of her so-called yarns," said Tiina. "She thinks she's really saying something."

"You fell asleep when Uncle Veikko told his stories too," said Tanja.

"I'm going to kick the shit out of Elga next time there's a fight," said Johanna.

They crept forward, ready to encounter a lynx, but after a while they lost patience and picked up speed. Lynx aren't easy. Hunting them requires patient waiting, mostly without reward, and they needed to get to the market on time.

"Can you eat lynx?" Tiina asked.

"I'd rather fry earthworms," said Tanja.

Tiina retched. "Fuck!"

"People used to chew earthworms during the war," Tanja said. "Veikko told me fried worm doesn't taste as awful as it sounds. Kind of like chicken, actually."

"Elga said that if you took all the earthworms in the world, they'd weigh twenty times as much as all the people," said Tiina.

"Idiot! Let's sit down for a minute and have a smoke," said Johanna, pulling the bag of cigarette butts from her pocket.

"I'm dying for one . . . imagine getting a puff on a fresh straight."

"Did you notice the way Laura smelled the other day?" Johanna said.

"Not just smoke. Dude sweat," Tanja said.

"Do *you* know how men smell?" Tiina said, grinning.

"I sat and bounced on the old man's knee often enough," said Tanja.

"The ship sails, the mast impales," guffawed Tiina.

"There's something dodgy about Laura," said Johanna. "She'll be the first one to rat us out, I'd bet on that. Her tongue's loose. Runs from farm to farm like a cat."

"Can you see any farms from our little croft?" said Tanja.

"Some bugger's been there leaving bottles behind," Johanna said. "Of course riffraff and drifters are going to come to our ancient forests."

"Would they hand out smokes and make out?" said Tiina.

"Laura's got something going on: this, that, and the other on the sly," Johanna said.

"Nah, she's just nearsighted and muddleheaded. I doubt that's going to—"

Tiina interrupted Tanja. "What about Simone then? Talk about crackers," she said with a lunatic's gurn.

"Advanced-level kooky and easier to put in her place," Johanna said. "But Laura's just crazy, you know? One of these days she'll pinch the rifle from me and shoot every last one of us."

"I'm worried what they'll get up to while we're away," said Tanja.

Johanna nodded: "Or not get up to. I gave Aune a stern talking-to before we left. She at least understands what you say to her."

"Check out the wild raspberries. Let's get in," said Tiina, throwing off the backpack.

Tanja bellowed: "Ow! You just dropped a ton of luggage on my foot."

She sat on a stone, massaging her foot, face twisted in pain.

"You can take it, come on," said Johanna. "Let's pick some and have a little lunch."

Tiina swallowed down food faster than the dogs. Every time she ate, she tried to beat her last record in speed-chewing.

"Don't eat any more of those," Tanja scolded. "The ladies in town will get moist panties when they spot sweet wild raspberries."

Tiina went on stuffing her face.

"No, no more meat either. I'm shutting the pantry right now."

As Tanja packed away the food for their journey, it was obvious her injured foot was troubling her. Tiina stared lustily at the food. Belched as she always did after eating.

"It's getting dark so quickly now," she said.

"The moon is fine. Tomorrow night it will be full," said Johanna.

"So will we . . . full of booze!" said Tiina.

"We forgot something," Tanja said. "We should have asked Elga to write some signs."

"Ah, people can see with their own eyes, can't they?" said Tiina.

"We need the prices to be clear, otherwise they'll just walk past the stall," said Tanja. "Who of us can write reasonably?"

"I did go to school a little at least," said Johanna. "You know . . . before the old man completely closed the door."

"Were you so rubbish you had to stop?" said Tiina.

"Not at all," Johanna said, hurt. "The teacher actually said some pretty nice things. Well, I mean, not in everything . . . conduct and behavior I wasn't so hot on. And sewing. We're not made that way in our family. That's just how it is."

"I thought you'd never learned anything," Tiina said.

"Who told you that?"

"Elga."

"Elga's the daughter of a slimy pig," said Johanna.

"What are you saying about the old man?" said Tanja, shocked.

"Look at her. A feeble body. Tiny nose. Useless at everything but reading. She's not like us."

"Are you seriously suggesting Mother . . . ?"

"That's what it looks like," said Johanna.

"The old man wanted you to come hunting . . . so you had to stop?" Tiina mused.

Johanna nodded. "There was other stuff too, of course . . . a lot happened in the short time I was at school. The old man was hunting illegally, maybe he was up to other things I didn't know about. Everyone had a still going in our neck of the woods, so it can't have been that. We were being hounded by the police, social services, child health. We got rid of the telephone. Sometimes they banged on the door, so we hid."

"We hid in the root cellar. I remember how cold it used to get, sitting there for ages," Tanja recalled.

"Suddenly Father had decided," said Johanna, "to break all contact with the outside world. No bugger's going to come in here and break up our family, he said."

"And what did Mother say?" Tanja asked, massaging her sore foot.

"She snuck off to the pastor when the old man was out hunting. Lapped up all those holy words that the old man had forbidden. She and Simone had that hocus-pocus in common."

Tanja shivered: "Must be down to thirty degrees now, right? How many pelts do we have? Look, my whole foot is black and blue. I hope it can handle the last few miles tomorrow."

Johanna got up "You'll manage it, we'll take it slowly on our way to the cave. I'm guessing there's less than a mile to go."

Tanja progressed with great effort.

"We must buy new sneakers. And winter boots. Before we know it, everything will be white."

They trekked slowly in silence. Tiina stopped, attentive: "What was that?"

"An owl, dummy," said Johanna.

"No, the rustling."

"Wild animals can smell the flesh," said Tanja.

Johanna squashed a mosquito against her cheek and pointed: "I can see the cave now. Put the bags right at the back. We mustn't lose anything."

On that last stretch they became aware of how bone-tired they were.

Tanja shared out minimal portions for their evening meal. They went to bed early.

"I'll stay out here and keep the fire going for the time being," said Tiina.

AS USUAL, JOHANNA WAS THE FIRST TO WAKE UP. SHE CRAWLED OUT into air fresh from the night's rain. Her feet ached as she prowled around the cave and then peed standing up like her father. A wood pigeon cooed, a squirrel came hopping along and darted up to the top of a dead pine. That twisting tail that drove the dogs to their wits' end. She looked down at her boots, they were much too big. Clown-size. She'd lied about having the same size feet as her father.

She picked a handful of lingonberries and grimaced at their sourness, but it kept the scurvy at bay for a day. The bilberries were either dry or overripe. She tore leaves from the bilberry bushes, dropped them into her mug, and heated a pan of water. She aimed the rifle at the squirrel, but then put the weapon down. They wouldn't have time to grill it today and people at the market weren't ready to eat squirrel. She slurped the bilberry tea, dreaming it was coffee. She sensed her father at her side—his great thighs and copious stomach, the nose-tantalizing smell of his sweat. His focused gaze on the edge of the forest, a gaze that never stopped scanning for game. The aftershave he'd left behind was all gone. Might there be a few coins left over so she could buy some? If the others were allowed to buy some small thing, perhaps. They needed a more reliable watch. Not for the forest, but it was useful for keeping track of market days, that much was true.

"Any more tea?" Tanja asked in a dazed voice.

"Go for a piss and pick some. It's everywhere. Eat some lingonberries."

"Ouch, my fucking foot. Throb, throb, throb," Tanja moaned, turning to shout, "Up you jump, Tiina!"

"Quiet! I need my sleep, I was on wolf-watch last night."

"You do realize we have to get to the market on time, don't you," Johanna said. "Where are we going to get paper from?"

"How fancy has your ass gotten?" Tiina yelled from inside the cave.

"I meant paper to write prices on."

"We can write on our bellies," said Tiina.

"What if our bellies are empty?" Tanja said, longing for a sandwich.

"The first thing we'll do is buy a bottle of whiskey," Tiina said.

"I've got the old man's hip flask with me," said Johanna. "You know, the lucky one."

The parking lot was completely full before the market traders had even laid out their wares and arranged the price markings for strips of sweets in ten flavors and various kinds of cotton candy. Several stalls were selling glass beads and leather thongs embroidered with silver thread. As tradition dictated, people could pick and choose from pyramids of root vegetables. They could buy salt-fermented gherkins, funnel chanterelles, and freshly spun honey. The customers had begun to wander from stall to stall, surveying them as they went. Everyone wanted to be first, so as not to miss some tidbit at a knockdown price. Kids were lifted onto the pale pink horses of the little carousel. The repetitive pling-plong melody the mustachioed carousel operator had to listen to for six hours straight must have been driving him barmy.

This was a place to find jumble-sale bargains, even if there was always one seller at least who had an eye for which designers were hip, which jugs were valuable, which glasses they could charge ten euros apiece for. People from roundabout—young families, expectant couples with precious cargo, nesting—fingered patinaed cutlery. Buyers from the antique shops of much larger towns and cities jostled for space. They always made their way alone, striding briskly through the wares on offer, then gone just as quickly.

Between a stall selling chunky knitted socks and another with locally produced halloumi and chorizo, the sisters had found a spot to show off their berries, bearskins, game meat, and foxtails. They'd managed to borrow a marker from a trader selling ring gun caps. Johanna's tongue poked out, steering the lettering across Tiina's bared midriff.

"Write under my tits! 'Sweet wild raspberries five euro,'" said Tiina.

"Write 'lingon eight euro a liter' above my belly button," said Tanja.

That did the trick. Bearded, denim-clad guys with motorbike helmets under their arms swiftly formed a first row. Women in patterned dresses pulled vainly at the arms of their polo-shirted husbands. The men stood firm in the second row of onlookers and got the first laugh of that market day.

Tiina had sold two cartons of lingonberries before Johanna had even had time to write the price on Tanja's midriff. As Tiina lifted her top to loud wolf whistles, she spotted a dried-up spinster with an SLR camera. Tiina looked her up and down. Orthopedic old-lady shoes, a pastel green cardigan, and cute bangs. This chick had the nerve to take pictures of them. Tiina fixed her with a murderous look, and a simple little *I'm-going-to-kill-you* gesture made the spinster lady lower her camera and withdraw to the back of the queue. There's nothing sweeter than seeing a wuss back away in fear. Tiina grabbed the hip flask and swigged in satisfaction, then passed it to Johanna and Tanja. "Let's sell some skins. We'll get all the goods we need for the winter." She picked up a foxtail, placed it between her legs, and began to belly dance. The men in biker getups applauded and held out their own hip flasks in enthusiastic generosity. A slim-built man with upright posture and a confident demeanor stepped forward and introduced himself as a fur trader. He pointed to Tiina's chest and said,

"You're selling gold much too cheaply. Your sisters who were here in the summer knew the art of getting paid."

Tiina flew into a temper, pulled down her top, took off her jacket, and flexed her biceps.

"Nowyoulistenhere. Wanna arm wrestle?"

"No, God no," said the furrier with a laugh. "I'm a bad loser. I want to do business. You're the only ones with something worth buying at this yokel market."

Johanna stepped forward: "What kind of business? I'm the boss here."

The furrier shook her hand firmly.

"Onni Kvarnholm," he said. "What are the other two Red Riding Hoods doing on this lovely summer's day?"

"They're back at home, hunting bears and butchering," Johanna said guardedly.

"Send them my best wishes. We had a damn fun weekend. Those two sure could party . . . right, show me your furs."

"My fur, you mean?"

Tiina wiggled her hips, holding the foxtail like a furry member.

Onni shook his head in amusement: "You sure know how to show those furs off to their full advantage. Lay out everything you have."

With self-satisfied expressions, Tanja and Johanna laid out the bear, beaver, and rabbit skins. Last of all came the shining foxtails.

"Wow. A fine sight. What do you want for the lot?"

Johanna, Tanja, and Tiina looked at each other. Never in their lives had they thought they'd want Elga standing next to them.

"Five thousand" was the first number Johanna hit upon.

"Any chance of a bulk discount?" The furrier laughed.

"We don't deal in discounts. These are first-class wares we're selling," Johanna said insolently.

"That number's pie in the sky and you know it. I can pay one and a half."

"Four," Johanna said cockily.

"Joker. Let's call it two and say no more. Come to my place for some meat stew and cognac and we'll settle the deal. For future sales, too. I'll drive you to wherever you're staying tonight. Are you at the Stadt Hotel?"

"You want meat too?" Tiina asked.

"I have meat, though of course it depends on what kind of meat you have. I suppose I'd be tempted if the steaks were particularly tender."

"We'll put the skins to one side if you keep your promise. You can come and drive us there at the end of the day. We walked here."

"I'm impressed by your mettle. Here's my card if you need anything. Call me."

Johanna took the card and put it in her trouser pocket, and the furrier vanished into the melee.

"Now we have to sell the meat," said Tanja.

"Let's focus on the women. What did you do with Laura's bundles of sticks?"

"Did she say what we should charge?" Tanja asked.

"Old women are tight. We'll charge five euros each," Tiina suggested.

A middle-aged woman in banana yellow knee-length shorts and a pale pink polo shirt stepped forward and peered bluntly at the sisters. They saw the woman's pupils expand in terror; she concealed a rattling cough with a petite hand upon which glittered three big gold rings. She placed her order in a voice that was accustomed to giving orders. "Please put aside ten pounds of bear meat for me. I'll pick it up at closing time. Write it down! Ellen Beaverfeldt."

"We'll remember that name," Tiina said.

"Thank you!"

THE FUR TRADER REALLY DID WANT HIS GOODS AND TURNED UP AS promised. He showed them to his sky blue SUV and opened the trunk.

"Put the meat in the cooler here. You'll sell the rest of it tomorrow. You can pack away the furs here. You'll have to sit on some of them in the back seat."

Johanna was about to get into the front seat like the leader she saw herself as, but she was pushed aside by Tiina, who was bouncing up and down.

"Can I drive?"

Onni was just settling into the driver's seat, but he stepped out and Johanna moved back so he could sit up front.

"Of course. Jump in!"

Tiina took a firm grip on the steering wheel.

"Belts on, girls," he said. "The police round here have a keen eye for trivialities."

Onni noticed the driver's big toe was peeking out of a hole in her sneakers. They were on the verge of complete disintegration.

"I see you've walked far," said Onni.

"Gonna buy some new ones tomorrow," said Tiina.

Once she realized the car didn't need a key to start, she backed out and stepped on it.

"Fucking hell, Tiina, this isn't motocross," Tanja yelped, laying a calming hand on her sister's shoulder.

"This motor's got some bang. Is it far?" asked Tiina.

"Seven miles of road, then three on gravel. I got this last year. If you want to buy my old ride, you're welcome to."

"We live in the wilds, no cars can get out there. Maybe a helicopter," said Tanja.

Johanna fixed her with her sternest keep-your-mouth-shut look.

"Wow, *those* kinds of wilds," said Onni.

He looked in the rearview mirror and watched the sisters in the back seat. Sturdy girls, both, he thought, thick necks like Russian female athletes.

"That's why we have the best animal skins," Johanna said. "The wildest specimens."

"Who do you sell to?" Tiina asked Onni.

"I have my contacts, mostly overseas. Here in town, people don't understand the charm of real furs anymore, aside from a few society ladies. The Russian market is the most profitable. And the Chinese. There's real money there. No one in this country has serious money anymore."

They sat in silence for a while. Onni laid a hand on Tiina's when she yanked the gear stick too hard.

"Easy, easy."

The skin contact made her jump.

Johanna was thinking about money. They had seventy left of the hundred-euro note. And Onni was about to give them a fortune. They could buy all the important things they needed for home. A sense of calm spread through her.

"As I said, my freezers are full of meat. It's furs I'm after," said Onni. "I'll drive you to where you're staying tonight. Stadt Hotel or Fiona's Bed and Breakfast?"

"We're staying here!" said Tiina, pointing out across the tree-tops. The sun was already close to setting.

"In the trees?" Onni looked amused.

Johanna nudged Tiina's back and Onni went on.

"There's a lot of chanterelles right here, I can tell you that for free. But surely you're not going to stay the night in the forest? I have a guest cabin, why don't you stay there tonight? Make coffee for yourselves in the morning if you wake up before me. Here! Slow down and turn right at the sign."

Dense mixed forest on both sides, a narrow, dusty dirt track. Smoke billowed when Tiina changed gears, and gravel rattled against the wheel rims. Onni raised his voice: "Slow down here. Goddammit, slow down! That's more like it, yes. Turn into the ranch. Park on the left."

They were greeted by birdsong. They looked up at a large

wooden house with two floors, a veranda with gingerbread trim. Through a forest glade they saw a lake, a good-size jetty, a rowboat, and the largest sauna they'd seen in their lives.

Tiina pointed to the sauna.

"Do you have a big family?"

"No, but I like to have big parties and invite my business partners. Heikki Leskinen came to many a party here. People in town tell me he was your father."

"Our old man's dead," said Tiina.

"Damn shame that man's gone. The way they flocked around him! Both men and women were wild about him."

Johanna, Tanja, and Tiina looked at the ground. They tried to summon an image of their father at a party. Or surrounded by people on any kind of occasion.

"I'm sorry for your loss. I share in it: Heikki became a friend. He was an asset, in any situation. Please, come in!"

Onni stepped into a pair of leather slippers adorned with baby fox heads, carried in the cooler, and Tiina helped him with the skins. On the big outdoor porch they met a bear about to attack. Johanna stood close to the bear, checked the claws, stroked its belly.

"That was shot by your father, you know."

Onni opened the door to the living room and turned to the sisters, who stood on the threshold of a great parlor, the ceiling of which must have been over twelve feet high, with walls covered with stuffed deer and elk heads. There were even zebra skins, stretched alongside paintings in huge gold frames, all with themes taken from nature. Armchairs were crowned with animal heads, the floor was covered with colorful, boldly patterned rugs. An enormous fireplace and a TV screen covered half the wall. Right in the middle of the room was a long table that would have seated a whole hunt.

"Welcome! Please, make yourselves at home while I go and warm the soup."

"Where's the can?" said Tiina.

Onni gestured toward the main bathroom and to a smaller one off the hall. Tiina was there in two great strides. A scuffle, something tumbled from the wall and crashed to the floor. The door to the bathroom opened and slammed shut.

Johanna went into the smaller bathroom. In the glow from the lights in the bathroom cabinet, she peered with surprise at the reflection of a face she didn't recognize. She took a step back, ran her hand through her hair and got stuck in the tangles. Examined the leathery, freckled cheeks. *Is this the skin of a human being?* Gray tidemarks on her neck. She washed it, rubbing so hard it flushed red. Until she'd seen the sparkling tiles, the washbasin with both hot and cold running water, she hadn't realized how she stank. Gray flakes of skin in the basin. Should she wash, and take the edge off the sour smell? Open up an abyss of baked-on earth, filth, and sweat?

She pulled off her shirt and washed her armpits, *What a resplendent bush of hair!*, soaped her arms. The filthy water stained the glistening washbasin. She wished she had a clean top to put on. They must buy new shirts tomorrow. She pulled down her jeans and washed her ass and crotch. She put the soap back in the cup, not noticing the hair and dirt that now covered the bar. She opened the bathroom cabinet, picked up the razor, and inspected exciting bottles containing various fluids intended for shaving and skin care. She unscrewed caps and lids and sniffed them. She tried to decipher the minuscule script on one of the men's scent bottles in particular, wishing once again that she could read properly. She recognized it as her father's brand, unscrewed the top and brought her nose to it. She closed her eyes in bliss. She stuffed plasters, a few painkillers, and an unopened bar of soap into her coat pocket.

Stepping into the parlor, she caught the delicious scent of the soup. Her nostrils flared and her stomach screamed for food. When had they last visited a furnished home? When they were at Teacher Leena's house? Electricity, flushing toilets, mirrors, sofas, and a dining table. Five months ago. She'd grown so quickly unaccustomed to all the things that belonged in a home. If you could call the farm they'd been raised on a home—she supposed it was more of a tumbledown shack. In any case, it had stopped functioning as a home when the old man died.

When Johanna stepped into the parlor, she heard the sound of an extractor fan and clattering plates from the kitchen. She sat beside Tiina.

Tiina flared her nostrils and sniffed demonstratively.

"You smell like the perfumed slags at the market."

"And you smell like a pigsty. I realize that now."

Tanja whispered in Johanna's ear: "Can we trust him?"

"You know who he reminds me of?" Tiina interrupted.

"The old man, actually," said Johanna.

"If Father had been slim. And not as coarse and hairy. But he has something . . ."

Johanna's brow furrowed and she raised a finger pointed like a candle's annihilating flame at Tiina.

"Father's rules!"

Stern eyes on Tiina, rapping her own forehead with her knuckles.

"Wake up!"

Tiina sighed.

"Those saucy little fox-cub slippers. Yeah, what the fuck can I say . . . they're the last thing Father would have worn."

Onni entered the room carrying a large gilt tray on which stood a silver ice bucket with a bottle of champagne sticking out of it. A firm grip on the cork, a resounding pop. He filled four frosted glasses, sparkling eyes looking on.

Onni held up the bottle and it caught the evening sun that was shining in through the window, making both the bottle and Onni's hair shimmer.

"Russian. The best. Baron Mannerheim's favorite."

"Who?" said Tanja.

"Good Lord, has no one taught you that? School? Heikki?"

They said nothing, didn't want to give away too much to this new acquaintance.

Johanna held up a glass and looked right into the fizzing wine.

"I thought fizz was only for old ladies."

"Show me a man who refuses fine champagne," said Onni. "Your father never—"

Tiina spluttered. "The bubbles are going in my nose."

"Sip it!" said Onni. "Watch."

"Don't you have any porter?" she asked.

"Drink up. It sends a delightful tingle through your body. Then I have something to tell you."

He raised his glass toward the feeble sun as the last rays before evening shone in.

"Kippis!"

Three thirsty sisters drank without responding to the toast. Tiina's fizz-related skepticism was long gone.

"No toast?" said Onni.

"No need," said Tiina.

And just like that, the glasses were empty.

"I'd like to see the old man sipping lady drinks," Johanna said.

Onni responded by refilling the glasses.

"Heikki could neck a whole bottle of Russian champagne. My Russian guests were impressed. He was a legend to them. No one but him could take down those big bears single-handed."

The sisters felt themselves growing in stature, they lapped it up, as though the praise was meant for them. And in a way, it was. Johanna was puffed up, drinking, having a good time.

Onni looked at Heikki's offspring and threw up his hands. "I'm glad the interest has been passed down."

Johanna looked him squarely in the eye: "He chose *me* to hunt with him.... I was his right-hand woman. I'm the first huntress now."

"Hmm, you can't always have been with him, or I'd have had the honor of meeting you before. Heikki would come here to sell the season's skins. He'd sleep in my guest cabin, and I'd take him out to the Stadt. He always wanted to go there, to dance with the ladies. That man had rhythm in his big body."

The girls looked at one another, brows quizzical. Johanna grew obstinate: "Are you sure you've not got the wrong bear hunter? Heikki's a pretty common name."

Onni looked at each of them in turn: "Heikki's in all of your faces. I was able to sell the skins for a good price via my contacts in Ulaanbaatar. Well, now for my most important question. Would you like to continue the collaboration? I'll buy beaver and lynx too."

"How will it work?" Johanna said.

"Like it did today. You deliver and get paid for the lot."

"We still haven't seen the money," said Tanja.

Onni grabbed his cell phone.

"Give me your account number and I'll transfer it now."

"We want payment in bills," Johanna said.

"That's a lot of cash!" Onni raised his eyebrows.

"Banks get their claws into you, they control people," said Johanna.

"Can we exchange the skins for things we need instead?" Tanja asked.

"That's more complicated, but sure. The main thing is for us to start working together," said Onni.

"We need a new quad bike. Our old one's clapped out," said Tiina.

"Not even you can drive a quad bike all the way through the enchanted forest and the marshland to the cabin," said Johanna, immediately gasping for air. Now she was the one giving too much away.

"Maybe we could drive halfway and hide it somewhere," Tiina suggested.

"You reckon it'll still be there?" Tanja said. "There's a lot of thieves knocking about in the forests. Maybe we can get another cart."

"You could save up for a snowmobile with caterpillar tracks, that way you can use it all year round," said Onni.

"What does one of those cost?" Johanna asked.

"No idea. You'd need to take out a loan."

Johanna waved her hand dismissively and assumed a resolute expression.

Onni grew animated: "There are seven of you. You're enterprising.

You'll be able to create a little empire for sure. What do you need? Write a list so I know what shops to go to."

For the second time that market trip, they discovered, to their surprise, that they missed Elga. Johanna's meager writing skills did not extend to a shopping list.

"Reckon we'll have to do the shopping ourselves," Tanja said. "There's a lot of stuff we need."

Onni picked up the bottle, it was empty. He stood up and set the glasses on the tray.

"I imagine you're all hungry."

He went into the kitchen, turned on the oven, stirred an enormous iron pot on the stove, then brought in the steaming soup and set it on the table. He walked around the room, switching on strings of fairground-bright lights that were strung from the ceiling. The sisters' eyes followed him. Back into the kitchen. He took the pirogs out of the oven.

"Bon appétit, my friends. My famed meat stew . . . and here's the porter. Made by a little brewery in town."

Tiina got a real kick out of this: "Rice pirogs! Beer!"

"Help yourselves. The freezer is full," said Onni.

They chewed, choked, coughed, slurped, dribbled.

Onni looked on, both amused and concerned by his guests. "When did you last eat?"

"Day before yesterday. Bilberries and—" said Tanja.

"A sandwich at the market," interrupted Tiina. "Do you live here on your own?"

"I travel a lot for work. A woman would have a dull time with me."

"Women adjust," said Johanna.

"Don't you get lonely?" said Tanja.

"Occasionally, if I'm home alone of a weekend. But I get a lot of visitors. You're here now, of course!"

"We live a hundred miles into the forest," Tiina said. Johanna was tipsy and had forgotten the importance of secrecy.

"A hundred! Well I'll be. Did you walk with all that load?"

They all nodded.

"Your legs must have muscles of steel. Your arms too, I see."

Tiina pulled up her sleeves and showed off her biceps, flexing them.

Onni stared at Tiina's powerful, dancing muscles and gripped one delicately, giving the arm an air-kiss.

"So you have no bank account, no car, no snowmobile?" he summarized. "You're living like my great-grandparents did a hundred years ago."

He went out into the kitchen to fetch more porter. Returning, he said to them: "Girls, girls. Don't you ever want to just have fun? You're so very young. It all sounds so strict. You have a cell phone at least?"

They shook their heads.

"So if you break a leg you can't call the doctor?"

"The body heals. It's made that way," Tanja said.

Tiina thought the conversation was getting depressing: "We've got a chainsaw at least. But we'll need to take gasoline and oil back home."

"We can sort that out tomorrow," said Onni. "When can you next deliver? You can have my old phone, it works fine. But you'll need a contract."

Johanna waved him off. "We're not in any registers."

"Oh, in that case I'll get you a prepaid card. We'll need to be able to arrange the next meeting. Or . . . I'm guessing you have no electricity?"

They shook their heads.

"Buy a gasoline generator. But then how would you drag that a hundred miles? My, my, girls, you're really not making things easy for yourselves." He leaned forward, looking them in the eyes. "Heikki had the same odd ideas."

Johanna's gaze didn't falter. "You shouldn't put out to the authorities. Shouldn't mix. You're safer that way."

"He mixed with me in any case. You can stay with me too, whenever you bring skins. I have a triple bunk bed in the guest cabin."

They nodded silently. Tiina belched loudly and said: "Let's settle on a day right now. We'll be here with the goods."

"Agreed. It's a pleasure doing business with Heikki's excellent daughters. You look so much like him . . . it's unreal. Your sister too, the one who stayed here last time. Though Elga, who stayed at the market, she looked different."

Johanna's face clouded.

"Did Simone sleep in the guest cabin?"

With a secretive smile, Onni got up to fetch liqueur glasses and dessert.

"Mi casa es su casa. Let's have some vanilla ice cream and cloudberries."

Tanja got up to go to the bathroom and realized the alcohol had made her legs unsteady—the lines on the zebra skin were fuzzy. She looked in the mirror and flinched. Her mother's stern features, worry lines between her eyes. She touched them with distaste, sat on the toilet seat: a real toilet. So unfamiliar, yet natural, so nice to flush everything away. She washed her face with ice-cold water, pulled off her top and washed under her arms. The guest towel was already filthy. Who was this oddity they'd ended up being hosted by? Was he telling fibs about their father? Why wasn't Johanna more on her guard? Whatever. It was wonderful to eat, to drink well, to have a little fun. This man with his fox slippers truly did have an ability to make everything sparkle, and it wasn't all down to the booze.

By the time she was back at the table eating ice cream, her doubts were nowhere to be seen.

"Tomorrow we must get rid of Laura's junk," said Tiina.

"What kind of junk?" asked Onni.

Tiina went to get the box, then lined up the little figures on the table.

"Oh, look at these little cuties!" Onni exclaimed, to the sisters' surprise. "Look at this girl with the owl face. And the sad elk with its broken crown. I'll take a whole box. My mother has a big birthday coming up this winter, and I'd like to keep a few for myself. They'd look great on that mantelpiece, don't you think?"

Then he bustled off into the kitchen and they heard the sound of clattering china. He came back carrying a tray of coffee cups and a bottle of cognac, to whoops of delight. He laughed. "It's nice when your efforts are appreciated."

He wiped his hands on a napkin and walked over to a sideboard by the wall, lifting a flap and putting on an LP of Russian pop hits. He sang along with the chorus, danced a few steps, and then began educating them on the Russian star.

"An unbelievable prima donna. Do you have any idea what kind of audience you get if you make it in Russia?"

"Don't you have any country music?" Tiina asked.

"Sadly not, sadly not," said Onni, serving the coffee.

The cognac bottle was soon empty, and then everything began to blur and sway. They tottered out into the late-summer night. Took a sauna, beating themselves with birch whisks, then jumped into the lake. "The full moon tonight is even bigger than that Russian's voice," said Onni.

At three o'clock the sisters were in the bunk beds. Tiina woke with a thumping head and a pulsating groin. She went outside naked and pissed a hard stream. She looked up at the house and walked in the darkness with only the moon to guide her, through the garden, in through the unlocked front door, right into the hall—without knocking over the bear poised to attack—past the parlor and into the fur trader's bedroom. The door was ajar, as though he were expecting company.

Around six she returned to the guest cabin and clambered into her bunk. By then, Johanna, who'd been sleeping in the top bunk, was awake.

"You smell like a whorehouse," she hissed.

"Whoops. I took a piss," said Tiina.

"Aftershave stink."

"You're fucking nosy. We arm-wrestled . . . I won."

"The rules, Tiina. The rules."

"Blah blah blah, stop nagging. Sleep."

TANJA WAS WOKEN BY TIINA'S SNORING. SHE WAS LYING ON HER BACK, mouth agape. Johanna had fallen asleep again and was still sleeping. Tanja picked up her clothes from the floor and strode down toward the lake, then dove in. On the jetty was a bottle of shampoo and beside it a soap dish. She washed her hair, soaped herself, and swam in the foam. It was a long time since she'd felt that sweet sting of shampoo in her eyes. She lay outstretched on the jetty in the morning sunshine, warming her body. Her pulse was rushing in her head, she gagged sourly. She heard clattering on the wooden balcony of the house. Was Onni up so early? She rolled onto her front and looked up at the balcony. The fur trader waved and pointed, indicating that breakfast was served.

To begin with they talked in low voices to avoid waking the others. Tanja was shivering from her swim. Her eyes snagged on Onni's fox slippers. His dark brown silk dressing gown glimmered with its gold-patterned design. He passed her a towel.

"Here! Dry your hair. Borrow Oksana's dressing gown, it's hanging in the bathroom."

He put out a coffee cup, a basket of rye bread that was black as night, and a large wedge of cheese. Tanja stared at the holes in the cheese.

"You lot make great party guests, I must say. If you have a headache, I've got the cure: raspberry-flavor effervescents."

Tanja shook her head in spite of the throbbing in her temples.

"If you want pirogs instead I can heat some up in the oven?"

Tanja nodded.

"Pirogs and bread and cheese."

"Drinking makes you hungry," Onni said.

Tanja closed her eyes, enjoying the strong coffee and eating the flavorsome cheese. She cut five slices and spread a thick layer of butter on the bread.

Onni unfolded a map on the table in front of Tanja.

"Please put a cross where you live so I know where to find you. We could take turns when meeting up."

Tanja took the pen, held it cautiously like an unfamiliar tool.

Onni pointed.

"We're here. Where do you live?"

Tanja drew in the air above waterways, forests, and mountains. She wrinkled her brow, dropped the pen. Shook her head, full of loathing at her helplessness.

Onni put the map away.

"I'll ask Johanna. She went there with Heikki. That man's sense of direction was unparalleled." He reached for a notepad.

"Write a list of what you need. Then I can plan which shops we should go to."

Tanja held the pen above the white paper. She pressed it against the paper, so hard the nib broke.

"No one can read my handwriting. I'll say it out loud and you can write."

"Okey-dokey."

"Gasoline. Chains for the saw. Oil. Kerosene. Coffee. Dried yeast. Dried milk. Flour. Oats. Salt. Ketchup. Rice. Nails and screws. Wood glue. Cigarettes. Oooh, brännvin, of course."

"We need to use up all those bills you earned," Onni reminded her.

"Warm boots. Winter coats. Trousers."

"Do you want to buy my old quad bike?"

"We won't get far with it, not over the swamps."

"May I ask a frank question?" he said.

Tanja stiffened, as though she expected something harsh to come out of Fur-Trader Onni's mouth.

"Why do you make life so difficult?"

"We're following tradition."

"Which tradition? Heikki didn't live in the wilderness, you know, he wasn't far from the shops."

"He wanted to protect us from evil powers . . . he thought we were strong enough to handle it."

"Are you absolutely sure he had your best interests at heart?"

Tanja frowned. Wasn't the man in front of her her father's friend? Onni leaned forward and looked her in the eye.

"Brilliance requires a certain degree of madness. Glorious men are not always so kind to their loved ones."

Tanja thought for a long time. She looked down at her sandwich.

"He wanted the best for us. Pines and spruces behave the way people should behave."

"They stay quiet?"

"A pine is never quiet."

"Oh? What do they say?"

"All the things people never say to us."

They heard steps from the hall, and presently, Johanna appeared. She eyed the breakfast table greedily.

"Good morning!" Onni said. "Do you want warm pirogs or bread and cheese?"

"Coffee first."

Onni put a carafe in front of her and she fumbled with the lid. "What a weird thing."

"Just pour." Onni showed her. After a while he added: "So, I guess Tiina's not getting up."

"She's a stealthy cat who hunts at night," Johanna said.

Onni cleared his throat. Johanna turned to Tanja.

"Wake her up if you're done. Otherwise she won't have time for breakfast before we have to leave."

"The cured bear meat will sell quickly. Take my word for it. Then we can go shopping."

He passed the list to Johanna, who stifled an attempt to sound out the words. . . . She balled her fists under the table, it felt like she was exploding inside.

"Didn't Heikki teach you to read?"

Johanna looked up, her demeanor all dark defiance. Tanja got up and went into the house, mumbling something about going to wake Tiina.

"Didn't let you go to school, didn't teach you—"

"One more word and we'll take the skins and leave," Johanna said threateningly.

"All I'll say is that even good men have sides that don't smell so sweet."

When Tanja came back out onto the balcony, she sensed a stifling atmosphere. Johanna's clenched fists on the table, knuckles whitening. Onni thought, *I'm not dealing with cats that scratch, I'm dealing with boxers.*

"Tiina's half dead. I'll make her some sandwiches," said Tanja.

Onni nodded. "Then we'll have to leave. Get the meat out of the fridge. Don't forget the other box of stick creatures."

Then Tiina was in the doorway, hair pointing in all directions. She walked over to the table and grabbed hold of a sandwich, stuffing it in her mouth. Voice gruff: "You drive, Onni."

Tiina poured herself into the back seat, leaned her head on Tanja's shoulder, and snored.

Chapter Twelve

When the noisy, cantankerous sisters had departed the cabin, peace reigned and those left to work from home reveled in it, at least for the first day or two. But it soon became clear that they were dependent on those coldhearted hunters and butchers: every night they went to bed hungry. One morning Aune was awoken by Elga kicking her in the shin and talking in her sleep, right in her ear. The first nights of frost came, and she was forced to seek warmth from Elga, to hold her bony back. Her thoughts were a noisy jumble. *Let them remember to buy covers and blankets. Let them not drink the men under the table and repeat Elga and Simone's mistakes.* Who can resist a cold, strong beer after half a year without? None of them could resist an intoxicant, and once they'd started, Old Nick himself would climb up their throats and scream for more. *Skål. Kippis. Cheers.* Aune pictured Tiina, drunkenly singing her fucking country songs, putting so much into it you'd have thought she was cheering from the bleachers at the ice hockey world championships. *Walkin' after midnight doo doo doo doo.* Patsy Cline sung it miles better. And yet another pint would be ordered before the last one had been drained.

The previous day, Laura's face had been yellow-white and her legs wouldn't carry her. Soon they'd have to force her to move into the house, however stubbornly she insisted on seeing out the winter in Spruceside. Homeless people did it, so why shouldn't she? Yes, but homeless people had lean-tos, sleeping bags, and tents. Or they stayed in hostels when the temperature dipped to minus twenty. Let Tanja remember to buy Laura a warm sweater. She was so thin.

Perhaps death will come to all of us in our sleep this winter, Aune thought ominously. Once the neighbors' boy John Niskanpää had said that the best way to go was to freeze to death: you slip into a pleasant daze and dream sweetly. Drowning is the worst, it takes a long time for your lungs to fill.

Aune went on thinking: How long would it take you to die if you lived curled up in a broken tree? She looked up at Simone, who resembled some prehistoric bird. She was speaking in tongues, reeling off biblical phrases wildly.

"LAUDATE DOMINUM."

Whinnying, mumbling, hissing, suddenly shrieking from her trance:

"YOU ARE DISGRACING YOURSELVES IN THIS DEN OF THIEVES."

They threw pieces of meat up to her. Sometimes she caught them. When it rained, she tipped back her head and threw open her mouth. When it wasn't raining, flies flew into her mouth.

It had now been a long time since it rained. A long time since they'd eaten meat; the dogs were listless. Let them catch a fish today. Aune wouldn't have the strength to cart stones about with nothing but crowberries and wild mushrooms in her belly. Her belly that rumbled and screamed. She ate the skin around her fingers, chewed her knuckles. Simone was going to dry out soon. Let Laura finish the ladder so they could bring her down.

A time of tedium. Laura was waiting for more nails and glue, Aune for books. Tanja had promised to bring a manual on how to build a root cellar. The roof was the tricky bit, they couldn't figure it out. Soon they would have rolled all the stones they could find to the site where the root cellar was to be built, all the stones it was possible to shift without a crowbar. Elga had calculated that they could position two small logs in parallel and push the stones up the logs. Genius! Now, with their log rails, the work of moving the stones was much easier.

Aune rolled stones, rolled and rolled. She pondered new stories and came up with one about the horny capercaillie who'd ranged the forests when Elga was little. Once it had set upon Elga, thinking it would get laid. Tiina was ready to give it a beating, but the hormone-crazed bird would not give in. Tiina was twice the attacker's size, but he thought he was king with his red-painted eyelids. He pecked with his beak and boxed with his wings. When Tiina hit back, he got even angrier. Tiina backed off and the capercaillie reared up cockily. He'd won. But the sweetness of his victory was short-lived: the next day the family dined on roast capercaillie.

On better days, Laura sat by the site of the root cellar, working on the totem pole. She and her sisters worked together in silence, enjoying the stillness. Laura's neck was bent, her eyes close to her work. How could they get her to an optician? And how was Aune going to get to a dentist? Now, with Tanja gone, at least they were spared a wallop on the back if they complained. It was awful to witness how she swallowed everything Johanna said, playing queen to her older sister's king. They talked about the old man as though he were the great god Ukko himself.

Please, Aune fretted, let Tanja bring writing pads, pens, and books from town as I asked her. Otherwise Elga's going to run away soon. She hasn't been the same since she got beaten up. A bitter expression has taken up residence in her face—she looks at us accusingly, her eyes sharp as knives. We're all guilty.

Was Elga more disappointed with her lot than the rest of them? It is said that he that increases knowledge increases sorrow. But if you are without knowledge, Veikko said, you're a sea without fish. Their old man always said people study to make others slave on their behalf. And perhaps that was true in a town where many people go to high school, but in this little wilderness society it was the ones with the biggest muscles and the ice-cold hearts who had the power.

Aune stared ahead of her as she rested. Her arms ached. With no food, your head starts spinning. With no food, you don't even have the strength to walk to the bilberry patch. *It would be at least two days until they came back,* she thought wearily. When she closed her eyes, fish pirogs floated before her, hunger pangs seared her jaw muscles. Shame Tiina had taken the pipe with her, smoking angelica dulled the hunger.

From a distance, that stone over there looked like a white farmhouse loaf. Could it really be a loaf of bread? Could it have been blown here by the wind? She saw the spiders' webs binding together the ferns with glimmering gossamer threads. Is that how it looks inside my brain when I'm coming up with a story? Now the Laura spruce was moving. Stubby, filthy little feet stuck out of the opening. Aune hoped she had the strength to go fishing. She'd stopped speaking, completely.

"they're coming! they're here!"

Aune heard Tiina's raucous voice from miles away and called to the others. Elga stood and stared in the direction of the shouts. The dogs rushed off to greet them.

"Come on! Let's go and welcome them home," said Aune.

"I'd really rather not," Elga huffed.

"Come on! Bring some water. We'll help them carry everything this last bit of the way. They might have a tasty morsel for us, I'm faint with hunger."

How could three young women make so much noise? A herd of elephants was thundering toward them; Tiina whistled, Tanja imitated a crane, Johanna lowed. They could see them crossing the dry swamp: Johanna in the lead, with a walking stick and a rifle over her shoulder. Her backpack bulging at the sides, thank God. Tanja close at her heels, limping, resolutely upright, her whole body straight apart from her arms, which were flailing about. Tiina brought up the rear and appeared to be several feet taller than the others, with some kind of sack attached to her skull like a peculiar kind of headgear. A huge leather bag hung from a rope around her waist.

Aune and Elga were walking as fast as they could with their

stomachs screeching. Aune announced their presence, calling a hello. Elga, with her skinny legs, lagged behind her older sister.

"We've brought you some cold water," said Aune.

"Honeys, we're home!" Tiina said, sweat glistening on her forehead.

She put down the bag of flour in a thicket of lingonberry and drank thirstily from the bottle. "Carry this the last stretch, will you, Aune? Elga, carry me home! I'll ride on your shoulders."

Johanna gulped and gulped. "Hi, by the way. Hi," she said afterward. Tanja drank and Tiina got the dregs. Three mosquito-bitten faces, chapped mouths, scratched cheeks.

"Do you have anything I can stuff straight in my face?" Aune begged.

"Tobacco. Chips," said Tiina.

Elga and Aune binged so fast on the bag's contents that Elga choked.

"Haven't you caught any fish?" Johanna asked breathlessly.

"A few pike is all we've had. And we found some sour cherries," said Aune.

Johanna shook her head like the parent of impossible children.

"You take this sack, Elga," said Tiina.

Tanja had cut off her hair and it was barbed with rough clumps. Elga and Aune stared at Tanja's shaved head.

"I used the furrier's clippers. Just went like this: 'vroom.'"

Johanna's braid was still intact, she stood in front of her sisters with a proud look on her face: "We sold the lot."

Aune clapped her hands together.

"What a relief. Now we'll be fit for the winter."

When they'd taken off their packs outside the cabin, Tiina lay flat on the ground and kicked off her loose, battered sneakers. The soles of her feet black, the balls and ankles blistered and streaked with blood. Tanja's foot was black and blue. Johanna's feet were speckled red with mosquito bites.

"But . . . didn't you buy boots?" Aune said, concerned.

"It was so hot," Tiina said. "You don't think about winter things when it's like that. But Onni gave us the old man's town boots."

"Which Onni?" Aune asked.

"The furrier. He was friends with the old man."

Tanja looked at Aune.

"You're always going to forget something. We'll have to sort that out at the Christmas market . . . and take turns with the two pairs of boots we do have."

Johanna sat down on the big rock in front of the house and stretched out her legs. She caught sight of the little heap of rocks that absolutely no one could mistake for a root cellar under construction.

"What the hell! Is that all you've done? We've just trekked two hundred miles with a load fit for ten massive guys. You lazy asses. Laura hasn't even finished the ladder."

"She needs nails and glue to finish the work," said Aune.

"I bought some," said Tanja. "You can help unpack. I need to rest a bit."

Johanna looked over to the edge of the forest.

"Is the psycho still up on her column?"

Elga nodded. "She's refusing to come down. She opens her mouth and eats what flies in."

"Hope she swallows a big fat pigeon," Johanna said bitterly.

"Do you remember Symeon the Stylite?" said Aune. "Veikko used to tell the tale."

Johanna roared.

"Tiina! Go and get her down. Let's have an end to this Jesus gibberish."

"Watch it! She's got a knife," Aune said.

Johanna stilled herself.

"Ah well, I guess she'll fall down once her muscles have wasted."

Tiina strode over to the pine column and shouted to her sister that there was some smoked sausage for her if she jumped down.

The reply was swift: "May the soles of your feet burn! May the devil's black seed sprout in your loins. May your stretched, sullied bellies split asunder, and the sinful shoot be feasted on by sea eagles."

Tiina laughed, didn't let it get to her, adding to the temptations: "Pirog? Church wine? No? A pack of cigarettes, then. The ones in the green pack, the forbidden ones."

"I am the one you most fear, you godless wenches."

Johanna went to stand next to Tiina. She spoke calmly but firmly to the unhappy soul on high.

"Think of our father's words. You're making an enemy of yourself."

She wasn't used to looking up to talk to someone on a higher level—her neck grew stiff in the awkward position.

"Our father had a pact with the devil."

"You don't know what you're saying, sister. A strange voice is talking through you."

"Our mother was on the side of purity. You go where your genitals lead you."

"You too, Simone. You too, we heard it in town."

"Liar! Your tongue is turning black."

Now Elga too was standing with them, trying to speak to the saint on her column.

"Mother abused us. Including you, Simone."

"Our most esteemed mother did what she could to save our souls. Now it is I who must watch over my damned—"

"You're Simone, not a surveillance camera," said Elga.

Johanna lost her patience and turned on her heel.

"Where's the next nitwit?"

"She's been puking. Now she's in her nest under the spruce," said Aune.

"What's she been gobbling?" asked Tanja.

"The vomit of a marten with a tummy bug," said Elga.

They looked over at Spruceside, where Laura's feet were sticking out of the opening.

"Shall we jump up and down on her toes?" said Tiina, walking over to her sister's aerie.

Laura groaned.

Tiina added a call: "Hello, baby. Come out to your loving sisters. Now you can glue the bear paws on the totem's trap. Tomorrow we're going to have a höstblot. We've plenty of brännvin."

Tanja kneeled down and peered in at Laura, who was lying on her bearskin on a layer of bracken leaves. She was clutching her stomach, whimpering.

"Come out and have some porter, it's mild on the tummy. We sold your figurines and bought you nails, screws, glue, paint, brushes, and a fine file. Everything you could need."

Laura groaned in agony, seeming unresponsive. Tiina called, "Come on, folks! To the tarn. Bring a bag of beer and some sausages. Did you get the buns, Tanja?"

Johanna held up her father's leather boots, which had been on Onni's porch. Tanja took over their father's old ones. She was mortified she'd forgotten to buy hiking boots. What on earth were the others going to wear on their feet when the snow came? The sisters stood around Johanna as she took a sensual delight in pulling on the undamaged boots. The leather smelled good enough to eat, the shaft reached her knees. Aune touched the boot and sniffed her hand. The memory of her father: the feeling it gave her was far from sensual.

And Johanna got a feeling that was just as far from sensual as she went round the back of the house toward the tarn.

"Goddammit! What a stench! Have you been shitting three feet from the house? Don't you realize you need to go into the forest?"

"Stop bickering," said Tiina. "Let's swim, sisters!"

The dogs rushed around their humans' legs, glad of the group activities. Tanja was barefoot, limping slightly. Her foot hadn't recovered after Tiina dropped her pack on it. Tiina dashed after them in the rattlesnake-patterned flip-flops she'd nicked from the furrier.

"Fucking tiny feet for a man. Did you know he files his heels? Ouch, look! I'm walking on huge blisters!"

"I bought some bandages," Tanja said.

"The day you see me fussing around with that shit I'm done," said Tiina.

Elga and Aune trudged after their sisters. The sky and the forest were spinning, their legs were limp and resigned. Tiina lifted Elga onto her shoulders.

"Carried like a baby."

Elga boxed herself free, hissing curses like an angry dachshund.

ONE SHIMMERING, CALM EXPANSE WAS STORMED BY FIVE NAKED BODIES. Johanna dove in and swam with strong strokes, her long braid like a snake down her back, its tuft reaching all the way to the cleft of her backside. Tiina alternated crawl and butterfly, her splashing almost drowning Elga, who was swimming peacefully along. With both hands Tiina gripped Elga's head and pretended to save her from drowning, at which Elga flailed about like a trout just pulled up into the boat.

Aune took a quick dip, got out, and dried off. She ate dill chips while getting a good fire going. Across the tarn: Screams. Laughter. Howls. High waves made the beaver's lodge rock like a riverboat.

Tanja, Tiina, and Johanna sat in a row on a log by the fire. Johanna squeezed water out of her hair. Elga and Aune sat on a log opposite. Hungry drool. They ate and got greasy faces and fingers shiny with fat. The porter's benediction. Five varieties of hot dog belch and Tiina's cascades of farting as a cadence. Their feet, their poor, swollen feet. Another round with the bottle, farewell to aches and pains.

"How the hell did people manage during the war? Here we are, stumbling around all feeble after just a week."

The full moon shimmered on the black water, which had regained its composure. Snatches of mist settled. The reeds rustled as a breath of fall found its way between spruce and pine, running a cold hand across the girls' necks. The beaver looked out and returned to work on its wintertime home.

"Now we have food. For a while, at least," said Johanna. "Tomorrow it's back to work for you, or you'll get a slap. You have to gather mushrooms, berries, and nuts, otherwise we'll send you to the penal colony."

"Now I want you to tell us everything that happened, so we can feel like we've been on a market trip too," said Aune.

"We slept in a cave," said Tanja. "Then the fur trader bought everything, though not the meat, because he already had plenty."

"A little more detail, if I may. Show me you're Veikko's kin."

"The fur trader wants to partner with us. Father did it, they were buddies," Tiina said, her cheeks flushing.

"Can we rely on the man?" said Johanna.

Aune and Elga were all ears.

"Father did," said Tanja.

"Onni wants flesh," Johanna said with a glance at Tiina.

"But I thought he didn't want any of the meat," said Tanja.

"Don't think for a minute those red marks all over Tiina are horsefly bites. Fur-Trader Onni sucks the blood of young damsels." Johanna was stoking the fire.

"Are you going against Father's rules?" Tanja asked, bewildered.

"This furrier really might split the tribe," said Johanna.

"Do we have any choice? Our business with him could mean our survival," said Elga.

Tanja nodded.

"We need to make sure we get plenty of bear, fox, and especially lynx. Ahead of the next market the trader will come to the forest with his snowmobile to collect us. We'll ride with him to market and sell the meat."

"We need to be done with the root cellar and the sauna before winter comes," Johanna said. "Five of us can work. Or four."

Aune wanted to show they hadn't been lazing around.

"Laura has a couple of skis ready but she's at a loss with the fixings. You need metal. We've got leather to work with, but we don't know how to fix the ski boots on. Oh, and another thing: we don't have any ski boots."

"We can tie our regular boots on. That's what they used to do," said Johanna. "Father would have knocked this root cellar up in half an hour."

"The root cellar we had at home was actually a bodge-job," Elga protested.

Tiina shouted, "Stop talking shop now, we've finally got something to drink!"

She rummaged in her backpack and put on her best Father Christmas face.

"I brought presents for everyone." With great ceremony, she handed out T-shirts printed with a picture of copulating pigs.

"And what does this say?" said Aune.

"Making bacon," said Elga.

"It's in English. What does it mean?" said Tiina.

"If you don't get it, I'm not going to explain."

"Where did you buy these?" Tanja asked, pulling on her shirt.

"Get? They were deadstock at some store in town so someone was handing them out for free at the market. These ones have a different design."

"Porn Star. Hmm. Quite clearly something obscene," said Elga.

"You keep that, Tiina, and give one to Elga. It suits you two best," said Johanna.

"Nuh-uh, our sanctimonious Simone should get one," laughed Tiina.

"Great. That'll keep our upper bodies covered for another year or so," Tanja said.

Tiina went on rummaging in her bag.

"I've got more for you."

They whooped and stamped their feet with joy as they were each handed a multipack of cigarettes. Eager fingers pried them open and they drew the first puffs deep into their lungs, their toes. Elga coughed. Johanna rolled her eyes.

AROUND MIDNIGHT, WHEN JOHANNA'S SNORING AND GRUNTING could be heard for miles around, Tanja snuck away to Laura in Spruceside with water, hot dogs, and bread. She was still delirious. Tanja held a cold, damp towel to her hot forehead. She crept out of the spruce shelter and stood quietly with her thoughts in the light of the full moon, the night air holding the promise of a raw fall. She stood at the bottom of the saint's column.

"Psst. We've got a message for you from Onni the furrier."

Whimpering. Guttural sounds.

"He sent a message to you in particular."

Whinnying. Sniffling.

"He sent a present."

Coarse noises came from Simone's throat. "You're fibbing. You're all fibbers."

"Come down and you'll see. Here's the package."

"Trickster."

"It's beautiful."

"So you claim to know beauty?"

"I'll put a pile of bearskins down here to give you a soft landing."

"Perhaps I shall come down to walk among you the day you take away the barbed wire."

Tanja was silent. Simone really was seeing things. Well, at least she'd tried.

"I'll put the present here. Good night."

The dogs lay down for their watch. They went from the nervy one on her column to the sick one in her Spruceside.

That night all living creatures felt the chill. The bears went into hibernation with their bulging bilberry bellies. They would sleep well now, untroubled by shots.

TANJA AWOKE SHIVERING AND SAT UP, RUBBING HER ICE-COLD NOSE. Johanna lay on her back, loudly. Tiina was grinding her clitoris itch particularly hard, as usual after a night of drinking. Aune and Elga lay back-to-back, warming each other. Their clothes were in a heap in the middle of the floor.

On the steps Tanja met with white, white, white. The first snow had come early. She pulled on the boots and leather jacket and walked over to the column. Empty. The saint had climbed down. The skins were still there, but the gift was gone. She couldn't have gone far on her wasted legs. Tanja searched for footprints, but the snow around the pole was untouched. She walked over to Laura's den and peered in. Her sister was sleeping soundly, no longer clutching her stomach. Tanja didn't want to wake her, perhaps she was on the path to recovery. But Simone? Where had she laid her head?

Tanja did a few rounds of the cabin, moving in circles all the way to the tarn. Not a trace of Simone, who must have left her perch before the snowfall. Tanja stopped, looking up at the trees in case her sister had climbed into the branches of a spruce. She called across to the other side. Not a rustle from the beaver.

Wounded feet don't fare any better in Father's oversize boots. She slipped and swayed, was forced to stop and catch her breath. The sky was gray and grim, and the fresh snow looked set to stay; perhaps it would snow more. She stumbled home and woke her sisters. Aune cried out, while the others were remarkably unmoved by the fact Simone was gone, as though they'd long since discounted her as a living being.

For months now they'd thought of the tribe as six people. If Tanja had believed in God, she would have said Simone had ascended to heaven.

The late risers staggered up and made their way out to the sitting logs in the yard. Johanna had wrapped herself in the sheepskin, Aune and Tiina were wearing windproof jackets. Tanja pulled a bearskin over her shoulders and said anxiously, "You see the column? I can't find her."

They shouted: "Simone!"

"She can't have had the strength to go far. She must be somewhere," said Aune.

"Seems she's taken the dogs with her," said Tanja.

They shouted: "Killo! Kiiski!"

Aune and Elga got up to go out in search of them, but Johanna stopped them: "Have you ever heard of a tribe that adapts to its weaklings? The snow will soon be here for real. We all know what needs doing right now. And the dogs will come back, believe me."

The coffeepot began to sing on the fire, their nostrils flared, the pieces of bread with smoked sausage went down beautifully. That's how every working day should begin, for every living creature. Where had the dogs gone? They usually scented sausage from miles away.

Johanna looked hardened—a level of hardness the sisters had never seen before. She was talking with food in her mouth about the plan for the day.

"Today you're galley slaves. Elga, you instruct us on how the root cellar roof is to be built. And someone has to shake some life into Laura. Pole number two needs to go up tonight, the fangs need to go on and the face needs painting. Then the planning huddle and the höstblot."

Tiina smacked her lips.

"Oh, that needs dancing in. All hail the fall sacrifice!"

Johanna went on giving orders.

"First, you'll have to drive this unruly flock to work. The root cellar must be finished by the time we return from the hunt."

"Are you and I going hunting?" Tanja asked, surprised. After all, they had ample supplies of sausage and bread.

"If we don't find any animal blood, one of us will have to be sacrificed at the pole."

Aune's short laugh that broke off.

"What's this new game?"

Johanna's smile was cruel and stiff.

"No höstblot without blood."

Four sisters looked at each other quizzically. Had any of them understood what Johanna was on about?

"I'm sure we'll get something. If not bear, then elk at least."

"Otherwise the weaklings will have to give some blood. They've got to be of some use," said Johanna.

Johanna fetched the rifle and her backpack, sat on the front step, and pulled on her boots. Tanja too.

Soon Elga and Aune were watching their backs recede. Tanja was limping on her injured foot.

"Let's do this!" said Tiina. "I'll pass the stones, Aune you lay them. Elga, you sort the plan for the roof quick as you can."

Aune protested.

"If Simone is out there dying somewhere, we'll regret it."

Tiina waved her off.

"She was already lost."

The night before the höstblot, Simone was racked with chills on her column. She inched her way down and landed spread-eagled on the bearskins. Snow fell on her hot cheeks and freezing body. She crawled round the column and dug in the snow, searching in vain for her present; they'd been bluffing as usual. She got up determinedly and tried to walk, but fell on feeble legs. She slithered a short distance along the ground and lay stretched out in the direction of the swamp.

Mother was calling from there, she wanted to go to Mother.

To leave this roughneck den of sin for good and be united with Mother's pure power. The call gave strength to her weak, frozen wrists, helping her bear the ache in her skull from the cold. Her hair was so stiff you could snap it in pieces.

Stoically she nestled into an ever-rawer cold. The call grew clearer, stronger: *Mother, I'm coming. Mother, I'm close.*

Snow fell in the cold night of winter come early. On bloody knees she was there. She let go and fell softly.

Mother's warmth.

THE GROUND WAS BARE AGAIN AFTER LATE-FALL SUN WITH LONG SHADOWS and damp air. Five naked bodies warmed themselves around a bonfire. Johanna with loose hair and a foxtail skirt. The fire rose serene and grandiose awaiting the moment when it would die back to reveal the perfect embers on which to roast two freshly shot hares. They stole brushes from Laura and painted each other's faces with patterns of ash mixed with hare's blood. They drank beer spiked with vodka to invigorate themselves for the raising of the second totem pole. From within Spruceside Laura could be heard howling in her bed, the pain in her belly seemed unbearable. Elga stuck on the bear teeth. Johanna and Tanja dug a hole with support stones.

Tiina wound the rope around the pole.

"Me, Johanna, and Tanja will raise it. You two hold it in place down there."

Yells. Bellows. Howls. Groans.

And then the pole was upright. They swigged and swilled, beer ran down their breasts, they leaped around shrieking in a flailing dance, shadowboxing against each other's collar bones. Tiina sang in a strong voice,

Blue moon of Kentucky keep on shining.

They drank, gulped, laughed, and bellowed.

Tiina only knew the verses of the country songs, she reeled them out again and again.

Johanna whistled and everyone looked up, wondering why she was interrupting the wonderful whirling, the dance, the foot-stomping, the shadowboxing, the ecstasy.

"My sisters, my tribe. Sit in a circle before me. It's time for my announcement."

She stood with an assured expression on a tree stump and, as usual when she gave a speech, she became curiously eloquent. An unfamiliar voice issued from her alcohol-fuming mouth. Clear, not yet slurred, and without the stammer that used to slow her down.

"We were born from the same bloody crevice. We have strong bear's blood in us. I see you stalling, trudging about half-zombified. You still don't understand the gravity of this. Yes, Tanja does. You can sit here close to me. Tiina, you're one with us, at times. You have the strength, but you don't control it. The next time you ask us to look on as you somersault between the logs you've felled, you'll taste the whip. We have no time to applaud your arts. Do you hear me?

"I see how some of you have opened yourselves to men, your bodies are marked. Maybe more of you than I know have opened your legs. I warn you and repeat: We must work as one body. One single, powerful body. One of us is gone, but she was weak. What's worse is that the dogs are gone. We must hope they've caught a scent and taken off, found shelter in some cave, and are on their way home.

"Winter will soon be here. Fell spruce and scotch pine. Chop wood. Dry wood. Gather birch bark. We need to bring home food. Seven . . . no, six mouths to feed. That means hard graft. We have two pairs of boots. Two sets of winter feet. We'll have to take turns. We'll have to catch the bear before he beds down for the winter, perhaps he already has. We need ptarmigan meat and black grouse and arctic-fox tails for the furrier. We'll meet him halfway, at the cave, on the first of Advent, so keep track of December the first. Your task, Elga: count the days. He'll bring food and alcohol for us. Now we have salt to cure meat with. If I see any of you behaving like slack dicks, there'll be punishment in store.

"From now on you'll obey me, or the tribe will die out. If we mix with others, we'll be weakened. If our father trusted the fur trader, we too must . . . try.

"We're born bear hunters, not harlots. Get it into your heads, you bawdy creatures! Rabbits are supposed to copulate, not you."

She pointed at them each in turn and then swept her arm over her sisters as they listened.

"We," she said, and again: "WE! We have built our own nation. By spring, our land will be marked with four totem poles. We rule here, wild, liberated. We live on our strength and our rage. Our great father is with us. He's in the snowflakes. He's looking down from the moon. He's the wind that blows in our hair. Gives us food that sates our bellies. Our father didn't believe in God and Jesus and all those things that ruined our sister. But one time he quoted straight from the Bible: 'I am with you always, to the end of the age.'"

Johanna took a sip from the bottle of blended nectar and sent it round the circle. She raised her voice, "Are we one body?"

"Yeahhh!"

"Will we survive the winter?"

"Yeahhh! We'll survive anything."

DARKNESS FELL EARLY, A MOON OF GREAT PROPORTIONS LOOKED down at them and lit the scene as they imbibed. The mist was so thick that the creatures round the fire didn't notice a thin shadowy figure bent in agony stumbling toward the circle. The blood was running down Laura's thighs, from her genitals thick bloody clots pushed through; she collapsed, whimpering, by the fire. In the darkness no one noticed at first that one of the clumps had the suggestion of toes.

Aune sobered up the moment Laura collapsed. She and Elga tried to carry her into the cabin, but Laura insisted on going back to her den—she wanted to be left in peace, wouldn't let even Aune sit beside her. Something nasty welled up in Aune. She walked up the bare hillock behind Spruceside, bent over shuddering, her body vibrating from the convulsions, up and out came chunk after chunk of meat. Her breath ragged, she rubbed her mouth with snow. The acid, the revulsion. In the dawn light she looked over at the empty column that had been Simone's home for a couple of weeks. Strange tracks below it, which animal could make those kinds of furrows? A hand, a human footprint. But they'd have to search when it was light. She blinked sleepily and then went to bed. She pictured the times when she and Laura had played for hours in the brook as children. Building clay figures. Focused and silent. She fell asleep, kicking restlessly.

Simone was her first thought when she woke and stretched out her body on the bearskin—her fingers stiff, feet numb with cold. *Laura, the dogs, Simone*, went the echo in her aching head. She stood up, stiff and clumsy, blew on the embers, and added wood. She dressed, put her feet into Johanna's dad-boots, and saw snow-white spruces through the frost marks on the window. She tugged at Elga's arm. She looked up woozily.

"Laura," Aune whispered in her ear. Elga stood up unsteadily, so cold, she was shivering. They stepped out into soft, fresh snow that reached their knees. In Spruceside Laura lay motionless. The sisters carried her into the warmth of the cabin, laying her between two bearskins. She was still breathing, at least. The others were still sleeping deeply with boozy snores.

Aune felt Laura's hot forehead and her own hungover brow, which was almost as warm. She was nauseated by the thought of the fetal blood and membranes being pushed from Laura's body. She recalled what her sisters had said after it happened. Recalled every word spoken there by the fire.

Johanna said: "Good job that sorted itself out. Means we won't have to."

Tiina said: "Do you all understand what happened to Laura?"

Johanna said: "Not even here are we free from the cocks. We'll have to arm ourselves."

Elga went back to bed. But Aune couldn't relax. She had to go searching. During the night, more snow had fallen, but faint furrows were still visible in the snow by Simone's tree column. Aune followed the tracks, which led toward the great swamp. All was cold and silent in the forest. She plodded on, grateful for the leather boots, even though they were several sizes too big. Something glowed in the snow a few yards ahead of her. She stopped short: a mane of red hair where the forest gave over to swamp. Every step was hindered by the snow. She called her sister's name. Silence. A few yards more, heart pounding. As she reached the bundle, she fell to her knees, pulling Simone's body into her arms, slapping her cheeks. She laid her skinny, lifeless sister down beside her, tried to pump her heart into action, but you can't wake someone who's already dead. Aune felt a howl deep down as she held her hand over Simone's stiffened heart. The worn clothes weren't worth inheriting. She took the knife. In her pocket a rolled-up plastic folder with a sheaf of papers inside. She took out a sheet, densely covered with words written in ink. Could Simone write? She looked at the last page and was astonished to see the name: Louhi Leskinen.

Aune made her way home tracing her own footsteps, the plastic folder pressed to her heart, trotting as fast as she could, snot running. She tripped, got up again, tripped. Barged into the cabin.

"Wake up, everyone, wake up. Simone!"

Johanna whined a reply, "What's the crazy lady up to now?"

Aune stamped her foot. Now it was serious.

"Quickly, it's starting to snow again. Hurry!"

Aune paced anxiously on the doorstep while the others readied themselves. Tanja pulled on one of the pairs of their father's boots. Johanna searched for the others, moaning.

"I have them," Aune said. "I'll show you the way."

Johanna cantankerous in worn-out sneakers, Tiina barefoot, Elga in Laura's not-quite-clogs that weren't worthy of feet.

"Follow the trail from the column," said Aune. "Walk toward the great swamp. She's there."

The snow was falling hard. The spruces bent and crouched under the weight of the snow. An icy wind pinched their cheeks. How could the way to the swamp have grown so long? Aune walked in front, trampling the path with their father's boots. They got stuck, tripped, and swore all the way to the swamp. They stomped about in the place where Aune had found the body, afraid of treading on Simone's body.

"She should be here. Next to the dwarf birch. I dug a hole."

They searched in a ring around the birch. Steam from their mouths, frost-frozen manes. Searching in vain.

Johanna was so cold she was trembling. She looked suspiciously at Aune. "Was it really here? Fuck, my feet are dark blue."

"We have to get home," said Tanja. "Otherwise we'll freeze too."

Johanna trudged off back to the warmth of the cabin. "We'll look again tomorrow."

AS DUSK FELL THEY WERE SITTING IN THE CABIN, ENTANGLED around the fire. The wind howled and tugged at the door, snow flung itself against the window.

Still no one had mentioned the word *death*. No one wanted to speak the word out loud. Simone had to be brought home, that was how it was phrased.

Another anxious night. A feeling of ruin, that powers they had no control of had taken command. The dogs still missing. Yet another gray-cold morning in silence. Not even the coffee could bring them joy. Their disquiet could be silenced only by once again treading the snowed-over path to the swamp. Aune and Elga shivered as they trudged off to search for the missing body. They circled the dwarf birch once again and realized, to their despair, that they would be forced to wait for the thaw before they could find Simone. Their feet corpse-stiff. The snow had let up, a few delicate, silent flakes fell, shimmering in the light as a weak sun peeked through. Elga wrapped her bearskin around her shoulders.

They walked in silence toward the lake. They still hadn't recovered from the drunken blowout; Simone's death and Johanna's chilly reaction to their unhappy sister still preoccupied them both. Aune stopped and wrapped her bearskin tighter.

"We'll find the body in spring at least . . . unless the wolves do. Maybe the wolf already has . . . I don't get how we're meant to be able to fish in these clothes, even if we can cut a hole in the ice with a saw and drill. We can't exactly jump up and down to keep warm."

"Johanna's revenge," said Elga.

Aune nodded.

"I thought she was thawing a little at the pole dance there, but then we got a real punch in the jaw."

"How are we meant to have any respect for her?" said Elga. "Someone who has no idea how ridiculous she is, has no idea how we laugh at her behind her back?"

"She thinks she's saving us. Blind faith," said Aune.

Elga stopped and turned suddenly toward her sister.

"I think about running away every single day. If I stay here, I'll lose it, like Simone. But where can I run to? Our parent's ruined house? To town, where I'll be thought of as someone to be pitied?"

Aune sighed. She couldn't think of anything sensible to say. When they'd made their way puffing and wheezing through the forest and spotted the lake a few hundred yards in front of them, Aune asked, "Can I trust you?"

"Why do you ask?"

"The atmosphere Johanna's whipping up is going to have us competing for her favor in the end."

"You know me," said Elga.

"Sure, but if it's the only way you can get food, if you're punished every day?"

"Okay. You can trust me," said Elga.

Aune looked at her sister, looked her right in the eye.

"Swear."

Elga put her hand to her heart.

"Right. I want you to read for me."

"Did you manage to get hold of a book?" said Elga, brightening. The Don Quixote she'd brought back from the market was still too difficult.

"A diary Simone kept closest to her heart."

"Could she write?!"

"No, but Mother could. That's if I've understood the words, the little I was able to read."

"Mother!"

Elga stopped, her features hardened, the lines of her mouth narrowed.

"We have to read indoors, but where?" said Aune.

"Let's head out tonight and read. When the others are at home we can take the winter clothes," said Elga.

"We need a reason. Since we're not allowed to borrow the rifle."

"We'll think of something. Let's hurry to the lake, we need to get our blood flowing."

They stood shivering at the edge of the lake, their teeth chattering, and dropped the line into holes they'd made before, the ice thin and easy to saw through.

Elga stared down into the deep.

"Bite now, little chars, please bite," said Elga.

"Can you see that spruce over there?" said Aune.

"The very thick one?"

"Let's hide in it and start reading right now. I don't want to wait until tonight. But first we need a bite. Think of six hungry gullets," said Aune.

Elga ran in place and wrapped her arms around her body, shook her fingers.

"Look. My hand's purple, I've hardly got any feeling left."

Aune intoned: "Think of saunas. You're sitting in the sauna, your body is warm and soft. The sweat starts flowing, your legs are all red from the heat."

Bite. Pike. Bite. Char. A few morsels for each of them. Survival for the time being, but no full bellies. A salmon trout, please stay on the hook!

Snow fell in great flakes. They crawled into the spruce's shelter. Thought of Laura as they sat on one bearskin and laid the other over their shoulders. They took off their sneakers and massaged their feet, blowing on them. Blew on their hands.

"Okay, there's nothing for it," said Elga and wriggled out, pulled down her trousers, crouched, and peed on her hands. Yellow patches in the snow. Cold behind.

Aune wrinkled her nose.

"Dammit, now it's going to stink of piss while we're reading."

"I need to be able to hold the paper."

Elga held up the first page in the bundle, which was actually the last page of the diary. The pages seemed to be randomly placed in chronological disorder. Elga cleared her throat, staring at the beautiful handwriting. She pursed her lips and frowned.

"I don't think we should be reading this."

"Come on, read it, please!"

"The kids have gone into the forest. I can't manage them anymore. Everything around me is harsh and ruined. I have to write. Seven daughters forming one single, steely body that frightens me, constantly in motion with hard knees, fourteen hands thrashing, fourteen feet kicking. Seven pairs of eyes looking at me with contempt. Bawling, shrieking, howling they are wrestling in the mud over by the marsh. Blood gushing, dried blood on their foreheads. Half a tree's worth of twigs and leaves stuck in their tangled hair. One day there's going to be a terrible accident.

"Every day they almost beat each other to death. They don't seem to feel much pain. Not for a moment do they sit still, aside from Laura, who does everything spectrally slowly. Her watery, dreamy gaze spooks me, everything about her is directed inward, she sits there drawing or forming twisted creatures out of pine cones and sticks. No one can reach that child. She doesn't seem to know what's going on around her.

"Why did Heikki set on me of all people? Why did we have seven kids? He wasn't the slightest bit in love with me, not even that first time when we met at the barn dance. He danced surprisingly well, given how drunk he was and how large his body. I was intrigued too, and noticed how the other women, their cheeks pink, whispered about him, the bear hunter. Look, what a huge man. A magnificent man. Whisper, whisper. What's that grand man doing with that gray little mouse?

"Yeah, why did he only want to dance with me? We ended up in the forest. I remember to this day how I thought his body and his pounding cock were going to end my short life. I remember how I gasped for breath. The pressure on my chest. A tongue the size of a Sunday steak stopping up my mouth. He got off, pulled up his trousers, slurred out 'thanks a lot' as he fumbled with his fly and wobbled off through the forest, leaving me lying there where he'd brought me down.

"My belly swelled, something living was kicking in there. Out came a girl, surprisingly enough. Heikki and I didn't marry, but we stayed together. He was smitten with the baby. He saw her, took her in his arms. Goddammit, you're just like your father, he chuckled. My middle name is Juhani, and she shall be called Johanna.

"Heikki had not a penny to his name, but he owned a run-down farm with a barnyard, a few clapped-out cows, and a small rye field. I moved in, the working days were long. Heikki would be off hunting and I took care of the farm and the children. Veikko was the only one I was close to, but he couldn't take over his grown sister's jobs. My brother had been like a father anyway, he'd taught me to read and write. But you have to keep that a secret or I'll kill you, said Heikki.

"You'll need to keep those girls with an iron hand, they're wild. That will be your task, while I'll bring home the meat.

"He spoke to Johanna—just like an equal—while I was like the mist over the fields on a damp August morning. And yet he always wanted to empty himself in me. I knew it would happen every time he came home from a week or so in the forest, dragging the bear he'd shot. He'd be especially ardent then. His gaze intense. This is how it is to sleep with a cold-blooded reptile, I thought. It always happened after he'd been sitting in the sauna for an hour, he would have drunk twenty porters or more. I think he was repulsed by my face, by my breath. I couldn't understand why he didn't find some damp moss to lie on and just shoot his load there. Why he had to grip my throat and push me up against the wall, or hold me down on the table, pressing my head against the tabletop and thrusting into me from behind. The first time I could yell from the pain, but not the others. Baby Johanna would wail like a pig when I screamed, until he started holding his enormous, blood-stinking paw over my mouth. When he came with a *great roar, there was not a peep from Johanna. It was like she knew it was a different kind of shriek."*

Elga sighed, folded up the paper, and tucked it close to her chest as protection from the damp. Aune was silent, her expression sorrowful.

"My feet are dying. Let's go home."

They walked slowly, saying nothing. The pike and char swung on a stick. Might that make six morsels?

As they limped the last stretch, dusk was already falling, the crescent moon was in the sky. Johanna and Tanja were in the yard, skinning a hare. Tiina was trimming a spruce trunk and beaming all over with the joy of getting to hold a machine and fire up a motor.

Johanna yelled, irritated, "Two measly roaches. So typical. God, you stink."

"Your faces are all rosy. You been jerking off?" said Tiina.

"We're not as horny as you," Elga said in a tired voice.

Elga and Aune fetched a towel and washed the stench of fish from their hands in the snow. Then they went into the cabin and shivered, each wrapped in their bearskins. Elga was on the verge of sticking her blue-frozen fingers in the flames.

Hunger. That hunger. They sat and stared straight ahead with their mother's words whirling inside them, until Johanna whistled to tell them the hare was done roasting.

The sun shone as Elga and Aune walked toward the lake with fishing rods over their shoulders. They were no longer wildly hungry. They'd slept deeply all night. There'd been enough meat on the hares for several mouthfuls and the fish had made a little extra.

Tanja had baked rye buns, which helped their bellies, helped their mood. The ingredients they'd brought back from town would make one more dough. They had to keep close tabs until the Christmas market.

The snow had hardened and it was even more difficult to make progress. They would take a few steps on the hard crust, then plunge through and get a shoe stuck.

The first thing they did when they got to the lake was to sit under the spruce. Elga took out the bundle of paper she'd been keeping close to her chest, took a deep breath, began to read.

"*Johanna got in a temper when the twins arrived, she'd had sole right to my breast and my knee. When the children slept, Heikki stuffed my mouth full with his cock. My mouth is small and I gagged. If Heikki hadn't steered his cock in there, there would have been even more children. It was as though he could sniff out my ovulation. Or perhaps the devil saw to it that an egg was released just after the hunt. It seemed the seed that swam into me after a successful hunt was made more potent by the death of the great animal. He named the twins Tanja and Aune. The names came from two plump young redheads he'd fucked for fun as a lad.*

"*He'd be away for weeks while I looked after the newborn twins, the unruly Johanna, the cows, and the field. I was skin and bone, and surely ugly as sin. He forbade me from getting a mirror. Every time I heard his heavy footfall on the steps, the way he hung up the rifle, I froze like ice. It was what it was. Out came yet another kid with a slit between her legs. He lifted the child in his arms, held it up toward the ceiling. Soon I'll have a whole harem, he yelled, and laughed so hard the beer bottles by the sink rattled.*"

Elga stopped. Her hands were shaking, not only from the cold.

"I think we'd better do some fishing so we can catch something before it gets too dark."

"No, read! Keep going," said Aune enthusiastically.

"*And so there I was again, with twice the belly, this was after several miscarriages. I took them as a gift from God. Aside from one: I gave birth to a dead boy and got a fever well over a hundred. Alone and inconsolable with the dead baby, I called for an ambulance. Heikki, who was out hunting, was furious when he heard about it. Registered with the authorities! You damn traitor bitch.*

"*Let the next one be a boy, I thought, every time my belly swelled. A boy will know he won't be like me and he'll dare to turn to me, to help me with my jobs on the farm. Or even take pleasure in the day's tasks. A boy would speak to me without contempt. Perhaps I'm wrong.*

"*My daughters do me harm. With cold eyes they suck everything from me, while they sparkle and gurgle at Heikki. They want to be close, to sit on his lap, become one with his essence. At the same time, he talks about me with words that make them look at me with distaste. The older they get, the more scared of me they become. Scared of becoming their mother. Their father's knee is their salvation.*"

"Here's a new date," said Elga. "She wrote it a long time ago."

"*I gave birth to twins again. When I saw their sex I lost it, the remnants of my will to live were gone. One of the babies kicked me in the back at night and had an iron grip. The other is feeble and whiny, her arms constantly wrapped around her waist.*"

Elga folded the papers with a snap and stuffed them inside her top.

"My name's up soon. Time to go home."

HOW LONG DOES IT TAKE A PERSON TO STARVE? FREEZING TO DEATH IS significantly quicker, of course. The cold is not the worst. If hunger makes you dizzy and mirthless, starvation disfigures. The snow is whirling outside my window as I write these lines about the sisters' unlucky first winter of freedom. It's going to be minus twenty tomorrow. People in town are worried about their heating bills, the oldest remember the wartime winters when the record was minus fifty-eight.

Fur trader Onni Kvarnholm couldn't go into town without being asked where it was the sisters lived and how they were surviving the record-breaking cold of that winter out in the wilderness. People from miles around talked about the bear hunter's descendants—they'd made an indelible impression at the fall market. No one believed Onni when he assured inquisitive souls that he didn't know where the Leskinen girls were holed up, only in which direction and that it was a hundred miles away, toward the border. *They'll make it through the winter*, he said to these curious folk, *given how skilled the eldest was at hunting, just like her renowned father*. In truth, though, he was concerned. They had plenty of water in their snowbound forest, and they'd be able to shoot the odd bird for sure, but would they be able to get the goods they needed for the Christmas market? Furry creatures sought shelter in bitter cold. Not even thick-skinned types like them could hunt with any success at minus forty.

Onni Kvarnholm called their cell phone in vain. He could only hope they would turn up at the cave on the first of Advent as arranged. But they'd agreed to call and firm up the plans as to what goods they'd be able to deliver this time. The cell-phone battery must have died, and perhaps they hadn't understood how to use the portable charger he'd sent along with them.

On the first of Advent, dressed like a polar explorer, he waited and waited in the cave. Something had happened to the girls, he could feel it. He wouldn't be able to get a search party together in this cold. Not even the hardiest would dare make their way out to the cabin.

On the second of December, Onni Kvarnholm got in touch with a good friend who owned a number of drones, some of them very large. This fellow thought it sounded like an adventure—just think, he might be the one to find these famous girls. The plan was that they would first progress as far as they could with the snowmobile, and then send out the drone. It was a dangerous trip through the creaking, crunching, hard-frozen landscape.

On the drone images they could make out a log cabin with a little outbuilding near a tarn and a great swamp located five miles or so south of Troll's Mountain. There was no smoke from the chimney, so Onni Kvarnholm called the emergency services, and a helicopter was dispatched to fetch the sisters.

The pilot reported that when the two paramedics were lowered next to the cabin, it was covered with snow all the way up to the roof. A snow shovel was lowered and the door was dug free. In the airless interior, a few dazed waifs lay piled on top of each other. Six women intertwined, in the little body heat that remained.

They managed to revive the woman with the long braid and knee-high leather boots right away; her cough was heinous, a clear sign of pneumonia. Four of them were heavy, in spite of their skinniness. Two of them were as light as maple leaves.

The helicopter trip back was perilous, through the whirling snow in minus twenty. When the woman with the boots got some food inside her and came to, she hissed like the devil himself and bit one of the paramedics on the hand, lunging like a rabid dog.

The Town

CHAPTER THIRTEEN

What happens after a catastrophe? How is the work of restoration to occur? Where to begin when absolutely everything has gone wrong: your tribe is wounded, your leader under lock and key. For the first time, the sisters go through whole days in complete isolation from each other. Enjoyable for some; for others, tinged with fear.

Two camps formed, like a country divided by internal conflict over how it should be governed. Apparently, it's not possible to live together in the long term with different understandings of what freedom and independence are, or what constitutes gainful employment.

In any case, the health and social services had a finicky task on their hands, as there were exceedingly few traces of the girls and their parents in the records.

The girls were in such a bad way the authorities thought it would be easy to civilize them into fully fledged citizens, and by extension, much-needed taxpayers.

In that they were mistaken.

WHITE, WHITE, WHITE. A SNOWY CAVE? NO, A WHITE-PAINTED ROOM with a window, darkness outside. Strange beeping sounds from a machine beside the bed. A glass of water on a little table. Laura sat up and drank until her thirst was quenched. She moved her arms and legs. Put a hand to her belly. Strange, the pain was gone. But why was there a needle in the back of her hand? It was stuck there. Who'd put her in this blissfully comfortable bed? She'd never laid in a bed of her own made up with a coverlet, pillow, and sheets. Well, one time when she was little, at Uncle Veikko's house. It felt good to have smooth sheets against her legs, the cover pulled up to her chin.

The warmth was befuddling. She remembered the pain in her abdomen in Spruceside, remembered how it shot through her nether regions so hellishly she was forced to go out to the others. How she collapsed, bleeding, at her sisters' bacchanal and a bloody bundle ran out of her.

Laura recalled scenes from the cabin, uncertain if she'd experienced or hallucinated them. Recalled excerpts, short, hard, sometimes meandering episodes:

Cutting open a hole in the ice. Jigging. Freezing. Freezing. No gloves. No hat. Face frozen solid like a mask to be lifted off. No fish. Hunger.

Johanna's ragged cough as she plodded home with red-frozen hands and an unused rifle. Even Tiina sat, defeated, by the fire. There was nothing in her traps. The animals were hiding, keeping warm as best they could.

"In all my life I've never experienced such a terrible year for ptarmigan." Johanna repeated this sentence again and again as the cough rattled up from its hiding place inside her skeleton.

Now Laura was in the midst of it, she was back on the croft: Snow fell and fell and fell. Her nostrils froze together as she lay in Spruceside. One night, Elga and Aune came and carried her into the warmth of the cabin, laid her down on a warm bearskin. She had a deep aversion to having her sisters' bodies so close, but right then she was grateful for their warm breath. *Where are the dogs? Where's Simone?* She remembers falling asleep before the answer came. Days of eternal hunger, they sat unmoving, all of them. Stilled the hollow feeling with boiled water.

The dried meat gone. Hot dogs, chips—yes, everything—eaten. No vodka, the cartons of cigarettes but a sweet memory. Aune pulled on Father's boots and set off for the forest to gather old man's beard for soup. It was warming and nauseating, suppressing the hunger pangs for a while. Tanja shoveled her way through the waist-high snow to the toolshed to bring in some wood. She tried to disrupt the snow's sense of order with the spade. To loosen it and dig down. But the snow was determined to stay there, stubbornly solid and hard.

The evening sky shimmering pink over a blue-tinged blanket of snow. The evening cold. The night colder. The morning coldest. They laid the bearskins in a row and lay body to body for warmth. "Ring Onni," said Tanja. "We need to get help," said Tiina. "The phone's dead," said Johanna. "Give it here," said Elga. But not even she could bring it to life.

Will I soon be as dead as the old man, as Mother and the phone? Laura recalls thinking in that impotent moment. She fell, powerless, into a daze. Awoke to alarming noises from Johanna, who was seized by cold fever, lay shivering on Father's camp bed, under the old man's pelt.

The wolves howled in the distance, calling their adventurous cubs home for the night. Laura was the only one who heard them.

TWO WOMEN IN GREEN AND WHITE CLOTHING CAME IN THROUGH THE door. Laura looked and closed her eyes again. What did these strangers want with her? Why was she lying here? Had they all been taken prisoner, ending up right in the hell Johanna had warned them about? Aside from the beaver film guy, she hadn't seen a single outsider since they'd left the farm in May. The women in green and white had a strange way of moving, their mouths looked unsettling from underneath.

"How are you feeling?"

"I don't know," Laura said to the green and whites.

"Are you in pain?" the nurse asked.

"The aching is gone," said Laura. "Where am I?"

"You're in the hospital. You're no longer in critical condition."

Laura looked at the name badge on the nurse's chest, the letters blurry.

"A good friend of yours, Onni Kvarnholm, told us your names. Are you Simone?"

"No, I'm Laura, Laura Leskinen. Someone has put a needle in my hand."

"It's a drip, for nourishment. I'm afraid you'll have to stay here until your levels have improved."

"So I'll get better?"

"You will. We've removed everything from the miscarriage. You're receiving antibiotics for the infection, and pain relief."

"Where are the others?"

"Wait a moment while I fetch your notes," said the nurse. She returned with a look of concern on her face.

"We can't find a Laura Leskinen in the system. Nor your sisters. What are your parents' names?"

"Heikki and Louhi, they're dead. Simone too."

"Have you *never* accessed healthcare?"

Laura grew nervous. "What happened?"

"You were found unconscious on an abandoned croft in the wilderness. The air ambulance brought you in."

"Are they dead?"

"Three of them have a drip, just like you. Soon, any day now, you'll be able to sit and have a coffee together. Tanja's in a more serious condition, but it's not life-threatening. One of you—there were six of you, I believe?—wasn't admitted here. I can't speak for her. Onni Kvarnholm mentioned that she was his primary fur supplier."

"Johanna. Where is she?"

"In the psychiatric ward. Other end of town."

Laura woke in darkness, smelled unfamiliar, stale smells. If she hadn't been lying comfortably in a real bed, freed from the stomach cramps, she probably would have cried out. Someone was breathing in the room. Someone was snoring a strange, unobtrusive snore. Not the nocturnal rattles of her sisters. Was there a man sleeping in the same room as her? Prickly thoughts made their presence known.

She recalled Johanna's mocking questions: "Who did you spread your legs for? Which fucking beaver film guy? Why didn't you say anything? If we meet the enemy, we're to come together as warriors. What is it that your thick little head can't grasp? What do you mean you didn't realize what was happening? You know what people do when they hook up? What? You read the Niskanpää boy's porn mags, didn't you? What do you mean, it went so fast you couldn't keep up? Well, well, we'd better just be thankful it didn't turn out to be a kid. This is all for the best."

The world was spinning. Hard voices. Soft voices. The beaver film guy. The gentle waters of the tarn. Her mother's bony hands. Her sisters' shoves. How she was forgotten when her mother bore yet another girl. If the fetus had grown and she herself had given birth, the child would never have played with other children, only with five boorish women. Okay, so Aune and Elga were reasonable enough.

She'd suspected something was up when her belly began to bulge despite the fact she was rarely full. At first she thought she was unwell, but her monthly bleeding stopped completely, and then she understood. She who'd always felt feeble found new strength to begin with. Her little breasts swelled, her nipples darkened, grew tender, she could no longer sleep on her front.

Why didn't the fetus want to stay? Perhaps her food was too unvarying. Perhaps it cared to eat something other than bear meat. But people had grown from such nourishment before. The fetus got cloudberries and chanterelles. The feeling that her belly was going to explode . . . Aune washing off the blood.

Where was Aune?

THE SOCIAL WORKER INTRODUCED HERSELF AS RITVA HALONEN AND tried to shake the hands of the five skinny young women. She asked them to say their names, she was an ace at memorizing things. She noted cracked teeth, missing teeth, sunken cheeks, red-chapped skin, tangled shocks of hair. But also that they were tall, several of them with sturdy frames, and of course, that they looked unnervingly alike. Aside from one, with her perky little nose and watchful gaze.

Ritva put out some chairs and bade them sit down. She sat opposite them, iPad in hand. One of them, Tanja, her facial expression stiff and tense, put down her crutch on the floor beside her. Her right foot had been amputated due to frostbite, the hospital had said. Ritva's eye caught on the girl's T-shirt print, and she raised her dramatically penciled eyebrows.

"Do they still sell those shirts?"

"They were giving them out at the fall market," Tiina said.

"Some trader figured they were unsalable," Elga added.

"That one with the pigs was popular when I was a kid," said Ritva.

"Did you have one too?" asked Tiina, brightening.

"No, but my boyfriend did. He didn't last long," said Ritva, and Elga laughed.

Tanja lost her patience with the small talk, keen to get to the point. "Where's Johanna?"

"In the psychiatric clinic, I don't know any more than that, unfortunately."

"Find out then," said Tanja, severely.

"As soon as I find anything out, I'll let you know, of course. You can trust me on that."

"We don't trust anybody, especially not anybody in this town," said Tanja.

Ritva nodded, noticing the sisters' tired eyes. She'd see to it that they got coffee and something to eat after the meeting.

"So do you only come to town for the markets?" Ritva asked.

"We hate town," said Tiina.

"The forest is lovely, but it must be tricky to be a hundred miles from the shops."

"Every trip to the market is a story in itself," said Aune, even though she hadn't joined the escapades at the market herself.

"What have you got against town?"

"We have our own lives," said Tanja.

Laura looked carefully at the tattoo on Ritva's upper arm—a dragonfly.

"A blue-green damselfly. Isn't it lovely?"

"We would have been fine, if it hadn't been a famine year," Tanja said.

"Our fur business is going excellently. We simply had bad luck, with this record winter," said Aune.

Ritva gave an empathetic nod.

"You're fighters, I understand. Between you, you have a lot of skills and knowledge. Your friend Kvarnholm tells me that you, Tiina, are skilled with engines. Wouldn't you like to train as a mechanic?"

"Nah, I can do it all already . . . did he really say that . . . that I was . . . skilled?"

"Yes, and if you want to, you can get a qualification. Then you can drive by yourself."

"We already drive, and we train ourselves."

"No qualifications needed here," said Tanja.

"Can we see Onni?" Elga asked.

"He's on a business trip in Ulaanbaatar, it says in this email. He'll be home in two weeks. He'd be delighted to help you. He has some money for you, he wanted you to know. He'll transfer it once you have a bank account."

The next sister Ritva turned to was Laura.

"You are a talented craftswoman, according to your good friend. We currently have an award-winning artist working at the adult education college."

Laura pictured a large class full of strangers and shook her head.

"I have everything I need in the forest. The best clay is there . . . My target is a thousand figures."

"Think it over. You might find inspiration, learn new techniques. I actually have one of your little figures, a little girl holding a bear. What are you working on at the moment?"

Laura had never been asked a question like that. *What are you working on?* She perked up.

"Totem poles."

"I love totem poles. Are they miniatures too?"

"Nine feet tall."

"Wow. Do you have photos . . . no, you don't have phones or computers. Do you have a regular camera?"

They all shook their heads.

"I know that you, Elga, got some private tutoring with exceptional results. Wouldn't you like to continue? You can have the same teacher."

"A hundred miles is a bit far to come for school," said Elga. But a hope was sparked.

"You can stay at the adult education college while you're studying. Think it over. Tomorrow you'll be discharged. Onni says you can live in his guest cabin for the time being, you know where the key is. Remember to bring in the newspapers and any post."

"Someone else can do that," Tanja said sourly.

"Onni was just making a friendly offer. This is how things stand: we're sending a construction team to repair the roof and the chimney at your parents' house. When it's finished you can live there. The farm is in the forest at least, even if it's not old-growth forest."

"Who's paying for the roof?" said Elga.

"You haven't paid any taxes, of course, but on the other hand you've cost this district very little. The local authority can cover it."

"Johanna would never accept this," said Tanja.

"Do you accept it?" asked Ritva.

"We have our rules. We're a tribe," said Tanja.

"Is there anything the tribe needs that I can help with?"

"Gas. Then we can take one of the old bangers from the farm," said Tiina.

"May I ask if you have a clock? The time's gone so quickly, we must agree our next meeting."

"We're not complete Neanderthals," said Elga.

"Great, let's say next Monday at ten? We'll see if your sister Johanna can join us then."

"I doubt it," said Elga, who hoped her wristwatch would show the right time. The battery Teacher Leena had given her was running out of charge.

"If you're okay with living five miles out of town, I know an old croft there. You could reach it by snowmobile in the winter."

"If you know about it, lots of other people will too," Tanja said in a contrary tone.

"Actually, only me and my mom do. People are scared of swamps, they think they'll get swallowed up. They've heard about some horse getting stuck and being lost in an old story . . . my mom's dead and I never go there myself. If you want, I can show you the way."

"The forest doesn't have to be untouched, with five-hundred-year-old trees, for it to be good enough for us," Aune said, kindly.

"As long as there's a brook with black clay," said Laura.

"There is! I'll show you a photo," said Ritva and tapped a few times on her iPad, before getting up and showing it to Laura. Aune leaned over one shoulder and Elga the other. Tanja looked hostile and Tiina seemed about to fall asleep.

When Laura lit up at the sight of the photo, Tanja caught and held her eye demonstratively.

"You're squinting, Laura. I think you need to see an optician," said Ritva. "How about you, Tanja, where would you ideally like to live?"

"I'm going home. We all know why we live on that croft. It's our destiny to live where our father hunted."

Ritva looked at Tanja and nodded.

"I get it. Last question. There were a lot of questions today, there always are at these first meetings. A researcher from the local history association is trying to get in touch with you. She wants to write about your legend of a father in the association's yearbook. I assure you the quality is generally very high."

"We don't mix, we told you already. How many times do we have to—" said Tanja, but Aune interrupted, "I'd be happy to meet her. Since I'm in town anyway."

Tanja gave Aune a stern look, but she had no intention of stopping.

"Our uncle Veikko Huovinen worked frequently with the local history association."

Ritva clapped her hands together.

"Veikko! His voice was pure magic! What a shame he died, but he was an old man, I guess. People would drive a hundred miles through a blizzard to hear him speak, going as far as they would to dance. Well, this brings our meeting to a close. You'll find coffee and biscuits in the room at the end of the hallway. Here are some bus passes, food tokens, and a card for gasoline. Hand over this voucher at the sports store to buy winter coats and boots. Don't forget hats and gloves. It's going to be below zero tonight."

PTARMIGAN IN A SNARE. FOX IN A TRAP. "LET ME GO!" LEGS UNMOVING, ARMS tied down. Only the tongue free. "Let me go, you bastards!"

The room cold. No windows. She spoke out loud: "Dear Father, can you see me now, prisoner of these townspeople? Beloved Father, they want to drag me over to their side. By force they brought me from our little home, carrying me off to weaken me, to make me feeble and innocuous. That we had died there in the cabin, a united soul and spirit."

She took stock: her cough had relented at least, the fever too. The hunger was gone, as was the cold. If only she could remember what had happened that night. Mouth dry. The cough so violent her collarbone had snapped. The sounds of engines growing closer, closer, until the noise above the house was deafening. The sound reverberating against her eardrums. Men's voices. Men making a racket outside, shoveling their way in, stomping around the room, and checking on each of them, *they're alive*. The men grabbed hold of her, she was unable to put up a fight.

Father, you helped me kick, helped me battle the enemy, three against one. They gave me an injection, the evil swine. I felt all my muscles melting, the world went black. What have they done to my sisters, Father? Without me they'll fall into any old trap. Men's hairy embraces, they'll climb up onto men's laps. You warned me, dear Father. I won't budge an inch, but my sisters are weak by nature. Was Fur-Trader Onni your weakness too? Were you enchanted by his cigars, by those gilt trays of delicacies and drinks?

Johanna sat up when the consultant walked quietly into the room and took a seat beside the bed. Demonstratively, and with eyes black as coal, she stared in the opposite direction, straight at the wall. Refusing to look him in the face.

The doctor said a soft hello and asked how she was.

"And why am I your prisoner?" Johanna said angrily.

"You were a danger to yourself and my staff," the doctor said in a calm voice.

"Your staff. Listen to how you speak about people. 'My!' When it comes to my life, I make the decisions."

"You were biting and hitting and we gave you something to calm you—"

"You strapped me down and pumped me full of drugs."

"We were just trying to help—you resorted to violence."

"When the panther is captured, she must defend herself."

The doctor hesitated before asking his next question. He cleared his throat.

"Do you remember what happened in the cabin?"

"I'm not telling you."

"You were snowed in, in a house in the wilderness, some of you unconscious from malnourishment."

"What does that have to do with you?"

"It's illegal to allow human life to be lost, if there's a possibility of saving it."

"Everyone makes their own choices."

"You don't think something would have been lost if you and your five sisters' lives had ended?"

"We have our rules to follow."

"Your rules?"

Silence. A long silence. Head still turned away.

"Would you consider telling me about your rules?"

"They stay within the tribe."

"Do the tribe's rules work?"

"They were starting to . . . but now everything I've worked for is . . . going to hell."

"Do you want to carry on with the rules?"

"I've sworn my oath. The rules or death."

"There's no alternative in between?"

This provoked Johanna. "I want to see my sisters."

"They're in the hospital."

"I want to see them NOW!"

"You'll be able to have visitors in a few days."

"So you think you can decide for me?"

He looked at Johanna's averted face, saying nothing. He scratched his mustache and coughed.

"I take it you're the leader?"

"Our father's firstborn, his chosen deputy on the hunt. I've learned to ensure the tribe's survival through him."

"Would you like to tell me what you've learned?"

"If I have no ammunition, I know exactly where the spear must land to topple the bear."

"Without giving away your rules . . . could you paint me a rough picture of how you want to live?"

"In the forest, with the springs, the lakes, the waterfall . . . far from people."

"Who do you see as your tribe?"

"My sisters, the same blood flows in us."

"The life you live is risky . . ."

"And here in town? The snow is black, the sky filthy yellow."

"You were on the brink of starvation."

"We had bad luck. A record chill, a bad year for ptarmigan. I would have brought home food if I hadn't got pneumonia. We were about to make big money for the tribe."

"Do you think you'll find harmony if you return with your tribe?"

"Harmony? I want to be on our croft, that's all."

"Wait out the winter, would be my advice."

"I only take advice from our great father."

"In a week your lungs will be fully recovered. Would you like to eat in the dining room or in here?" She turned to face the doctor and gave a smirk, followed by a grimace of disgust.

"I told you, I don't mix with others."

"In that case a tray will be brought to your room."

"Give me three porters."

"Unfortunately we don't serve alcohol."

Chapter Fourteen

"Prepare yourselves," said Tiina and pulled into the farm, making the tires skid on the filthy snow. Laura and Elga, who'd been sitting either side of the driver, jumped off. Aune climbed down from the back of the quad bike and stretched her legs. The sisters inhaled deeply: raw, damp air flowed through their noses, stinging throats. In a simultaneous movement they looked down at their new, lined winter boots that kept out the wet and the cold. Eight dry feet, forty warm toes. Their coats held up against the rain, and they had hoods. It would never occur to them to put a hat on their heads. Maybe a Russian ushanka like the old man, but you couldn't get them in the shops. Gloves were for pussies.

"Look up there!" said Tiina, pointing.

The roof had collapsed in the middle, and the chimney had tumbled down into the house.

"Oh, no!" said Aune.

Elga sighed heavily. "That hovel should be leveled with the ground. It's not like we can expect any insurance money if we set fire to the miserable heap and report it as an accident."

They trudged through muddy slush into the farm. The ten car corpses were still there, alongside piles of tires and hubcaps. A rusted-through harrow, a red Ferguson in an advanced stage of disintegration, and a bicycle with no wheels.

"How come Tanja ended up back at the hospital?" Aune asked as they walked slowly toward the front porch.

"She got some swelling in her foot," Tiina said. "An infection."

"Where did you sleep last night?"

"Here, in the barn. Couldn't face seeing Onni . . . with some bitch." She pointed at the barn. "The roof's in one piece and there's a little hay left in the loft."

"I almost miss the cows," said Aune.

"It's okay, there's company. Lots of rats this year, big families," said Tiina.

Laura stepped into the woodworking shed and found treasures on the workbench. Here were all the things she'd longed for out on the croft. She picked up each tool in turn as though it were gold bullion she'd found: A plane! A file! A bow saw! A load of nails and screws of different sizes. Glue! Though that had dried up.

Dragging her feet, Aune walked onto the porch, pausing where she'd sat with the dogs at night, leaning her heavy head against them. The loneliness she felt in her breast when her sisters showed off to their father, even Laura and Elga at times. Was it real, or did they feel compelled? She couldn't determine. True, she too boxed and wrestled with her sisters, even competed in the crawling races. *The traveling storyteller must have strong knees*, Veikko always said.

Here on the porch she'd listened to the tawny owl, the cuckoo and the barn swallows. Repeated words she'd picked up from

Veikko, whispered wonderful phrases. She was curious about this local historian, hopefully Tanja wouldn't put a stop to it.

She looked at Laura, who had just come out of the shed, and she remembered how the two of them had sat for hours by the brook as Laura carved graceful little animals from a bundle of worthless wood with a whittling knife. Every figure that came into the world got a story of its own.

She was brought back to the present as Elga pointed up at the roof, where a gang of squirrels were playing on the broken tiles.

"Do you remember what Veikko said about seeing several squirrels on the roof?" said Aune.

"Nope," said Laura.

"It means conflagration. Fire to come."

"The sauna's ashes already," said Elga.

Tiina stomped round in the ruins of the kitchen. The chimney had crushed the kitchen table. The rafters creaked and groaned, ready to give in.

"It's like the house was bombed," said Elga as she walked into the demolished kitchen. "How are those social services people going to rebuild this?"

"There's nothing but shit here," said Tiina.

Aune stood among the wreckage. The only thing left intact was the firewood chest Veikko used to sit on to tell his stories. Aune saw it as a sign, a path was shown to her. How could she bring the chest? It stood there like an ornament, a pulpit. Her gaze swept across the junk. The wading boots definitely needed to come. The fishing rod. The thick wool socks their mother used to knit in a rage—they were coming to the wilderness, along with the basket that held them.

They'd have to let Ritva know the roof had fallen in, anyway. She looked up at the collapsed rafters. The creaking and grinding: they were risking their lives just being here. She asked Tiina to help her by carrying out the chest, while she gathered up her other finds and put them out on the steps.

"What's all that junk?" said Elga.

"Imagine if we'd had woolen socks in the croft. Waders. I want to keep the firewood chest, but I realize it's going to be impossible."

"Weirdly, the sauna stove still works," Laura said. "Let's move it into the workshop, it can go in the abattoir. We need to find wood," she said with surprising vivacity.

"There's wood in the chest. Let's take it to the workshop," said Aune.

She walked over and ran her hand over the chest.

"Ah, it's too heavy."

A rumble and a crash as roof tiles slid down and hit the ground. Laura and Aune stood in the middle of the farmyard—safest place to be—in case the whole place collapsed. Tiina stomped around, grabbed the wood chest, and carried it, groaning, to the workshop. There was a boom as she dropped it once she got there; a wonder the whole thing hadn't turned into matchsticks. She put out stools, got a fire going, it smelled of blood in the poorly cleaned abattoir. Then out strode Tiina with a huge clown's grin across her face.

"Last one to the brook's a loser, bitches."

They ran, tearing off layer after layer, dashing naked the last few yards.

THE SAUNA STOVE'S HEAT MADE THEIR COLD-STIFF BODIES SOFTEN. They sat in silence, aside from Tiina's humming. Aune grew philosophical in the heat. She thought about their way of life.

"Do you want to go back?"

"Weird question," said Tiina. "We can't live here."

"Depends what you mean by *can't*," said Aune. "I'm asking what you all want to do."

Laura thought of the workbench, how easy her work would be with the right tools. Though of course, she could build a bench out there in the old-growth forest, if she had help carrying things.

Tiina was more vocal: "Look at these bodies! Just look how lynxy we are. Made for the wilderness."

"The forest is a given, but you could live thirty miles from town, in the house Ritva mentioned, instead of the very last outpost."

Tiina protested, her whole body making it clear what team she was on.

"You're selling us out to some social services woman . . . just as Father said. They make offer after offer, then they've got you."

Aune appealed to her sister. "Tiina, you can have machines, quad bikes, snowmobiles, whatever you want. I can see you with a workshop of your own."

"Tell that to Johanna, she'll kick you where it hurts. You can drive a snowmobile anywhere you want."

"I want to live closer to town, anyhow," said Elga. "Closer to books, paper, and thinking minds."

"Are you getting all wet over that math genius again?"

Elga grew agitated. "That's rich coming from you! Your whole belly was bright red from rubbing your muff all over Fur Trader Onni."

"Aren't you a perv, staring at my body," Tiina said spitefully.

"You do insist on shoving it in our faces," Elga snapped back.

Aune tried to steer the overheated discussion in a new direction.

"Onni's been in touch with key worker Ritva. He wants to meet us next week."

"Then I'm not seeing no key worker on Monday."

"And how many days can you go without food, you think?" said Aune.

"Don't we have a rifle here?" said Tiina.

"We'll have to visit Tanja at the hospital and Onni's got our money. And we must find out where Johanna—"

"Maybe they'll lock us up in the psych ward too," said Tiina.

Elga butted in, her voice contemplative. "How crazy was Johanna? Something happened every day at the croft. Did she go as psycho as Simone? It was like the worst sides of both Mother and Father in a single firecracker."

"She was busting her gut to stop us getting . . . completely lost," said Tiina.

"That in itself is proof," said Elga.

"What are we going to do if Johanna doesn't get discharged? If they keep her on the psych ward?" said Aune.

Tiina flexed her biceps. "Then we'll go get her. I'll storm in and—"

"She really might get institutionalized," said Aune.

"She's not that fucking bonkers," said Tiina.

"I do want to live in the forest, of course, somewhere a little more old-growth than here," said Aune, "but not so far out in the wilds." Laura agreed.

"We're fated to get away from those controlling bitches at the authorities," said Tiina.

"It'll pass in the end," said Aune. "In any case, we'll have to go back when the ground thaws to bury Simone."

"Feels weird to think there are only six of us now," said Elga.

"Killo and Kiiski," said Laura sorrowfully.

No one said anything.

"Did you know that dogs and humans have walked alongside one another for twelve thousand years?" said Elga.

"How did they figure that out?" Aune asked.

"Carbon dating. They start by taking the—"

Tiina clapped her hands over her ears. "Stop! Got to go out and pee."

She returned with brisk strides, her whole face lit up like the sun. With a wiggle of her hips, she held up an unopened bottle of Jaloviina brandy.

"The old man had stashes all over the place. In the old privy! Okay, girls, time to quench our thirst and still our hunger."

"I can't get my head around why we didn't buy any food," said Elga.

"We bought clothes. Shopping is hard work when you're not used to it."

Aune splashed some water on the birch logs and sprinkled a little on her sisters, one by one, with a theatrical gesture, a pastor's pious expression. Tiina beat them with the birch bundle until their bodies glowed and the dried-out twigs were in pieces. She hummed the verse of a country tune about moonshine in an off-key voice, pausing to gulp from the bottle. Laura declined the bottle the second time it was passed round, for her a single sip was enough. She grimaced: the beaver film guy's whiskey, the nausea.

Suddenly, the door was heaved open. Ice-cold air flooded into the heat. Who was that, standing in the doorway? Who was that, snorting amid the steam?

A rifle was pointed at them, a figure in thin white clothing and long boots stepped into the sauna's heat.

The old man's leather boots.

Aune got a rifle butt in the stomach and collapsed onto Elga, clutching her abdomen, gasping for breath.

"Johanna!" Tiina exclaimed in delighted terror.

Johanna stepped out of the boots, pulled off the hospital garb, opened the door, and threw the clothes out. Raising the rifle to her shoulder, she aimed at them, one by one. Muttering something about getting rid of this hellish psych-ward stench. Then she sat down next to Tiina and walloped her sister's knee with the flat of her hand.

"Budge up, Judas! Sucking the devil's rotten cock. You thought you were rid of me. Eh?! As soon as you were alone for a minute you sucked those social bitches' titties. Give me the bottle!"

She gulped, gulped, reached the bottom, grimaced with enjoyment.

"How did you get here?" squeaked Aune.

"Ran. Dodged that ass of a psych doctor who thought he was going to break me and turn me into the compliant type. Slack little boy cock. Easy to deal with."

"Why did you end up there?" asked Aune.

"Resistance. You wouldn't know what that is. None of you know, you milksops."

She brayed like a sheep.

"Were you that ill-treated?" said Aune, who'd recovered from the blow to her belly.

"What do you think?!"

"Well, at the hospital everyone was very nice," said Aune.

"But I was stronger than him. I'm stronger than anyone. Yeah, even you, Tiina, because you don't have the mental strength it takes."

She looked at Tiina and tapped her temple as she said it.

"You've got to think coldly, Tiina. It's all in the mind."

"Have you spoken to Tanja?" Aune asked.

"I've not seen anyone apart from the doctor," said Johanna.

"Tanja stayed behind so they could sort out a prosthesis. They cut off her foot."

"I called from the loony bin," said Johanna. "But the old bag on her ward just said she didn't have a phone. I shouted at them, 'Can't you carry her to a phone?!'"

"People have phones in their pockets these days, but maybe you hadn't noticed," said Elga.

"Watch it! Soon you'll be dangling like a dead beaver from one of the butcher's hooks here."

They all sat stiffly, trembling in the heat. Johanna's rage would not be mollified.

"Tiina and I are going to sleep here in the sauna tonight: I'm going to give you a good talking to, sister. You other nitwits can sleep where you want. Tomorrow we're heading back to the cabin. We'll have a roof over our heads there, we'll keep ourselves to ourselves."

"We were starving, Johanna," said Aune.

"Because I got sick. That's not going to happen again," said Johanna.

"Without Tanja?" said Elga.

"We'll get her out somehow, I'm sure. I'll take the rifle with me. Good job the old man had them hidden all over the place."

"Is Tanja going to hop there?" Elga persisted.

"Tiina can carry her. We need to get some use out of you, Judas."

Laura, Aune, and Elga limped silently on trembling legs out into the snow. Three hearts pulsing with fear faced the hard chill. Loose snow that had frozen to ice cut their feet as they hurried over to the porch, put on their clothes, and grabbed a few of the moldering overalls that were hanging in the hall. Shivering, they made for the barn and up into the hayloft. On with the overalls and their coats. They lay close, whispering, barely audibly for fear Johanna might be listening somewhere.

They jumped: terrifying shrill laughter from the sauna, turning to screams.

Aune sat up. "We have to save Tiina."

"Tiina's a lot stronger than Johanna," said Laura.

"Johanna's got the gun," said Elga.

"I think it's best we get help in town," said Aune, shaken. "There's nothing we can do by ourselves."

"Okay . . . Ritva," said Elga. "Tiina's got the key to the quad bike. We'll have to walk all the way."

"How can we get away without Johanna noticing?"

"The worst thing is, we need to go right now. Johanna's three sheets to the wind, but when she sobers up . . ." said Elga.

Laura went on: ". . . We'll need to be a good way into the forest."

"We can't take the road and hitchhike, in case they're looking for us," said Elga. "I can see Tiina half-standing on the quad bike, like one of the Furies."

"Get your coats on. We'll take the forest road to town."

Silence in the forest, not a sound was heard. The branches crisply frost-white against a sky with a hint of pale-green glow. How many degrees below zero could it be? The aching cold in their cheeks sobered them, the thought of Tiina in the sauna—difficulty breathing, steam from their mouths. Let nothing bad happen, imagine if they beat each other to death while drunk.

The snow fell, it was in a hurry. It fell thick and it stuck. Father used to say that: *snow that sticks*. There was a difference between snow and snow—any serious hunter had to learn that. At least now they had boots and coats with hoods. Their feet weren't used to heading into the winter warm and dry. They sent a grateful current of thought toward Ritva in town. Could she sense the well-meant beam of appreciation as she lay there, hopefully dreaming, in the witching hour? The sky darkened again as the moon was hidden behind black clouds.

When the alcohol left their bodies and their thoughts had cleared, the hunger came. Their stomachs had gotten used to regular mealtimes while they'd been in the hospital, so they'd stayed quiet. One seldom notices a sated stomach.

Laura turned to Elga: "One of the Furies, you said. What are they?"

"Furious goddesses. Do you remember, Veikko's tales . . . a Fury with armed backup from Johanna. An avenging Fury who wants to punish us for leaving her in the devil's clutches."

Laura was dragging her feet, exhausted. The miles they'd put behind them thronged in her body. What did words mean when Johanna and Tiina might be killing each other at that very moment? She was surprised to find herself longing for the hospital bed, for conversations with the scatterbrained young nurse, Mostafa. But now the most important thing was focusing on putting one foot in front of the other.

A calm night. Not a branch stirred. The crunching of the sisters' footsteps was loud in the frigid silence.

On stiff legs and with the tips of their noses frozen, they stopped to gaze at the filthy gray-yellow light over the city and its starless sky. The darkness seemed hard and unwelcoming beside the city's streetlights. The closer they got to the outskirts, the filthier the snow grew, and the heavier the air felt to breathe.

Why are people drawn to the city's grime? Is it to avoid having to trudge through the snow? The drifts at the croft were always chalk-white and shimmering pale blue in the moonlight.

Why did the townsfolk want all this noise in their ears? The muted roar of the bypass road grew, making Laura's heart grow restive, beat faster. The sisters passed an industrial estate ringed with a barbed wire fence. Mechanics' shops, small sawmills, and furthest in, the old paper mill, shuttered, the smoke no longer belching from its tall chimneys. The white smoke that had been a sign that here the work kept up around the clock, here were jobs for the town's inhabitants. The traffic roared: 18-wheeler after 18-wheeler and a truck full of chickens. Laura heard their panicked cackles, pressed her hands to her ears, and grimaced, taking a beat to shake off her discomfort.

Reeling from exhaustion they made their way across three roundabouts, passed a huge parking garage, and were soon treading the town's sidewalks.

"Town center," Elga read. "This way."

WHEN RITVA HALONEN SLIPPED ON THE WALKWAY UP TO THE SOCIAL SERVICES office it was still pitch-black, but it had finally stopped snowing. Even though it felt a little early in the season, she'd put on her nonslip winter boots. Little cuties. She often used the language of love when talking to her boots—life was easier now that she didn't have to fuss about putting snow grips over her shoes. She stopped, dug out her polishing cloth, wiped her glasses. Now she could see clearly. To the side of the entrance three people were huddled together on the bench. Some homeless people perhaps, though they didn't tend to hang out there at night—they had their tents pitched out by the recycling center. And on a grim night like this, the church should have opened its doors.

Ritva plodded up to the entrance, pausing to brush the snow from her down jacket and hat. She stomped her boots, cursing the fact that the council had bought a pig in a poke when they appointed that shitty company that didn't have the capacity to salt and grit the roads. People were falling on their asses, breaking their wrists and femurs while that low-down company was seeing out its contract.

She tried to push down the stress in her belly over the fifty or so cases she had to deal with that day. Her acid reflux filtered sourly up into her throat. There'd been a real feeling of powerlessness among local residents since the paper mill shut down. Her meetings could be emotional, or sometimes loud and heated. So she made a point of being there two hours before the others, to ensure she was fully prepared. First, she had to down two espressos to wake herself up.

She was holding up her entrance card to the reader when the three figures got up and came toward her. Young, pale, exhausted faces were visible within the hoods of the jackets. She said good morning and tried to go past the girls, but they pressed in on her, and for a panicked second she thought she would be robbed and pushed over.

"We've got a meeting with Ritva Halonen at ten on Monday," Aune said resolutely.

"That's me. But today's only Wednesday."

The sisters didn't recognize her in her giant woolly hat, with her scarf wound up over her nose, and Ritva didn't recognize the sisters.

"We are six sisters. We need urgent help."

"I have a lot of cases. People in this town live difficult lives."

"The Leskinen sisters. The bear hunter Heikki Leskinen's daughters," said Aune.

"Is it you? Have you walked all the way from Kvarnholm's place?"

"From the farm, our parents' farm," said Elga.

"Oh my giddy aunt."

Ritva gasped for breath when she thought of the work she had ahead of her. She fought back the instinct to invite them up to the office, others were in front of them in the queue. But something about their anxious faces and hounded body language indicated something serious. She showed them in and asked them to sit on the sofa in reception to wait until she took a break for breakfast. One of the girls grabbed her arm—the strength in that grip, the implacability. She stopped.

"Our sister escaped from the mental hospital. She's on the farm with Tiina, threatening her with a rifle," said Elga heatedly.

"She may kill," said Aune.

"I'll raise the alarm!" said Ritva. "I have the address for your farm, right? Sit on the sofa and get warm. The bathroom's down the hall. I'll make sure you get some coffee."

She slipped out of her boots and into slippers and went briskly up some steps. Through the glass doors the sisters watched her down-jacketed back recede.

AS SOON AS AUNE, ELGA, AND LAURA HAD CLOSED THE SAUNA DOOR BEHIND them, Johanna rested the rifle on her lap with its muzzle pointing at Tiina, who sat stiff-backed with fear.

"So, Tiina. Even you've been licking those busybodies' asses, eh? I never thought I'd see the day."

Tiina's legs were shaking. Her voice trembled:

"We got money for food and winter clothes . . . she was actually really . . ."

"And that's exactly how they get you . . . I've told you a million times . . . they invite you in, get a bite, and then BAM, the ax falls. Kvarnholm is our enemy."

"That man saved your life," Tiina said, pleading.

"Oh yeah, great. And for what? I've been locked up in the loony bin."

"We could have been dead. How did you get here anyway?"

"Knocked out the nightwatchman. The staff will realize at eight a.m. But by then you and I will be far into the forest."

"Are we going to leave Tanja?"

"We'll go and get her. We can't stay here. When the psych people start looking, this is the first place they'll come."

"She's got problems with her prosthesis."

"Come on, we're going there."

"We're pissed as farts . . . and you want me to drive?"

"When has that ever stopped you? Huh?"

Tiina sighed and looked at the gun, thoughts rushing through her head, which the fear had quickly cleared. Her legs were trembling—they usually jittered with restlessness, but now it was pure mortal terror.

"Are you with me?" said Johanna, militarily.

"I'm sitting right here," said Tiina, her voice uncharacteristically squeaky.

Johanna's eyes were small, very small, her mouth a thin line. She stood up, raised the rifle to Tiina's temple.

"You even sound like Elga. Full of yourself. You've joined Team Elga, admit it."

"I'm with you," Tiina said lamely. She was disgusted by the weakness in her voice. Where was it coming from?

"The others are hare droppings. Am I right?"

Johanna pressed the end of the rifle against the side of her sister's head.

"They're betraying everything our Father fought for. So I have to tidy up. You and I are going to make a clean sweep of it. A great big bonfire."

"Arson?"

"Can't be helped. Then we'll flee to the croft."

"But the helicopter guys know where it is."

Johanna slumped and was silent awhile. She closed her eyes, her back bowed.

"Do you need to rest a little?" Tiina ventured. "You've walked all that way . . . even warriors have to rest sometimes."

Johanna opened one eye.

"Do you know how hard I've fought?"

"Yes, tell me how I can help."

"It hasn't been easy to keep the flock together . . . six wild minds."

"Seven," said Tiina with a grin.

Johanna gave a short laugh.

"Yeah, seven."

Tiina stood and took a step toward the door.

"And where might you be going?"

"For a piss."

"She who pisses at night needs a sentry."

Tiina opened the door and a polar wind whipped her. She stepped out into the darkness, slipped on a patch of ice, and landed on her rear. Johanna laughed loudly and playfully poked the rifle under her butt. For once Tiina squatted to piss. The heat rose from the snow, there was so much piss wanting to come out, her legs trembling, about to tumble again. She got up and hurried toward the door of the abattoir, into the warmth.

They sat down, added the last chunk of wood, poured water on the glowing rocks.

"Do you remember when Father used to come home with his load of meat and furs?"

Johanna recounted the story of how he had once returned with a whole bear propped upright on the cart. The sisters screamed with the thrill of it: the bear was dead, but it exuded power, just like their father, who'd dragged home the body to sell it to a taxidermist.

"We always got resin to chew on and bear paws to play with. We tore at each other with the claws while the old man took saunas and slept for two whole days."

"At least two days, but first . . ."

". . . he'd neck a load of porter."

"Yeah, that's how he taught us to count. One porter, two porters, three . . ."

"He'd down everything in the store cupboard, then collapse."

"Over Mother. Remember her screams?"

"And we'd go to the brook and wrestle."

Tiina beat her breast.

"I always won."

"I let you win, sometimes, from the good of my heart."

Past days formed scenes in their minds, they felt the heat from the stove warm their faces beautifully and the tops of their thighs burned red. Tiina closed her eyes, no longer able to stave off sleep. It took her as she pictured Uncle Veikko talking about the sandman.

"Hey, Tiina, are you asleep?" Johanna asked, kicking her in the thigh.

Tiina looked up.

"I have to slee . . . just a little."

Tiina closed her eyes again, listening to Johanna's breathing, it grew heavier, turned into a rattle. Coughing. Snores.

WHEN THE TRIO IN TOWN HAD BEEN TO THE BATHROOM, WASHED COLD hands in hot water and stared at their pale, alcohol-strained faces and their lips perished from cold, they fell asleep against each other on the sofa. One of them had her feet on the table, which gave Ritva pause—she didn't like that uncouth behavior. What's more, they stank in their barn-splattered overalls. They were snoring loudly, and Ritva went over and prodded them gently, only to be met with whinnying, drool-smacking, rattling coughs and an unwillingness to join the waking world.

Ritva communicated the impasse: "Unfortunately, there's no one we can send before lunch. The police are investigating a femicide. But I've reported it to the psychiatric hospital. They're short of people too, but they'll send someone as soon as they can."

Aune sat up, horrified. "A murder? Last night?"

"Tiina!" Elga and Laura said at the same time.

"Yesterday evening. Here in town, to the east."

They breathed out.

"Stay here for a bit. You're sleeping at Kvarnholm's place, right? And you got bus tickets?"

"Johanna's got Tiina in her grip," Aune said anxiously. "There's no knowing what she'll do . . . now we've betrayed her."

Ritva laid a hand on Aune's shoulder.

"There's nothing we can do for the moment. I'll get some lunch for you. What would you like?"

"Pizza, pirogs, pancakes, sandwiches. Anything," said Aune.

Ritva dug around in her handbag.

"Here's a phone for you. And here's Onni Kvarnholm's number."

Elga received the gifts with great formality.

Ritva showed them patiently how to use it and the three of them followed her instructions with wrinkled noses. The ringtone made them jump. Ritva looked at her own phone, muttering, *Good lord, some people never let up.* The town's financially challenged residents knew exactly when Ritva opened for business.

"If you have questions, go and see Laila at the reception desk over there," she said, taking a deep breath before dashing up to her office.

The sisters slept deeply, very deeply on the sofa. They didn't wake, despite all the people passing, but at the scent of pizza their eyes snapped open. Ritva put down a box for each of them and some cutlery.

"This is how things stand. It will be a while before your roof is repaired. The guys don't want to take on such risky work in this weather. They're going to go over there and cover up the areas where the house is completely open. You'll have to squeeze into the guest lodge at Kvarnholm's place and wait for the move. I'll find out whether the council have any empty apartments. And wait a moment, you're Laura, right?"

Laura nodded.

"Right, right, that's you, yes. I've booked you in to see an optician at one on Monday. The same day you're due to have a meeting with me. Kvarngatan 3, just off the main square. Then you'll be able to sit right where you are now and read that information sign by the entrance."

"Oh!" said Laura, looking at the word salad on the sign.

Ritva's phone beeped. She read aloud:

"The police and the people from the psychiatric hospital are on their way to the farm. They'll send me reports when they're there, but right now I have to get back to work."

She half ran up the stairs. Cursed Rolf the electrician, who should have been there that morning to fix the lift. She popped a heartburn pill into her mouth.

Aune wandered around the room. Laura stood at the window, looking out over the town in the dim daylight. Out on the forecourt a woman was approaching in thin sneakers. She was holding a little child of perhaps five years old by the hand. The woman slipped just outside the door, pulling the child with her as she fell. She lay there, unmoving, and Laura was about to go out and help her up. Then the little girl yanked on the woman's arm so hard and so resolutely that the woman got to her feet.

The woman limped in holding the child's hand and went over to the reception to check in. She blew on her cupped hands, blew on the girl's hands. From the sofa, the girls heard that she was here to see Ritva. Her voice was weak and nervy. Laura saw the girl's thin back in her light jacket, and in front of her, her mom's broad back as they went up the stairs to the office. The girl's short legs struggled up the high steps while her mom held the banister, dragging her sprained foot.

Laila the receptionist was standing in front of the sofa, trying to get their attention. Elga looked up from the cell phone, Laura and Aune from a free paper about Christmas events in the town.

"Ritva wanted me to let you know that they said on the news that two of the Leskinen sisters have been arrested—one suspected of kidnapping and intimidation."

The sisters looked at each other anxiously. Laila went on, "Ritva has asked you to come back on Monday for your appointment."

Aune, Laura, and Elga put their outdoor clothes on slowly, and walked out into the cold with flushed cheeks and shaky legs. The path from the entrance had just been gritted. They wandered awkwardly with their hands in their pockets and their eyes on the grains of grit. They only looked up when they heard a police car pass on the high street, heading toward the town square. What if Johanna and Tiina were in the back seat with bruises and handcuffs. Aune stopped to light a cigarette with trembling hands, and the others followed her example. Dusk was already falling, the streetlamps were coming on.

"Should we use the bus tickets?" said Aune.

"I've never taken the bus," said Laura.

"I have," said Elga. "But where do we get the bus to Onni's?"

Aune looked around.

"Let's stand at the crossing and ask the first person who passes."

The piles of plowed snow were a sooty black, spotted yellow with dog piss. They were on their third cigarette by the time a dog walker in a bobble hat came toward them with a heavyset Welsh corgi on a leash. It looked like the dog was going to topple onto its behind when it tried to take a shit. *"Good dog, Timo!"* said the owner.

Aune walked over to the woman and asked her where the nearest bus stop was. The dog sniffed the hems of Aune's overall, excited by the scent.

"Where are you going?" the woman asked, peering at their stained overalls.

"Past the paper mill, so about seven miles out of town," said Aune. "To Onni Kvarnholm's place."

This woman didn't seem to react to the name.

"Do you know the address?"

They shook their heads.

"Which direction is it in?"

They responded by all pointing in different directions and the woman gave up.

They realized that Elga had the best sense of direction of all of them, and took the direction she pointed in, all the way to Onni's place with a fretful headwind in their faces.

They arrived late in the evening, and were met by silence and the soft darkness.

The moon shone over the lake.

Chapter Fifteen

Onni's cabin was so cold steam billowed from their mouths. The sisters turned on the radiator, which immediately started to wheeze in shock at being put to work. They went to bed in their clothes, Aune climbing up to the top bunk. Laura wanted to sleep closest to the ground—every time she remembered her fear of heights she pictured Simone's face; pictured her sitting up in the fork of the tree. She had violent visions of Simone's fate. Wolves sank their teeth into her body, wolves ate up the dogs. Laura lay awake for a long time, listening to the wind, her body tense. She tossed and turned. Would both Johanna and Tiina end up in the nick, or in the mental hospital? Three left and one with only one leg. What would the old man in his heaven say about his wounded flock?

The others were awake too, thinking dark thoughts until the early morning. If they were awake, they might as well talk.

"I know one thing," said Elga.

"Tell us," said Aune.

"Where Onni locks his bottles up and where the key is."

The reaction came surprisingly slowly.

"I never thought the day would come when I'd turn down an offer of booze," said Aune, "but I don't feel like it. The urge has gone."

"I'd rather have a snack," said Laura.

"Come on! Russian fizz! Celebrating Johanna being in the clink."

"Oh, okay then," said Aune.

AUNE POPPED THE CHAMPAGNE CORK THAT HAD BEEN WEDGED tight in the last bottle in Onni's store. Elga switched on the fairground lighting. Elga and Aune gulped down the breakfast champagne and ate pirogs that weren't quite warm. Laura sipped at her half-full glass. The hunger made the partially thawed pirog taste delicious.

Elga saw a note on the kitchen table—the reminder from Onni to bring in the post. The mailbox was a fair distance away, and the wine fizzed in her legs as she walked. The air was raw, the sky gray, a vague sun tried in vain to penetrate the clouds' dominance. Onni Kvarnholm's mailbox was stuffed with envelopes and newspapers. She recognized the kind of letters—the old man had always torn them up.

Elga thumped the heap of newspapers down on the table, holding up one to show the headlines: *Leskinen Sisters Arrested*.

They stared at the photo for a long time. Naked bodies, blankets over their heads. Handcuffs. Elga read the caption.

"They got them in the sauna."

She raised her eyes from the paper and looked at the other two. "Are we free now, for real?"

Aune reacted angrily: "Don't you feel anything at all for your sisters?!"

"Tiina's still my twin," said Laura. "She carried me on her shoulders when we were little."

Elga didn't feel the slightest bit sentimental. "They've written a little story here. They call it 'The Leskinen Case.'" Aune and Laura listened rapt as she read aloud:

"Last week, during a record cold snap, six defenseless young women were found unconscious in a derelict cabin deep in the forest by the border. They received treatment at the hospital for exposure and starvation. One of the sisters suffered more serious injuries and has been kept in for further assessment, another was admitted to a secure psychiatric unit.

"The girls are the daughters of the late bear hunter Heikki Leskinen. Following in their father's footsteps, the girls are a popular attraction at the market, where they sell bearskins among other treasures of the forest. They are also suppliers to the fur trader Onni Kvarnholm. The girls who recovered are now in the care of the local social services."

"Defenseless . . . ! It's like we're helpless children," said Aune indignantly.

Elga went on reading the paper, chewing bread and slurping down the fizzy wine—soon the bubbles in the champagne began to catch irritatingly in her throat. Laura doodled on a piece of paper. Aune sighed and asked Elga to read the article about this year's bear survey. She'd managed to pick up that much as an almost-reader.

They shouldn't have opened the champagne. A few glasses

of the sticky drink made them thirsty for stronger stuff. Clear liquor, that was the best thing for a session, they'd gulp it down and calm their nerves.

"Drinking just a little is more of a torture than a booze drought," Elga declared.

"Onni will be back tomorrow, and he'll surely stock up. I'm sure we'll manage until then," said Aune.

Laura put her nose to a photo of a bear, she couldn't wait to get glasses.

"This bit's about us too. A reader's letter," said Elga and the others held their breath.

They leaned over Elga as she read aloud: "*The moment some riffraff turn up out of nowhere, the council's always ready, but they treat law-abiding, unemployed residents any way they please. If we have a car or a dog, we have to be content with pennies, no matter that we've been paying taxes all our working lives. We're treated with suspicion, while the real villains are treated like kings.*"

Full of anger and raging shock they put on their coats and went outside. They walked deep into the forest where the snow glittered white and the air was clear. They sat down in the mouth of a cave, looking out at the snow drifting silently down. Each flake took its time before landing.

Laura hushed them, then said, "Can you hear the bear breathing as it sleeps?"

"I can," said Aune.

"Can you hear the beaver making babies in its lodge?" Laura went on.

"Yeah, but they're called cubs," said Aune.

Elga rolled her eyes. "You two are crazy."

They sat there all day like that. The best cure for anxiety was to become one with the floating snowflakes.

WORN OUT, THEY WENT TO BED EARLY. ELGA LAY READING WITH THE lamp on until Aune asked her to turn it off. At around three they were woken by a car door slamming, then another. They lay there, tense and alert. A woman's loud laugh and Onni's high voice.

THE PLEASANT SCENT OF COFFEE AND A TANG OF MUSK MET THEM AS THEY opened the door to Onni's house. They stopped short on the threshold. The woman looked like a Russian boat whore, or a 1950s American film star. But of course the girls couldn't make those associations. They'd never been to the cinema, or seen a film on TV. They stared: stiff-sprayed, back-combed hair and masses of pale pink eyeshadow. The woman swung her foot in high-heeled, sequined slippers.

"Good morning, girls. Come in and say hello. We've got freshly brewed coffee and Russian rye bread."

Onni was wearing a silk dressing gown and he too was swinging his foot: the fox head came to life. He lit a cigarillo and offered one to the Russian. The ashtray was overflowing with lipsticked cigarette butts and half-smoked cigarillos. They appeared to have been up since their arrival.

Onni gestured to the woman.

"This is Oksana. A very good friend of your father's, from Novosibirsk. Your skins go to her company. Russians are simply crazy about furs. Oksana wants real bearskins. Not a matted pelt from some poor animal that's gotten lost and started digging about in the refuse bins here in town. You can't trust the Swedes anymore, they've given in to fake fur."

Oksana got up and shook each of them by the hand, the sisters got tangled in all these limbs.

"Aune, Laura, and Elga. Three of Heikki's seven daughters," Onni informed her.

"A pleasure," said Oksana.

Onni served them coffee, pushing the basket of warm rye buns and apricot jam toward them.

They ate and ate and ate. Piles of crumbs gathered in front of them.

Oksana laughed.

"You're uncommonly like him—maybe not you so much." She looked at Elga.

"I heard all about the drama on the news," Onni said earnestly. "What do you think? Johanna . . . will they keep her in the psychiatric hospital?"

The sisters looked at each other and squirmed, finding the question uncomfortable.

"She's . . . what's it called . . ." said Aune.

"In the nick, we don't know any more," said Elga.

All of a sudden, Onni was every inch the businessman. "I realize I won't be able to get any deliveries from you at the Christmas market."

Oksana stiffened. "That's not good news. Christmas is when I sell most."

Onni looked at the silent sisters, his voice growing more cautious. "Wouldn't it be good for one of you to get your hunting license? Take this opportunity while you're in town?"

It was the last qualification any of these sisters wanted.

"It's mostly Tanja and Tiina who hunt with Johanna," Elga said.

"But who will pick up the baton when she's ill?" Onni asked.

"She's never ill," said Aune.

"This winter was an exception," said Elga.

"Wouldn't it be good for one of you to learn to sew furs? Then you could make fur hats to your own design. Laura, might that appeal to you?"

Laura didn't answer, she was clearly considering the idea.

"Who makes the cone art?" Oksana asked, pointing to the figurines on the mantelpiece.

Aune and Elga pointed to Laura.

"Breathtaking. Pure poetry in their features. I've heard about your totem poles. Do you have a website?"

Laura looked at the Russian, her face a question mark, and wondered where one might buy apricot-pink eyeshadow like that.

"They've been living like hermits," Onni explained. "They're not online, don't have electricity. Are you going to go on in this spartan fashion? If so, you should fix yourselves up with solar roof panels, then you'd at least have light to work by and enough power for a little fridge."

Oksana grew excited: "Take photos of the totem poles and send them to me, however you like . . . let's say by regular mail. It's always fun to get letters, as long as they're not bills."

"I gave you that phone, you can take photos with it," said Onni.

"Johanna's got it," said Aune.

"I've got the phone we got off the social worker," said Elga. "We'll sort it out when we go back to the croft." Inside she was thinking: *If we do.*

"Do you have a pen and paper?" Laura asked. "I can draw the poles."

"You're just as charming as your father, you know?" said Oksana. "People are so insipid these days. Robots who say 'grrreat' all the time. Right? Not much is great about this world."

"It's true, there aren't as many personalities these days . . . well, there's you, dear Oksana."

Onni stroked Oksana's cheek. He knew she was fishing for compliments.

"You don't follow the crowd. And neither did the good Heikki, he had style. Always conducted himself elegantly when we were out on the town, despite his rather worn clothes. Would you like to see some photos of your father?"

The girls mumbled a dubious "yes," afraid of what they might see. Onni pulled out drawers here and there in the kitchen and placed several color photos in front of the girls.

"We always took a photo before the dance at the Stadt."

There he was, as big as a house, in a wolf fur and ushanka. And there he was, in Oksana's arms. There they stood, all three of them, arms around each other. Oksana in the middle, surrounded, her face delighted, in thigh-high leather boots and beaver skins.

"He could dance," said Oksana. "The women buzzed around him and the men clenched their fists in their pockets . . . they were mad with jealousy."

Onni noticed how uncomfortable Heikki's daughters were with all the photos, all this bewildering information about their father. Onni, who had a genuine gift for putting his guests at ease, suddenly took the conversation in another direction.

"I'll get the money out for you today. But you can't go around carrying bundles of cash. People in town are so desperate since the mill shut down that they can sniff out anyone wandering around with cash in their pockets. Ask Ritva to open an account for you. Send her my regards. I'll help you with it."

"I can manage an account," said Elga. "Can I have a cigarillo?"

"PLEASE, MY DEARS, SIT DOWN," SAID RITVA. "WELCOME TO OUR SECOND meeting."

Tanja walked in first, refusing to look Ritva in the eye. She put her crutches down alongside her chair and stretched out her leg with a grimace. She'd been discharged, but it still hurt when she used her remaining foot. Aune said hello to Ritva and sat next to her twin sister. She eyed her ungainly shoe nervously, there was a prosthesis concealed within. Elga and Laura gave Ritva a friendly nod and each took a seat. Tiina was the last to enter, lolling sulkily on a chair.

"I have some news to share—" Ritva began.

Tanja interrupted her: "Is Johanna going to jail?"

"I know nothing aside from the fact that she's in the psychiatric hospital. I'm afraid investigations of this kind can take a long time. The police in this town cover too large a district. I'm sorry."

"Well, find out then!" said Tanja angrily.

Tiina looked down at her hands, which were busy crumpling a cigarette packet. The police interrogation had crushed her. Johanna's aggression in the sauna had made her realize for the first time how alien, how dangerously moody her sister could be. Tiina had been sheltered until that point. She looked at Elga and Laura in a new way. Was this how they'd felt all these years? Fear lurking perpetually beneath their breastbone. The only one who hadn't yet felt the clamp of Johanna's vise was Tanja. But still, Tiina didn't want to talk about Johanna in here with a stranger like Ritva, who seemed eager to tell them something.

"I have good news too. I'm happy to say the council would like to buy your parents' home from you."

"That old magpie's nest!" Elga blurted out.

Ritva went on, "We haven't been investing enough in culture . . . and the house could be turned into a hunting museum, with stuffed bears and stories from our local hunting history. Your father will be the bait. The politicians responsible for culture are in the process of coming up with a name for the museum, something involving Leskinen, of course."

Tanja stared at Ritva coldly.

"It suits you now then? Our father was pursued by the authorities all through our childhood, hounded by the police. He was branded a poacher and all kinds of other things."

"It's true," said Ritva. "But now he's dead and we don't have many famous people in our district."

"We'll never sell!" Tanja roared.

Elga turned to her sister, "Are you going to live there?"

"No, but I'm not going to let our father's name be shat upon by the enemy."

"Your father's name will be honored," said Ritva. "Now I . . . as your so-called enemy . . . would like to set up a bank account in your name."

"We deal in cash," said Tiina.

"If you have an account the council knows everything about you," said Tanja.

"Well, do you have something to hide?" asked Ritva.

"We just want to keep to ourselves," said Tiina.

"And I want to make sure you survive. I won't have time for you later, I can promise you that. Another question. The local historian has been in touch again. She has written about your uncle before—she emailed the article to me."

Aune held out her hand to take the printout from Ritva and looked at Elga with a nod.

"It's hard to believe he's dead," said Ritva. "If I saw that Veikko Huovinen was appearing somewhere I was always in the front row."

Aune's face lit up as though an internal aurora had passed through it. Ritva addressed her directly, and the sourpusses Tiina and Tanja sighed loudly at everything that was said.

"Yes, the historian traveled round the county with your uncle, telling stories. Now she's keen to write about you, as I mentioned before. She might even turn it into a book. What do you say?"

"No!" said Tanja.

"They'll make common gossip of us," said Tiina.

"I'd be happy to meet her," Aune said. "Veikko taught me—"

Tanja interrupted her, "Like hell you will!"

Aune locked eyes with her obstinate sister. "Would you stand in the way of our uncle and father being honored? On your conscience be it."

"This will all end badly," said Tanja.

"Why do you think that?" asked Ritva cautiously.

"Johanna will be furious, I'm already furious." She turned her head to face her sisters. "Don't you see the trap? This woman is reeling you in with sugar. Then they'll take our lives away from us."

"You can figure out together what you want to do about your parents' house, the bank account, and the historian," said Ritva. "Here are the contact details. You do as you please. My next meeting starts in a moment. You're not the only ones living difficult lives."

Elga met her in the middle. "I'll take on the bank account. Aune can meet the local historian."

"Fuck you all!"

Tanja got up and made for the door haltingly on her crutches. She turned around and bellowed, "You're coming with me!"

"I'd ask you to keep your tone civil," said Ritva sternly.

Tanja pointed a finger. "Pull your cunt over your head and you'll have a nice fur hat!"

She tore open the door, steaming with anger over the sisters who remained. She leaned her crutch against the wall and limped out.

It took every ounce of Ritva's will to restrain herself, to quell the urge to laugh out loud. None of her clients had ever said anything so funny. She struggled to keep her tone formal.

"The council has two empty apartments they've placed at our disposal. Is it working, living at Kvarnholm's? Otherwise please let me know. There are five of you after all."

Tiina corrected her, "Six. And we're forest folk, we'll stay forest folk. Spruces don't call other spruces riffraff."

"If you're going to book a new appointment—"

"We won't," said Tiina, getting up.

"In that case, I wish you all the best. Here are some coupons so you can get some new trousers. You need them. You know where to find me. Look after yourselves."

THE JACKDAWS WERE HOLDING A MASS SCREECHING CONCERT AS THE leaden sky hung over the Lily of the Valley shopping mall. Aune, Elga, and Laura were walking along a gritted precinct where every other shop was boarded up. They stopped outside shop windows decorated for Christmas—they flashed, shone, and blazed red. They came to stand outside a toy shop with a giant mechanical Santa in the window that nodded at all the children walking past.

"Can you remember us ever getting any presents?" said Aune.

"We lit candles for the cows. That was our Christmas celebration," Elga recalled.

"Father grilled each of us a Christmas apple on a stick. But wait, didn't we get packages from Uncle Veikko?" asked Aune.

"Once we each got a wooden donkey he'd whittled himself," said Laura. "The ears were pinned on with tiny nails."

"Where did those donkeys end up?" Aune wondered aloud.

"I want nails like that," said Laura.

"Father used them for firewood," said Elga. "Apparently, donkeys burn particularly well. 'I'll set light to you soon,' he said to Mother. I remember how he laughed and laughed."

"You laughed too," said Aune.

"Did we?" said Elga. "Didn't you?"

"No, actually. The old man was a real swine. There, I said it."

She didn't say it in an accusatory way at all. The others tried to remember. Elga looked at Aune skeptically.

"You say that now we've got the answers."

"What answers?" Laura asked.

"Pages torn out of Mother's diaries. We'll show you."

"She couldn't write, could she?"

"She could, we'll read it to you this evening."

Laura was confused. She walked along frowning, then tugged on the handle of the door to a candy store. *Closed on Mondays,* Elga read on the door. Laura found a cigarette butt outside the door—two!—she stuffed them in her pocket. They walked into the warmth of the mall. The stores had not yet opened. The sports store where they'd planned to buy their trousers was also closed on Mondays. They walked back and forth, looking at the ironmonger's sign, pressing their noses to the glass of the liquor store, gazing at all the bottles with their pretty labels.

At first it felt good to be in the warmth of the mall, but they soon grew sweaty in their coats and overalls. Their cheeks flushed and the sweat made the stench of manure rise up into their noses. They hadn't noticed the smell back home, but here in town they could almost touch it. A new scent infiltrated their nostrils as a man with a huge beard hurried past with an enormous bag of wrapped presents in each hand. One store must have been open after all. The beard smelled like their old man would have done if he'd poured a whole bottle of aftershave over himself. They all started coughing and went back out onto the street.

Aune pointed to a sign. "Look! Over there it says Café Me . . . me . . . trow . . . poll. We can afford three coffees, right?"

Elga sounded it out: "Met-row-pol. That's how you pronounce it. Not 'me' as in 'me and you.'"

"How are you meant to know that?"

"By listening to people. How they talk."

They stopped in the doorway and looked around: old-fashioned armchairs with patterned cushions, coffee tables in dark wood adorned with lace doilies. Great big plant pots by the windows, holding weeping figs. Tables piled with newspapers. A gray-haired woman in a hooded jacket sat on a sofa, hunched over a laptop that was open on a table. On a blanket alongside her was a hairless dog in a neon suit. She looked up from her screen.

"Please close the door, there's a draft!"

They stepped inside and went over to the counter; looked at the biscuits, the pastries, looked at each other. Their mouths watered, but they didn't have the money. Not yet.

Aune ordered. "Hi, three coffees." She held out a bill.

"We're cash-free," the barista said.

"Then how do you pay?"

"Card or transfer app."

"Oh, then we can't pay."

"You can pay with a bill, it's just I don't have any change. You could get some cake to bump up the total?"

Aune and Elga chose princess gateau, Laura went for chocolate cake with whipped cream. They stared at the cakes. Strings of saliva from their mouths.

"Sugar?" asked Aune.

The barista pointed at the short end of the bar where the sugar shakers were lined up.

"Sugar cubes?"

"Don't have any."

Aune grabbed a shaker and looked at her sisters with a disappointed shake of the head. They chose a table, sat down, and set to the coffee and cakes with eyes closed in delight, eating so greedily Aune's and Elga's faces got covered in cream and Laura's mouth was ringed with chocolate. The hairless dog jumped down and sat on the floor beside Laura, looking at her with the beautifulest begging expression. Laura put her plate full of chocolate cake crumbs on the floor, at which point the woman on the sofa jumped up and jerked her dog back as though tearing it from the jaws of a wolf.

"Chocolate, for a dog?! It can be fatal, you know." She took the neon dog in her arms, stroking it and smothering it in cute phrases.

Elga went up to the barista who was speaking on the phone about the murder. "I hope they find her. Not a trace yet. Yeah, it's always some dude getting angry when his girlfriend breaks up with him. They can't handle it. Hang on, I've got a customer."

"I can't find any ashtrays," said Elga.

The barista's brow knitted in astonishment.

"There's a smoking ban."

"Smoking ban?"

"Yeah, everywhere in town."

Elga grew irritated, saying loudly to the barista, "If you don't want us in your furnished interiors, we'll go outside and sit at one of the tables there."

"I'm sorry but you're not allowed to smoke out there either. You'll have to go to the park. If you turn left at the door and walk down the street, you'll soon see it."

They trudged lethargically to the park with the vague sense that something went wrong every time they set foot in public. In the park there was nothing but restless jackdaws and a few dog owners with lap dogs in winter coats. The snow got even more piss-yellow, the trash cans overflowing with dog poop bags. Magpies searched the ground for treasure.

"Killo and Kiiski would have killed us if we'd forced them into girdles like that," said Aune. "Weird how empty it feels without them."

Laura nodded with a lump in her throat. Every day she missed the dogs and the hens. Whose necks could she wrap her arms around now they were no longer there? The animals made her feel less transparent.

In one corner of the park there was a snowed-in stage with an artfully carved roof, and in front of the stage, rows of benches. They sat down and puffed away. Laura looked up at a big building on the other side of the river.

"Look at that weird castle."

"It says . . . wait a minute . . . Lib-Libra-ry and Gal . . ."

"Books and girls?" Aune said, taken aback.

"Don't rush me! Gal-ler-y."

"Let's go there this afternoon, once I've got my glasses," said Laura. She took out a cigarette butt and placed it voluptuously in the corner of her mouth. She passed the other butt to Aune.

In silence they looked from the freezing ducks to the fancy building, the arts center they'd soon be stepping inside. A man was fishing from the narrow bridge that led there.

Elga looked at her watch. It showed the same time as the big clock over the entrance to the gallery.

"Your time has come, Laura. You'll find your way to the square, it's over there, straight ahead. We'll wait here."

They trundled round the park a few times. Rummaged in trash cans, finding beer cans to trade in for the deposit, and some bits of bread left over from a kebab. A pregnant woman in a padded coat waddled slowly through the park. Elga and Aune looked at each other and said with one voice, "Lygia!"

They both had unpleasant memories of the fight at the Rec, and wondered whether Buster was the child's father. They sat down on a bench and stared into space.

"How can it take so long to go into a shop and buy a pair of glasses?" said Aune impatiently.

They amused themselves by collecting spat-out chewing gum; the pieces were frozen and hard but grew soft and pliable after a while. They'd got enough for a thick wad each. Who could blow the biggest bubble?

And then she appeared. Her stride uncharacteristically steady, her back straight, a glow to her face. A rare smile.

Aune and Elga looked at her: round spectacles with thin temples.

"It took forever," said Laura. "I was shut in a little dark room with this old woman and had to look into this great big weird machine."

"You went for the glasses like the pastor had," said Elga in surprise.

"The optician said these were the ones that fit best on my nose, they were happiest on my face. Yes, that was what she said."

She removed the frame from her face and held it up carefully, as though it were a big, sacred spider with delicate legs. Then she put the glasses back on, and surveyed her sisters, seeing them clearly for the first time.

"You look like you belong to a totally different crowd," said Aune.

"These ones are just on loan. I have to pick up the glasses made up to my prescription in two weeks."

"Okay. Come on, let's go to the gallery!" said Aune.

On the bridge over to the arts center they stopped to look at the eddying black water that had little ice floes clinking on its surface.

"If Tiina'd been here . . ." said Aune.

". . . she'd have been jumping from one floe to the next," said Laura.

A breath of cold wind grazed the sisters' throats. Steam rose from the river water. The mallards along the shore were chattering with hunger, huddled body to body.

"What shall we do about Tiina and Tanja?" said Aune.

"Think them away," said Elga.

They walked shoulder to shoulder up the palace steps, the walls of the lobby were covered in posters. Elga read, Aune practiced her reading, and Laura was excited that she could see the letters. Storytelling evenings. Author visits. The gallery's Christmas exhibition.

"The Forest My Father," Elga read.

"What do you mean 'the forest my father'?" said Laura.

"That's the name of the exhibition," said Elga. She pointed and read out a notice about storytelling events in the spring. "Something for you, Aune."

Laura stood in front of the gallery poster's reproduction of a painting of chalk-white birch trunks on which the black patches formed bat heads. She was drawn into the gallery, while Aune and Elga walked cautiously into the library. Laura was alone in the large hall, which was painted as white as the room at the hospital. She walked as slowly as the leader of a St. Lucia procession between the paintings and sculptures, going up and stroking the pieces, and touching a grass-green carpet of moss ringed in birch wood. She pressed lightly on the carpet. Then she touched the oil paint on a painting of a group of young children playing with bear cubs. She found herself having to take a few steps back to see.

The children were tugging on a thread that was hanging over the bough of a birch tree. They'd tied the thread around a piece of meat and thrown it over the bough. Three bear cubs were jumping for the meat, but they couldn't reach it. They jumped and fell, and one of the cubs was sprawled on its back. In the entrance to their winter lair, the female was lying, watching the game.

It was just as Veikko had told them: how he and Mother had teased bear cubs. Laura struggled to picture her mother caught up in the game, it seemed impossible that she would have romped about with bears. Veikko had said they knew it was important not to take the dogs with them, and certainly not adults, because then the mother bear would attack. But children could be tolerated.

Kids will be kids. It's a familiar refrain. And of course, children want to play, but what about adults? What are they to do when they want to keep playing but don't want to be a threat to the animals?

How could Veikko's story have ended up here? Laura tried to make out the artist's name, but the letters merged with one another. She took another step back into the room and observed the details of the painting. She discovered a squirrel in the pines behind the children.

In a glass-fronted cabinet there were little wooden figures and some clay miniatures. She walked closer and stopped short in front of an elk and a beaver. She grew dizzy. What were they doing here? Who could she ask? She looked about her, still alone in the great hall.

The next painting looked like a photograph of a girl phantom in a tarn dotted with white waterlilies. A man with a long beard was sitting in a rowboat, trying to catch the girl's spectral image, to grab her with his hands, as though she were a salmon trout, but she slipped from the old man's grip.

Laura tried to make out the title, recognized the name Aino, she damn well knew that Kalevala story by heart. She stood there for a long while, gazing into Aino's eyes, *you can't take me*. She touched Aino's face.

A real person suddenly appeared behind her and said, in a stern voice, "Excuse me!"

Laura jumped. She turned quickly, frightened.

"Please read the signs!" said the gallery attendant.

The man pointed at sign after sign bearing the words, *Please do not touch the artworks*. He noticed how bewildered Laura looked and decided she must be that rare thing: a tourist, or perhaps a person of no fixed abode. Newly homeless, not yet completely broken physically, he thought. The attendant repeated in English, but Laura looked even more quizzical. In the end he lost his patience, walked over to the painting, and gestured to show a hand stroking its surface before slapping the hand away. Laura nodded. She had understood, and yet not. Couldn't you do anything in this town? She steeled herself and pointed at the glass-fronted cabinet.

"Where did those come from?"

The attendant was pleased to be asked a question. A welcome departure from the standing around that came with the job.

"Those are works by local artists and craftspeople."

Laura pointed at the beaver and the elk.

"We don't know her name. But we know it's one of the seven hunter sisters who live out in the wilderness. Beautiful craftsmanship."

"I made them," Laura said proudly.

"You?" The attendant was startled.

"Me, Laura . . . Laura Leskinen."

The attendant grew excited.

"Then I must speak to the curator immediately. Do you have time? She's on a break, but we can knock on her door."

He did. And got a *Yes yes, come in if it's important*.

The attendant peered in.

"We've got a visitor. One Laura Leskinen, she made the elk and the beaver."

The curator got up from her chicken salad and welcomed Laura, grasping both her hands; her smile reached from one earlobe to the other. Laura couldn't quite bring herself to look this stranger in the eye, even though her eyes were friendly. Instead, she looked at the curator's worn jeans, with large holes where her kneecaps peeked out. Over the jeans hung a black-and-white-checked shirt that was several sizes too large. Chunky lace-up boots with a thick sole that looked like car tires. Laura's gaze traveled up again but to just above her pupils, avoiding the terrifying black gravity in the center of her eyes. Round spectacle frames identical to the ones she and the pastor had.

"My name's Tova. What an honor. Take a seat. Cute glasses, by the way. You want coffee and baklava? I got some absolutely fresh ones from the Greek place. You sit down too, Ove. You could do with something sweet."

"No, thanks. I've already had a break."

"There's no one in the gallery anyway," said Tova.

The attendant declined once again and backed out, shutting the door. The curator looked at Laura, who was looking shyly down at the table.

"Your figures are really well liked, I'd even say loved. People are really touched; with a few simple elements you create poetry. It's genius, to my eyes."

Laura looked up at Tova in confusion.

"We'd love to collaborate with you. Would you like to have an exhibition of your work here?"

"I've got almost a hundred of them, though they're back at the cabin."

"Bring them here and we'll fill the place and break our visitor records. We really need more visitors."

"We'll be going there in the spring," said Laura.

In a daze, Tova pushed her glasses up her nose. She pushed the baklava toward Laura.

"Have another!"

Laura did. The sweetness of honey filled her mouth.

"I should probably go. My sisters are waiting in the library."

"Here's my card. Get in touch and tell me your plans. Write your name down here and we can put it in with your figures. You must take the credit."

Laura took the pen that was held out to her. Trembling, cheeks flushing, she wrote in a child's hand: Laura.

The curator took the paper from her.

"Leskinen, right? Everyone's heard of the bear hunter."

Elga ran her hand along the spines on the science shelves and pulled out one book about chemical formulae and another about equations, while Aune sat in an orange corduroy armchair, flicking through an anthology of Finnish folktales. In her pile she also had an illustrated copy of the epic tale, the *Kalevala*, a little book with the tempting title *The Lazybone's Kalevala*, and Veikko Huovinen's *The Sheep Eaters*, about some men of the forest who barbecue sheep, drink, and ruminate on existence.

During their nights in Onni's cabin, Elga had patiently sounded out words with her. It took forever to sound her way through the sentences, but she was reading. She was nearly there. She'd nearly arrived. A tickle of delight in her belly.

AUNE LOOKED OUT THROUGH THE ENORMOUS WINDOW: IT WAS snowing. The streetlights were lit, even though it was only two in the afternoon. Her feet were sweating in the heavy boots, she opened the zip to get in a little air. There was a faint smell of dust as she sat there reading folk tales. A smell she wasn't used to. She was at home in scents like manure, barnyard, dog hair, dry gravel, pine needles, blood. Not dust. It smelled different, good. She took the stack of books and went to the counter.

The librarian was wearing a striped top and had a long beard.

"How much does it cost to borrow the books?"

"It's free," he said in a cheery voice.

"Free?" said Aune with surprise, looking at the pile of books.

"But you need a library card, of course."

"I want one of those."

She was given a form and a pencil and asked to fill in her address, phone number, and ID number.

"I don't have an address," said Aune.

"Your ID number then?"

"Eyes? I've got two."

The librarian looked confused.

"Is your identity protected?"

"Our father was careful to keep it that way."

"So you can't ask your parents what your ID number is?"

"They're dead."

"Are you a refugee?"

"Not exactly."

"Where will you sleep tonight?"

"At Mr. Kvarnholm's place—the fur trader, until spring."

"Onni Kvarnholm! You can put down his address, that'll be fine."

"I don't know it. . . . We just moved in. He lives where the forest takes over."

"I'll look it up. It'll be fine. One moment. Put your name down anyway."

He gave Aune a bag to put her books in and a receipt to show she could keep them for three weeks.

"Thanks!"

She walked over to Elga, but couldn't find her by the science section, and she couldn't find Laura in the art gallery. She went outside. There they were, among the snowflakes, smoking manically by a little garden. It seemed people who visited art galleries dropped their cigarettes after just a few puffs, with a long way to go until the filter. They were talking over each other. *It was funny to see Laura so talkative,* thought Aune. Apparently all it took to loosen her tongue was good vision, something sweet, and a few paintings.

Aune held out the bag.

"I get to keep them for three weeks. For free!"

"No way!" said Elga. "I'm going back in, wait for me."

THEY WERE SITTING TOGETHER READING ON THE BOTTOM BUNK, WHILE the hissing gas radiator stole all the oxygen and gave them headaches. Onni Kvarnholm had brought over some extra woolen blankets for them, like a doting mother. The sounds of Oksana's high laughter and raucous Russian rock music came from the house.

"You think she's moved in?" said Elga.

"He did say he doesn't believe in monogamy," said Aune.

"A horny old whoring goat," said Laura. "That's what Johanna says."

"For once I think she's right," said Aune.

"And yet she refuses to believe that the old man was having his end away," said Elga.

"He was a womanizer too," said Aune.

"That's how Mother got so nasty and bitter," said Elga. "And I was her life's last great torment. Yet another cockless brat."

"We looked after you," said Aune.

"Sure you did!" said Elga, voice full of recrimination. "Like when you stood behind me and said *fall backward, fall backward, we'll catch you* and I hit my head on the ground."

"I wasn't exactly the leader of that game," Aune said defensively.

"But you joined in."

"I don't remember."

"You were too little."

Since they'd gotten into childhood memories, Aune suggested they might as well read the last part of their mother's diary.

"Can I try?"

"I don't get it . . . did you write for Mother, Elga?" Laura wondered.

"Absolutely not, Mother avoided me. The loathing was mutual." Aune explained.

"She wrote it herself, but kept it a secret from everyone apart from Simone. Our father didn't want us to be able to read."

"Old bastard," said Laura.

"Yeah, old fucker," said Aune, and began to read what remained of the diary.

"*My dear brother tells me I must teach them to read. I must not deny them the power of stories to thrill, like the thrill of God's light. It can leave you hanging, but not hungover. Veikko praises my imagination. I've been given a gift, he says. And of course I do feel it. But none of my daughters has any knowledge of my feeling for words. They don't know that many of the tales Veikko tells are my stories.*

"*There wasn't a penny to spend on toys when we were young. I would give Veikko ghost stories for his birthday. Tales about little children in houses with guests in the attic. About little children who lived in a cave in the forest near the swamp when they buried their dead mother.*

"*The words formed a bond of imagination between Veikko and me. Why do you do this to your daughters, dear sister? Veikko says. But Heikki always says that those who study and write do so in order* to have power over others. Everyone who works with their head has an oppressor's soul deep down.

"We kept it secret. My secret gave me a rush when the girls were around. I felt like a killer bear when I wrote. I reigned supreme then. The rush I got was stronger than their worship of brännvin.

"I've given birth in the fields, in the barn, in the attic. When Elga came along I gave birth on the kitchen bench like any other woman would. The Niskanpää woman was there to help and she pulled out the unwanted child. She looked at me with pity when she caught sight of the child's slit. I pretended she wasn't born, that was my only salvation. Heikki accused me of having got knocked up by someone else. She was nothing like her sisters, she was made different. 'The pastor or the huntmaster?' he fumed. How could I prove it was neither of them?

"Heikki was seldom home and for me it was hell just getting through the day, what with all the animals and the rye field. It was impossible to get the girls to lift a finger. It was like Heikki and the girls had their own lives. More important lives. The boozing. The motors. The wrestling. They had other things to do, and they took care of Elga, the smallest child I'd borne. Small but with a shrill voice. Her cries even drowned out Tiina's.

"There was an electric fence between us. We took detours so we wouldn't get shocks. My own girls looked down on me. When I went down to the lake, wet through with sweat from the harvest, they were all lying around exhausted after a swimming competition. The hum of their voices died down the moment they caught sight of me. Their hostile, penetrating gazes locked on to me as I took off my sweaty rags. They looked my body up and down, eyes snagging on my round, dimpled thighs. Turning their heads away in revulsion, whispering to *one another. As I stumbled into the water on tired, wavering legs instead of diving, I could hear their muffled snickers.*

"Over the years the rage grew, but where anger rose, my fear rose too. My terror ate me from within. I was afraid to let my dread of them show.

"Seven daughters.

"One day they'll kill me."

Chapter Sixteen

What does it take for a chief to let go? A lot. The leader doesn't want to lose face, the leader fears the lonely darkness. Going from a tribe to abandonment is painful. But then begins a new power struggle. That's been the way throughout human history.

JOHANNA STIFFENED WHEN THE DOOR OPENED AND THE CLINIC'S senior psychiatrist entered cautiously. *Is this the executioner at the door?* He said hello and sat on a chair by the bed. Johanna saw herself as the enemy's prisoner in the white torture room. She'd had a taste of freedom, but now she was locked up again. *Is this what it is to be dead?*

As usual, she turned her head away, refusing to meet his gaze.

"How are you?" asked the doctor.

"What do you think?!"

"I'm sorry, but the police were required to take action, you attacked them, threatening them with a rifle."

"I was defending myself."

"You were in a nervous, violent state, that's why you're here."

Silence. The doctor crossed one leg over the other. Sat that way awhile before remembering it restricted blood flow.

"Can we talk?" he attempted quietly.

"Shut it!"

"If you agree to talk, we can take you out of isolation. Give it some consideration."

"I only talk to my tribe."

"You kidnapped and threatened your sister."

"She betrayed me. They all betrayed me. They broke the rules."

"Which rules?"

"Our father's rules. Now everything's been sabotaged."

"And what will happen then?"

"The tribe will founder. The tribe of the bear will thrive."

The doctor just caught a laugh before it slipped out.

"Are you planning to try and assemble the members again?"

"I've given up. My underlings have got no balls."

"Could that be liberating for you?"

Silence.

"The game is over. I was too weak. Father is punishing me, he's disappointed."

"Your father's words have been a powerful force in your life."

"The strength, the light, the struggle against all weakness."

"You are a force in yourself. Is it impossible to meet your father eye to eye?"

"He's dead! Don't you realize that?!" Johanna shouted.

The doctor sat quietly, not a sound could be heard in the room, apart from Johanna's breathing. He got up quietly, went out, and shut the door.

The doctor massaged his sore neck as he sat at his desk and read patient records. Now and then he looked up from the screen and looked out into the half daylight. The monstera by the window hung apathetically. It was up in the thirties out there, the snow was shrinking, melting, was this wolf-winter finally coming to an end? The muscles at the corners of his eyes were twitching. He was struggling under the weight of a certain anxiety, conscious of what constituted appropriate behavior, conscious of professionalism, he didn't want to jeopardize his good reputation in town. He was afraid of revealing to his staff that he harbored certain feelings toward this patient.

He got up and looked out over the grounds. Grit-flecked heaps of snow, gray sky. He was in the habit of examining his feelings—was trying now to analyze this new interest that filled him with heat and vigor. Was his eagerness rooted in his familiarity with the myths this family, the bear hunter and his daughters, were swathed in? They were the talk of every dining table, their adventures had become watercooler fare. Unhelpfully, all this added an extra frisson to his encounters, even for a man of high moral sensibility. Or perhaps it was the rather dangerous, masculine act she put on that had begun to titillate him? She was extremely imposing.

He sat down again, looked at the clock, swallowing and swallowing again as the door opened. When Johanna entered, he greeted her as neutrally as he could manage. She sat in front of him, slouching in the chair and brushing her hair, which glinted and shimmered. After just a few weeks, she'd assumed a more balanced demeanor— the blackness in her and her poorly developed impulse control had responded very well to the serotonin-boosting medication. She had even started washing her auburn hair, which flowed all the way down to her rear. But it could never be cut, she was decided on that point. He took in her broad forehead, thick eyebrows, and oval nostrils.

"You keep it so hot in here," she said.

"And here I was, thinking it was cold. There's a draft from the window even though I've closed the vent."

She took a packet of cigarettes from her trouser pocket and stuck one in the corner of her mouth.

"You know smoking is forbidden."

"Not for me."

"We have rules that must be followed, even here. It applies to you as much as to all the others."

Johanna sighed and got up so quickly her chair toppled backward.

"Then I guess I'll go outside."

"You'll come back here and sit down! Here."

Johanna stopped in the doorway. Something in the doctor's metallic, commanding voice made her turn and come back to sit once again in front of the desk. She shoved the brush in her trouser pocket.

"What do you want to do once you're discharged?"

"I don't want to hunt, that's for sure."

"In spite of your skill?"

"Don't feel like it anymore."

"What do you find fun?"

"Nothing . . . well, smoking, drinking. That's fun."

"Nothing else? Do you play any instruments?"

"No fucking way!"

"Do you read books? Any favorite authors?"

"None. Not even my uncle. Everyone's constantly going on about him, but he was deadly dull."

"Do you play sports?"

"Nah. Well, wrestling."

"We've got a good team here in town. You could join when you—"

"A team! Get it into your head . . . we're solitary forest folk, we'll stay forest folk."

"You could become a biologist, working in the field."

"Fucking geeks. I'll take off to the forest, to my croft, and find something there. Live on fish, berries, nuts."

She leaned forward, she was close now.

"You coming out for a smoke?"

"No, thanks. I'm not a smoker."

She stood abruptly and he said gently: "Tomorrow, same time."

Weeks turned to months. The conversations continued. On this particular morning, the spring sunlight was shining sharply in through the window, the windowsill was dusty. The monstera's leaves were dusty too. The doctor was forced to lower the blinds so he wouldn't be dazzled.

As always, Johanna turned up a little late with an air of cigarette smoke and an intensity that brought the office to life.

"Hiya." Her arms a windmill.

"Good morning, how are you today?"

"What are you doing, sitting here in the dark?"

This morning too she sat down in the chair in front of him and conducted her usual ritual: brushing her freshly washed auburn hair. The consultant leaned back in his chair and watched her, she no longer averted her eyes. Lately she'd been making progress, she'd put on a few pounds and her face had new color. Her cheeks were no longer hollow, the dark rings under her eyes were gone. She glowed.

"You'll be discharged on Friday next week. Do you have anywhere to live until it's possible to make the journey out into the forest? Could you stay with your sisters?"

She shook her head determinedly at the word *sisters*. Standing up and pacing the room, she went to stand by the window and looked out, smiling to herself when she saw the luxuriant magpie nest in the upper boughs of an elm tree.

"Please come and sit down. We have a few practical details to iron out."

On this particular spring morning she made an abrupt turn and looked earnestly at the doctor. She stood like that for a long time, then she walked over and sat down on his lap, putting her arms carefully, caressingly, around his neck.

He stroked her back gently, felt the weight of her body, her smoky breath.

On this morning he thought: *I am a human being. I am a man.* No man, no human being could dismiss such a sincere gesture of intimacy, such a craving for affection.

AUNE STOPPED IN THE DOORWAY TO CAFÉ METROPOL. HER HEART WAS thumping: so many people, so close together, in such a small space. The noise rammed into her, along with the stuffy air. She was glad to have new trousers so she wouldn't smell of manure.

Young people, younger than she was or of the same age, were at every table, drinking coffee with milk from large glasses, talking nonstop, and laughing. A young woman opposite a young guy, close, closer, mouth drawn to mouth. A more mature woman fiddled with her phone absentmindedly, laid it on the table, gazed out dreamily. Beside her on the floor there were several tall bags containing rectangular packages wrapped in Christmas paper.

In the very back corner a woman was reading a book. She looked up and waved at Aune. The woman got up from the table and held out a hand. "Sunniva."

Aune nodded and looked at the clean, white hand with long, witchlike fingernails painted black. She looked up at Sunniva's face, her pale skin, her well-combed, glossy black hair and red-painted mouth. Black lines on her eyelids. Her gaze returned to the hand's pointed nails. She didn't shake Sunniva's hand; instead, she held her own out in front of Sunniva's, their fingertips almost touching. She smiled and nodded.

"So nice to finally meet you," said Sunniva.

How does she know? thought Aune, taking a seat opposite her. The hum and the chatting voices invaded her head. Her eyes darted around and she squirmed on the hard chair, accustomed as she was to always resting her backside on bearskins.

"Seems to be a lot of people cutting school today, or maybe they're off," said Sunniva. "The acoustics aren't great but the coffee's the best. These days so-called baristas scald the coffee into oblivion. Or they put far too much milk in the latte and you start wondering where the coffee's gone . . . Have you tried the coconut macaroons here?"

Aune shook her head.

"Exquisite. I'd love to treat you to one."

"Coffee," said Aune.

"Latte? Cappuccino?"

"Coffee. Regular coffee."

She thought with disappointment of the sugar cubes; they must remember to buy some.

Sunniva went over to the counter and chatted with the girl behind it. She came back holding a tray with a coffee glass and some milk, and a cup next to some kind of glass apparatus containing coffee. Aune stared at this contraption. Two plates, each holding a large macaroon.

"Marie promised me they're freshly baked," said Sunniva. "She's the one Metropol girl who can reasonably call herself a barista. But enough of that . . . I don't know how much Ritva told you about my idea."

"Just that you were a local historian and you wanted to meet me."

"I'm actually a nurse, but I've gone part-time. From now on I'm going to live simply and indulge my hobby."

"Hobby?" said Aune, curious.

"Local history with a focus on people in the area who've chosen unusual ways of life. Like you and your sisters. By the way, I bought something from your market stall back in the fall."

"It would have been my sisters you saw."

"You're very alike. Really."

Aune smiled and said: "Did they behave?"

Sunniva laughed. "I heard from Onni that you're as skilled a storyteller as your famous uncle Veikko. We actually appeared together a few times . . . even here in town, on the stage in the park. I'm a huge fan."

"You know Onni?"

"An old flame, from way back. Back when we thought a relationship that lasted a month was big news. We're friends now. He told me you were the author in the family."

"I tell stories."

"Have you written them down? Could I read them?"

"They're in my head. Word for word, sentence for sentence." She tapped her temple.

"You're quite the dompteuse, Onni says."

Aune felt she should ask about the word, but she stopped herself. The worst thing she could think of was seeming stupid. Right now she was being stupid with the coffee apparatus, she needed help to press the grounds down into the bottom.

"We're staying in Onni's guest cabin, but I don't know him all that well. My father did."

"Your father is a legend, but of course I don't need to tell you that. I would like to write your family history for an anniversary anthology our local history association is putting together. To tell the story of your upbringing in the wilderness. And I want to work together with you."

"The farm wasn't in the wilderness. . . . It wasn't until recently that we lived out in the forest."

"All I want is for you to describe it. It might end up as a *book* as well, I've been talking to a lovely little publishing house who are interested. Of course, when it's published your name will be on the cover too. How does that sound?"

Aune frowned and looked down at the black-and-white squares of the floor.

"It would be your debut. Wouldn't that be cool? We'd split the money, even though the fee's just a token—everyone in the association is a volunteer. That's how it is in the arts."

"What would I do?" said Aune.

"What you're good at: telling stories."

Aune fixed her eyes on the floor again, picturing Johanna's enraged expression. Sullying Father's name by breaking his main rule. On the other hand it would be a form of redress. For everything they'd been called—at the dance, at the tobacconist's. Bog witches. Marsh Marys. Filthy sluts. She wouldn't be able to ask Johanna, nor Tanja or Tiina, they wouldn't get it. Elga and Laura probably would . . . She looked at Sunniva's full red lips. Her smile exposed a gap between her front teeth. Aune kept her mouth closed, she knew how her front teeth looked, in Onni the dandy's house there were plenty of gold-rimmed mirrors.

Sunniva tried to suppress her eagerness to share another

idea. She couldn't move too quickly. Don't force it, build trust gradually—she'd learned that through past collaborations. But she placed particular faith in this collaboration. She felt it, a thrill through her body.

"You don't need to decide now. Think about it for a few days and let me know. Right, now we have to try these macaroons."

Aune wolfed hers in two bites: sweet, buttery, crumbly.

Sunniva wrote her phone number on the receipt and handed it to Aune.

"How will you get to Onni's?"

"On foot."

"You're going to walk all that way in this wet snow? I'll drive you. They said there's going to be a storm later."

Aune would have preferred to say no, to start processing the encounter and everything that had been said, to try to guess the meaning of certain glances and tones of voice. She considered Sunniva, her bright eyes and the butterfly earring on one earlobe. It looked like something Laura might produce.

She heard herself say something unexpected: "That would be . . . great. Thanks."

SUNNIVA OPENED THE CAR DOOR, TOOK A BRUSH OUT OF THE GLOVE box, and swept the wet, heavy snow from the roof, windshield, and rearview mirrors. She stamped the slush from her boots before getting in and opening the door for Aune, who stared at the digital symbols on the dashboard, the strange little lights and gizmos that glowed in the darkness. Aune turned to see the back seat with its three seat belts. She looked shyly at Sunniva's slim nose and narrow nostrils. Who gets strapped in by those belts? The car was completely free of junk, as though Sunniva had just picked it up from the car showroom. How the hell did she start the car without a key? Everything was eerily quiet. When Sunniva backed out of the parking lot the engine didn't make any sound at all. Aune thought of Tiina's roaring, puttering, growling, creaking, steaming, gasoline-stinking motors.

Sunniva switched on the windshield wipers and the news on the radio.

Storm alerts. Murderer still not found. The book bus discontinued.

"It's real icy, so we'll need to crawl along. The council's late gritting as per usual. Do you have anywhere to be?"

Aune shook her head.

The wind whipped up, the snow whined, a peculiar glow made it difficult to see. Once they'd passed the industrial estate and driven out of town the streetlights left them to their fate. The wild animal warning signs appeared.

Sunniva drove in tense concentration with the coniferous forests lining both sides of the road. An 18-wheeler had forgotten to turn off its brights and for a while they were terrified, dazzled by the light. After each downhill slope the dip was slippery as glass. Sunniva jumped as some hazard lights flashed orange—there was an abandoned SUV in the ditch.

It wasn't far now, but the unpaved road to Onni's was narrow and potholed; the windshield wipers whisked a valiant monotone. Aune blinked drowsily and tried to think of something to say. She was nervous to the pit of her stomach, sitting so close to this unfamiliar person. What did people say when they didn't know each other?

"Sorry for not talking, I have to concentrate on the road."

The wind howled and the moon looked like an ice pick swathed in tulle. Aune stamped off the snow on the steps to the cabin. She brushed down her coat and went into the warmth where the gas radiator was hissing; the air was compact.

Elga on the bed with the cell phone in her hand. Her fingers moved about on the receiver—or whatever it was called, Aune didn't know.

Nose in the air, sniffing it like a wolf scenting. "You smell of coffee and perfume."

"I washed with soap at Metropol."

"How the fuck did you get home? This wet snow is coming down in spades."

"That local history woman drove me. What are you up to?" Aune sat down beside Elga.

"I'll be able to do this soon. I know how to call someone and use the bank. Tomorrow we can get out some money with our card. What did she say?"

"She wants to write about us."

"You and me?"

"About seven sisters and their famous father, the bear hunter."

Elga laughed in her face. "Who's interested in that?!"

"The local history association. People in town. People talk about us. Everyone knows the old man. By the way, she knows Onni."

"Oh!"

"They were together for a bit."

"What did we say? Womanizer."

"They were young."

"That long ago? Goddammit, please tell me you'll say yes. You could be the first of us to make some money of your own."

"Apparently the association will do this book basically for free. Sunniva says we'd share the money we get from sales."

"Lay it on thick! Make us really exciting. Have the readers gasping for breath. We only need to go out in public to make people take three steps back in fear. Did she seem good?"

"What do I know? We drank coffee."

"You'd know if she was a nitwit. It's obvious right away."

"I don't think so, but we'll see. I was nervous."

"Are you going to drink coffee again?"

"I got her number. I'll call when I've decided."

Elga held out the phone.

Aune fended her off with one hand. "I have to think first, you know."

She blushed. She got up and turned off the heater. Opened the door a little to get in some air, but some force pulled the door outward. The wind whined, the snow whirled. She thought how hard it was to make decisions when others have always decided for you. Once again she pictured Johanna's angry face. Was she still in the mental hospital? Where were Tanja and Tiina sleeping? In the hayloft on the farm?

Aune closed the door and climbed in beside Elga.

"I wanted to ask Laura first. And then the others. Where is she?"

"With Kvarnholm and one of his colleagues, she's learning to sew fur. She'd gone from curled up to unstoppable in no time. Some people are easily pleased."

"Can we ring somebody about Johanna? We at least need to know what's going on with her."

"She's an asshole, but she's also our sister. I'll call Ritva and the loony bin tomorrow."

Aune put her hand in her pocket. The receipt with Sunniva's phone number was in there.

"And Tanja and Tiina?"

"Yeah, where did they get to? Not that smart of social services to give us only one phone. What's the point of having a phone if the only people you know don't have one?"

THEY SLEPT HEAD TO TOE TO STAY WARM. THE HEATER WAS switched off, otherwise they'd faint during the night. They'd fallen asleep with library books and pens in the bed, accustomed to sleeping on bumpy surfaces. Aune was slumbering on a book about Russian opera divas she'd found on Onni's bookshelf. Before she fell asleep, she pictured Sunniva; everything Sunniva had said over coffee and coconut macaroons replayed in her head.

The storm howled. It wanted to tear up the cabin and toss it into the forest, but the sisters were tired and they slept a deep sleep. They awoke in the middle of the night to the sound of somebody stomping on the steps. That somebody thundered in and struggled to close the door behind them, bringing with them a wind sharp as ice.

Epilogue

Epilogues have always bothered me. Dostoyevsky should have held off. Afterwords flatten and smooth, putting things neatly in their place. But now here I am, writing an epilogue, and it feels totally right. The final sentences I've formulated might feel hard, but the sisters are young, we don't know how they will develop, if they'll come to think differently as they mature.

Would the book about the bear hunter's daughters have been more exciting, or less, if they themselves had written it? We'll never know. I wanted to share my pen, to share my thoughts; in vain I made offerings of coconut macaroons. But where the Leskinens are concerned, oral storytelling will always win.

I suppose it's a little odd to try to formulate a story that is not mine to tell, to enter into a family's experiences when they lie so far from my own. One thing is clear: Mother Louhi wrote with a vividness I don't possess, she was the true author. In spite of that, I wanted to try: Louhi is dead, and I was asked to write the story of this unique family. Their unusual life is the stuff of this community's cultural history.

The lead-up to the end must of course be the spring market. With this, the circle is closed.

THE QUEUE FOR THE ICE CREAM KIOSK WAS AT LEAST THIRTY YARDS long. People were almost twittering as they talked. The spring market attracted record crowds, and after a long, savage winter came a sudden heat wave. An elderly lady supporting herself on a cane collapsed in the melee and sank onto the grass.

The temperature had risen fifteen degrees in two days and many of the town's inhabitants had stripped off a layer too many: shorts were tight and tops sleeveless. Didn't they have mirrors at home?! Couldn't they see their bark-white legs? Skin unused to sun was suddenly exposed to blazing rays. At the stall selling cuttings and plants, it was all the traders could do to keep their wilting saplings watered.

Of course, my eyes sought the Leskinen sisters in particular, curious what sales tricks they'd learned since the last time. Of course, I was hoping for something wild and bold: a colorful scene from the market would make the perfect ending to my book. After all, this was where the townspeople had the honor of meeting them—those winter visits to social services had turned out to be extremely short-lived.

A lot had happened since my meeting with Aune at Metropol. It didn't turn out as I'd hoped, and perhaps that's for the best, since it forced me to use my imagination. It has certainly been beneficial for me and my adaptable nature to spend time with the Leskinen sisters through my writing, and to try to inhabit their way of thinking and reasoning. Now I dream that the buyers will be queuing up to read about the sisters as enthusiastically as they do to see them live. It seems people can't get enough of these stubborn, uncompromising young women. Dangerous, many would probably add.

The season's offerings were predictable and I felt a certain weariness as I trotted along past the tables. The same licorice cables, the same fucking rhubarb jam. But then the din rose and through a knot of people I caught sight of the Leskinen's red manes. Electricity jolted through me: thank God! This year they had two tables, with two sisters on each. At one, Tiina danced her famous risqué foxtail dance, drawing as many punters as the ice cream kiosk. Tanja offered their guests a sip of moonshine from the customary hip flask. People drank, wolf-whistled, clapped.

The sun beat down and Tiina and Tanja took off their coats and shirts, in the end dancing in nothing but jeans and their father's fishnet tanks. The audience stared at the bushy hair in the girls' armpits as they sold smoked elk meat to their customers. This meat was what sold fastest these days—the customers preferred it to the heavier bear meat, which the sisters tended to keep for their own needs. It was different with the skins.

Two women with brand-new hunting licenses stroked the bearskins for a long time, but in the end settled on a beaver skin each. As they were paying they got confirmation that it was going to be a good year for ptarmigan, and that the bear tribe was thriving as much as ever, meaning business was brisk in spite of Onni Kvarnholm's strange and sudden decision to relocate his operations to Novosibirsk. It's a shame, he's been essential for the genesis of this tale. Our old passion came close to reigniting when I interviewed him.

A couple of tables along from the athletic Leskinens, visitors could find the more delicate sisters. This is where Aune stood, spellbinding her audience with tales of the wilderness and asking them to share theirs. Alongside her stood Laura, reticent and artistic, selling her much-loved stick figures and cone art, alongside a new kind of clay figurine with heartbreaking, tortured expressions. She also sold beautifully sewn ermine-fur caps.

I pushed my way through to listen to Aune. It was phenomenal how she charged her stories with her voice, creating drama, sometimes with whispers, sometimes with shouts. At that moment she was telling of a girl who'd decided to live in a tree and never again set foot on the ground. Aune waved when she caught sight of me, and I went over and greeted her as she came to the end of her tragic tale. We hadn't seen each other since meeting a second time at Metropol, over macaroons again, when she'd delivered her firm "no." I was forced to respect that no, even if it stung. The local history association's annual was published without Aune Leskinen's contribution. She wanted to spellbind listeners, not readers. It was impossible to convince or persuade her that the one didn't necessarily exclude the other. Aune was happy that their story would be told anyway, built on witness statements and make-believe.

I am a little ashamed to have used them. What do I know of what went on in their heads out in that cabin in the woods? But I stopped quibbling over right and wrong and set the story of the bear hunter's daughters free. People want to read. People want to be shocked. The local history association's annual has broken sales records and I've traveled the area telling the story.

When does a tale reach its end? Never. It goes on for all eternity. This is where the unavoidable epilogue comes in.

The sisters' lives still captivate people, leading to all sorts of gossip over beer and coffee. Tiina and Tanja returned to the cabin in the wilderness as soon as the snow cleared, and they've made a good living for themselves there. They grow potatoes, field peas, and have even managed to start up bines of hops in their greenhouse. They keep their home-brewed porter, which is meant to be heavenly, to themselves. These days they hire a helicopter for market days and for the ptarmigan hunt.

Aune and Laura went for Ritva Halonen's tip about the abandoned house closer to town. They've put solar panels on the roof, which has meant lamps to work by, an electric stove, and a fridge. They've had a smaller sleeping cabin built alongside it, so they each have a house to live in.

Laura has built herself a large, wide workbench by a picture window. She lines up all her tools before her—she finds herself falling in love with her tools as much as with animals. She calls her little Dremel multitool Cutie-pie.

The world had become more intelligible with glasses: from her window she watches squirrels, foxes, jays, and a confused, attention-seeking elk, a yearling calf who lingers about the house.

The animals live their life under her watchful eye, and when she takes her daily turns to the forest tarn, the lost elk calf accompanies her. Once a year they meet Tanja and Tiina, and Laura buys skins from them so Laura can make the winter caps that are so sought-after. She sells them not only at the market but at the Leskinen Hunting Museum in their fully restored parental home, where Elga is the curator.

Over the years the construction work was taking place, Elga completed both her middle and high school education. During that time, she's had Laura create totem poles, which have been much acclaimed, not least by the museum's younger visitors.

Elga has turned the attic into a comfortable apartment. It's here that she unwinds after a long day of visitors and chattering schoolkids. The paperwork follows—those calming numbers, the ones that remind her of Matti the math genius, who's at college in the US. The admin might involve an invoice after Aune, sitting atop the firewood chest, has once again drawn a full house for one of her storytelling evenings. People love the lack of pretense, the feeling of being in somebody's home. Yes, there's a lot of history in the walls of that house, the visitors are even delighted by the cafe in the barn. It's impossible to scrub away the stable smell, but those peculiar townies are content.

Did she succeed in renovating away the scent of Mother in the attic room? Had her cries soaked into the walls?

Elga lies in her alcove, clenching her toes in the socks her mother had rage-knitted. She tries to inhabit the exhaustion her mother must have felt when her working day came to an end, the grunt work that included the crops and the farm, as well as the children. Did she work herself to death? The words from her mother's diary ring clear in her head. Her dread and her daughters' joy when the hunter, her town-loving, party-hard husband stood in the doorway.

In a way that still astonishes Elga, the room gives her strength. She tries to imagine how her mother felt as she was about to birth her seventh child, hoping that it would be a boy at last.

The unwanted girl-child came into the world through a hole located close to the orifice that pushed out feces. She thought of it with disgust, but it wasn't only unwanted, impoverished children who were born unpleasantly close to that source of foul-smelling dung. Even royal newborns emerged from the same hole.

That's how it was with children.

Screaming and terrified they come into the world.

Children are marked by their upbringing, and any child of sound mind tries to break the rules and find their own way. *One day I'll make my own decisions*, the child's inner voice says. *Wild and free at last*, they think as they reach young adulthood. But the child soon becomes aware that the rules are in their bones, both an iron girdle and a sense of home. At first, the grown child is crushed by this realization, but eventually they let go and begin to act as their character dictates.

Routine offers a sense of security. You get up in the morning and you know what needs doing and what doesn't.

And Johanna? you're wondering. Yes, what has happened to Johanna? I have no insight, she remains a mystery. She betrayed her tribe scandalously. She never visits her sisters, not even Tiina and Tanja out in the wilderness, and she never turns up on market days. The sisters used to speak about her anxiously when they met. They wanted to understand, but they couldn't. *The last person you would have believed it of.* The moment a man wanted her, she opened herself, sat on his lap—that's the way Elga sees it.

The strangest thing of all? Johanna has moved to town. She's even settled down in the fancy part of town, with its enormous mansions and huge verandas. The sisters sometimes drive past the house out of pure curiosity. They never see a soul in the yard, except a gardener who prunes the tall rosebushes.

In wintertime, Aune and Laura take the snowmobile out into the wilderness and visit Tiina and Tanja and their new hunting dogs.

They visit Simone's grave alongside the final resting places of Killo and Kiiski. No one wants to hear about how and where Tiina found the remains.

Tanja and Tiina live according to their father's rules and never meet a soul aside from their three sisters. Over time Johanna has become unmentionable.

The tribe has broken up, but the bond between the five sisters remains. No one even gives a thought to meeting a man and having children.

No one has given birth.

Convinced—yes, absolutely sure in their belief in the fateful legacy of their mother: Doomed to have daughters.

A NOTE FROM THE TRANSLATOR

Seven uproarious sisters. Drinking, hunting, wrestling, and backbiting their way to freedom in whatever form it might take. When I first came to read Anneli Jordahl's *The Bear Hunter's Daughters* I wasn't really sure what to expect. She's a versatile and deeply political writer who has turned her imaginative hand to many subjects, but I'd never read anything by her that was as playful, almost fantastical, as this novel. I started on the first page and was immediately charmed, both by Jordahl's flame-haired protagonists and by the ebullience of her prose.

When the book was acquired and I was asked to translate it, I was excited that I would get to spend time with these women and their bawdy, chaotic ways, though I have to say I was quite intimidated by them and felt relieved that our encounter would take place via the page and not in person. I wouldn't last five minutes in their presence—they'd sniff me out as the townie I am and eject me from their precious forest.

And what a forest. One of the greatest challenges of translating this novel was the descriptions of landscapes that simply don't exist in the tame environs of southern England, where I've lived most of my life. In fact, I've never even been to the area of northern Finland

A NOTE FROM THE TRANSLATOR

Jordahl imagined as the site of her heroines' hideout. It's quite different from the forests of the southern half of Sweden I'm more familiar with, where millennia of human habitation and forestry have stripped whole swathes of land of the biodiversity they once held. But the dense, old-growth wilderness of Jordahl's imagination and the sisters' remote croft is full of vast trees, rare lichens, and wild animals large and small.

Luckily for me (and for you, dear reader), the vividness of Jordahl's descriptions made it easy for me to picture the scenes she'd dreamt up, and thus to recreate them in English—the clear, still lakes and fresh-scented swamps studded with cloudberries, the mountains with their abrupt switches in weather, the rowdy seasonal markets in town.

And so I immersed myself in the sisters' world and got stuck in, carried away by the pace of the writing and the bright light it casts on Jordahl's imagery. I was so in love with the sisters that I heard their voices in my head as they romped about the forest. I crouched with Laura as she whittled her little clay figurines, listened along with Elga as she sounded out new words, squeezed Tiina's rippling biceps as she threw herself into building projects, felt Johanna's frustration as the others slipped out of her control (though to be fair, she should really chill out), nodded along to Aune's yarns full of mystical beasts and lovelorn spirits, perched with Simone atop her tree stump during her last, desperate days, and warmed my hands by Tanja's skillfully built fires.

In short, I lived in the world of this book for several months and I loved it. I hope you will too.

Nichola Smalley
London, Summer 2025

About the Author

ANNELI JORDAHL is an author and literary critic. She has written several works of nonfiction, as well as critically acclaimed novels, including *Like the Dogs in Lafayette Park*. *The Bear Hunter's Daughters* was shortlisted for Swedish Radio's Novel Prize, the August Prize, and France's Prix Fragonard.

ABOUT THE TRANSLATOR

NICHOLA SMALLEY is a translator of Swedish and Norwegian literature. In 2021 she won the Oxford-Weidenfeld Translation Prize, and her work has also been nominated for the International Booker, Bernard Shaw, and Warwick Prizes. She worked for several years in publishing and has a PhD in the use of slang in contemporary Swedish and English literature. She lives in London.

Here ends Anneli Jordahl's
The Bear Hunter's Daughters.

The first edition of this book was printed
and bound at LSC Communications
in Harrisonburg, Virginia, in February 2026.

A NOTE ON THE TYPE

Cut as a private version for the Nonesuch Press in the early 1930s, Bulmer was first released for general use in 1939. It was initially designed circa 1790 by punchcutter William Martin and used by William Bulmer, owner of the Shakespeare Press, in a number of prestigious works, including Boydell's *Shakespeare*. Narrower and with a taller appearance than Baskerville, Bulmer adopted the modern face of Bodoni but retained vital qualities from the old-face style. A contemporary digital revival has been created by Robin Nicholas at Monotype Imaging and is based on the 1928 revival by Morris Fuller Benton.

HARPERVIA

An imprint dedicated to publishing international voices,
offering readers a chance to encounter other lives and other
points of view via the language of the imagination.